WAREHOUSE OF THE DEAD

Ferrel D. Moore

ISBN-13: 978-0-9898669-4-1

To my lovely wife, Beth
And my two children Kate and James,
Kate's two children Mat and Harley
My brother Thom and his wife Joyce

The Mine

"I'm not going in there first," Gregorio said, turning up his nose. "It's dark, and it smells bad, like something died."

"What do you expect? It's an old mine," I said. "Besides, I'm right behind you."

He was right, though. The smell was so strong that I could taste it. We were ten miles out of town. The afternoon sun was about halfway down in the sky, but the heat and humidity were suffocating. I hated Mexico. The people were okay once you got past the customs and the language thing, but the country would never be the same for me since Gregorio and I had found the Almacen de la Muerte, which means "the Warehouse of the Dead" as they now called it in the Mexican papers.

Gregorio wiped his wide, dirty forehead with his shirtsleeve. "How come you always go in last?"

He was twisting his shoe in the gray and red dust like he was exterminating a cricket with his cuffed and stained work boots. For once, he had the laces tied. He did that for good luck. For some reason, that bothered me.

"You got a gun, so he's not coming at you from the front. He'll try to hit us from the back. But don't worry about me, though," I said. "I'll just duck. Maybe you should duck, too."

"Asshole. What if he hits us from the side, like from a branch tunnel we don't see?"

"Get moving," I said. "We go in, we see what's there, and we get back to the air conditioning. That a plan or what?"

"You know, we should take some more men."

Gregorio wasn't afraid. He just liked to argue. It was how he worked himself up. He was a solid man, bigger than me, maybe about six feet two. He had a broad nose, a wide forehead, and he looked like some kind of an Aztec warrior. Except for the dirty jeans and the wide leather belt with the Caterpillar Truck logo . Shoulders like a construction worker, but with a narrow waist. Hands big enough to crush a melon or snap a neck.

We smelled pretty ripe since we'd been out in the sun all day scouting the fields, but neither of us smelled as bad as what was coming out of the tunnel. I read somewhere that the average temperature in Mexico was 81 degrees Fahrenheit. They must have averaged that in the Mexican Ice Age. The average humidity is always too wet.

"You want an army, Gregorio? I'm telling you; this guy works alone."

He turned to me and shook his head. "He's connected."

"Come on, will you?" I said. "We're wasting time."

But he had a point. I just wanted to keep it simple. Find the kids, dead or alive. Go home, report in, and collect the cash. There were worse ways to make a living, but they didn't pay as much.

I raised the barrel of the twelve gauge to my forehead and pushed back my hat. The metal was almost as warm as my skin. I looked directly into Gregorio's dark eyes. There was no fear or hesitation in them, only a hard shine.

Finally, he shrugged and slid his red-checkered bandanna up and over the lower half of his face, so that he looked something like a Mexican bank robber. He had his police flashlight in one hand, the black Glock in the other. The Glock hung easily in his grip. People that are scared squeeze a gun handle so hard their knuckles almost pop through their skin. I had never seen Gregorio scared.

While Gregorio kept an eye out, I pulled my bandanna up over my mouth and nose, too. It didn't stop the greasy smell, but it cut it down a little.

The tunnel, an abandoned silver mine, was set into the side of a small hill of hard-packed, red-brown dirt outside of Guadalajara.

Weeds clung about the mouth of the entrance, their roots like thick fingers grasping the ground.

Gregorio flicked on his flashlight and began walking into the shadows, the beam cutting through the darkness like a light saber as he played it back and forth.

The halogen lamp strapped across my chest sent a circle of white forward and onto the back of his white cotton shirt. The shadow of my shotgun barrel cut across it, making it look like he was wearing a "No Smoking" sign on his back.

We walked forward as quietly as we could. There wasn't much point since our target was probably long gone — at least the way I figured it. Or dead. Gregorio had a point. People died in Mexico and were never heard from again. It wasn't as bad as in Chile, but it happened.

Guadalajara was a dangerous town, even for Mexico. But the way I looked at it, any country whose favorite vehicle was the Volkswagen Beetle deserved what it got. You couldn't drink the water unless you'd been vaccinated. Couldn't sleep with the women unless you'd been vaccinated. And mordida—graft—was the basic currency of Mexican business. Nothing got done unless you juiced the right people. If you thought about it, it was a lot like Detroit, only hotter.

We were the only noise, the only movement through the heavy air except the occasional rustling of thin leather wings beyond the bobbing haloes of our lights. The odor grew stronger; I could feel it coating the lining of my mouth. I had to alternately tense and release my muscles to keep from throwing up into the bandanna.

It wasn't much of a mine. A couple of four by four by eight wooden braces the color of well-done meat. Crunchy pebbles that ground between the metal rails and our boots, and hard dirt walls too low for comfort. Rusty lanterns hung from spikes pounded in by someone long since dead.

"Used to run train cars in and out of this place, no?" asked Gregorio.

"Looks like," I said.

"Pretty crappy mine, eh?"

Gregorio had a pregnant wife and a kid, a five-year-old boy named Bruno. That bothered me as we walked. My own life was kind of empty since the accident—except for the hit and run types. I turned a valve a long time ago in a factory now dismantled and sold for scrap. It killed half of the town. It was like Bhopal, India, except on a smaller scale. Two hundred and twelve dead taxpayers. Twenty-one plant workers. All dead except for me. Hard to hang with a good woman after that.

"You see anything move, you shoot it," I reminded Gregorio's back.

"Si, Madre," he said without looking back.

We found them twenty suffocating minutes into the mine. Seven bodies in various stages of decay, bound by chains and manacles. They were lined up against the packed dirt wall in the cut-away as though they were on display; gruesome, bloated mannequins profiling the latest in death apparel. They were so swollen from internal gas their clothes had cut into their skin. Their necks were truncated in disgusting stumps. Their heads rested between their purple-black bloated legs. But I could still tell that the skin from the eyebrows up had been cut and peeled back like I had seen it before.

Someone had posed them carefully and was proud of his work. The cut-away was a carved-out space to the side of the tunnel, dug in maybe six feet, braced and supported. I turned and scanned the area constantly, while Gregorio checked the bodies. It was like being a human lighthouse with the lamp strapped across my chest as I turned and turned, looking for someone to shoot.

Gregorio was bent over the third body from the left, hunkered down on all fours. The smell, the bodies that were now rotted carrion, chewed and eaten by cave animals as though they were so much meat, was too much for him. I heard him retch as he pulled down his bandanna and turned my head as he threw up on a body.

He yanked away from me as I took his arm. There wasn't any reason for him to be ashamed. He knew it. I knew it. We both felt like shit. But there it was. As he struggled to get to his feet again, I bent over once again and reached out for his arm again, realizing too late my mistake.

The shadows out of the corner of my eye were moving. Black against black in motion, big and coming toward us quickly. As I turned, I fired upward at a slight angle, shooting completely by instinct. The flash blinded me, and the noise deafened me.

Later, when I got out of the hospital, I would learn that I had shot him squarely in the crotch, which was some consolation for the miner's pick that he'd stuck into my right arm.

*****

Where I live, you get a good look at the Detroit River. It's on all sides, so it's tough to not get a good look at it. Soldier's Point is a half a mile long and a quarter of a mile wide. Roughly. From the top of the lighthouse, you can see both the American and the Canadian sides. The light up top works, but I rarely get the chance to fire it up anymore.

My lighthouse is one of three structures on the Island. The other two are my work shed and an open-sided pole building where I store some of my junk.

The island is mostly rock and trees, with just enough open fields to keep it from making me feel claustrophobic.

There are basically two ways on and off the island. You can use a boat or a helicopter, the way that Allen Hemlock does. But a good swimmer can make it just the same, do what he or she came to do, and then exit the same way if they didn't feel like or didn't want to steal onc of my boats.

Still, I have always felt safer when I'm home at Soldier's Point. I'm no different from the next guy in that regard. After the accident at the factory, I like to be alone more than most people.

I had the place on a ninety-nine year lease when I first took possession, but I've since bought it outright. Hemlock says that I've turned into a hermit, but I like it that way. I like to wake up in the morning and know that I'm alone, know that there's no one there to depend on me. After killing half a city, living around other people has been kind of iffy.

The day was like my mood. Dark clouds hung heavy in the sky. Heat lightning occasionally flashed like minor skirmishes in an impending war in the clouds. Hemlock was due at any time, and I was making my second tour of the island on foot to work of a head of steam. I was going to like what Hemlock had to say.

I didn't look up as his helicopter came in from the north and passed overhead. There was no danger of rain yet; it always seemed to wait for him to disembark and go inside before it started.

He had that much pull.

Gregorio had saved my life in Guadalajara. He'd stopped the bleeding as best he could, drove me back to the hospital, and screamed at the nurses and doctors until security escorted him to the waiting room.

Mexico had armed men at every hospital I had ever visited. They were prepared for armed assault, although I still can't figure the logic of terrorists attacking an emergency room. I decided it must be a Spanish thing.

Even the admissions counter in a big Mexican hospital has as much protective bullet-proof glass as any US bank, as I saw on the day that I was checked out. Gregorio had been there to help me out of the wheelchair if I needed it, but I was damned if I was going to ask for his help.

He was the first person I talked to after surgery. The doctors, who spoke passable English, prodded me with a barrage of questions when I was conscious. I ignored them. I'd talk to Gregorio. Period.

The Mexican police had had other ideas, but I didn't give a shit what they wanted either. At my trial for the Great Gas Release, I'd had enough of any kind of government authority to last me for the rest of my life. And the press. Allen Hemlock would spring me. Mordida was his middle name.

The first thing that Gregorio had said to me was, "Hey, amigo, you blew his balls right off. Nice shooting. Too bad about your arm, though."

I told him to bite me, but I slurred the words and had to repeat them.

*****

Hemlock was waiting by the front door of the lighthouse when I finished my walk around the island. The sky continued to darken, but I hadn't felt a drop yet, although I knew the rain was coming. He had a woman with him; nice looking enough if you liked small-breasted librarians. She wore black slacks, a thin white sweater, and was carrying an expensive looking black leather briefcase. Her blond hair was bobbed behind her head in a bun, and she wore overlarge wire-rimmed glasses that made her eyes look smaller. She looked as though she had come to research the lighthouse's history.

Next to her, Hemlock, who was six foot four, looked like a giant cowboy. He dressed as he always dressed when he came to see me—jeans, turtle-neck sweater, and a tan colored chamois jacket. The black hat that he wore tilted back on his head was the same color as his boots. If it wasn't for his Mr. Roger's face, he could have passed for Clint Eastwood.

He pushed back a lock of dried grass-colored hair from his forehead as I approached and smiled a broad smile, showing his perfect teeth.

"Scott, it's good to see you," he said.

He stuck out his right hand and then withdrew it just as quickly.

"Sorry," he said quickly, "I wasn't thinking. Is your arm doing any better?"

I ignored him and said, "Who's your friend, Allen?"

"Ah, forgive my bad manners. This is Dr. Kris Stouffer. Dr. Stouffer, this is Scott Brown."

"Nice to meet you, Mr. Brown. I've heard a lot about you."

She smiled. It did her face a lot of good.

"Just Scott. Are you another arm specialist?"

"Pardon me?" she asked.

"Scott thinks that you're a medical doctor, Kris," explained Hemlock.

"Oh," she said, and her cheeks flushed the color of faded roses. "No, I'm sorry. I heard about your arm. I'm not a medical doctor, I'm afraid."

"Then what are you a doctor of?"

"Why don't we go inside?" suggested Hemlock.

The lighthouse has everything that I need inside. I like the fact that it was round; I've never liked corners. Things can hide in and around corners. Nastier things than dust bunnies. In the center of the room is the spiral staircase that goes up to my bedroom on the second floor and keeps on going up to the big light itself on the third level.

The place was in a shambles when I bought it, but still structurally sound. I redid the floor with ceramic tile. Ceramic tile is clean and shiny looking, and doesn't require a lot of maintenance to look good.

The room is like a big clock face. The door marks six o'clock. The kitchen on the far side of the circle at twelve o'clock, which is dead north, is laid out simple; I've got a cast iron Dutch oven that I bought at a flea market and restored myself. I like to cook, and I do it pretty well.

The oak wood island five steps away from the Dutch oven is for chopping and dicing and it's at least fifty years old. When they closed Joey's Stables and Restaurant, I picked it up just for the cost of hauling it away along with a lot of their other "classic" cooking equipment.

The rest of the place is simple and clean, which is how I like things. One four-foot-long semicircular couch and two chairs that are the color of fresh, white typing paper are between six and nine o'clock to your left as you come in the door.

A glass dining table with striped green and vermilion cloth chairs is between nine o'clock and the kitchen still anchored at twelve. Whenever I'm home, I keep a vase of flowers on the glass table. Every day I change the water in the vase. I don't like to look at dirty water; I drink too much of it when I'm on the road.

Between twelve and three o'clock is your basic Steinway baby grand. It's glossy black buffed, and so clean you can straighten your tie from your reflection- it was buffed better than a teenager's first Corvette. I play some, but mostly I just like to look at it. The rest of the time, I listen to the stereo.

My desk, the bookshelves, and a computer are halfway between three and six o'clock. The downstairs terminal is tied to the main hardware upstairs on the third floor where the big light is. I don't know what the former owner did with all the extra space up there, but me, I've got high speed access wired to a bank of computer muscle ranged around the light. The system is the eyes and ears for Soldier's point, connected to the pressure plates, the infrared monitors, the microphones, and a few other electronic niceties. It's also, via the satellite dish, my gateway in and out of the Web, which means to the rest of the world.

The round windows, three feet in diameter, are at seven, nine, twelve, three, and five o'clock. They give a great view, let in the light, are made of one-way glass, and will stop a nine-millimeter bullet at point blank range.

All in all, I've got a nice set up.

* * *

*****

Two minutes after I'd seated Dr. Stouffer and Hemlock on the couch and sat down myself after getting us all Coke's, the rain started pounding the island as though it knew Hemlock and his guest were now safely inside. The lightning flashed brightly occasionally to give us a show through the circular windows, and the thunder rolled in right behind it. The pilot out in the copter must have had a good seat for the fireworks.

"This really is an interesting home you have here, Mr. Brown," repeated the librarian, who was really a doctor for the second time.

I ignored her. The first time she'd said it, I'd told her thanks.

"You going to tell me what this is about?" I asked Hemlock.

"I'm sorry about your arm, Scott," he said.

"You told me that. I'm sorry, too. Hector was a lot sorrier."

Héctor Ramirez was the name of the asshole down in the Mexican tunnel that tried to put a miner's pick in my skull. He was the one the papers were saying killed the children.

"Yes, I imagine so. But I don't think he'll be killing any more kids, thanks to you."

"He never did it in the first place, and you know it. Somebody sent him there to kill us. He knew we were coming. "

Dr. Stouffer was watching me closely, the way that shrinks did.

"And why do you think that, Mr. Brown?"

She asked it the way that a shrink would. She might as well have asked why I thought I was a street lamp, or inquired where my last alien contacts took place. I'd had enough probing from shrinks to last me for the rest of my life; she should have known that.

"Quit jacking me around," I told her.

I didn't like mental health professionals. They didn't do much for me when I needed them. They just made the nightmares worse.

She reacted the way that a shrink would. Her blue eyes narrowed slightly, but her composure never cracked.

"Why do you feel so strongly about my question?"

"Because you and Mr. Hemlock already know that he wasn't the killer, and this is my house. If you want to play games, let's go to your house, okay?"

"Fair enough," said Hemlock. "Fair enough. Let's stick with why we're here."

"I'd appreciate it."

"I've got another job for you, Scott. But I'm worried about your arm."

"You mean my mental health? Is that why you brought your shrink along with you? Thanks, but I don't need therapy. I need exercise. I lost a lot of muscle mass, some nerves, and the shoulder joint is screwed, but I don't intend on being the one-armed man for the rest of my life."

"You seem like you have a lot of repressed anger, Mr. Brown."

"I've got my share, Kris, and it's not that damned repressed."

"I'd much prefer," she arched, "if you would call me Dr. Stouffer. I spent a lot of time getting my degrees."

"Well, Kris," I told her with a straight face, "here's the way that it is. I respect the fact that you've got your degrees. I just don't care."

I wasn't interested in a fight. She was a little snobby and a lot condescending, but that wasn't the point. The point was that she'd crossed the line by talking down to me like I was a patient. I wasn't about to cut her any slack. No shrink ever cut me any.

Hemlock tried to smooth things over. "You see what I mean, Dr. Stouffer? I warned you, but please don't take it personally. He's a just little bit rough around the edges."

Her face was still screwed up, and there was a little more color in her cheeks than she had before she came through my front door. But I'll give her this much — she just nodded her head in his direction. At least she had enough brains to not continue the lecture.

When you're right-handed, you automatically reach for things with your right hand, whether or not your arm is with the program. When I brainlessly reached for the can of coke on the small brass and glass table between where they sat on the couch and the armchair that I was sitting on, a jolt of pain went up my arm like I'd brushed against a live wire. Colored stars flared and lit up the room as I screwed my eyes shut to keep back the tears. My teeth clamped together, cutting through the inside of my lower lip; I could taste salt and copper.

Dr. Stouffer was looking straight at me when I opened my eyes again, a wide-open clinical stare with a touch of sympathy and a dash of worry thrown in. I glared back at her. Shrinks can manufacture sympathetic looks on a dime. They're trained to do it. They can turn it on when it suits them. It was a waste of time to guess if her concern was genuine. Shrinks perform as naturally in the theater of the mind as an actress emotes on stage.

"I need you, Scott," said Hemlock softly.

The tremor in my arm had subsided. My body was under control again. The pain had disappeared to wherever it is in the human anatomy it is that it hides.

"What is it you need me to do, exactly?"

With the rain splattering against the bulletproof windows and the light outside the windows being blown away by the storm to be replaced by the dreary dusk that precedes the night, Allen Hemlock told me why he had come and what he wanted me to do. It was the first time he had ever lied to me, if you didn't count the last twelve years.

"Dr. Stouffer has a theory," he began.

"That's nice."

"I'm going to let her explain it to you," he continued, as though I hadn't interrupted. "Doctor?"

"Thank you," she said in the way that professors do before they begin a lecture. According to her body language, she had completely recovered her composure. Unless, of course, she studied body language and was just trying to communicate that she had recovered her composure, in which case I was wrong. All of which proves that it's useless to waste time trying to figure out shrinks.

She laid her briefcase on the table, unsnapped the locks, and took out a newspaper the color of old pasta and handed to me

"You want me to read it?"

"Look at, if you would, the headline story."

I did as I was instructed. It was headlined International Gifted Children's Group Visits Riverview. The picture showed an assembled group of smiling children of ages that seemed between five and sixteen gathered in what looked like a school auditorium.

"Do you recognize any of the children?"

There she was, right up front. About three rows back. I couldn't recognize her photo, of course. It was her old man that tipped me off, kneeling next to her. The beard and hair were black, but the eye patch was the same. He was smiling in the photo. The last time I had seen him in Mexico, he hadn't been smiling. Maybe he would have been if I'd found his daughter alive.

"Yeah."

"How many?" she persisted.

"How many?"

"How many? You mean that there's more than one?"

"Take another look."

This time I really looked. There were more familiar names in the story that I recognized from countries that I had visited over the last several years to look for the living, but finding only the dead.

I knew suddenly that those photos and the story below them contained the key to unlock a Pandora's Box of horrors. What I didn't know, and what was making me madder by the second, was how she knew about it and I didn't. The other thing that bothered me was that I didn't know how she was tied in with Hemlock.

"I can see that you recognize some of the others."

"I do. This is the laundry list."

"Yes," agreed Hemlock, "it is."

"Who found it?"

"Dr. Stouffer found it. She's pieced a great deal of it together for us."

"Nice work," I said.

"Yes, well, we think the killings are linked to this group of children."

"Is that all that you know?"

"There are other things."

"Look," I said, "Mr. Hemlock's pilot gets paid to wait, but there's no reason to drag things out for him. He's got a wife and family and would probably like to get home at a decent hour. So why don't you just tell me how you found out about all of this? After you've done that, Mr. Hemlock here can tell me what he wants me to do for him."

She crossed her legs and folded her arms across her chest, then unwound herself and put her palms down on her thighs as though to smooth a dress that she wasn't wearing. Body Language 101 was going right down the drain for her.

"There are reasons why I can't tell you about how I found out about the children. Patient confidentiality restrains me from—"

"You told Allen here, didn't you?"

She looked at Hemlock for support. He shrugged and spread his hands.

"I'm afraid I can't tell you anything, Mr. Brown."

"A little while ago, it was Scott," I reminded her.

"I can't tell you."

If Hemlock wasn't there and my right arm wasn't so pathetically useless, I think I would have gotten up, gone around the table, and choked it out of her. She sat there with her scruples, knowing what I had gone through to find those kids. She knew where I had been and what I had seen. On the other hand, I still had one good arm; I could have slapped it out of her, but it would have taken twice as long.

Instead, I asked her again what else she knew.

"Whoever is doing this is in a class by themselves," she said. "Not your average killer."

"Not counting," I said, "the trail of dead bodies."

"In fact," she continued, "I have reason to believe we are dealing with an organized team or group of teams rather than an individual."

That made sense. Hemlock and I had talked about it before, but it was just talk. We just didn't know where to take it.

"Maybe it's one person with a tight-knit group of associates. Maybe. But I think it's an organized group. The person or persons responsible for these murders are deranged but brilliantly gifted when you consider what they've gotten away with. Perhaps it is even one of the children in the photo itself."

When I looked down at the smiling faces in the faded newspaper, I felt sick. What kind of sick person would target a group of innocents that happened to be gifted? Or was that why they'd been targeted? Worse still, maybe it was one of the gifted people in the picture, all grown up and psychotic.

"You contacted Interpol, right?" I said finally.

"Interpol personnel are potential candidates. They certainly have the ability to commit murder on an international scale. Who would suspect them?"

The ultra-rich had their own way of looking at things, but this was taking it a bit too far.

"I know what you're thinking, Scott," he said, "but Interpol's been involved in this for a while, and they never came up with the link provided by Dr. Stouffer. Maybe it's because some of their people are involved."

"You mean to say that just because they walked right by the fact that all the children involved were gifted, you think it's smart to keep the one piece of information that might bring it together from them? You've got an international list of victims and potential victims here, with the added possibility that now one of these happy faces in the newspaper photo might be the killer. If you tell Interpol what they need to know, they might get results, or maybe even save a few lives. You want to keep all of this back just on the possibility that the killer might be with Interpol? That's bullshit, Allen."

"I've got my reasons," he said.

"Yeah? Well, I've got my conscience. What's happened to yours?"

It was a low cut. Dr. Stouffer tried to say something, but he held up his hand. From my experience, it was bad manners to interrupt a billionaire.

"My conscience is doing just fine, thank you." His fists clenched and unclenched as though he were testing a new set of bionic hands.

"Then tell me why you really want to hold out on the only police agency that might help us."

He brought his hands to his face and leaned forward. It was a pathetic gesture that must have taken a chunk away from his pride. I would have felt sorry for him if he wasn't so filthy rich.

"I have a problem," he said when he was finally able to regain his composure and uncover his now not smiling face.

"Yeah, I figured. What is it?"

He took a deep breath.

"My son was at that conference."

"Oh."

John, his son, the only heir to Allen Hemlock's fantastic fortune was a write-off. He'd been in and out of trouble with the law, in and out of drug addiction, and, as far as I was concerned, in and out of reality as far back as I could remember. For the last few years, he had been a born again something or other. World ambassador for some weird Christian sect. But he was a certified genius.

"He could be a victim," he added.

"You mean he might be the murderer, don't you?"

Hemlock covered his face again.

John Hemlock

I didn't like the deal, and I could have gone it alone, but they were holding out on me, so I decided to play along long enough to make sure that I found out what it was they were hiding. Besides, Allen Hemlock could exert amazing influence. He was, as they say, a good friend and a seriously bad enemy. With a phone call or two by him, I would be cut out of the information loop and frozen out of the action. And I wanted to stay in that loop so I could catch the killer or killers myself.

Before they left, I learned what I could, and made a show of resisting Hemlock's request, but in the end, I agreed to continue tracking whoever was responsible for the death of all the kids. I also agreed to pay special protective attention to his son, John. Not that the other kids weren't important to Allen, of course, but they weren't heir to the Hemlock fortune.

To tell you the truth, if someone had pointed a gun at John Hemlock in my presence but was hesitating to pull the trigger, I believe that I would have egged them on. The world can be a better place if you kill enough of the right people. It's not my philosophy, just an observation.

John Hemlock lives on Grosse Isle, the big island that you can see from the light cage at the top of my house. There are two smaller islands in between in the line of sight, but they don't amount to much. On clear days you'll see the local artists working there, sketching this and that, painting just what the world needs. Sometimes I wonder how we've survived so many years as a species faced as we are with the critical shortage of island and boat paintings to hang in our motel lobbies.

The smell of wet grass, freshly mowed, was in the air as I got out of the car. The sky was as clear as clean glass and the nine o'clock sun was moronically happy in the sky.

Getting out of my Reatta was a pain. It's a low hung sports car with not much space inside. I felt like a wounded pilot crawling out of his cockpit after crash landing on an island estate. No respectable pilot ever crash land in a trailer park.

John Hemlock's home was paid for by daddy's bucks, of course, as had everything else in his life. It was one of those large, red brick homes with an arch domed door that makes you feel like you should be properly dressed before you knock. The lawn, all two acres of it, was trimmed and landscaped with perfectly sculptured shrubs.

The smoothly interlocking red and gray slabs leading to the front door fit together as neatly as a finished puzzle. They looked as though they were power-washed every morning to eliminate dirty footprints.

You can tell a lot about a person by the sound that their doorbell makes. When I pushed the white button that was inset neatly into the brick a few inches from the doorframe, I heard classical music. Push a button, start the orchestra. Beethoven would probably have never written a note if he had known that his music would be used to announce visitors at the front door.

When the door opened, it was Angel, the Hemlock maid that opened it. Angel was a twenty-ish Nicaraguan beauty with glossy black hair and dark eyes. I had heard stories about her family being burned alive while she watched when she was only eight. Everybody has a past, some darker than others, and if you look at them hard enough, it seems as though you should be able to see some of it in their eyes. Angel's eyes, however, showed nothing.

If she noticed the way my right arm hung, she never gave me any indication. I think that I could have shown up at the front door dragging a dead body behind me, and she wouldn't have looked surprised.

"Is he in?" I asked.

"He's expecting you," she replied.

"There'll be a lady coming along to join us."

"She's already here, Mr. Brown, in the study."

"Wonderful."

Was there the hint of a smile on her face before she turned to lead the way? I rolled the thought over in my mind as I followed her down the thickly carpeted hallway.

Dr. Stouffer was waiting for me, sure enough, pacing near the room's single large window that looked out onto more of the never-ending lawn. She was wearing a thin white blouse that was almost sheer in the morning light. The outline of her apple sized breasts showed plainly through the fabric. With her hair knotted behind her head and her black linen skirt, she had the professional, reserved look that some men find attractive. When she turned to face me and adjusted her glasses before saying hello, I couldn't tell if it was another body language thing or whether her glasses really needed to go up a notch on the bridge of her thin nose.

"Good morning, Mr. Brown." There was a slight tenseness in her voice; the two of us hadn't exactly left on the best of terms the night before.

"Morning," I said. "All ready for the interrogation?"

She wrinkled her nose in disapproval. "Mr. Brown, I want to caution you that no direct questions concerning any involvement of John Hemlock will be tolerated under the rules of discussion that we agreed upon last night."

"We're just here for coffee, is that it? I happened to be in the neighborhood and decided to drop in? He knows what I think of him; you don't think that our coming here together is going to set off his early warning alarms?"

"We are going to stick to the plan. As you may or may not have gathered from last night's conversation, John is a former patient of mine. He has experienced enormous difficulties in the past, and we are not going to treat him as though he were a criminal. Allen would not stand for that, and neither will I."

"Stand for what, Dr. Stouffer?" It was John Hemlock himself.

He stood in the doorway looking thirty years old, rich, handsome, and charismatic. He had a full head of wavy blond hair and a finely boned face with a dimpled chin. His skin was so smooth and healthy looking that it actually seemed to glow. He was tall, and although not muscular, had the athletic, health-club build common to so many rich young men. Fat cells were not in vogue anymore.

His eggshell blue suit and open collared white shirt gave him the look of someone you could be comfortable around. The suit complimented the mauve colored carpet. Dr. Stouffer must have put him through years of color therapy.

"Hello, John," I said. "You're looking fit these days."

He grinned shyly. At least he didn't blush.

"I'm a bit pale," he replied. "I never can seem to get or hold on to a decent tan. It's nice to see you, too, Scott. Father said that you wanted to ask me some questions. Why don't you sit down?"

"Let's all do that," I told him. "We can take a load off of our feet and talk about old times."

Ignoring the look on Dr. Stouffer's face, I took a chair in front of the massive mahogany desk that dominated the room. She took the other, moving it forward an inch, I suppose, so that she was closer to her former patient. I had never met a psychiatrist or psychologist that wasn't a closet control freak. Dr. Stouffer was obviously no exception, and here she was trapped in a room with two screw-ups, one of whom who had targeted the other.

John slid into the red leather chair behind his desk and folded his hands carefully in front of him on its glass top. Bookshelves lined the walls, covering a variety of topics, most of which were religious in nature, some of which were in English.

"Can I bring Angel back to get you anything?" he asked with a smile.

"No thanks," I answered for both the doctor and myself.

"Father told me about your arm. I was sorry to hear that you were injured. How did it happen?"

"Some prick tried to put a miner's axe through my skull when I was down in Mexico."

"You're very lucky to be alive," he said.

"He wasn't so lucky."

I was getting tired of people telling me how lucky I was. Why people had to keep giving their opinion on how lucky I was or wasn't escaped me.

"Yes. Well, how is that I can help you? Father said that I might know something that could be of assistance."

"Mr. Brown would like to ask you about something that happened a long time ago, John," put in Dr. Stouffer gently.

I saw the shutter behind his eyes snap open and close as though taking a picture for future reference.

"The International Gifted Children Conference, that's what I want to know about, John. Some of the kids that attended have gone missing. Some have gone dead. I say kids, but they're older now. A few are about your age. "

While Dr. Stouffer glared at me, I pressed on.

"I think that maybe something happened at that conference, or maybe that something else other than the conference links these kids together. Since you attended, I thought you might help me out. Do you know anything?"

"That was a long time ago," he said.

"I figured a guy with your Mensan memory might be able to handle the time difference."

"That's very flattering, Scott, but it was just a conference. The only thing that really stands out in my mind is the day that the boiler exploded. That actually obscured most of the associated memories. It was an immensely traumatic event."

Last night, Dr. Stouffer had showed me the subsequent clippings. Four children had died in an explosion that ripped straight up and blew open the floor of the auditorium. It was officially declared an accident, a terrible tragedy and blah, blah, blah. Nothing that would lead me to a killer.

"I'm interested in people, John. Can you help me with that? Was there someone that was there that shouldn't have been? Someone that seemed like they didn't belong. Maybe an incident between people, like a confrontation. Or someone that you remember that seemed cold, or different. Can you remember anyone like that?"

He leaned back in his chair and closed his eyes, making a good show of it and impressing Dr. Stouffer in the process. I wonder if she knew that John Hemlock had tried to put a letter opener into my eye one night a few years back. Probably not. Then again, I doubted she would think it relevant, now that he was "cured."

John Hemlock had the kind of memory that even The Amazing

Kreskin would be proud of, but while he pretended to work at remembering what happened back then, I looked around the room again at the books on his wall shelves.

He had everything from the Prophecies of Nostradamus to the complete works of St. Augustine. There were books in Latin, books in ancient Greek, books in Arab, books, books, and more books. On his desk, however, there was only one book—*The Coming of the Beast*, by Thomas Argyle. It was an inch thick and hard covered, with inset gold lettering.

"You've been doing some light reading?" I asked.

"Mr. Brown," said Dr. Stouffer, "could you at least let him think without interruption?"

"I'm sorry?" asked John, as though he hadn't been paying attention.

"I was asking about the book on your desk. The Coming of the Beast. It sounds a little heavy."

"It's a serious topic. But as I remember, you're not much interested in the Bible or its prophecies."

His tone wasn't accusatory; it had more of a flavor of light derision sprinkled with a little superior sadness.

"I'll leave that to you, John. Everybody's got to have a specialty."

"Scott isn't a believer, Dr. Stouffer," he said.

"I'm a realist. You go down a few tunnels with me, and you might be, too."

"The Bible is truth," he said, politely wagging his finger in my direction. It was a manicured finger at that. "Truth has relevance for all ages. Prophecy is especially important with the coming of the End Times."

"I sorry," I said, "we've had so many false End Times that I was confused. What was I thinking?"

"Mr. Brown," said the good doctor, "everyone is entitled to his or her theology. Because Mr. Hemlock's is different from yours is no reason to ridicule him."

"Thank you, doctor, but I am well used to Scott's irreverence."

"But it's no excuse. After all, we've come here for your help."

I couldn't help it. I hate all that End Times bullshit. Seems like a new one is announced every time there was a slow news day. And she was all worked up and self-satisfied by the chance to defend her pet patient. Then again, he hadn't ever tried to poke a letter opener in her eye.

"Well, just for the record," I put in, "as far as I'm concerned, the Beast isn't coming. He's been here for a while. Which brings us back to the murdered kids. You remember anything helpful yet?"

"I agree with you that the Beast is here. Does that surprise you?"

"Seen him first hand, have you John?"

"Mr. Brown."

"I told you, Dr. Stouffer, it's all right. He can't bait me. Scott and I go back quite a way, back to the time before I was saved. I was quite a different person then, wasn't I, Scott?"

No matter what he said, there was tension in his voice that wasn't there when we first started talking. And I knew he knew something. Otherwise, his daddy wouldn't have sent Dr. Librarian along to protect him.

"I can't tell any difference. You seem like the same person to me. Maybe your lady friend here thinks you're different. I know better."

"I was quite the bad boy, Dr. Stouffer," he continued. "I even tried to kill Scott, didn't I, Scott?"

Dr. Stouffer's head had been going back and forth between him and me like she was a spectator at a tennis match following the ball. When John dropped that tidbit, though, she stopped swinging her head and looked at him with great concern.

Now that's rich, I thought. When she hears he tried to stab me in the eye, she feels sorry for him. Go figure.

"You don't have to talk about it if it makes you feel uncomfortable, John."

"Yeah, John, we wouldn't want to upset you."

"It doesn't upset me to think about it."

I looked at Dr. Stouffer and shrugged my shoulders as best I could. My right shoulder didn't actually move that much.

"I told you, he's pretty much the same as I remember him."

"Allow me to explain, Scott. It doesn't upset me to remember the bad things that I did because I know that I have been forgiven. I know that you, however, are still living in darkness and can't understand, which is why you scoff at the reality and meaning of the Beast."

"Why don't you explain it to me?" I asked. "Enlighten a poor soul living in the darkness. Help me out."

The camera like shutter behind his eyes snapped shut again. He was photographing the moment for his high-IQ'd brain to put into storage for his viewing enjoyment at a later date. The lady had to be blind not to see what he was really like. Blind or in love. They were two equally depressing possibilities.

"All right," he said, "I'll do what I can."

Dr. Stouffer turned a smug look toward me, but I ignored her. What did she know? She was too educated to think.

"My life was saved on the day of the boiler explosion, Dr. Stouffer. That conference was my road to Damascus."

When Dr. Stouffer turned a blank look to him, I helped her out.

"The road to Damascus. You remember the conversion of Saul to Paul in the Bible, don't you? Saul was out and about throwing Christians in prison and having them executed. One day, on his way to the city of Damascus to do more bad things, a brilliant light appeared out of nowhere and blinded him. That's what blinding lights do, though, isn't it? They blind people.

"Anyway, it blinded Saul, and when he went blind, he heard the voice of Jesus talking to him. Jesus was already dead, by the way," I added in a confidential whisper.

"Jesus tells him he will have a new name and a new job description. He's got to go around spreading the good news and suffering for the name of Jesus. Have I got this right, John?" I asked innocently.

"Yes, although your telling of the story leaves something to be desired."

"Okay," I continued for Dr. Stouffer's benefit, "so now you know what the road to Damascus is all about."

I would have bowed to emphasize the point that I had showed her up, but it seemed inappropriate.

"Thank you for that lecture," she said with a small but recognizable sneer that warmed me all over.

"That conference," repeated John, "was my road to Damascus. I was blinded for three days, you see, just like the Apostle Paul. Only instead of a blinding white light, the light that I saw was orange-red, and my world was filled with smoke, burning flesh, and the smell of sulfur. My vision was that the Beast had come into the world somewhere, and that the battle for men's souls had begun. A voice told me that I was to become a student of the Word—"

"That's slang for the Bible," I whispered to Dr. Stouffer.

"And take it to my heart," finished Hemlock in a louder voice. "I was a sinner, and if I didn't repent and practice the goodness of the Lord's word, I knew then that I would fall into the hands of the Beast."

Dr. Stouffer couldn't seem to think of what to say. I've got to admit, I couldn't think of anything much to add myself. John helped us both out by continuing his testimony.

"In my three days of blindness, I saw what I had been. I had been a hedonistic, amoral, and violent person. There was no excuse for the things that I had done, no way to make amends. I could only seek forgiveness from God and change my ways. I became a new man in Jesus."

At any moment, I expected him to hold up a placard with a toll-free number so that we could phone in our love offerings.

"It was, of course, you, Dr. Stouffer, who guided me through the changes in my life. For that, I am eternally grateful. I will never forget what you have done for me."

And, he could have added, I would like to thank all the little people who made this possible. The women that I beat up and raped, the drugs I took, the people I used, and, of course, my father's endless supply of money and his lawyers, who kept me out of prison.

"Between yourself, Brother Thomas, and Jesus," he continued, "I have a certain peace that I would never again like to be without."

"Thank you, John," glowed Dr. Stouffer modestly, "but it was your commitment to change and your hard work that made those changes possible."

"I stand rebuked," I said, "and maybe I have been a little bit of an asshole."

He was watching me carefully, waiting for the sucker punch.

"So, tell me," I continued, "what was it like to hear the voice of Jesus? I mean, just for the record, what did he sound like? Did he have a deep voice? Did he have a Middle Eastern accent, or did he speak English like a native? Help me out again, John. What exactly did Jesus sound like and how did you know it was him?"

Before he could answer, a young woman came into the room. I felt her come up behind me before I actually heard her footsteps or heard her speak.

"Oh, excuse me, I didn't know that your friends were still here."

Her voice could have come from a music box; it had that tinkly-pure quality. When I turned to see her, I saw she had that ethereal presence of the ballerina that spins airily while the music box plays a haunting tune.

She was thin bodied, with a small porcelain colored face framed by soft brown waves of hair. Her dress was a blend of Easter egg colors, bright and happy, innocent and expectant.

"I can come back," she said apologetically.

"Please stay," John said eagerly.

Dr. Stouffer's face lost its misty-eyed quality, and she stiffened noticeably.

"Dr. Stouffer, you know my wife, Christine. Scott, I don't believe you've had the pleasure of her acquaintance yet."

Leveraging myself to my feet with my good arm, I stood to meet her.

There are some people that you meet in life that you don't even feel like you deserve to be in the same room with. Christine Hemlock made me feel that way. She smiled and extended her hand. I felt like I should fall to one knee and pledge myself to her service.

Instead, I took her delicate left hand in my own-callused grip, and shook it gently. As I released and took my hand away, I realized she knew about my injury, but had said nothing about it, had not drawn attention to my problem. I liked her already.

Hemlock rose from his chair and walked around to where his wife stood, and he took her hand, intertwining his fingers through hers.

"Have I interrupted you?" she asked.

"No," said Dr. Stouffer in her professional voice, "I think we were about through. Mr. Brown, is there anything else that you can think of to ask?"

I shook my head no. For the first time, I saw approval in her eyes. Scott was following her script like a good boy.

"Nothing comes to mind. John's been as helpful as he could, I suppose. We're following a twelve-year-old trail, so I didn't expect much. Mrs. Hemlock, it was a great pleasure to meet you. I hope to see you again someday."

"Perhaps you could come to dinner, one week from tomorrow night," Christine asked. "Brothers Thomas and Peter are coming; we're having a fund raiser for the new outreach program. I'm sure that they would love to meet you. John has told me very little about you. I don't know many of John's father's friends. Please say yes. You're welcome to come as well, Dr. Stouffer. The two of you can come together."

"Scott's very busy doing something for father," said John.

"Oh, I'm not that busy," I said quickly. "Dr. Stouffer could be my date. What do you say, doctor?"

She should have said no, but I think that the shock of hearing me call her doctor had numbed her brain. "That would be... yes, I can come. I think that I'm free."

"Oh, good," beamed Christine, "it will be such a special evening with you both here.

Special, I thought, was not the word.

Bob Alby

Dr. Stouffer may have thought that it had been a total wash, but I didn't. I left her behind after agreeing to meet her later for lunch, and drove to the office of Bob Alby— one of two people in the area that I actually counted as friends. There were plenty of people that I knew on sight and exchanged limited pleasantries with, such as the people who ran the marina where I parked my boat, the convenience store attendants, and the local waitresses where I ate, but Bob Alby, Leroy Croton, and Charlie Kim, my Hapkido instructor, were the only three people who really knew me. Monica Thomas knew me in a different way, but I'll get to her later.

Bob Alby published the Gibraltar Gazette. Really, that is its name- the Gibraltar Gazette. It was a small town paper with a circulation of slightly over three thousand readers. The Gazette sold for fifty cents per copy at the local gas stations and in scattered newspaper boxes, but was also distributed to all of the homes in Gibraltar on an honors basis. If you wanted to pay, you did. Most didn't. If it weren't for the advertising and the coupons, Gibraltar wouldn't have had its own newspaper. It wouldn't have been that big of a loss. After all, we still had Blockbuster Video.

The world headquarters of the Gazette was in a mostly deserted strip mall off of Gibraltar Rd. sandwiched between the Comely Cosmetic Shop and the Bulk Food Granary. I parked the Reatta next to one of the five other cars in the cracked blacktopped asphalt parking lot and got out swearing to myself as I maneuvered free relying mostly on my good arm.

Both the Mexican doctors and the real ones back in the States had told me that I might never regain the use of my right arm, and that I should prepare myself for that possibility. They were wrong. I was going to have two good arms. It was important that when I found the killer, I could wrap both my hands around his windpipe and slowly squeeze the life out of him.

Dr. Stouffer, her educatedness, had missed the whole point of our conversation with John Hemlock. John had heard a voice telling him that the Beast had arrived. He was blind at the time, so the question was, who was doing the talking? I didn't buy the Jesus bit. Whoever had been doing the talking was our man, unless it was all in Hemlock's mind, or he just made it up. In that case, Hemlock was most likely the killer. Either way, the owner of that voice was going to die. I just needed a while longer to get better before I was able to choke whoever it turned out to be so I could do the job myself.

Bob was in his office, sitting behind the art form of chrome and Formica that he called his desk. I could barely see his broad, pock marked face behind the monitor.

"Hey, editor," I called out, "I've got a hot story for you. Seems the owner of the local paper has been banging the—"

"Hey, hey, hey," he cut in. "Watch your mouth, this is a respectable rag I run here. We don't need any smut stories."

"It might boost your circulation, you know, by adding a little spice. While you're at it, why don't you try getting a decent website?"

"We don't sell spice," he said standing up, "we sell community oriented journalism. And I don't especially like technology."

Bob Alby looked like the average person's stereotype of a Mafia gangster. He had black slick backed hair that was so greasy that the joke around town was that he combed his hair with the same thirty weight motor oil that he put in his car. His neck was so thick and muscular that he had a hard time getting shirts that could button around it. Bob still lifts weights as religiously as he has ever since the tenth grade. He's a hard man to fit into a suit.

"Community oriented journalism. That's what you call it?"

"With a straight face. You on for poker tonight? Leroy's hot. Says his astrology chart tells him that this is the luckiest day of his life."

It was Friday night, and every Friday night that I was in town we played poker. When I got back from Mexico, Leroy had presented me with a hand-made card holding stand.

"Count me in."

"Good. Monica coming?"

"I don't know. She's still pretty pissed at me," I said.

"You know your problem? Lucky in cards but unlucky in love. That's your problem. You should just marry her and settle down. Enjoy the rest of your life."

"I don't think so, buddy. She's not my type. I'd like a woman that's less screwed up than I am."

"Whoa, that was low."

With my good hand I pulled a chair around to the side of his desk, and sat down. Bob did the same, sinking back into the leather chair behind his desk.

"Yeah," I said, "but it was called for."

He held his hands up, palms toward me. "Okay, okay. So what do you want? You're here for something, right?"

I nodded.

"I need some help. You know the clowns that Johnny Hemlock is tied up with, the New Apostles of Christ?"

"I know a little bit about them. Why?"

"I'd like to know a lot about them. I'm going to run the databases on them, but I want to know more. You got a handle on anybody with their organization that I could talk to? Anybody that's maybe as pissed at them as Monica is with me?"

"No, but I could look around, Scott. Let you know what I find out."

"I'd appreciate it."

"You on a job?" he asked.

"Same job."

"Johnny's not involved in this, is he?"

"I don't know, but I hope so."

Bob's newspaper was mostly empty space. Before 11920 Gibraltar Rd. had become the headquarters for the Gazette, it had been a convenience store. It still had that look to it. The office was mostly empty space, three desks, a couple of computers, and a bunch of fold-up buffet tables. The linoleum-tiled floor still had the rust colored discolorations and marks from where the counters and racks had been, and there was one seriously disfigured spot where the freezer had stood. Calendars and notices were nailed or taped to the square pillars. On the pillar nearest Bob's desk hung the bright red fire extinguisher that he had hit me in the head with when we had first met.

That day was a bad day for me. I hadn't slept well the night before because of the bad dreams, and the night sweats had come back.

Sometimes driving seemed to help clear my head, so I had gone out for a cruise down Gibraltar Rd., hoping that the car motions and highway sounds would take my mind off of the flashbacks of dead men laying on their backs on hard factory concrete because an asshole named me turned the wrong valve. No one cruises Gibraltar Rd. for the scenery unless they like to look at weeds and drainage ditches.

I'd gone about five miles driving in a fugue state when this sun-bleached green pickup truck came tearing past me just as I was slowing down for a brown and white patched beagle that was crossing the road a ahead of me.

I yelled whatever obscenity came first to my mind and whipped up my middle finger to punctuate the point.

The dog never had a chance. I saw the rear lights on the truck flash briefly like the driver was thinking of stopping, but then he gave it up and kept going. The dog under the wheels when his brakes went on, so that his front wheel slid with the furry mess under it for a few feet. I slammed my palm down on the steering wheel and swore again.

When the driver let off on his brakes and kept on going, the dog's body came out from under his front wheel and was run over by his back one. The truck bounced as though it had gone over a speed bump and kept on going.

I stopped on the side of the road, and got out in so much of a hurry that I left my door open when I ran over to see if there was any chance that the dog survived.

Dogs are dogs, they're not people, I know that, but when I kneeled down next to the beagle and lifted its head gently, there was still life in its eyes. It could have bitten me, but it licked my sleeve instead and whimpered. Its body was flattened too much for the dog to live; it probably had a cracked spine. I couldn't think of what to do, so I just patted its head.

Around its neck was a collar, and on the collar was a shiny metal heart with the name "Pete" stenciled on it. When Pete finally shivered and died, I dragged his body to the side of the road and tossed it into the drainage ditch. I didn't have a shovel with me, and Pete had no objections, although I can't say that I felt good about doing it.

A mile further down the road, I saw the same pickup truck parked out front of the Gibraltar Gazette. I parked a few feet from it, got out of my car again, and went inside. Bob Alby, who I didn't know from Adam back then, was sitting at his desk in the middle of the floor. Two part-timers were wandering around carrying papers and looking busy. There was a big, bearded guy in sweat pants and a T-shirt standing in front of Bob's desk with a clipboard in his left hand and money in his right probably trying to get his lawnmower ad in the paper at the last minute.

I didn't hear what they were saying, but I walked right up behind the guy with the beard and said, as nice as I could, "Hey buddy, is that your green pickup truck out there?"

He turned to look at me, an ugly, friendly expression on his face, and said, "Sure is. Heart and soul of my business. Why?"

I supposed he was trying to tell me that he used the truck in his business. He was a contractor of some kind, I imagined, but I really didn't care. I grabbed the front of his T-shirt, yanked him toward me, and head-butted him square in the nose.

He yelled like I'd cut off his finger.

When I kneed him in the crotch, he yelled even louder.

I spun him around hard and threw him up and onto a desk. He missed the point-up message spike, and landed on a wire cage full of memos, still screaming. The part-timers started running for the door, their faces wild and frightened. Papers had scattered when the bearded wonder hit the desk, and as he rolled over it and smacked onto the floor, he must have tried to hang on to the desk because it tipped over with him and slammed down onto his back.

He lay like the beagle had on the highway. There was blood on the floor, pooling by the side of his face. I felt as good as I ever had before

Bob Alby came at me from behind and nailed me with the fire extinguisher and dropped me like a stone.

"... and I'll call you," Bob was saying. "Hey, are you listening to me or what?"

"Sort of. I was just remembering the first day that I had the pleasure of meeting you."

His face was blank for a moment, then he broke into a wide grin, showing a good set of teeth unfortunately stained by years of cigarette smoking.

"Hell of a way to meet, eh?" he asked.

"Fuck you," I said, "I've still got a dent in the back of my skull. It's not bad enough that I've got only one good arm now, but I've got to go through life wearing this disfigured head on my shoulders."

"You weren't that good looking to start with. What are you complaining about?"

I left the newspaper and headed towards the lunch appointment requested by Dr. Stouffer. Monica and I were supposed to have lunch, but she wouldn't show for half an hour past when we were supposed to meet just to make me wait, so what was the point of going? She would get mad, but she was always mad when she didn't get her own way. So I decided to tie up with Dr. Stouffer.

Sometimes I hang on to things too long.

Monica fit into that category. The thing was, not only was she a good looking woman, like most redheads that I've seen are, but she also had a good brain. She was a lawyer, and she took that seriously enough, but she wasn't too good in the faithfulness department, which is a big thing to me. The breaking point had come about two years ago when I had found out that she was banging the same guy that had run over the damn dog. That about did it for me.

When I was married a thousand years or so ago, I had never once cheated on my wife. Never. I went crazy for a while after the accident, like sex was going to validate the fact that I was still alive, according to one shrink. Another said I was trying to take myself down as low as I could go by sleeping with any woman willing to do it with me. I had some baggage. I admit it.

Scott Brown turned a valve and killed a town. It was a crappy rhyme, but it made the point.

Shrinks weren't always wrong. It's just that I eventually figured it all out for myself, so what had I paid them for? It was a new valve, no one knew it was defective and, yes, I was supposed to open. It wasn't supposed to break and send toxic gas into the air.

My wife Becky and my son William lived in the town that I gassed. They weren't among the survivors. You could say that I had cause to be screwed up. I should have died along with them. Sometimes I hang on to things too long, but I didn't have a choice when it came to the after-shock of emotional numbness. Anyone that kills their wife and kid, even by a complete and total accident, is never going to be right. That's what I figured out on my own.

*****

There were no restaurants proper to take a lady like Dr. Stouffer to in Gibraltar, so we had agreed to meet in at Julio's in Trenton. It wasn't one of the uptown restaurants like she was used to in Farmington Hills where she had her practice, but it would have to do. I wasn't meeting on her turf. I got there ten minutes early, but she was already in a booth, waiting for me. Another shrink trick.

She was drinking a glass of wine, probably to ease the strain of our meeting. Although it was an even bet that she saw me coming in through the door, but decided to conceal that fact by looking down studiously at a spiral notebook when I sat down.

"Studying for finals?" I asked.

I mentally ticked off three seconds off before she looked up.

"Ah, Mr. Brown. You're here."

"Yes, I am. And early, too. But not as early as you."

"I was in the neighborhood anyway," she said. "I've never been here before, so I decided to look early to avoid being late."

"Uh-huh."

"Is there some reason that you find that suspect?"

"Lots of them. But let's skip ahead. What did you find out from John-boy?"

"Pardon me?"

"Ooh, astonishment. A difficult emotion to portray correctly. Good job. But you stayed around after I left, so that means that you were poking around in his head, or trying to. So what did you find out?"

"You are an irritating man. I understand that you've had a difficult life, but-."

"You don't understand anything about me, so don't even try. Now, what did you find out?"

She took a deep breath, a cleansing breath, as I think they call it, before she answered.

"I wasn't 'poking around in his head'. We were just talking."

The waitress interrupted to take our order. Her name, according to the nametag pinned to the tightly stretched fabric over her left breast, was Julie, and she had the kind of pretty face and full but firm figure that made older, less attractively well-endowed women uncomfortable. Julie's hair was thick and full and shiny black and needed to be touched. I felt sorry for her. Looks like hers were trouble. Maybe she'd get lucky and get fat.

Dr. Stouffer ordered the Pasta Alfredo, and I ordered a black coffee.

"You're not hungry?" she asked when Julie had left.

"I never eat lunch," I replied.

The truth was, however, that even though I gotten reasonably proficient with feeding myself left handed, I wasn't about to go through the ordeal of doing it in front of her. The idea of her watching while I fumbled around with my food was an appetite suppressant.

"I always eat lunch," she confided. "I'm hypoglycemic."

"It must be hell. Now what did you find out?"

"You can't badger me Mr. Brown. Your aggressive behavior might serve you well when you're dealing with an adversarial situation, but I am not your adversary. We're on the same team."

"Thanks for that. Now, before we go any farther, let's get a few things straight from my side of the table."

There was no perceptible change in her posture, no stiffening of her back, no compressing of her lips, but her eyes seemed to focus on me, ready to see some aggressive behavior, some sharp words that she could file away in her psychiatrist brain for future use in analyzing exactly what type of antisocial humanoid that I was.

"First," I said, "although my personal experience with John Hemlock was bad enough, and I kind of hate his guts—that isn't relevant. We're looking for murders. They are beyond amoral. I hate what they've done to those kids more than I can ever explain. So, believe me, I'm not hung up on pinning this on John. I want to pin it on whoever hurt those kids. John Hemlock is just a distraction Allen threw at us because he's paranoid. I don't blame him for that. His own kid, no matter how worthless I think he is, is important to him.

"Next, when we find out whoever is responsible, I can hunt them and take them down. That's all any of this is about to me. If John Hemlock is innocent, then so be it. If he's not, then we take him down like any other murderer. I don't answer to anybody. I should have bought it with my wife and kid, which I think Allen already told you about. I don't answer to anyone because what could they do to me that be worse than what I've already done to myself?

"Third, there is nothing personal in the verbal tactics that I use on John Hemlock or anyone else that could yield useful information. We need efficiency more than we need sensitivity. There are still kids on our list who are alive, and we've got to keep it that way. None of us know how much time is left or when and where they'll kill next. That's the way I see it. I just don't want to show up too late. That's what I've been doing since this started and I absolutely hate it."

Dr. Stouffer seemed disappointed. She waited before answering, hoping, perhaps, that I would eventually lose control and launch into a diatribe revealing my truly sinister side or my hidden plans for revenge. I had both, but I wasn't going to let her know that.

Eventually, she gave up. Not entirely, of course. I knew that we would be plowing this same field again in the future. Some shrinks, particularly women shrinks, are like that. They go over the same ground over and over ad nauseam. Certain men do it, too, but they're a lot easier for me to dust off.

We were about five minutes into her Pasta Alfredo when my phone began to ring. I excused myself and headed for some privacy at the back of the restaurant.

If you've never tried to work a smartphone with one hand, you know it's not as easy as it sounds. If you're sweating, it pops out of place like a greased pig slipping through your fingers, and you have to start all over again. I should have bought a Bluetooth a long time ago.

There was a message on my voice mail from Allen Hemlock: Ukraine. Five kids from the master list were missing. Leave immediately. I should have expected it. John Hemlock began to look a lot less promising as the killer, but he was still an asshole.

I would have to finish my lunch with Dr. Stouffer some other time. Tomorrow night's poker game would have to wait. I had a plane to catch.

*****

It was the summer of 1988. It was going to be the worst night of my life. I had been working in the plant since four thirty a.m. and was going through the motions more than anything else, dreading to go home. Becky had made it plain when I was called in to work that she had enough. Enough of me, my ways, and the job that had worked me seventy to eighty hours every week. We had a child named William, she had reminded me, who couldn't recognize me as a father because I wasn't home enough. When I wasn't working, I was working out. She had gone to her lawyer about filing divorce papers. That came out in the trial along with everything else.

It had been okay before we were married. It was "cool" back then when I split my time between working, working out, and dating her. I was going to put enough money away to open my own martial arts dojo, then quit the job, and split my time between teaching my students and being with her. The problem came when, in the third year of our marriage, I lost my job shortly after William had been born.

Eventually, I had found another with a company that treated plastic with fluorine gas to make them resistant to chemicals. My title was "chemical operator." It was a start-up venture, but I didn't care. I didn't have any experience as a chemical operator, but that didn't matter. I had worked as a lab technician in my last job, I could pronounce the word "fluorine," and I was obviously strong enough to handle the manual labor side of things. In my job interview, I had told the manager that I wasn't very smart, but that I could lift heavy things.

At the trial afterwards, the prosecutor had made a big deal of all three points: I had trouble at home, I was burned out from working too many hours, and I lacked professional experience. He didn't like it when I told him from the witness stand that it applied to well over half the working men in America. It wasn't a good comeback, but I was under a lot of stress.

It was three o'clock in the afternoon, and the wind was blowing toward town, a fact that didn't sink in until after the accident. I had the acid suit on, my air hose was turned on and connected, and I was going into the fluorine room to change over valves on the hydrogen fluoride delivery system.

You have to understand that hydrogen fluoride and fluorine eat the hell out of everything that they come into contact with, so that, as a part of maintenance, it's necessary to change over from one system to the alternate, and then replace the alternate on a regular basis. It's just part of the job. The alternate system had never been used, never been tested, but was supposed to be identical to the primary system. It wasn't my job to make sure of that; I was just a valve turner.

When we had been building the plant, I had worked the extra hours, because the company had been behind their construction schedule. Now that the system was operational, we were working the extra hours to supply the customers for the company's new business. Hence my problems with Becky.

I had called her twice during the day. She had hung up on me both times. I remember thinking that if I got off of work early enough, the flower shops would be open, and I could pick her up a dozen roses. But at three fifteen, I went into the fluorine room to change over the system. By four forty-five o'clock, she and William and a lot of other people were dead, and I lay unconscious on the floor.

They died painful deaths.

Boris Zankov

I had been to Russia before, but never to the Ukraine. In the post-Soviet Union era, it was important to keep these things straight. Although without the natives to inform you, a person would be hard pressed to tell the difference.

Allen Hemlock's private jet touched down in Kiev, the Ukrainian capital, at seven fourteen a.m. their time on the following morning. Boris Zankov, who steered me past the usual customs monstrosities, met me at the airport. Zankov was Hemlock International's dirty tricks guy in that part of the world.

With a global network like Hemlock International, one thing that I had learned was that you needed men like Gregorio, Zankov, others, and myself to keep things running smoothly. Before the accident, before I went to work for Hemlock as part of his covert operations group, I would have never dreamed that worldwide corporations needed or used people in that way. I now know that the giant multinationals are larger than most of the planet's countries, and that they have the same needs.

Still, it's hard to believe the things that go on in most of the big companies. Most people live in a dream world in that regard. They believe the TV ads and ignore the reality. But if you really think of it, where there's big money, there's big power, and where's there's big power, well, you get the picture.

Hemlock International turned over eighty billion dollars US per year. That's likely more than the gross national product of Canada. Allen is the sole owner. He could have been President of the United States if he'd wanted to, but, as he said, then he'd have had to move into public housing. Billionaires have their own way of looking at things.

Zankov's background was KGB, or whatever it is that they call it these days. I suppose I should have judged him. Maybe he should have judged me. After the accident, however, I guess I got out of the judgment business. He had always done what we had paid him to do, and that was all I really cared about. Whatever he used to do for the Russian government was past tense.

We left Kiev airport driving Zankov's green Lada, which, although it was built like a truck, he drove as if it were a sports car. Zankov was the epitome of a movie spy. He was handsome in a dark sort of way, complete with the square chin, broad shoulders, and a narrow waist. On the day that he picked me up from the airport, he dressed in a worsted brown tweed jacket patched on the elbows, a cream colored turtleneck, and brown pants that told me he was just aching to be on the cover of a Western men's magazine. He was so noticeable that it was hard to for me to figure out how he had survived as an agent.

"So," he said as we drove down the crowded, polluted streets of Kiev, "you are here again when is trouble. Why you not come to visit us when times are so good?"

"Nobody needs me when times are good, Boris." I was still a little grumpy from sleeping on the plane.

"Times always are good," he said, turning toward me with a sly wink, "when there is money to be made. And there is always much money to be made. Surely your Mr. Hemlock must have taught you that."

"I get paid pretty damned good, Boris, but I'm not much into making money."

He laughed hard, and thumped his palm on the steering wheel. The fact that we were crowded hard on all sides by pollution-belching Russian cars that put up a dark cloud like a herd of buffaloes on the run across a dry plain didn't seem to bother him.

"Me," he said, when he had finished laughing, "I am not ashamed to be capitalist."

"Good for you. Now tell me about the kids."

Kiev was a cross between Detroit and a Moroccan bazaar. Cars jammed the streets, people jammed the sidewalks, and business was transacted everywhere. When we stopped at a stoplight, teenagers banged on the glass, shouting at us and waving briefcases in front of the windshield. When the signal changed, Boris floored the gas pedal, and the car jumped forward. The children adroitly twisted their bodies and got out of the way, waiting for the signal to change so that they could repeat the whole mess again.

"We go now to bad place, my friend," he said, and his face changed expression. "They were found too late for me to be help. I sorry. They find each one but one."

"All but one? You mean that there's still one unaccounted for?"

"Unaccounted? Please explain. How does this mean?"

"It means that you can't find one."

"Yes. I see."

"Where are we going, specifically?"

The car turned a corner so fast that it felt like it would tip over.

"We go to old train line. Underground. I have friends who be there."

"Friends? You mean like in police?"

He smiled over his shoulder, and I saw a glint of steel. Russian dental work. It could screw up the best looking faces.

"No police. My men. You know I now have own security business? Twenty men and more are employees to Boris. Former associates. Three of best protect this place against someone go to it by mistake."

"You've kept it from the police?"

"Mr. Hemlock has so instructed me. I cannot disobey him. He pays me big money. He tells me to protect this place, so I do it."

The sky was bright and sunny. I used to think that bad things could not happen on such days. Now I know that they happen in any weather, anywhere. The thing to remember is that good things do, too. Sometimes. If I didn't try to keep that in mind, I think that I would have gone crazy. I'm close enough as it is.

"Hemlock had you check the master list? That's how you knew to look for them?"

"Yes. But by the time I was told, they all gone."

"But you didn't find them all?"

"As I said, all but one was in old train place."

"You searched it thoroughly? Completely?"

"Of course."

He said it matter of factly. I tried not to think of what it must have been like. Looking for what you did not want to find. Dreading that you would find it. Smelling the bad smell.

"How much further?" I asked.

"Very close. Smoke?"

From inside his jacket, he withdrew, then extended a crumpled pack of Marlboro's, which were still bartered in the former Soviet Republics.

"No thanks."

Zankov shrugged, and then lit up.

After a minute or so I said, "Christ, can't you at least roll down the window?"

"Why?" he asked with a grin. "The air outside so much worse."

"Fucking country," I muttered under my breath, then rolled down the window on my side of the car. It wasn't easy with my left hand, but it was better than dying of cancer before we got to the underground railroad. When the window was halfway down, the handle came off.

"Push back on. Is frequent happen."

I laid it between us on the seat.

"Ah," he said, "I forgot."

"Yeah, well, it's getting better. I can't pick my nose yet, but it'll get there. At least I can move my fingers."

"Try first to pick your ass," he said with a grin, "is much easier to reach."

God, I miss Mexico, I thought.

In a soot covered part of town that looked remarkably like either photos of Berlin after the bombing raids of World War II or certain parts of Detroit, he pulled the Lada over to a curb.

"We are here," he announced.

"Figured. I'll take the nine-millimeter now."

Zankov looked at me, then up and down the street. "Is not a

dangerous neighborhood."

"Give it to me."

"But my men," he protested, "are inside. Is perfectly safe."

"Give me the Beretta, Boris. I'm not getting out of this car without a weapon."

"Okay, okay. But I tell you it is safe. Besides," he said as he leaned over and opened the glove box and revealed the weapon inside, "with your arm..."

I took out the gun, checked it out, and slipped it into my left jacket pocket.

"I shoot just fine with my left hand. Now let's get to it."

Zankov led the way through an old building, stepping around the dusty dead bodies of shriveled rats, avoiding the broken glass and the scraps of dirty brown metal. There was a smell to the building as we followed the hallway—not the bad smell, but a dry, sour smell, like an old man's breath.

We passed a room full of laboratory benches and equipment, another full of filing cabinets. Gray-white dust covered everything. The walls were faded and hole marked, and chunks of plaster lay on the tiled floor.

Filtered light shone through the building's greasy, dirty windows. The sky outside was still, I imagined, bright and sunny. The clouds, what few there were, were probably still full and pillow white above Kiev's polluted skies. But as we went further and further into the building, the polluted Ukrainian day seemed bright by comparison. The light became dim, and the air felt heavy. I kept my hand in my left pocket and my finger on the trigger.

As we were approaching the end of one hall, there was a man standing in the shadows before a metal door with an AK-47 slung across his shoulder. He stood casually, dangerously. Men that carry weapons and have a stiff body posture respond more slowly, in my experience, than do men that are relaxed but alert. Men like this guy up ahead were good to keep an eye on.

"What's his name?" I asked Boris.

"Katerina," he said under his breath. "Her name is Katerina."

"He's a she?"

He nodded sharply, as we approached the guard, "She is wife. So watch, please, your mouth."

"You brought your wife in on this?" I asked. I couldn't believe it.

"She is employee of security business. Former Major in KGB. Now vice president for security company. Very efficient. Very good."

"Did it have to be your wife? I mean, you had some choices, Boris."

By then, we were too close to her for her not to be aware of the conversation. I could see that she was indeed a woman, and not a very attractive one at that.

She had a hard, thin face and thick glasses. Her hair was brown and short, and her mouth was just a dark slash in the shadows. She was a few inches shorter than me, but with an AK-47 involved, size wasn't really an issue.

"I volunteered, Mr. Brown," she said in a surprisingly feminine voice and using better English than her hubby.

We stopped three feet from her.

"I'm sorry, Major," I said. "I didn't mean for you to hear."

"Former Major Katerina Firyubin. I am now only Katerina Firyubin. You may call me simply Katerina."

So instructed, I said, "My apologies, Katerina. It is a nasty business."

"Very," she replied. "My husband is not unaffected, regardless of how he appears. We have no children ourselfs. Yet we hope to much soon in future. It is very terrible business."

Boris's face was uneasy. He smiled, he frowned, then smiled briefly again.

"My wife and I, we would much like to know how is it you know of this terrible thing in the Ukraine and our own police know so very little of nothing?"

Rules of the game. I couldn't tell him anything.

"I'm just following orders, Boris. Mr. Hemlock says go to the Ukraine and check things out, I go. He's the boss. I don't know what he knows."

"Do you know why these little ones and no others?" asked Katerina.

Gregorio was easier to deal with than these two. He knew the score going in. He might bitch and moan about certain things, but he hardly ever put me on the spot. These two started out by playing hardball.

"We know of what you found in Mexico, Taiwan, Japan, Spain, and elsewhere," said Boris.

"Somebody's been busy," I agreed.

They both went quiet on me at that point. Two armed KGB pros who wanted to know something, and they didn't look like they would take bullshit for an answer. I didn't feel too good about the situation, considering my bad arm. The question was, how far did they want to take this? How important were the answers to them?

"I have read of killings like these, of what was done to bodies," offered Katerina finally.

"How do you mean?"

"No, Mr. Brown," she said firmly. "No answers without exchange."

Apparently, she had gone as far as she would go.

"You must understand what we have seen in our lives," said Boris sadly. "I think I need speak no further for you understand. But this..."

He spread his hands apart, not knowing what to say.

I had the picture. Two family members in the KGB. The stories that they must have shared over the kitchen table. Or not. Maybe they hadn't been able to speak freely in their own homes—microphones in the salad bowls and all that.

"All right," I said at last. "Deal. First, we look at the bodies, then I'll tell you what I know and you do the same for me."

"Deal," nodded Boris.

"I agree," said his grim faced wife.

"Then let's do it."

As we went down the stairs, Boris held the big flashlight, and I mean the big flashlight. It was more like a search lamp. Katerina held a standard flashlight like I did. She'd had them stacked against the base of the wall, waiting for us to take along.

I had had a choice between holding a flashlight or a gun. It was a tough call for me, but I chose the flashlight. I'm not afraid of the dark, but I like to know what I'm up against.

The metal steps made it impossible to walk quietly. A deaf man could have heard us coming. But it was supposed to be safe.

I went last, like I always did, but I didn't like it much.

The husband and wife team of former spies were better in one respect than Gregorio. They kept their mouths shut on the way down. By the time we reached bottom, though, I was missing a little mindless chatter. It would have been nice to have him there just so that I could have told him to shut the hell up.

The door at the bottom of the stairs, when we finally got there, opened with a screeching noise that would have done a parrot in heat proud.

"Do not worry," said Boris without looking back, "all is secure."

"Hell of an early warning system you've got."

"Is not hotel," he said.

There were mechanic's lights strung alongside of the wall that made the flashlights unnecessary. I exchanged mine for my gun and immediately felt better.

"You've been busy," I said.

He didn't respond, but kept walking behind his wife.

The parallel with Mexico got my nerves talking to each other. A tunnel, railway tracks, and children's bodies somewhere up ahead. The only real difference was the size of the underground railway. The smell was fainter, mixed with the cloying odor of heavy oil. I didn't know how far the tunnel went, but I was grateful for the dilution of the bad smell by whatever passive ventilation the place had.

"Hey, Boris, what was this? Public transportation?"

They both stopped and glowered at me at the same time. I could tell that they had worked together a lot.

"Please to be quiet," he said.

"I miss Gregorio," I explained.

He shook his head at the same time as she did, then they both turned and continued walking again. He broke rank, though, when I heard him mutter something in Russian.

When we rounded the bend up ahead, the smell of death and fresh blood hit me simultaneously, and I knew we had trouble. The crumpled bodies of two men were lying one across the other in the shape of a cross about ten feet ahead of us.

I dropped to a crouch and turned, fanning the area behind us with the Beretta. Boris and Katerina did the same, each covering a different area. We stayed like that for what seemed an eternity, waiting for something, anything, to happen.

Finally, I asked, "Last contact with your men?"

The answer came quickly from Katerina.

"Thirty minutes."

In a place like this, I thought, a lot can happen in thirty minutes.

"Katerina," came Boris's voice. "I see Sergie's body, but man on top, he is not Sasha."

Thank you, I thought, for speaking in English.

"You mean we've got an unknown?" I asked.

"I do not know who is this man."

I should have seen it sooner, the man sitting beside the other bodies. His eyes popped open, and he raised a pistol. With a muffled sound, he fired and hit Boris. The barrel turned to me and I dove toward the ground just as Katerina let loose with the AK-47. My head was turned to him as I went down, and just before I hit the stones face first, I saw his head explode into wet mist and fragments.

She could have gone for a body shot.

*****

I've never felt so out of place in my life as I did at the Eastern Orthodox funeral. I couldn't understand but a small portion of the language. Boris, like Katerina, had made Kiev their home, although they were Russian by birth. They had lived in Kiev, Katerina had told me bitterly, for over twenty years.

The fact of the funeral, the size and solemnity of the stone church, the ritual performed by the bearded priests, were all too much for me. But it was the old women that hit me hardest. I had known Boris only slightly, and I felt grief for his passing, but seeing the old women in their dark dresses, tears streaming down their cheeks, caused me to feel a weight of despair descend on me I have not felt for many years.

I cannot explain it even now, although I'm sure that Dr. Stouffer would have had a quick, canned response to identify the reasons for what I felt. I hadn't attended funerals for any of the children that I had found. I was afraid to go. I tried to keep them out of my mind.

Emotions as powerful as thinking about what had happened to them would make me unable to function. I'd been there before. It doesn't help. You can't do anything about anything if you can't think.

Before I had learned about the conference back home, my only thoughts had been about finding the kids, dead or alive. I had had no clue as to how the murders were all linked. Now that I did, I coupled that objective with finding the killer or killers. Anything else, such as trying to understand, was just wasted space on my mental hard drive.

There was the matter of getting paid. Hemlock paid me well for each job. That was beginning to bother me, too. Find the bodies, collect the money. I was beginning to feel like a ghoul for hire. Just once I would like to get there and find someone still alive.

But the old women in the Ukrainian church, they began to change things for me. They caused me to deal with the fact that children and young adults were not only dying, but being hideously murdered. As I sat in that church, for the first time, I closed my eyes and could hear their screams, feel a fraction of what their terror had been.

After the gas plant accident, the only thing that saved my sanity was to deal with the death count, including that of my own family, as numbers. Nothing that the psychiatrists or psychologists said had had any effect on me as long as I continued to see images of the dead in my mind, heard their screams, or felt their pain. Every day that I relived the actions and feelings of identifying the dead bodies of my family, I drifted farther out into the sea of chaos. I believe that I would literally have gone insane had I not thought of them as numbers in a larger catastrophe. I knew better in some part of my mind, but that part of my self was grateful for the subterfuge. It allowed the slow process of healing to begin.

When Allen Hemlock had first sent me to look for the children of one of his employees in Spain who had disappeared along with three other children, I didn't get caught up in thinking of them as children, as innocents, as victims. I went about my tracking logically, methodically, coldly, and I found them. They were already dead, but I found them. And so, it continued. More countries. More bodies of children and young adults.

But my refusal to identify with the horror of what was occurring, I now realized, had blocked me from thinking the awful thought that all of these killings were linked. In my desire to protect myself, I had blinded myself as to the pattern that was developing.

It was the old women's grief that opened my eyes again, that caused me to go beyond sympathy to some amount of empathy.

I scarcely had contact with Katerina during the next few days of mourning, funerals, and more mourning. I attended Boris's funeral. I attended the children's funerals. I didn't break down and cry at the funerals, but back in my hotel room, I damn near drowned myself.

It was the morning of the fourth day when we actually met again in my hotel room. My plane was set to take off in a few hours, and it was the only time that we could talk. She had a busy schedule between the funerals, the press, and the police. Somehow, she had managed to keep me out of things. I didn't ask her how; it was enough that she had taken care of business.

"We have little time to talk," she said as she sat down near the window in the chair opposite mine.

"Yeah, and I made you a promise. I'll tell you what I know. Okay?"

She inclined her head, signaling me to continue.

While she listened carefully, I told her everything that I knew, starting with the conference for gifted children in Riverview.

"The reason I think that Hemlock had me get involved in the first place was because children of his employees started disappearing. They weren't all children of Hemlock International employees, you understand, but I was sent in every time there were children of Hemlock International employees. It was only after Dr. Stouffer uncovered the conference that I knew about the link.

"You see, Hemlock International sponsored the conference in the first place, so that they paid all travel expenses when a gifted child was from a family working for the company. Hence the large amount of children from company employees."

I went on to tell her about John Hemlock and what I knew about him.

"So," she said, "Allen is worried that son is maybe victim soon, or maybe involved, yes?"

Katerina Firyubin was a smart woman.

"Yes to both. Now, you said you had seen something like what happened before. Could you explain that?"

"You know, Mr. Brown, that KGB investigated much methods of torture and killing?"

"Yes."

"In many countries, we studied history of death. What we saw, with skin of head and hands cut and ripped away, it has been done before. In France and Spain, definitely, but also in your own country. I have seen drawings."

"Not all of the children had the skin from the forehead peeled back."

"Some also were drowned, yes?"

"Yes. But—"

She held up her hand.

"There is purpose behind these killings. You agree, of course?"

"If you can call it that," I said. "What do you think that purpose is?"

She was a lot more feminine than I remember her being when I first met her. It was as though her grief had made her more vulnerable, more delicate. Former Major Katerina Firyubin was still tough, but there was more to her. I began to see what Boris had seen in her.

"They look for something. It was same during Inquisition, and during witch trials."

"I don't understand."

"I will teach you, Mr. Brown. You have told me truth, I believe. Boris would not want me stop, so I have proposal for you. I will teach you, if you will help me continue, with or without Mr. Hemlock. This is now much beyond him. Is not about money. You will help me continue with you."

"Deal," I said simply. "Now, what do the Inquisition and the witch trials have to do with these killings?"

She smiled a grim little smile. "The Inquisitors, they looked also. They cut the skin of the forehead, and peeled back skin so to look for the mark."

"What mark?" I asked impatiently.

"The mark of the devil," she replied, "the sign of the Beast."

Revelation

From the Revelation According to St. John:

I saw thrones on which were seated those who had been given authority to judge. And I saw the souls of those who had been beheaded because of their testimony for Jesus and because of the word of God. They had not worshiped the Beast or his image and had not received his mark on their foreheads or their hands.

Charlie Kim and Monica

"Look, Allen," I said into the phone, "get this through your head. This is all about religion. I don't care if you're driving underneath some high-power lines, you stay on the line and wait until it clears up."

There wasn't a cloud on the horizon, but there was a storm brewing in my head.

I took a deep breath to calm down. "This group, whoever they are, they're looking for the mark of the Beast on these kids. That's why they peel the skin off of the foreheads and hands from them. Yeah, the Beast, that's what I said. As in the Bible. And that's why they cut off the heads afterwards. To show that, so far, all of these kids have been found innocent."

I listened impatiently while he rattled off his rebuttal.

"Okay, I know that's not what we think happened to all the kids, but—"

He hung up on me.

No matter, he'd call back.

Or cut me out.

The problem was, I'd jumped the gun, which is always a bad thing to do with Allen Hemlock. He was right. It hadn't happened to all the kids, just like I told Katerina. Whoever this group was, they were methodical, and they wouldn't be likely to let any slip through the cracks. So there had to be something that I was missing. But Katerina was on the right track, damn it. I was sure of it.

I was too tired. The night before hadn't been the best. I kept dreaming of men in white robes, beheaded children, and a dragon-man who emerged from a cloud of poison gas.

It seemed like every other hour I would wake up thrashing around and screaming. Once, after toweling off the sweat and finally getting rid of the night jitters, I dropped back into sleep and kept on falling into another nightmare. I was back, back in the Warehouse of the Dead.

The bodies were neatly racked in shipping crates, their skinless heads lying beside them. Gregorio stood beside me, gripping his Glock, looking for something to shoot. We were in the grip of an unseen fear, something far worse than the lifeless bodies stacked around us.

I tried to say something to break the black terror that paralyzed us, but I could not move my lips.

In the swinging light and shadows from the single electric bulb that hung overhead, I heard again the sound of dry leathery wings.

It wasn't a good night.

*****

About an hour later, while I was updating all the facts we had in a file I'd titled Warehouse of the Dead, Hemlock called back. He didn't apologize—like I gave a damn if he did—but he told me to go see Dr. Stouffer and discuss my theories with her. Abiding by my end of the deal, I hadn't told him the idea had come from Katerina in the first place. This would give her time, she had told me, to push the investigation ahead in the Ukraine without interference from Allen.

I had my instructions. Go see Dr. Stouffer. What a crock of shit.

Before leaving, I printed out all my notes from the Warehouse of the Dead. It was a creepy title, but that's where it had all started, so that's what I called it. For added measure, I folded the slip of paper where I'd written the name and phone number of the contact that Bob Alby texted me. Thanks to Bob, I had the name of someone who had been in the Church of the Apostles but left because left on an unhappy note. Benjamin Franks was the guy's name, and I figured after I saw

Dr. Stouffer, I'd go visit Benny and his lovely wife.

My first stop after I left Soldier's point wasn't actually Dr. Stouffer's. I pulled the car into the parking lot of Charlie Kim's Hapkido Studio. I had been Charlie Kim's student for over twenty years, off and on. I went because I liked it, not because I was that good. And I went because I needed a place to hide from the thoughts of death that always seemed to find me. But there was a better reason, too. It was Charlie's rock-like spirit upon which I had rebuilt my shattered life after the accident. I've tried to tell him that a few times over the years, but he doesn't want to hear it.

Slim and trim, with a full head of black hair, a face that you'd swear belonged to a twenty-year-old, and a personality twice the size of his five-foot four body, that's the way to describe Charlie Kim. In action, he moves with the power of a snake and a tiger all rolled into one new deadly species. All without a special effects crew to make it look good.

The front and back doors to the dojo were wide open, as though to welcome me back. Charlie was seated all the way across the room, behind his desk.

"Hey, Scott," he yelled, "welcome back, again. You work out yet?"

Did I work out yet? I liked that. Not, tell me all the gory details of what you've been doing. Yeah, I liked that.

I took my shoes off, and bowed to him, then to the flags, both American and Korean. Some people have a problem with that. Try to make more than it is. Simple respect. Some people have their heads up their ass.

"Yes, Mr. Kim. I did. Every morning, just as you taught me." In his dojo, he was always Mr. Kim to me. Always my teacher. That changed on poker night.

He was across the mat in a few graceful bounds and shaking my good left hand between both of his hands as vigorously as he would a reluctant water pump.

"No, come on, Scott. I mean, did you really work out?"

I waited too long to answer.

"Ah-hah. I knew it. You were saving your strength just to work out for real with me."

He had big white teeth for a little guy, and when he smiled at you like that, you knew you were screwed.

"Yes, sir," I said, "I was waiting to really work out with you."

He stepped back, put both of his fists on his hips, and looked me over critically. His expression grew very serious.

"Ah, you know, Scott, it isn't good to lie to your instructor."

And he burst out laughing.

I had to laugh. It wasn't that damn funny. But I had to laugh. I needed to laugh.

"So come on, come over and sit down. Come on, first we relax, we talk, and then I beat the shit out of you."

I was in the presence of comic genius.

In the art of Hapkido, there's no fixed ratio between hand and foot techniques. You use only what works. It is an art for the young and the old, the physically strong, and the handicapped.

And for me, who was both.

"The point, Scott," Charlie said, after he had swept my feet out from underneath me and dumped me on the mat, "is that you've got to quit thinking of you current, temporary condition as abnormal."

The quality of Charlie's English depended on the point he wanted to make and the position that he wanted to make it from. One moment he sounded like he just stepped off of the boat, the next he spoke like an English teacher.

"Yes, sir," I said, as I struggled back to my feet.

I stood before him, my left hand behind my back like it should be, my right arm hanging at my side. The rule was, you stood at attention with your feet shoulder width apart, and your hands clasped behind your back. I had the foot position right.

"Sometimes, Scott, it's okay to think before you say 'all right.' This isn't the Marines. I want you to think. You must think for the sake of your own spirit. Okay, GI?"

"Yes—" I caught myself mid-sentence. He had instructed me to think, so I thought.

"Good, you are thinking now," he said with a smile. Then he winked conspiratorially at me and added, "but don't think all day, okay? I have to go to the bathroom sometime."

My uniform, which I had brought in with me and put on before we began to really work out, was stained with sweat, and stuck to my body as though it were glued to my skin.

"So, what you think, Scott? You understand what I mean? What you are now, it is now normal for you. As you change, your state of normalcy changes. When your arm improves until it is good as new, then it hasn't returned to normal, it has become a new state of physical being for you. It will be familiar to you, because you have had two good arms before. But always in life, there is change. If you don't see this, then you will fight like a handicapped man, and you will lose. You see?"

"Yes, sir, Mr. Kim, I think I do. It's just that I have a hard time accepting that this is now normal for me."

"So what? Why do you waste your energy on stubbornness? If I walked outside in the rain without an umbrella saying, 'Hey, it's okay. I don't need an umbrella, it wasn't raining yesterday,' wouldn't you think I was an idiot? It's okay to say the truth. Tell me."

"Yes, sir, I would."

"Good," he nodded, "then we are done for the day, because today you have really learned something. About life, I mean, not about falling on your back. You knew how to do that before you came in here. Now, quick, go shower and come back, and you can ask me what you came to ask me."

When I came upstairs, he was seated at his desk again, his hands cupped under his chin, and his eyes closed. I stepped quietly toward him, laid my duffel bag on the floor, and whispered a foot away from him, "Mr. Kim, are you awake?"

His head snapped back as though some had yanked a string attached to the back of his scalp. "Hey," he snapped, "don't ever do that when I'm meditating."

"Yes, sir," I said quickly, stiffening to attention.

"I'm kidding, Scott, I'm only kidding. See, I'm smiling. Sit down, relax, and sit down. Ask me your question."

There was no need to ask him how he had known that I was coming to ask for advice. I had known him for too long for that. So, I sat down.

"Mr. Kim, we don't talk much about what I do."

"Not necessary," he said, waving his hands.

"All I meant to tell you is that I'm after some very bad people now.

For quite a few years, I thought I'd been after a lot of different bad people that I just couldn't seem to catch. Now I think they're all part of one group."

Once I had started talking, it wasn't that hard to continue. As I spoke, he looked at me intently, not with a shrink-stare, but with the concern of a teacher for his student.

"The problem," I continued, "is that I don't know who they are. But I am beginning to think that they're tied to my employer, which he is, on the surface, refusing to acknowledge. I don't think that when push comes to shove, if I'm right, that he's going to help me. In fact, I think that he'll try to hurt me, and he's a powerful man. The reason that I am starting to think like this is the way he's handling things, which got me thinking that there's more to him than I originally thought. But it doesn't make sense. He's the one paying me to find these people."

"So, what is your question, Scott?"

"It's actually two questions, sir. The first is how can I fight an enemy when I don't know specifically who they are or how many they are?"

"And the second question?"

"When the time comes, how do I fight an enemy, my employer, who is not yet an enemy?"

Charlie Kim closed his eyes and steepled his fingers on the desk before him. While he contemplated, I looked around the dojo. The wall to the right when you came in the front door was covered with mirrors, so that you could watch your own workout. Two other walls were padded to about six feet, in case someone got thrown or kicked into one. The other wall was eight feet from where the mat ended, and on that wall were the club's trophies, flags, and Mr. Kim's credentials.

Before leaving Korea, Charlie had been a national sports hero, having won the World Tae Kwon Do finals. The plaque for that was on the wall behind his desk. I remembered as I picked it out that in the next-to-last match of that competition, he had broken his arm. The doctors had set it in a plaster cast, and as far as they were concerned, he was out of the match. But he went back into the ring when it was his turn and became champion. The one-armed legend. I had forgotten all about that. He hadn't mentioned it after it I lost the use of my own arm. Now, as he sat thinking in front of me, trying to solve my problems, I wondered for the first time why he hadn't brought up to me his own triumph over a temporary disability.

"Well," he said, finally opening his eyes, "I think you're screwed."

"I'm what?"

Big Korean smile again. "Screwed. As in, no help here. They're bogus questions," he said with a sly wink.

"Mr. Kim, they're very serious to me."

"Oh, I'm sure they are, but come on, Scott. Loosen up a bit. You want to know these things, but you already know the answers. You just don't like them."

Before I could respond, he kept going.

"Look. How do you fight an enemy when you don't know who the enemy is? First, it sounds like you've already got a good idea who your enemy is, but if you don't, just figure it out. It's what you get paid to do, isn't it?"

He had a point. I didn't like it, but he had a point. I'd been hoping for something with a little more try to take the pebble from my hand stuff.

"Now, for fake-question number two. Interesting, but again, you already know the answer. Do what you have to do, but don't underestimate your influence on your opponent. Okay? That's all I've got to add."

"Yes, Mr. Kim."

"Now, you might need some practice at fighting a friend who becomes an enemy. So, I have a suggestion. A serious suggestion."

He leaned forward again with his trademark big smile on his face.

"What is it, sir?"

He had my full attention now.

His right index finger shot forward, pointing over my left shoulder. "Go to parking lot. Get big practice, right now."

"What?"

I was so surprised that I forgot to add the "sir."

When I turned to look behind me, I saw what he meant. A red Corvette convertible, top down, was parked in front of the building. I hadn't heard it drive up. Standing in front of it, her long, tan legs spread wide beneath a short plain white dress, her arms folded tightly in front of her chest, and her red hair blowing slightly to the side, was Monica Thomas.

"Mr. Kim," I said evenly, "you are a shithead, sir."

*****

"So, the big, tough guy is hiding from me?"

She said it as I came out of the front door. Hello, I guessed, would come later, if things went well.

"Monica—"

There was no time to finish; it's hard to talk when you're ducking an intended slap to the face.

"Hey—" I began again, but had to cut that short, too, as she came at me with a slap from the other side.

This time, I caught her wrist with my left hand. It was a stupid thing to do. She swung at me again, and this time, as I tried to move my useless right arm to block, she caught me full on the left cheek.

"Would you cut that out?" I said when my eyesight returned. "Christ on a pony, but you're a bitch."

She looked like she was going to take another swing, so I hopped back a step to get out of range.

"Why? You deserved it."

She stamped her red high-heeled right foot down on the gravel to emphasize the point. I wish they would stop showing Gone With the Wind. Scarlett O'Hara is a bad role model.

"Because I won't give you what you want, when you want it? That's your problem."

"You don't have anything that I want," she snapped, and folded her arms tightly again just underneath her breasts. They were big enough as it was; she didn't need to pump them up like that. It was just natural for her; she couldn't help it.

"Then why do you keep following me around? If I don't have anything you want, then just please leave me the hell alone. I couldn't be a happier man than if you and your bang buddies would just leave me be in peace and quiet."

Charlie's place was on Fort Street, a Michigan state road that ran so far in both directions that I didn't know where it started or ended. It had two lanes going south, two lanes going north, and grass islands in between topped by the occasional protected species of trees. The traffic was getting heavier, and the drivers, I noticed, were slowing to look at us. Or at her. She looked great from any angle. She could cause a head on collision on a one-way street cutting though Podunk, USA.

"My what? My bang buddies?" She said it so quickly that her face only got red after she said it.

"Yeah, and don't take another swing at me or I swear I'll smack you back. Look, we're just through, okay? The sex was great, but I'm looking for something else now. I'm not into the open relationship thing."

For a moment I thought, Oh shit, she's going to cry. She didn't know what I did for a living. She hadn't seen what I'd seen in the warehouse of the dead, and she didn't need to know. It was enough to make my sex drive shrivel up.

Instead, she whipped out her right index finger every bit as quickly as Mr. Kim had, and said with a wicked grin, "You're living in the past, mister. You men can't take it when women do what you men have been doing for years, can you? What's the big deal about sex? That's what you men asked, and now that we say, 'Okay, what's the big deal?' and go out and enjoy ourselves, too, you can't take it."

"I don't have time for this bullshit. The gender war thing is just boring."

As I stepped forward, she did the same, and grabbed me by the crotch.

"Come on," she whispered, her face only an inch from mine. Her tongue ran slowly over her lower lip. "Come on, you want it. I know you like it." Her fingers tightened their grip slightly. "Just ask me, and we can go to the park and do it in the weeds."

When a woman has her hands around your privates, you have to be careful. And, smart as she was, there was something of the control freak about Monica that spooked me and annoyed me at the same time.

"No," was all that I could think of to say in the end.

"Or," she said, her lips pulling back in a slight snarl, "I could squeeze real hard and bust your precious balls. How about it?"

"Monica," I said, with genuine anguish in my voice, "how the hell is that going to look on the record of a great lady lawyer like you?

Wouldn't you be the least bit embarrassed to be brought up on charges of castrating a handicapped guy?"

Thank God, she let go, and went back to pointing her finger in my face again.

"You stood me up today for lunch. Nobody does that. You think that you're so perfect. Well, I know all about you and your failures and the nasty little things that you do. You just remember that and treat me with respect. I won't stand to be treated the way you treat me and be talked about the way that you do. I'll ruin your reputation in this town, mister."

Before I could answer that I didn't know that I had one, she spun around and got back into her car. Her chin tilted back haughtily as she started the engine, then backed out onto the highway without looking, almost running a tiny red Escort into a tree. She smiled sweetly at me, gave me the finger, and then roared away, her beautiful red hair flying behind her.

I jumped when I felt Charlie's hand on my shoulder.

"You see," he said from a foot behind and below me, "very good practice. Very life-like. Better than TV."

I didn't have to turn around to know that he had a huge damn smile on his face. Chances were, Monica wouldn't be at the game tomorrow night.

*****

Two loud raps on her front door, and then I stood there, waiting for it to open.

Her office told me that she'd left for the day.

I was surprised that she lived where she did. Her office address had read Farmington Hills; her residence was in a small town called New Boston, about a half an hour west of where I lived. New Boston is an intersection with eight or nine businesses, one of which is a feed store, which you could drive by and miss entirely if you happened to sneeze at the wrong time.

Dr. Stouffer lived about fifteen minutes west of this thriving metropolis. I had to follow a dirt road and make three or four turns past fields of crops of some kind or another. Probably corn. I don't pay much attention to fields unless I've got a reason.

She lived in a gray and white trimmed wooden farmhouse, two stories tall, that looked like one of those old homes yuppies buy to fix up into centennial residences with a brass plaque out front.

Gnarled apple and pear trees in the front yard, in front of the white, freshly painted front porch. The obligatory porch swing hung from eyehooks by new chains. Along the porch balcony were potted red flowers.

The driveway leading to the not repaired, washed out wooden garage was pea graveled. I was willing to bet that out back there would be a small red barn. There was no sign of her car, but the garage door was closed shut.

When the door to the house finally opened, I was surprised to see a big kid with a moon face, topped with a mop of mussed black hair. He had big gray eyes that were wide open with surprise and a kind of guarded wonder at seeing me standing there.

"Hi," I said, "My name is—"

"You're not grandma," he said, as though announcing it to me. His voice was a little high for a kid that big.

"No, I'm—"

"Where's grandma?"

"I don't know. My name is Scott Brown, and—"

"I only opened the door because I thought you were grandma. My mother will be upset with me. You got me in trouble. Are you a stranger?"

"No. Are you a lawyer?"

He looked at me quizzically for a second, tilting his head to the side slightly.

"Lawyer. Noun," he said mechanically. "One whose profession is to give legal advice and assistance to clients and represent them in legal matters. See Law. Page seven hundred and sixty-nine. American Heritage College Dictionary. Third edition."

He flashed me a quick, satisfied smile.

"You're an unusual kid, you know that?"

"Yes. I'm special. My mother says so, and she's a psychologist. Your name is Scott Brown, and you're not grandma. Do you know where my grandma is?"

"Is your mom home, son?"

"What's wrong with your arm, mister?"

"It's tired, kid. Is your mom home?"

I didn't get to see a lot of living kids, except from a distance. Hadn't talked with one for a long time. I needed a translator or some kind of a mediator.

"Why isn't your other arm tired?"

He wore faded blue jeans and a flannel shirt that would have fit any truck driver that I've ever seen. There was a thin roll of flesh under his round chin. A big kid, but not a bruiser.

"I don't know. I'm here to talk to your mother."

"You should have brought grandma."

"I don't know your grandmother, okay? I just want to talk to your mother."

"My grandma brings me presents sometimes," he said with a big smile.

I don't know what I would have said next if Dr. Stouffer hadn't come to the door, and gently pulled him away.

"Go to your room, Bobby," she said.

"I thought he was grandma, but he wasn't."

"Grandma will be along soon, honey."

She took him away, holding up her hand for me to stay where I was. I almost didn't recognize her with her hair undone, hanging just above her shoulders, and without her glasses. The simple red and white checked dress that she was wearing gave her a different look than the professional cuts I had seen her wear the first times that we had met. In a few minutes, she returned and came out onto the porch, closing the door behind her. Even standing as close as she was, it was a little hard for me to reconcile her with the psychologist who had first visited me with Allen Hemlock.

"Why did you come here without calling first?" she asked.

"Don't get so self-righteous. You did the same thing to me, remember? Besides, Allen told me to talk to you, and I'm just following instructions. That's a nice kid you've got there."

"You leave Bobby out of this. You came to talk. Let's go sit on the swing and talk. Bobby's a...a special child."

"How special?"

"He's been diagnosed as—"

"Forget it. I don't want to know. He just seemed a little different, that's all. I don't want to hear about the psychological box that he's been put in."

"That's my son you're talking about."

"Yeah," I said, "I know."

Her lower lip trembled a little, and then she turned and marched over to the swing. I followed her over, and we both sat down. She sat on the far side, which was fine with me. My good arm was in between us. After a moment's silence, I pushed back a little with my foot to set the swing in motion. It seemed like the thing to do.

"Did Allen tell you yet about the religious connection?"

"No," she said too quickly.

It could have been innocent. Maybe she was still mad.

"You want to hear about it, or are you still mad?"

She was looking straight ahead at her yard. Her face looked softer, more like a concerned mother than a psychologist.

"I'm not mad, Mr. Brown," she replied, but she didn't look at me.

"What, then?" I asked. "Do you always avoid looking at people when they come to visit?"

"I don't want my son involved in this. I don't want him to be exposed to any part of this investigation. He's very delicate."

"You think my coming here has involved him?"

It was a simple enough question, but she seemed to be thinking a lot longer than necessary to answer the question.

"Am I missing something here?" I asked.

"No, Mr. Brown." She finally turned to face me. "Tell me what you've come to say."

For the better part of a half an hour, I related what had happened in the Ukraine. She was a good listener, but that went with her job. It was around two o'clock in the afternoon by the time that I had finished. Neither of us said a word for a few minutes, and we rocked in silence, with the only noise being the sound of the chains grating on the eyehooks that held up the swing.

"It must be hard to put the images of those children out of your mind," she said sadly, talking, I think, as a mother. I wished she would get back to being a shrink. It was easier for me to handle her that way.

"It's not hard."

She stopped the motion of the swing with her foot and turned to look at me with what I can only describe as incredulous disgust.

"It's not hard?"

"Not for me," I said. "I don't have a visual memory. I'm sure you came across that in whatever files that Allen gave you on me."

"He didn't give me any files on you, Mr. Brown. I don't care if you believe that or not. And everyone has a visual memory to some degree."

"Not me. Lady, if I close my eyes, I can't even remember what you look like. I recognize you when I see you, but I can't remember what you look like, unless I'm looking at you."

"Have you always been like this?" she asked.

"As long as I can remember. It's a big help sometimes in my line of work. Sometimes, it's a pain in the ass. When it comes to dealing with kid's bodies, it's a blessing, believe me."

"Have you been tested for this condition?"

"No, and I'm not interested in being tested. I'm not a lab rat. I get by just fine the way I am."

I don't even know why I told her.

"Now, can we get back to the religious connection?"

My voice must have sounded angrier than I was aware. She stiffened slightly, the way that I had seen her do before.

"If you wish. I was just going to say that I think your memory may be somehow —"

I cut her off. "Yeah, I know. It's probably psychological. Now, can we get on with this, or do you want me to leave?"

"I was going to say that your condition may be treatable. But by all means, let's avoid the topic. You want to know if I think that it's possible that whoever has been committing these crimes is motivated by a bizarre religious conviction that one or more of these children is a follower of, or perhaps actually the Biblical Beast?"

"In a nutshell, yes."

"It's certainly possible, Mr. Brown, although I can't say that I am familiar with the idea that beheading a dead body in any way demonstrates their innocence before God."

I repeated the quote from Revelations that I had come across, wherein those who had been beheaded for refusal to cooperate with the Beast in the end times were recognized as innocent because they had been beheaded.

"That's not quite the same thing, is it?" she asked.

"No, but it makes sense, doesn't it?"

"Maybe. And you seem to remember what you read quite clearly."

"What I read and what I hear," I said. "I've got a good memory for those two. You have a category for that?"

"Not one that you'd want to hear."

She smiled tentatively.

I smiled back.

She looked good when she smiled- better than I did, I guessed.

"Not all of the bodies had their foreheads and hands skinned, did they?"

"No," I admitted. "I've taken all the names of all the children that attended the conference, and made a database for what's happened to the ones that have already died that I know about. I've sent out faxes and emails to get the entire picture. It might take a few days to get all the info that I need to complete the profile completed. We can look at it then. Together, if you'd like."

"Thank you."

"For what? I'm just doing my job."

A red Ford Escort came down the road and turned into her driveway. Through the windshield, I could see an old lady behind the wheel.

"Grandma?" I asked.

"Grandma," she confirmed.

"What happened to Bobby's father?"

"None of your damn business, Mr. Brown."

The Death of Benny Franks

Dr. Stouffer wasn't interested in going to visit Mr. and Mrs. Franks with me. She had an "appointment" of her own. It suited me just fine. She was beginning to get on my nerves, anyway.

I shouldn't have told her about my memory. That was none of her business, and gave her something to think about. Something to talk to Allen about.

You might wonder how it was that I tied up with Allen Hemlock in the first place. The answer is simple enough. Hemlock International, through a subsidiary, owned the company that I had worked for. The one that killed half the town. That one event, the release of a poison gas, had tied us together.

If it hadn't been for the accident, the chances of me meeting a man like him were slim and none. After it occurred, against the advice of his lawyers, I suppose, he decided to meet me face to face. Self-made billionaires only rely on the advice of others to a point.

Men like Allen Hemlock trust their own judgment, find their own facts, and make their own decisions when they're in a bind. The accident put Hemlock's company in a bind. In addition to all of their other legal problems, I think that Hemlock was worried not about me suing him, but about what I might say to the press. He had to know for himself, to make his own deal. And he did.

I gave him what he wanted. Silence. He gave me an offer that, at that moment in my life, was what I needed. There was no way for me to go back to a normal job. My wife and son and neighbors were dead. I wouldn't have lasted three months. I needed something hard and dangerous to do, and that's what he gave me. I kept my mouth shut about some things that I could have told the media, but didn't; he pulled me away from the limelight, away from normal life, and put me to work as a trouble shooter. A contractor—neither one of us liked the idea of me being an employee. I wouldn't look good on anybody's books.

*****

Hemlock was as good as his word. He had promised me that whatever training that I felt was necessary for specific assignments would be mine. No questions asked.

For an entire year, I trained until I thought I was ready, and then he gave me my first assignment. Canada. A company executive was being blackmailed for a trumped up indiscretion. That's what I was told. What he was really being blackmailed for was the murder of his own wife. It would have been a perfect crime if there hadn't been a witness. A greedy witness.

Allen's idea when he sent me was that I would find a way out of the mess. I didn't know how big of a mess it was until I got there. Our man disappeared a week after I arrived on the scene. He disappeared permanently. No trace was ever found of him. I had learned my lessons well.

The blackmailer got no money from us. But he kept his mouth shut. He was more worried about his own neck.

I don't want to you to think that I murdered the company man in cold blood. I didn't, but when he tried to shoot me and missed, I figured he was fair game.

*****

Mr. and Mrs. Benjamin Franks lived in New Trenton, a town of roughly twenty thousand people and almost as many fast food places. It could have been renamed Burgerland in the interests of accuracy.

Mr. Franks was a supervisor at one of the auto factories, and Mrs. Franks, Ducky, as her friends called her, was a secretary at a local accounting firm. They lived in a small brick house near Hazelwood and Elm in a nineteen fifties style, picture perfect suburban neighborhood where all the houses were the same size, complete with one big tree per lot, front yards that were all exactly the same size, and front lawns so perfectly green that you would have sworn they were Astroturf. Ducky, who looked a lot like the old pictures of Betty Crocker without the apron, opened the front door no more than a hands width to stare at me before letting me in. I had called in advance, and was therefore expected, but Ducky was having second thoughts about talking to me.

To calm her down, I gave her my canned story about being a freelance writer doing an article on the New Apostles for Bob's paper. I assured her that her anonymity was safe with me.

"I don't want to use names," I told her in a confidential tone. "In investigative journalism, we have to protect the names of our sources. Otherwise, no one would ever talk to us."

"Where did you say that you got our names?"

"That would be violating a confidence, ma'am. I never use the names of sources."

In the end, it was the Chihuahua yapping that got me in the door. She kept telling it to hush, pushing it away from the door with her foot, but it was determined to make a break for it. Its entire body was no longer than a hand and a half, but it had the energy of three dogs packed into its little body, and a bark more irritating than fingernails being dragged across a blackboard.

"Bunny," she snapped, "Bunny, get away from the door."

I'd yap, too, if I had to go through life with a name like Bunny.

"That's a nice dog, ma'am. Cute name."

She thrust back with her foot, and, Bunny after skittling backwards three feet or so, came right back at the door with his nails clattering on the tile.

"Damn you, Bunny," she said.

"Dogs have always liked me, ma'am. Can I pet him?"

She gave a heavy sigh, bent down and scooped the little rodent up in her arms, and opened the door.

"Come in, Mr. Brown. If I don't let you in, I think Bunny's going to have a heart attack."

So, I went inside.

Mrs. Franks was a fanatical housekeeper. She led me from the foyer over to a small living room across closely cropped, bone-gray carpet. The picture window in the living room looked out across their perfectly manicured lawn, framed by bowed burgundy drapes. I slid behind a cherry wood oval coffee table and sat down on the green and gold striped loveseat, while she sat down on the armchair directly opposite me.

Bunny, the little shit, sniffed my shoes. If he tried to hump my leg, I had already decided that I was going to have to strangle him with my good hand.

"Thank you for taking the time to see me, Mrs. Franks. I promise I won't take more than a half an hour of your time. Is your husband home?"

"He was supposed to be, but he got called back into work," she said. "You know how it is, being in management."

I smelled an impending divorce.

"I can imagine. Now, Mrs. Franks, I understand you were a member of the Church of the New Apostles for a few years, but that you left their membership. May I ask why? And please be open with me. As I've told you, no one will ever know what we've discussed or even that we've talked in the first place. I give you my word."

"Would you care for some coffee?" she asked.

"No, thank you."

"What happened to your arm?"

"I was in an accident."

"Oh, you poor man. How did it happen?"

"Someone wasn't paying attention to the traffic light."

She clucked her tongue. I was beginning to get impatient.

"I swear, the drivers today. I bet it was a teenager, wasn't it?"

"Yes, ma'am, it was."

"Did you know they quit requiring these kids to pass a road test?"

"Yes, ma'am. It's a shame, isn't it?"

"I guess you would know that as well as anybody."

"Yes, I would."

We sat there in silence for a few uncomfortable minutes before she answered my original question.

"We just couldn't take it anymore."

I let it hang.

"A person should go to church to be uplifted, don't you think?"

"I would think so," I said tentatively.

"We would leave the sermon feeling... bad about ourselves. Do you think bar coding is a sign of the Beast?"

"Bar coding, ma'am?"

"You know," she said emphatically, as though I knew exactly what she was talking about. "Bar coding. On products, like at the supermarket. The Universal Product Codes."

"Do I think that the Uniform Product Code is a sign of the Beast, as in the Book of Revelations?"

"Yes, now you've got it."

"I don't know much about that sort of thing, ma'am, but it seems to me that bar coding is just bar coding. I don't waste a lot of time trying to read conspiracies into my groceries. There are a lot worse things going on in the world."

She giggled. It's not a pretty thing to see a middle-aged woman giggle.

"Well, they take that sort of thing very seriously, very seriously indeed. Frank and I spent most of our time in the Baptist Church before we joined the Church of the New Apostles. Now, we're Baptists again. What are you?"

"Ma'am?"

"What religion are you? I don't mean to pry, of course."

"Of course. I was raised Methodist. Haven't gone in a long time."

"You don't have children, do you, Mr. Brown?"

I had a son, once. Now I don't.

"No ma'am, I don't."

She smiled a smug smile. Bunny jumped up on the couch next to me. I was sitting on the left side of the couch. There wasn't much I could do with my right arm.

"Bunny, Bunny," she called, "get off of there. Leave Mr. Brown alone."

"I'd pet him, ma'am, but my right arm..." I let the words trail off.

"Oh. Well, you just ignore him, and he'll go away."

And, after a moment or two of trying to look cute, he did.

"You were saying, Mrs. Frank, about the New Apostles..."

"Oh. Yes. It seemed that was all they could talk about. The End Times. The Beast. They actually believed that we were in the times described in the Bible. That's not so unusual, I suppose, but it was the way they really believed that the end times were here. That the Beast was here. And the way they stressed that nothing, nothing was more important than fighting against anything that could be interpreted as being tainted by the Beast. They kept soliciting money for the battle against the Beast.

"Listen to this," she continued. "Groceries and products that had bar coding were not to be purchased, because that was or could be from the Beast. Mr. Brown, have you ever tried to buy products that aren't bar coded? Where was I supposed to shop? Bar coding is everywhere. Just because the Apostles think that bar coding is of the Beast. Did you ever hear of Jesus mentioning bar coding in the Bible?"

"No, ma'am. I think the sign of the Beast, as best I remember, was supposed to be on a person's forehead or hands, not on their bananas."

She giggled again and then got suddenly serious.

"Their leaders, the Apostles themselves, they were spooky. They were all so convincing, and they had us believing whatever they said. It was like hypnosis. Especially Brother Thomas. He had..."

She struggled to think of the right word.

"Charisma?"

"Yes, that's it. Charisma. An educated man, though. But he always stressed that you were either for them or against them. He'd say that in the war against the Beast, there were only two sides. God's side, which was the side that the Apostles were on, and the devil's, which was everybody else."

I was about to ask her another question when the phone, which rested on an end table next to her chair, rang. She picked it up automatically, like most of us do.

"Franks' residence," she said into the receiver.

And then she went pale.

"Oh, my God," she said in a trembling voice, "it can't be. It can't be, there must be some mistake."

I didn't like the sound of it.

"That's not possible," she said, after listening to someone on the other end. "He's been around those presses all of his working life. There must be some mistake."

Bunny began to pace nervously in circles in front of his mistress.

"Yes, yes, I understand," she said finally, and hung up.

Bunny jumped up into her lap, looking for reassurance, but she just stared at me blankly.

"Mrs. Franks. What is it?"

"It's Benjamin. There's been an accident at the plant." Her lower lip began to tremble uncontrollably. "He's ... dead. His head, his head was crushed in a production press."

Benny and his dog Bunny. Now one half of the comedy team was dead.

*****

I arrived at the plant forty minutes later, and saw my friend Leroy Croton's, Sheriff Leroy Croton's, police cruiser parked in the parking lot near the door. Mrs. Franks had stayed home. There was nothing for her to do. Before leaving, I had called her daughter for her to give her the bad news and to ask her to come be with her mother, who was in no condition to drive.

The timing was too coincidental. Even Mrs. Franks realized that, and had shut up immediately. I doubted that, even after recovering from her husband's death, the widow Franks would ever again have anything to say to me or anyone else concerning the New Apostles. She kept saying over and again that she should never have let me in the door, never agreed to see me.

I had called Bob Alby from the car and told him what had happened. He would have found out soon enough as it was, but I needed Bob to hold off on exploring the obvious connection until I had talked to him in person. I didn't have many friends, and wanted to hang on to the ones that I had.

I was five steps from the front door of the place when Sheriff Leroy Croton came striding out. When on duty, Leroy always strode, rather than walked. Even his belly, which could have won first prize for the biggest melon in any state fair, adhered to regulations and didn't jiggle when he strode. And when Leroy strode, he covered a lot of ground. He was still a good three inches taller than me, even when he slouched.

The mirrored sunglasses were already in place, settled an inch above the ragged scar that ran along his left cheek, and he was in the process of putting on his official sheriff's hat when he saw me.

"Hey, Scott," he said with a puzzled look on his face, "what are you doing here?"

"Bob told me about what happened, and I figured you'd be here, so I thought I'd drop by and see what the hell happened. He couldn't get away, so he asked me to play cub reporter for him."

"How the hell did he know about this already?"

"Ears glued to the police band. You know Bob."

"Bullshit," he said with a tired grin, "somebody from here probably called him."

I shrugged. "So what's the scoop here, Leo? Any chance of me seeing where it happened?"

"Any chance of you telling me why you're really here?"

He was a friend of mine. I should have told him, but what did I really know? Besides, he was Sheriff Leroy Croton. There was really no way to keep this just between us two guys. It would have to go further than that, and that would mean other people being involved, and me being relegated to an outsider role.

No, I had the inside edge, and I didn't want to lose it. Not even to Leo. Not just yet.

While I was thinking it through, Leo gave up and said, "Okay, I'll take it at face value for right now. You want to see where it happened? I'll show you. Come on."

With a practiced motion, he whipped his sunglasses off, turned tail, and headed back into the building.

"The body has already been removed," he explained as we walked into the office and stopped before the bottled blond at the front desk.

"Get me Mr. Masters again, will you?" he asked her. "I need to go back in one more time."

"He's on the floor still, Sheriff Croton," she replied. "You can go right back. You being the Sheriff and all."

Bleached blond hair, an unattractive, thin pinched face, but the body of a calendar girl and dressed to show it. I didn't like the three earrings in her left ear, but I guess I should just be happy that she didn't have spiked hair.

As we walked through the door leading to the plant itself, Leroy said, "That's Elaine Marsh's girl back there, although you'd never know it to look at her. Elaine outweighs that girl of hers by over a hundred pounds. When she dies, they'll have to call a moving company to get her to the funeral home."

His voice was drowned out by the sounds of machinery at work. We walked down aisles lined with presses punching out parts. The screeching of metal being forced into new shapes offset a steady kerthunking sound. It reminded me of the sounds that pigs made when being herded up the ramp to be slaughtered.

The workers gave us guarded looks as we made our way down the aisles past the presses and the cages loaded with parts, casting furtive glances at us in between press operations. A uniformed sheriff walking through their plant after an untidy death was certainly not the average day for most of these people.

About three quarters of the way through the plant, we came to a windowless cinderblock room with a metal door marked "R&D". Inside, we found John Masters, the plant manager, and a bald-headed old man in a white lab coat wearing a nametag that said "Fred".

Masters looked at us in surprise. "Why, Sheriff Croton," he said, "I thought you had finished here."

I had seen a lot of men like John Masters in my time, and hadn't liked any of them. They were the men who folded their cuffs up inside their sleeves instead of rolling them up on the outside. The men who wore the white shirts and tried to look like working men. The ones whose pants and shirts were always too clean and pants too neatly pressed to actually be workers in a real factory. The men who liked to think of themselves as "the management."

He wore safety glasses with side-shields, had a gold Cross pen in his pocket, and when we came into the room, it looked like he had been bitching at the old man in the lab coat.

"Just a few more questions for you, Mr. Masters. My associate here wanted to see where it happened."

I nodded the short, clipped nod of an official sheriff's associate.

"Name's Brown," I said, "Scott Brown. This is the machine?"

It could only be the machine. The unit in question was the only press in the room and was a pilot or testing bench. Blood had stained the cheap gray and white-flecked tile floor, which looked like it hadn't seen wax since the day it had been put down.

If it hadn't been for the stains on the floor and the faint, but persistent odor of blood in the air that remained in spite of the lab's ventilation system, I would have had a hard time believing that anyone had died there. The old man in the lab coat didn't look as though he would tolerate anyone dying in his work area.

It was, after all, a testing lab, and not a likely place for a death. Four white washed walls, black topped benches littered with testing equipment and metal samples lining three walls, and the other wall, to my right as I had entered, obscured by stacked and labeled wire cage drawers full of tested parts.

In the far left corner was a solvent hood, and in the far right corner a paint booth. The testing press was in the center of the floor.

"How in the hell did his head wind up in the press in the first place?" I asked Leo.

"Oil, I think. Oil spot on the floor a couple of feet from the machine," put in "boss" Masters. "We think that he slipped, fell foreword onto the press, and hit the button with his hand as he tried to catch himself."

"And then just knelt there with his head on the bottom plate while the upper plate came down and squashed his skull?"

Not fucking likely.

"He must have hit his head and was stunned or unconscious," replied Masters, his voice cracking nervously as he shared this insight.

Leo, who had been watching me with interest, said, "There was an oil slick on the floor, with a slide mark across it, and the same oil on the bottom of Mr. Franks' shoes. Sounds pretty lame, Scott, but you had to see it before we gave them the okay to clean things up. I've got the photos being developed. But it looks like it happened just the way Mr. Masters here says."

Or had been planned to look that way. But the truth was, I couldn't see anything to indicate something to the contrary.

"He was alone when it happened?" I asked Masters.

"Yes."

"How do you know?"

"I saw him go in. I was standing where I could have seen if anyone else went in or left. I was the next person to enter the lab, and I was the one who found him."

Feel sorry for me, his expression said, but he looked okay to me.

I inspected the machine, looked around the laboratory for anything unusual, and came up empty. In deference to Leo, I made a good show of it.

It hadn't been an accident, I was sure of that, but, from the looks of it, it had been too clean of a job to prove that it had been murder. If it really was an accident, it was the stupidest industrial accident that there ever had been- except for the one that had happened to me.

The old chemist, Fred, was looking at me, waiting for the first question, so I decided to oblige him.

"This your lab?"

"Yes, sir," he said stiffly.

"Where were you when it went down?"

He seemed a little relieved by the question.

"I had the afternoon off," he answered, "to work at home. My computer is there, and I was writing some reports, doing some calculations. This PC," he said, pointing disdainfully at the unit on his lab desk, "is too old to handle some of the programs that I have on my home computer. I've asked several times for a better computer, but no one listens-."

"Budget constraints," said Masters, who seemed to find it natural enough to interrupt underlings or speak for them. "Everyone is always asking for new computers. But when we buy them, they're obsolete in six months."

"It doesn't even have a modem," sneered the old chemist, as though that were important in a room where a man had died a few hours before.

Still, I liked the guy okay.

"I know what you mean, Fred," I said, "it's hard to make the computer illiterate understand, isn't it?"

The old man nodded knowingly.

"Where do you go to church, Fred?" I asked softly.

"What?"

"I was just curious," I said. "You look familiar."

"First Presbyterian," he replied, "over on—"

"How about you, Mr. Masters?"

The boss didn't look too happy with the question. Leo noticed, too. When you've been a sheriff as long as he has, you get a nose for nervousness.

"I don't see what that has to do with anything," he said defensively.

"It doesn't. It's just that you look familiar, too. Where do you attend church, Mr. Masters?"

His eyes flicked back and forth between Leo and me. "I don't understand," he said, rubbing the palms of his hands together.

"Sure you do," said Leo. "Answer the question, Mr. Masters. Or is there some reason that you don't want to tell us?"

"No, not at all," said Masters quickly. "I, my whole family, that is, go to the Church of the New Apostles."

"I must be mistaken, then," I told him with a cold smile. "But maybe it will come to me where I've seen you before."

The "boss" smiled uneasily at me.

I'd be seeing him again, all right, no question about it. The dinner at John Hemlock's tomorrow night, where I was supposed to meet the illustrious "Brother Thomas," was looking more interesting with every passing hour.

The Meeting

Leroy bitched at me in the parking lot when we were outside again, but I had it coming. He wanted some answers. I wasn't about to give him any, though, until I had had a chance to get more information, and to think things through. The best I could do was to stall him until after the poker game. That gave me four hours.

Before I left, he tried bringing up the topic of Monica Thomas. He told me I was being an asshole, that I'd upset her. That I shouldn't treat her the way that I did. I knew, of course, that he wanted her, but he kept pushing her off on me. Kept trying to put us together.

After giving me the finger and driving off, she had gone to Leroy, her father confessor. Told him everything. From her point of view, of course. How, once again, I'd treated her like shit. It would have been pathetic if it weren't so damned predictable.

My friend Leroy Croton was a single heterosexual who never wanted to be close to a woman that he cared about. He had an experience that I could identify with, even if it was different than what had happened to me.

Years ago, Leo had fallen in love with a young woman whom he had met on a domestic violence call. Her name was Heather, and her husband, who Leo had only referred to as "the asshole," had been in the process of altering her face when Leo had arrived on the scene and shit-canned him, breaking the guy's arm.

Heather, rather than being grateful, had attacked Leo with fingernails long enough that they should have required a weapons permit. That's where he got the scar across his left cheek. After the initial shock wore off, he decked her. The first woman that he had ever hit in his entire life. She made a real impression on him. He made a real impression on her, too. He knocked her out cold.

Love's a funny thing. You would think that after a start like that, nothing could ever develop between the two of them. But it did. Leo fell for her badly. She needed someone to talk to, and Leo became her listener and adviser. Get out before he kills you, he told her. But she wasn't ready for that. In her mind, the asshole just needed help. Maybe some counseling.

Never get involved, that's the rule, no matter what your feelings. After a few more interference calls to keep the asshole from killing her, and a set of broken ribs, Heather divorced her husband and moved out.

Leo started seeing her as more than a friend, and eventually, they decided to get married. This was over a year later.

The ex-husband came back one night two days before the wedding, after learning that his ex-wife was going to marry the cop that broke his arm. When she answered the door, he shot her in the chest. She was dead before she hit the floor. Leo found her later that night, lying in her own blood.

The asshole was never found. He left town and was never heard from again. Leo never quit blaming himself. For what, I'm not sure. It wasn't his fault, but he felt like it was. I can identify with that. Truth to tell, it's part of the guilt-glue that binds us together as friends.

*****

There were emails waiting for me from Katerina when I got back, bringing me up to speed on her investigation. She had learned a lot. She was very motivated.

Gregorio had called and left me a voice mail. He had a few things to tell me as well. Things were looking up.

I had a voice mail from Monica, too, but I deleted it because it violated the FCC regulations against calling someone a motherfucker over the telephone lines.

According to the electronic counter, I had twelve additional new voice mails, but I didn't bother listening to them yet. I needed some time to think, to organize what I knew.

There had been two hundred and fifty seven kids at the conference. Four had died in the boiler explosion, leaving two hundred and fifty three. In the two years following that incident, fifteen of the children had died "normal" deaths. A drowning here, a fire there, a couple of car accidents, etc. All of this I had learned through the computer system by tapping into files that I shouldn't have had access to legally. The "normal" deaths brought the number alive down to two hundred and thirty eight.

A bus accident in Brazil had killed twenty-seven more a year later. It was, the Brazilian papers had lamented, a national tragedy for Brazil. That took the number down to two hundred and eleven, and so it went.

Over the ensuing eight years, the number of children left standing had been brought down to one hundred and twelve, and the methods of their deaths had become more grisly. But, since they were spread out all over the world, the pattern was understandably hard to detect.

It would have been easier to catch, I suppose, if they had all been members of Mensa. But they weren't. It would have been easier to find the link to the conference in the United States if they had not been killed in their own countries.

I was positive that Dr. Stouffer hadn't "caught on." Allen Hemlock could have called her in as a consultant to analyze the situations that he kept sending me to, but I doubted it. She hadn't figured this out on her own. She wasn't that kind of savvy. She seemed too decent for that kind of thinking. A patient had clued her in. My bet was that John Hemlock couldn't resist the opportunity to let something slip during therapy. He didn't want to be caught—he wanted some resistance. He wanted an opponent that knew enough to take him down, but couldn't. He wanted me to know that, even though I knew who was behind the murders, I couldn't do anything to him. That was my bet.

John Hemlock loved games, and he loved to win. All he needed to make these murders into a game was an opponent like me. Apparently, killing defenseless kids wasn't enough for him.

But did he actually believe that one of these kids was the biblical

Beast, or was he just a cold-blooded killer out for some fun? That was the sixty-four thousand dollar question. And where did the New Apostles fit in? A cover organization for his pathological pursuits, or were the leaders actually involved? The answer to that was worth another sixty-four thousand. The prize money was stacking up.

There was another outstanding question to be answered. Why had some of the kids died without any evidence of their foreheads and the skin of their hands being peeled back? Was the physical examination for evidence of the Beast a more recent idea?

Unless in the early days it was after the fact. Which meant that some bodies would have to be exhumed. Brazil seemed like a good place to start. A phone call would start the ball rolling, and then I might make the trip to see for myself.

Going through the police would be a bad idea, so the phone call would be to a friend of mine in Brazil. Until I found out something concrete, I didn't want to involve Allen Hemlock. Unless I missed my bet, his son John was seriously tied up in the killings, and I didn't want daddy trying to interfere.

Of course, it was just my gut instinct. There was nothing concrete to tie John Hemlock to the deaths. Only inference and supposition. In fact, if I looked at the matter objectively, the most that I could say was that the New Apostles seemed to be linked to deaths. I really didn't have proof that they were involved. Just an unlikely coincidence of timing in the death of Benjamin Franks.

I called Jorge Alvarado in Rio de Janeiro to tell him what I wanted. He answered the phone on the fifth ring. I told him. There was a pause before he replied.

"You want what?"

"I want you to dig up a body or two and check out whether the heads were cut off after the kids were buried. Unofficially."

"Do you know what you're asking? You want me to go into sacred ground and dig up bodies in the middle of the night to see if they still have their heads on? I have done many bad things in my life, but I am not a ghoul."

He was probably crossing himself as we spoke.

"Look, I'm calling you because you're a righteous guy, Jorge, and because you've got respect for the dead."

I capped a guy once who killed Jorge's sister and had sex with her after she was dead, same as he had with three other girls before. Jorge wouldn't turn me down, but he needed to know that it was for a seriously good reason. Hard to blame him.

"You call that respect for the dead? To dig them up after they are buried?"

It wasn't hard to imagine him on the other end of the phone, sweating profusely, mopping his forehead with his handkerchief. A guy could still get away with keeping a handkerchief in Brazil. When you weighed as much as Jorge and lived in a climate like Brazil's, there was a lot of mopping to do.

His shirts and white suits had to be custom made. Three hundred and sixty pounds takes a lot of extra stitching.

There was a loud series of creaks in my ear, and I could imagine him rocking his big brown leather chair back and forth to give him enough momentum to get to his desk so that he could lean his fat forearms on it for support. Hard to imagine a guy that big had had a sister slim enough to be attractive. Then again, before it had happened, he had only weighed as much as me. Since her nasty death, Jorge ate a lot more. Death by cholesterol didn't seem to scare him.

"Listen, Jorge, I think some bad men killed these kids. Don't believe what you read in the papers. I think that bus crash wasn't an accident. You got that? It was a set up to get at them."

"But why? Who would do such a thing, and why?"

His voice came in raspy spurts, like his breathing.

"Bad people don't have reasons, Jorge. I don't have to tell you that."

There was a full two minutes of silence on the other end. I was going to have a big phone bill come the thirtieth of the month.

"Yes, yes," he said finally, "you do not."

"This has to be done quietly, Jorge. It's dirty work, I know, but you've got to clean up afterwards. You have anybody you can trust?"

"Of course."

"Not 'of course', Jorge. No mistakes."

"If they should talk, my friend, I will slit their throats myself."

"I appreciate the thought, but that would be after the fact."

"Trust me," he said, "to do this right."

Famous last words.

"I do. When this is all over, or if anything happens to me, you tell who you need. Okay?"

"As you say."

"And, Jorge," I added, "send me some pictures."

*****

It was eleven o'clock, later that same night. Bob Alby, Charlie Kim, Leo Croton, and I had just finished our third hour of poker and our fourth six-pack of beer. I wasn't really paying attention to the game, but I was winning anyway. There were a lot of other things on my mind.

"I'm being beat by a one-armed man," moaned Leo. "I've got the luck of a single man in a lesbian bar. Son of a bitch."

"Ha," said Charlie, "son of a bitch. You know, I like that expression, but I have no idea for what it means."

"Son of a bitch?" put in Bob Alby, pushing his chair away from the table. "That's easy. A bitch is slang for a mean woman. Son of a bitch means the son of mean woman. It's slang."

"Then why do we say 'son of a bitch'?" asked Charlie innocently.

"It's a figure of speech," said Bob.

"You see, it has no meaning," smiled Charlie.

"It means something," said Leo. "It means I'm pissed off."

"What has the son of a mean woman got to do with you being pissed off? And what do either have to do with you urinating?"

"Where'd you find this guy, Scott?" asked Bob.

"At the rent-a-smart ass store. And a smart ass, Charlie, for your information," I said, "is somebody with their brains in their butt."

"You Americans," he replied, "are inscrutable."

"Break," said Bob, "I've had enough. You guys are driving me crazy. Fifteen minute piss break."

That was all it took. Charlie and Bob headed for the toilet, leaving Leo and I alone at the table. My mind wasn't on Leo, though, I was wondering if more children were dying while I was sitting there. Weighing the responsibility of calling Interpol with what I had against the consequences of going up against Allen Hemlock. With his kind of money, I might wake up one morning and find myself the prime suspect for the murders.

So, what I had done in the meantime, after calling Jorge, was to call in more private markers and put a watch on as many of the kids in as many of the countries as I could. It wasn't enough to match the kind of manpower that the countries themselves could bring to bear, but it was something.

"Time to talk," Leo said.

"I need a little more time. There's something I'm checking into that will tell me if I'm on the right track."

"What's the problem? Don't trust Bob and Charlie?"

"I thought you wanted to play a few more hands?"

"For once in your life, can you just answer a direct question?"

We had been friends for as long as I had lived in Gibraltar, but I didn't want to answer his question just yet. I had been playing on pure intuition, guessing that Allen Hemlock knew more than he was telling me, that the killings would stop for a while. My intuition had been wrong. Benny Franks would have agreed with me if he were still alive.

Sorry, Benny.

But Benny Franks had confirmed one thing for me. In some way, shape, or form, the New Apostles were involved. And that meant that either John Hemlock, or his New Apostles buddies, or both, were involved. Tomorrow night, at the dinner at John Hemlock's, I would have the chance to meet some of the key New Apostles, and after I saw them eye to eye, I was sure that I would know the answers to a lot of my question.

Allen Hemlock would probably be there; I would have to work around him. His son was involved, and I was sure that Allen knew it. It must be tearing him apart, but I couldn't sympathize with him. He had only seen photographs of what I had not only looked at but also smelled. Allen hadn't met Mr. Mining Pick in person, either.

Allen Hemlock, unlike me, still had two good arms, and, unlike the dead kids, his head was still attached. No, I couldn't sympathize with him. I would find out what I needed to find out, one way or the other at the dinner tomorrow night, and wherever it went from there, I would follow to the killers.

"Hey, are you listening to me?" asked Leroy.

Not really.

It had begun to sink into me that I was really just a valve turner again. I thought I was in control. Turn the valve, the gas was supposed to go where you wanted it to go. Wrong.

By working for Allen Hemlock, I thought I was free. He pointed me at the job, provided the money, and I got what I wanted. So long as it agreed with what he wanted. I thought that he'd given me the chance to do things my way. Achieve the results the way that I chose. Wrong again.

But I didn't think I couldn't go wrong anymore. I began to believe that, once set in motion, I was beyond judgment. I had big money backing me. Now I was beginning to see that, unless I did something different, I was still just a valve turner, doing what the company said. Not responsible for the consequences.

Wrong.

I was getting tired of being wrong.

"Yeah, I'm hanging on your every word," I said. "Sorry, I didn't mean to be an asshole."

"Well, you were," he replied, but he smiled a little when he said it.

"Leroy, I've got a problem, and I think I need your advice and your help, and Charlie and Bob's, too. I think I'm over my head on something. Can we wait until they get back?"

He gave me a curious look. "Must be a big problem."

"Bigger than me," I said, and I meant it.

Bob and Charlie returned a minute later.

"You guys get serious while we were gone?" asked Bob.

"Sheriff Leroy is not happy losing his money again," smiled Charlie. "He will arrest Scott now. Very bad man," he said, pointing at me. "Saw him in picture on Post Office wall. We will hold him down. You put cuff on. Only need one."

"Charlie, I need to talk to all of you. There's something that I need to tell all of you, something that you need to know about."

"You draw from bottom of deck. I know."

"I'm not listening to shit until I get another beer, especially if it's serious," said Bob. "We empty the fridge yet?"

"Not quite," I replied.

"Good, then I'll listen."

When he returned with his beer, he sat down at the table with the rest of us, and popped the top open on the can. It was a clean, uncomplicated sound. And then I told them about the kids. I didn't tell them what it was that I did for Allen. I didn't have to. They were my friends, so they left it alone.

I told them about Dr. Stouffer, John Hemlock, and the New Apostles. I told them about Jorge, although I didn't mention his name or country. "The reason I'm telling you guys this," I said, "is because of what happened to Benny Franks today. And because I need help."

Charlie hadn't heard anything about it, so I explained it to him. He listened without wisecracking, without interruption. When I was done, I went to my desk and got the papers that I had printed out for them, and distributed one copy to each.

"This is a list of the kids that attended the conference, and their... status. You can see that all the American children are alive. Charlie, there are five Korean kids listed, also still alive."

"Yes," he nodded. "And Korean police have not been notified?"

"No, Allen felt that there was insufficient evidence to notify police departments around the world. So far, according to him, all I have is a hypothesis to work with. When my friend exhumes some bodies, we'll know whether it's real or Memorex."

"I have... friends in Korea who can help," offered Charlie.

"Then I'd call them. I think those kids are in immediate danger."

"I've got an immediate problem, too, Scott," said Leroy. "If what you're telling us is right, then they've murdered a man right in my backyard, and I've got to do something about it. If we lock them up pronto, that should slow them down a little."

"Who would we lock up?" asked Bob. "Scott's right, he's got a theory, but you can't lock up a person on a theory. Do you know what Hemlock's lawyers could do if you did that? Whoever you did lock up wouldn't even spend a single night in jail, and you know it."

"Something's got to be done to send a message to these people."

"Yes, Leroy, but we have to have a plan."

"We? This is a police matter. And now that you've told me, Scott, I have to do something about it. I don't care how much money Allen Hemlock or the Church of the New Apostles have. We've got to run this through channels to get the kind of support that's needed to get this under control."

"You'll just drive them further underground," I told him. "They'll wait it out, and then start out all over again. They've got until whenever to get done what they want to get done. We don't even know their time schedule, whoever they are. And the other thing that I'm worried about is the three of you. If you get involved, you could be the next target."

"I've been a target for over twenty years, Scott," said Leroy. The way that he said it, he sounded a little like a movie tough guy. I had to give him that.

"I am too small to be good target," said Charlie.

"You're big enough to catch a bullet," I said.

"You know, I never tell you what I did in Korea," he said.

"Fathered lots of Korean children?" grinned Bob. "Is that why you left your country?"

"No, I was not that fortunate. I worked with... Korean government."

"And?" I asked.

"In Korea, it is a tradition for martial arts masters to sometimes work for the government to do certain things. It is not good work."

A look that was one part shame, one part duty, and two parts grim crossed Charlie's face. It would be a mystery to Bob, but Leo and I understood it well enough.

"You did wet work for the Korean CIA?" asked Leroy.

"Wet work?"

Leroy extended his right index finger and drew it across his own throat like a knife.

"Yes, you understand me well. It is shameful, but true."

"Am I the only guy around here who hasn't killed people?" asked Bob.

"Afraid so," I replied.

Charlie and Leroy nodded their agreement.

"This time," continued Bob, ignoring us, "there is no government organization to fall back on."

"There is if we kick this upstairs," said Leroy. "The Church's money can't shut down a police matter."

"Trust me," I said, "they don't have to shut down the police. They would just wait for however long it took and start all over again. That's why I need your help. All of you. I want these guys."

"You want me to put it on the wire services?" asked Bob.

"No. I think we need to move quickly and quietly on this. We've got to find out who's running this and take them down."

Leroy wasn't buying in; I could see it in his eyes. Bob Alby wasn't on board either.

"Look, just give me until Sunday night. It's Friday now, and I'm just asking you to give me until Sunday. By then I'll have confirmation of whether or not some of those kids listed as accidental death were accidents or not and it will give me a chance to get more information on John Hemlock and the New Apostles. We meet again on Sunday afternoon and, if everything is what I suspect it is, we can go public or do whatever we have to do."

"I can't ignore what you've told me about Benny Franks," Leroy told me. "I need to act on that now."

"You've got nothing to act on yet," said Bob. "There's nothing actually linking Benny Franks' death to the New Apostles. So, you've got a plant manager who attends their church. So what?"

"So, I can investigate."

"I want you to investigate," I told him. "Anything you find out can only help. But keep this in mind. If I'm right, and so far it's mostly intuition, someone or a group within the New Apostles have had people killed all around the world. They're fanatics, but they're not stupid. In all of the years in between the conference and now, they haven't been caught. Not one police department in one of these countries has brought them down. They've got an organization, and they've had all of these years to think this through. I don't think we'll find anything that directly links them to the deaths."

"It's hard to believe," said Bob, "that someone of Allen Hemlock's stature is trying to bury this. And if it's true, it's criminal."

"You're forgetting something. He hasn't actually tried to bury it. He's got me actively trying to track this down. His head's up his ass, though, since he thinks that his son might be an intended victim. I think John Hemlock is up to his neck in it. And, somehow or other, maybe unintentionally, Allen himself. But I've got to be able to prove it. Otherwise, he and his New Apostles buddies are going to walk away clean."

Leroy rubbed the scruff on his chin. He was one of those men who had to shave twice a day.

"Tell me again what you'll know by Sunday," he said.

"I'll know whether a group of the kids that died an 'accidental' death were actually murdered. That's one thing. And I'll have met some of the key members of the Church of the New Apostles, and will try to squeeze something out of them. That's two. And third, but not last, it gives a lady friend of mine a chance to see what she can come up with in the way of linkages. She's been hot on their trail since they killed her husband."

"She up to that kind of work?" asked Bob.

If Monica heard him say that, she'd ream him.

"Former Major in the KGB. Yeah, I'd say she can handle it," I replied.

"And I can go ahead locally investigating John Masters, the plant manager who's a member of the New Apostle's Church?" asked Leroy.

"Yeah, Leroy, I've got no problem with that. In fact, I hope you come up with something."

After a moment of silence while everyone considered the situation, Bob Alby looked off into space for a moment, and then wondered out loud, "I wonder why they haven't done anything in the United States?"

It was Charlie who answered.

"Too close to home. Wait until last for Canada and United States both. United States is a big country. Big police force. Kill far away to hide pattern. Right, Scott?"

I had to agree.

"I think you're right, Charlie," I said. "It makes sense. Plus, I think that we would have found the tie-in to the conference quicker."

"Also," Charlie continued, after looking down at his list again, "these deaths are not the work of one man who plans and directs. It, unless I make big mistake, the work and planning of many men."

"I don't understand," I said.

"You are good student, Scott, but you make big mistake looking only for one man." He tapped the list with his forefinger. "You see, there are too many methods of death. When so many die in so many locations, we would see an emphasis on one particular style."

"Hey," put in Bob, suddenly excited, "there are twelve main Apostles in the Church of the New Apostles, just like in the Bible. Maybe all of the Apostles are in this. That would explain two things: how they are able to handle something this size, and why the methods of death vary so widely, like Charlie says."

Leroy and I looked at each other as we considered the prospect. Twelve Apostles of goodness in the Bible, Twelve Apostles of darkness killing kids today. It wasn't a happy thought. But it sounded possible. Maybe. I didn't buy it myself; things get kind of complicated when that many people are involved.

"They'd have to be fucked in the head," Leroy said, shaking his head.

"Think about the Inquisition," I replied. "These guys are sick, but it's not like it hasn't been done before. In Salem, they used to throw suspected witches into the water. If they could swim, and didn't drown, then they were considered guilty and executed. If they drowned, they were considered innocent, only they weren't around to give a shit. Yeah, church people have been there, done that."

"There's something else," said Bob. "What in the hell could Benny Franks know that was worth taking the risk of killing him for? And whatever it was, he must have found it out close to home. That means that if we could find out what Benny did, we might have the inside track."

"Yes," put in Charlie with a big smile, "then we, too, would be worth killing."

"What are you smiling about?" asked Leroy irritably.

"At their misfortune, what else?"

The Murder

The following morning, I heard from Jorge. He was not a happy camper. If I spent the night in a cemetery digging up dead bodies, I wouldn't be a happy camper either. But I would rather have been there than in the Warehouse of the Dead.

I had gotten up early, ran a few miles, and then worked out on the bag with my one good arm and my two good feet. The pain in my right shoulder, which was always at its worst first thing in the morning, was getting tolerable. My balance when I was kicking was getting almost impressive.

Almost.

If you watch a lot of television, it's out and out amazing how quickly the heroes and villains heal. In real life, it doesn't work that way. If you've ever broken a bone, or been in an accident where you were cut up badly, you know what I'm talking about.

I'd just gone back into the lighthouse for a glass of juice when Jorge called and gave me the news. He and his helpers had dug up two bodies. Both of them were headless, with the skulls lying next to the bodies.

The caskets, he informed me, had been sealed at the funeral home.

"I'm right with you," I told him. "Somebody there was in the loop. Somebody knew what was going on."

"This is a terrible thing," he said. "I want to find the bastard and squeeze the truth out of him."

"They're dangerous people, Jorge. You don't have to be involved in this any further. You've given me what I need."

His voice took on an angry edge. "Now I want what I need. To find them and to kill them. They are worse than animals."

"We might need them alive to testify."

I counted off the seconds nervously until he replied.

"You only need them to speak, is that right?"

"Yeah. I need them to be able to talk."

"They will talk and talk when I am complete with them."

"Then do it, Jorge. But be careful. I don't want your head squashed in a press."

"What?"

"Just be careful."

*****

He said something back to me in Portuguese, then hung up the phone. It sounded nasty, whatever it was.

I was getting out of the shower when it hit me. Leroy was the quickest way to find out if I was correct, if he was willing to do it. I dried myself off—it takes a lot longer with one arm, believe me—got dressed which also took a while, and went upstairs to the room with the big light to call him.

"Leroy," I said when he picked up the phone, "this is Scott. I need some help."

"What kind of help?" he asked.

"Dr. Kris Stouffer, you remember the psychologist I told you about? I need you to find out if she was married with a different name ten years ago. She's got a son named Bobby. He's the one I'm interested in. I want to find out as soon as possible if his last name is different from hers. I think Stouffer is her maiden name."

"Why is this important?"

"Because I think that her son may be one of the kids on the list. It's a long shot, but if he is, it will not only explain a lot, it might give me some leverage with her to find out everything that she knows. Can you help?"

"I've got some other things going on today, including going to see Mrs. Franks to question her, but I'll get it done one way or the other and call you back. Consider it a done deal."

Charlie called me shortly after I hung up the phone to tell me that things in Korea were "under control." I didn't have to ask what he meant.

I felt like a spider in the middle of a vast web. A filament stretching to the Ukraine. Another to Brazil. Yet another to Korea. More filaments, more countries. And me in the center, waiting for information. I decided to take a nap.

*****

In my dream, Gregorio moved ahead of me. We were in the warehouse in Mexico City. We had gotten the lead only three hours ago from one of Gregorio's contacts.

"Hey, amigo," said Gregorio, "I don't like this place. There should be people here."

Our footsteps were soft, and I could feel the treads of my boots catching occasionally on the cracked and heaved cement floor. The warehouse was a metal building that covered ten thousand square feet or so. Free standing metal storage racks held everything from fifty-five gallon drums to crates and boxes and five hundred milliliter stoppered glass bottles.

"Who's going to steal hazardous waste containers?" I asked.

"There should still be security. This is Mexico. People steal anything."

"What do you want? An honor guard?"

He wore a sleeveless white cotton shirt and jeans. As he turned into my chest light, I could see his biceps flex.

"Si, that would be nice."

In the background, I could hear the spinning of the fans built into the middle portion of the walls pulling the air in from one end, sucking it out the other. It did little enough to relieve the stifling heat, but at least prevented the buildup of toxic vapors from any of the containers that might be leaking. The occasional flap of a loose belt motor sounded almost like someone knocking on the wall.

"Look," I said, "we've got to check this whole fucking place. Can we get a move on it?"

"My mother would say that this is a place that the demons come to rest."

I hated it when he brought up his mother. It was usually a prelude to a philosophical spiel. The woman was dead, but she kept yakking away through her son. Sometimes I wondered if she had ever said half of the things that he attributed to her.

"Long as they don't get in the way."

"You know why I like to talk in the bad places?"

Fuck, I thought, it was going to be a long night.

"No, it's a complete damned mystery to me."

"My mother said that demons don't like the sound of human voices."

Neither do I, sometimes, I thought.

"Well then, they ought to be long gone from this place, Gregorio. Keep up the good work."

"It's true."

"Hallelujah. Now can we get moving? We've got a lot of shelves and pallets here to check."

The shoulder strap for my shotgun was eating into my shoulder. I had added it myself two weeks before. It was supposed to make lugging the thing around for long periods of time a little easier. That was the idea anyway.

We were looking for big crates or drums. Something large enough to hide a body or two in. By that time, of course, I thought that the boys that we were looking for were dead. A fifty-five gallon drum was big enough to hold a body if you folded the person in half before stuffing them in. If they weren't all in one piece, well, they might be scattered between a few containers. I hoped not.

At first, I had thought they were runaways. They were teenagers, and in a place like Mexico City, runaways did not usually last long. The parents denied it, of course. Parents don't like to say that there's trouble at home. Gregorio and his guys had been thorough in their checking, though. These kids had actually seemed happy enough.

"Your guy, he said crates, right?" I asked.

"Close enough."

"What?"

"He didn't speak English, hombre."

Everywhere that we turned our lights, shadows popped up from the shelves and containers. Their constant appearing and disappearing made it seem as though crowds of oddly shaped spectators were watching us. When we moved, they moved. Dark ghosts were following us. The labels, where there were labels on the containers, were in Spanish. I recognized the chemical formula for sulfuric acid on one large jug with a glass handle on the side.

"Maybe we should separate," I suggested.

"Maybe not," replied Gregorio.

"Where do they take all of this shit? You know, if we come up empty here, maybe we can find them wherever they dump this stuff."

"This is where they dump this stuff. It's just a move to get money. The company gets paid to pick up hazardous waste and dispose of it. They get paid well. Then the materials get stored in some cheap building like this. When the building is full, the company disappears with the money. It's a good business these days in Mexico. Mordida," he added, "makes it happen."

"You should put that on T-shirts. Sell them to the tourists. You'd be rich," I told him.

Gregorio stopped, and I almost ran into him. He looked back over his shoulder at me, and then pointed to the stacks of crates that he had found.

"That's too many," I said.

"Uh-huh."

"Don't be afraid," I told him. "This is just a dream. Nobody dies in a dream."

*****

It was the phone ringing that woke me up. I was up and off of the couch downstairs so quickly that I cracked my shin up against the glass coffee table. It hurt like a son of a bitch.

"Yeah," I said into the phone after I had hobbled over and picked it up.

"Don't you sound in a good mood?" was the response.

It was Dr. Stouffer.

"I'm hopping around on one foot," I said. "Cracked my damn shin on the coffee table getting to the phone."

"And it was only me; no wonder you're so happy."

"Nothing personal. It just hurts like hell, and I was sleeping when the phone rang. I'm always grumpy when I wake up."

"I'll remember that," she said.

I sat down behind the desk, and, crooking the cordless phone between my shoulder and chin, rubbed my shin with my one good arm. The phone popped out as I kneeled over, and bounced off of the desk and onto the floor.

I always seemed to show my best side to Dr. Stouffer.

"Sorry," I said when I had retrieved the phone.

"What's going on over there?" she asked.

"Oh, the usual. Trying to do two things at once when I've only got one good arm."

There was a pause while she digested that.

"Why'd you call?"

"I need a ride tonight. Can you pick me up?"

"Sure. Think you can stand all that time in the car with me?"

"No. But I need a ride. What time will you be here?"

"How about six o'clock?"

"Fine. I'll be ready. You are going to dress for the occasion?"

"I'll try to look like I just came off the cover of a magazine, doctor."

"Now that's interesting," she said.

"That I can dress up when the occasion demands?"

Tying a tie would take me an hour, but I wasn't going to tell her that.

"No. That you just called me doctor."

"Don't hold me to it, Kris. I just woke up. I'm not firing on all cylinders yet."

She didn't comment, but the dial tone said it for her. So much for diplomacy.

The rest of the afternoon was spent on phone calls back and forth around the world interrupted only by a local call from Bob Alby and one from Leroy, who had found out what I wanted to know. It turned out that I was right. Dr. Stouffer's last name at the time of the conference had been Beleski. Bobby Beleski was on the list as having attended the conference. Another piece of the puzzle had fallen into place. I was feeling like things were getting under control.

Here's how it all started between John Hemlock and me. Allen Hemlock, who was perpetually pissing off someone, had received death threats against himself and his family, consisting at that time of his wife Mary and his son John. In spite of his easygoing appearance, Allen was ruthless in matters of business. You can't get to be a billionaire from ground zero unless you step on and squash a few people along the way.

By that time, Allen had come to respect me as his chief troubleshooter. I didn't work directly for him; I was contracted on a job-by-job basis. That's the way that I wanted it. After the accident, I was determined never to work for anyone else again as long as I lived. But he knew that, however nasty the job that he gave me, I always took care of business.

When Allen was threatened, he called on me to protect his family. It wasn't my type of job, I told him, but he wasn't listening to any of that. I told him to hire the best bodyguard service that money could buy, but he'd been down that road before—he wanted me. He wouldn't take no for an answer. I finally took the contract.

John Hemlock was then Johnny Hemlock, aged thirteen. He was a tall, gawky kid, and when his father first introduced me to him at the Hemlock estate, Johnny seemed a bit shy even for his age. This was about two years before the conference.

Wife Mary was quite a bit younger than Allen. Thirty or so years old. Five foot two. Long, blond hair, wide eyes, elegant cheekbones, and a mouth almost full enough to be called pouty. In spite of her good looks and great body, she seemed to be a nice enough person. Somehow, the money and her looks didn't seem to have gone to her head.

She didn't quite know what to make of me at first. Whatever Allen had told her about me, she was definitely nervous. She probably thought that I was on the psychotic side, just waiting for the opportunity to whip out a gun and start blasting away at the gardener or the pizza delivery boy. I hadn't even met them yet; it was much too early to say whether they needed to die or not.

Here's how bodyguarding works—the client says that they want to go somewhere. You tell them it's not safe. The client wants to do something. You tell them it's not safe. The client gets pissed. You ignore the client. The client gets more pissed. Then the client does something stupid.

After a solid week of me as a bodyguard, Mary Hemlock was about ready to pay the gardener or the pizza delivery boy to shoot me before I could get a round off at them. I couldn't much say that I blamed her.

Johnny was a different story. The kid acted like he worshipped the ground that I walked on from the day he met me. It was unnerving. I said that I've never been around live kids much since the accident. Johnny Hemlock was the one exception.

I had moved into the Hemlock mansion. Allen was absent the entire time, traveling the world. He had his own team of bodyguards with him. I was supposed to be taking care of his wife and child while he took care of business.

Allen traveled all the time. He lived the fast life, seemed to love his family, but didn't really know them. He should have put on a nametag before he came through the front door to make it easier on everybody.

Johnny, in particular, was starved for attention. I felt sorry for the kid at first. He hardly ever saw his father. Allen called home a lot, but the calls were short, and almost perfunctory. So, Johnny stayed real close to me; wanted to know all about me.

Mrs. Hemlock was slightly less obvious, but it became quickly clear to me that after a while- when she hadn't seen me kill anyone- she was starting to look at me more like a man than she was a bodyguard. It started getting difficult the night that she came downstairs in a sheer nightgown saying that she couldn't sleep because she was too tense.

Don't get me wrong, she looked good and I was horny, but, as I said earlier, I'd already started losing interest in casual sex, so I sent her back upstairs.

*****

Johnny always wanted to know how many people I had killed. Did they die right away when you shot them? Did being hit with a bullet really lift someone up and slam them against the wall like in the movies? How much did they bleed? Had I ever used a knife or a garrote? Did I dress in black when I went after people?

He was a cute kid, if you liked thirteen-year-olds who were fixated on violent death.

His mother started constantly pestering me to let her go out. To go shopping. To go to church. To see her friends, and bullshit like that.

I tried to explain to her she was safest in a controlled environment, like her home, until all this was over. She didn't seem to listen as well as she had in the beginning. We ended up in a lot of arguments.

The arguments fascinated Johnny. More questions. How would someone go about killing his mother if she left the house? How did killers stalk their prey? I smacked him across the face once when he got too intense about it. His mom didn't take that well.

She called me a tyrant, a dictator, and even a few unlady-like names. I didn't listen to her. I was looking at Johnny, who had wiped the blood away from his mouth with the palm of his hand and was licking it off while he stared at me. Something, I realized, was definitely wrong with the young lad.

Things went bad the very next day. Mary Hemlock seemed to have calmed down. Johnny apologized for asking me so many questions. I should have seen it coming. The mother had decided to sneak out and see a friend, and Johnny, the little prick, had decided to help her escape for the afternoon as a payback for me slapping his chops.

The kid and the mother were swimming in the indoor pool. Rich people can do things like that.

I sat on a folding chair, wearing trunks and a shoulder holster that held my Beretta. If you can think of something more boring that watching somebody else's wife and kid swimming while you baby-sit them, don't tell me. I don't want to know.

After about twenty minutes in the pool, Mary got out of the water and told me she had a headache. She said that she wanted to go upstairs and lay down. She held both hands to her forehead as though she were in pain and rocked back and forth for effect. I tried not to look at her wet body or the way her bikini fit. It's hard to concentrate on a woman's eyes, though, when only a thin yellow cloth restrains her breasts.

I called to Johnny, who was still in the pool, and told him he had to get out so that we could go inside with his mom. He threw a tantrum that literally echoed off of the white ceramic tiled walls.

Mary pleaded with me, begged me to let him stay in for a while, and assured me she was only going upstairs, that she would be perfectly safe. Please, she said, her poor boy had never even gotten out of the house even once since I arrived.

I should have told her that was the breaks, but with young Johnny freaking out in the pool, and mom getting ready to cry, I said okay, just this once. As she went through the door, I didn't even think twice about her leaving. I was too busy imagining jumping in the pool and holding Johnny's head underwater until he quit screaming.

With his mom gone, however, Johnny quit screaming and wailing and thanked me for letting him stay in the pool. He swam over to the edge of the pool and asked if I wanted to come in.

"Can't get my gun wet, kid," I told him.

"That's so cool," he said, and then paddled off.

He stayed in the water so long that his skin should have started to wrinkle, but my mind was kind of on hold, so I didn't think about it. Whenever I seemed about to ask him to get out, he would swim over to the side and start asking me so many stupid questions so that I had to tell him to swim if he was going to swim or to get out.

Eventually, I got tired of just sitting around and finally told him to get out of the water. With a quick glance at the pale blue dolphin clock on the wall, he swam over to the side and climbed out.

I threw him one of the fuzzy yellow towels that were stacked on a chair and he even said thank you, Mr. Brown, and smiled. For a moment, it crossed my mind that he wasn't such a bad kid, that he just needed his father around more.

He took his time getting dried off.

Finally, I realized he was stalling. There's only so much skin on a thirteen-year-old boy to dry off. It was his eyes that really gave him away, though. He kept watching me with a weird look while he toweled himself off. A second or two later, I had it figured out and took off to look for Mrs. Hemlock.

She wasn't in her room at the top of the fancy marble staircase. The maid hadn't seen her. The cook, an old man who had been with the Hemlock's for years, told me she had gone to see a friend. I got the name and number of the friend and called. She hadn't seen Mrs. Hemlock yet, although she was expecting her over half an hour ago.

I got directions to the friend's residence, threw on a shirt, and almost ran over Johnny, who had been following me around, watching my every move.

"You're coming with me, kid," I told him brusquely, and to emphasize the point, shoved him on ahead of me toward the front door.

He nearly fell flat on his face, but caught himself on a chair, and, after shooting me a nasty look, smiled beatifically, then kept going.

"You're not so tough," he told me five minutes into the drive. "All muscles and no brains."

"Shut the fuck up," I replied.

"Make me," he said.

I slapped him on the side of his head and bounced him off the passenger side glass. He was quiet for the rest of the ride until we found his mother's blue-gray Porsche pulled over behind three enormous trees in a field of knee high meadow grasses. There was no one in sight.

I took the Beretta from its holster and told Johnny to stay in the car, then locked the doors behind me and took off on a run. There was no need to be careful, I figured, since I knew what I would find.

She lay next to her car, stretched out on her back. The top of her head was half blown off. Not exactly a clean job, but they must have felt pressed for time.

I scoped the field, but saw nothing threatening. Whoever had been there was gone, long gone.Mary Hemlock was well dressed that day. She wore a thigh high cream-colored linen skirt and a pale white blouse. Beneath the blouse, I could see the outlines of her bra. Her eyes had the vacant stare of the dead.

I wanted to shoot something, anything. I wanted to scream and set off at a run after whoever had done this. I wanted to do so many things, but in the end, all I could do was stare at what used to be her lovely face.

Johnny came running up behind me, and I turned and instinctively pointed the Beretta at him. The look on his face when he saw his mother's body would stay with me in my nightmares for a long time, only to be replaced by horrific dreams of poison gas clouds, and then finally those replaced by nightly replays of my night in the Warehouse of the Dead.

He snarled at me, actually snarled like a wolf, baring his teeth, and came at me.

"You killed her," he screamed, battering me with his fists. "You let this happen to her. It's your fault. You killed her."

I stood there and took it. He was right. I had failed her. I had failed him. I had failed Allen. I had been beaten by a thirteen-year-old kid and his stupid, stupid mother. I had let Mrs. Hemlock sneak past me, and now she was dead.

"You killed her, you killed her, you killed her," he blubbered and continued to swing away.

He would have beaten me senseless if the rage at my own impotence hadn't risen up and consumed me. I reached around, grabbed him by the hair on the back of his head, yanked up hard, and then shoved the end of the Beretta up against his forehead.

"Shut the fuck up," I told him for the second time that day. "I can't take any more of your shit right now. I didn't kill your mother. Your stupid game did."

It was a cruel thing to say, and I had no defense for it, no excuse at all.

I dragged him back to my car, practically threw him into his seat, went around the car, got in, and posted the cops on the CB channel we used back before there were smartphones.

The kid was so quiet that I kept glancing over at him as I drove, trying to see if he had gone into shock. But he was strangely silent and composed. I didn't like the way he looked back at me once. Cold. Hateful. Like he had a camera behind his eyes that was taking a picture of me for future reference. It was a look that I was to grow familiar with over the years as being unique to him.

When we got back to the Hemlock estate, he got out of the car, walking like a robot, and headed into the house. He must have gone straight to his father's study to get the letter opener.

His right hand was behind his back when I entered the room. He walked straight up to me and, with his left hand, motioned me to lean over toward him, as though he had a confession to make or a secret to share that was only for me.

The rage that I felt was slowly being overcome by guilt. He was a boy whose mother was dead. The kid had just been playing his part in a game when he had stalled me so that his mother could get out. There was no way that he could have foreseen the consequences. I leaned forward to hear what he had to say.

If I had leaned a little closer, I would be missing an eye today.

Brother Thomas

Dr. Stouffer was sitting on her front porch swing when I pulled into her driveway, although I didn't recognize her until I got closer. It was the legs that confused me. She was wearing a sleeveless pale yellow dress, and her legs were tucked sideways. I realized I had never seen her bare legs. Her hair was down and hung about her shoulders in waves of gold with a touch of red that the setting sun shared with her.

I braked, put the car in park, turned the engine off, and sat looking at her, not wanting to spoil the Norman Rockwell simplicity of her pose. A house in the country. A beautiful woman gracing the front porch. The clear quiet of impending dusk and the smell of apple trees. Everything that I had wanted when I was younger.

She swung her legs down, picked up a yellow purse that lay beside her on the swing, and walked down the steps toward the car. When she stopped before the passenger door, I could see the graceful curve of her hips; her elegant fingers reaching for the door handle.

The door opened, and her leg came in, the fabric of her dress sliding upward a few inches; my heart beat a little faster. Her face came into view, her hand rested on the dashboard, and she lowered herself into the seat.

"You look nice," I said.

When I was a teenager, I had said something equally stupid to a girl on our first date.

"Nice?" she asked, a faint smile playing about her pink, glossy lips.

"You look fucking beautiful, okay?"

"Watch your language," she said primly, "we're having dinner with Christians tonight."

"Oh well," I replied, and turned the key in the ignition.

I drove faster than I normally drove, savoring the feel of the air on my face, the cloudless darkening of the sky, and the occasional glimpses from the corner of my eye of her blond hair.

There is something about being behind the wheel of a powerful, smooth driving car like the Reatta that is mildly sexual when your passenger is a good-looking woman with beautiful legs. You're in control. You're driving. You're going where you want to go. She's going wherever that is.

I wondered if it was good for her, too.

"Where's Bobby tonight?" I finally asked.

"At his Grandmother's."

"Sorry about my language sometimes."

A quick smile.

"I've heard worse. You wouldn't believe what you hear in therapy. Behind closed doors, that is."

"I suppose you can't tell me, either."

"I'll have to think about that," she said.

"Mind if we talk a little shop while we drive?"

"I think I can handle that."

"It's that or the radio."

"Lead on," she said.

So, I told her. Everything. Except what I had found out from Leroy about her and Bobby.

"You were talking with Mrs. Franks when her husband died?"

"When we got word that he had died. Yeah. That's the way it happened. A freak accident, that's what the official version is for now."

"But you don't think so."

It was a statement, not a question.

"No, I think he was rode hard and put away dead."

"You have such a way with words, Mr. Brown."

"It goes with my line of work. I don't usually get to see people at their best."

"Hmm."

"You're not going shrink on me again, are you?"

"I'll let you know," she said.

"Fair enough."

"You know, Mr. Brown, I've been thinking, and I can understand why me being involved with your investigation must be disconcerting to you."

"Mainly, I wondered why you were involved at all."

"Mr. Hemlock recruited my services. He told you that."

Things had started out going a little bit better. I decided to put a stop to that.

"I never thought that was the total story."

"No?" There was an edge to her voice that hadn't been there before.

"No," I said casually, "But that was before I learned about Bobby."

I heard her draw a quick breath, hold it for a while, then let it out slowly.

"Why didn't you tell me in the first place?" I asked.

"You had no right to pry into my life. I told you to keep my son out of this."

I didn't have to look at her, and I didn't want to see the disappointment and anger that would be there.

"Do you know what I've seen in the last couple of years, Kris? You want to hear what I found in Mexico? It would make you sick and douse you in nightmares. You don't want to see what I've seen, and I really mean that. And your son is on that list. I don't want anybody's kid to be on that list; I want this to be over."

"How did you find out? How did you find out about Bobby?"

"Something he said when I first met him gave me the idea. I checked it out. Now you want to tell me how all of this started? I'd like to know that we're on the same side. There's too much going on with too much at stake for us to be on different teams."

Chances were that she would lie to me. I had learned over the years to expect that from most people, which was why I valued those few lasting friendships that I had developed over the years. Mentally, I crossed my fingers.

"All right," she said at last, "you want to know? I'll tell you. Ethics or no ethics I will not let anything happen to my son. I'd ask you to swear you'd never tell anyone what I'm about to tell you, but I won't. If you did, you wouldn't be around much longer, anyway. Allen Hemlock would see to that."

It would have made me better to say something like Clint Eastwood or Jason Statham would have said. But they were indestructible movie heroes. I wasn't. So, I kept my mouth shut. Truth was if Hemlock wanted me dead, he could make it happen. I'd have a harder time getting to him.

"Here it is," she said. "I was John Hemlock's therapist after his mother's death. He hates you, do you know that? I don't think that's something that you don't already know, so I'm not breaking any confidentiality rules by telling you.

"He took his mother's death... badly. But John had problems before that. His mother's death just accelerated their manifestation."

"When I first met him," I said, "he hooked on to me quick. Wanted to know how many people I'd killed, what it was like when they died. Real big on pain and death. He wanted to touch my gun, wanted me to teach him to use it. Like I said, he was real big on pain and death. I'm not around kids that much, but even I could see that he was definitely not your normal kid."

"Fixated on pain and death. And control," she said. "That would describe part of it. You understand that being the son of a man like Allen Hemlock wasn't easy for him?"

"Yeah, I can buy that."

"Allen is a very demanding man. I don't know if you know just how demanding he can be, especially to a young boy. Allen is a human dynamo. John has never been like that. There's more, of course, but that falls under the category of confidentiality. But there is much, much more."

"You mean the abuse?"

I didn't know jack shit, but I was baiting her.

"You knew about that?"

I nodded.

"Like I said, the kid bonded to me. I don't know why."

She was thoughtfully silent for a minute, and then continued.

"He probably saw you as someone who could defend him from his father. Someone powerful enough to protect him from the beatings, and the humiliation."

Allen Hemlock, beating his son? Did she really believe that? Was there a chance that it could be true? I drummed my fingers on the steering wheel.

"It's possible, doctor. Yes, that makes sense."

"Doctor? Again?"

"We're on the same side now, aren't we?"

"Thank you," she said, and laid her hand on my shoulder, then softly withdrew it.

"You're welcome."

My mind was going through the options. Either little John was smart enough to fool the doctor or it had really happened. Which one was it?

For the moment, though, all that mattered was that she was convinced that John had told me most or everything that had happened or that he had contrived had happened between he and his father. She had confirmed beatings and humiliation. Had he said that he had been locked in a closet? Tied and left? Sexually abused? How to get the details from her?

"I didn't know whether or not to buy all of it, though, especially the sexual abuse."

"Oh, yes. No wonder he hates you now."

"I don't understand."

"Well, he told you the most humiliating parts of his life, hoping that you would protect him, but you didn't fulfill his expectations. Yes, I would say that his perceptions of the events would cause deep resentment, even hatred."

Had I really missed something like that? Was John Hemlock really an abused child who had been looking to me to defend him?

Nah.

Possibly.

He had, in fact, told me none of the things that I had told Dr. Hemlock. That being the case, how could he have expected anything from me?

Little boys with big secrets, or little boys with big lies?

"I've got to tell you he seemed to have a problem separating reality from fantasy back then," I told her.

"And very well read in the area of psychology."

"Pardon?"

"You have to understand that I'm not naive enough to believe everything that I'm told. Particularly when the patient in question was, I believe, as well read in psychology as I was."

We were crossing over the free bridge from Trenton to Grosse Ile by then. The Detroit River was dark and choppy. The Grosse Ile free bridge was built from metal grates, so that the tires made a grinding noise that, on that night, I identified as the sound of the waves abrading up against each other. To the north, I could see the orange-red glow of McLouth Steel far past the lights of homes and marinas lining the River Bank on the Trenton side.

"Come again?"

"John Hemlock is a genius, Mr. Brown. Gifted in more ways and to a degree that you can't imagine. He was, by the time that I first met him, more than capable of having invented the entire conflict. There was not a test that I could administer to him he was not fully conversant with what answers would yield what evaluations.

"He was reading on an adult level, from what his earlier evaluations showed, by the age of five. He had the intellectual capability of a John Milton without the moral discipline. I found myself erecting defenses against him very early on in our sessions. There were times, most of the time, in fact, that I felt like the patient.

"In matters of memory, he was almost eidetic, so that catching him in an unplanned anomaly was out of the question. In other words, he never tripped himself up by contradicting himself in what he said from one session to the next.

"However, there were, as you pointed out, certain topics in which his emotional intensity was more concentrated than normal. Unfortunately, there were and are no methods to measure such things.

"But there were times when I was certain, on an intuitive level, that the boy with whom I was speaking was simply a construct of an older personality behind his eyes."

"Nothing that you have been saying could objectively be defined as abnormal, though? Is that what you're saying?" I asked.

"Yes. That's exactly what I'm saying."

"Doctor, we'll be there in another ten minutes. Before we get there, it's important that I know how you became involved in this. Did Allen Hemlock come to you, or did you go to him?"

A deer strolled across the two lane road perhaps fifty feet ahead of us, and stopped. I slammed on the brakes. The tires squealed, and I felt the frame shudder as the ABS kicked in. The headlights quivered, and the deer seemed to shake with fright.

Dr. Stouffer straight-armed the dashboard and cried out. I clenched my teeth and tried to control the wheel with my one good arm.

We stopped with a lurch ten feet from the deer, who stared at us the entire time as though it were supremely confident that we would definitely stop.

"My God, look at it," exclaimed Dr. Stouffer. "It's just standing there, staring at us."

As though the spell had been broken, the deer bolted and took off at a run into the field, disappearing into the darkness.

"Plays a mean game of chicken, doesn't it?" I asked.

"Allen called me," she said, when we were in motion again. "He'd noticed a pattern developing in that he was alerted by human resources that an unusual number of the children of Hemlock employees were vanishing. The corporate security group discreetly began making inquiries and compiling records. A pattern began to emerge.

"Remembering my work with his son John, and fearing that after what happened to his wife so many years ago that John, too, could become a target, he brought me in to see if I could profile what type of individuals might be involved.

"When I was reviewing the cases that they brought to me, I recognized two names as being familiar. You see, when the conference was held here for gifted children, Bobby attended. Area mothers were asked to allow, where it was appropriate, some of the foreign children to stay with them. We housed a boy and a girl from England. They were both children of Hemlock employees in the UK. That's when I got suspicious.

"I got hold of a list of the attendees and cross checked them against the list of Hemlock employees, and, well, you know the rest. There was a definite linkage.

"There were some points that were difficult to reconcile at first, but there was a pattern, a frightening pattern emerging.

"You had been involved in attempting to track down what had happened to some of these kids, and when Allen learned what I had found out, he contacted you and we went to see you. I didn't know you weren't informed that I was coming until I got there."

It made sense, and it sounded like the truth.

"Do you mind if I ask you a question?" she continued.

"Go ahead."

"Why you? I don't mean to sound cruel, but when he hired you to protect his wife and son, his wife was murdered. After that experience, wouldn't you think that he would have hired someone else for this job?"

"I don't know," I replied. "I've wondered about that myself. I thought he hired you to bird dog me; to watch and see that I didn't crack. I'm just deniable muscle for hire. But that doesn't answer the question. There are lots of people like me out there. Why me? He's got a reason for picking me. Whatever it is, he's got a reason."

The gas-styled electric lamps atop the brick pillars on either side of the wrought iron gates of the Hemlock estate appeared in the headlights. Behind them, the lights of the mansion itself were visible.

"We're here," I announced.

When the valet had driven away with the Reatta, Dr. Stouffer took my left arm in hers. I felt like we were going to the prom.

"Shall we go in?" she asked.

"Let's," I replied.

Angel met us at the door, and seemed unsurprised to see Dr. Stouffer draped on my arm.

"Hello, Angel," I said cheerily.

"This way, Mr. Brown," she said, without so much as looking at me. "And good evening to you, Dr. Stouffer."

"Nice to see you again, Angel."

She took us to Christine, who stood in the hallway talking to two women of the middle-aged, filled-out persuasion, and a tall, white-haired gentleman who was eighty if he was a day.

"Oh, Mr. Brown and Dr. Stouffer, I'm so glad that you came. Everybody," she said, calling her little troop of three to attention, "this is Dr. Stouffer and Mr. Scott Brown. They're friends of the family."

Suddenly, Dr. Stouffer had top billing. Educational rank does have its privileges.

"And this is Brother Thomas Argyle," she said, indicating the tall thin man, "and Mrs. Peterson and Mrs. Boyle."

Mrs. Peterson, the one with the longer name, had the largest gut and the grayest hairs. Her dress was pale blue with white polka dots, and she wore a string of white pearls, but mostly I just noted that she had fleshy arms and a round, sagging face in desperate need of structural support.

Mrs. Boyle, appropriately enough, was sunburned red as a lobster fresh from the boiling pot. Her dress was white, with pale blue birds in flight faintly imprinted on the fabric. Taking in the two of them together was like looking at conflicting wallpaper selections. The opposing patterns made my eyes hurt.

Christine led Dr. Stouffer and the Lewis Carroll twins away deftly, and I was left alone to appraise the author of The Coming of the Beast.

I'd say that he had the darkly intelligent, piercing eyes I had expected, but he didn't. His corneas were the dirty gray color of the creek that I used to splash in after frogs as a kid. The faint, rotted smell of water swollen driftwood came back to me when he smiled and said hello, and told me how much he had been looking forward to meeting me.

He extended his bony, liver-spotted hand toward me, then jerked it back and away as he remembered my disability.

"My apologies," he said with a thin, tight smile.

In a surreal silence, I watched his mouth form the words. His perfect teeth, I realized, were dentures.

Fake teeth, fake smile.

"Brother John has told me so much about you," he continued, as though there were no tension between us.

"What a surprise," I said. "He's not said a hell of a lot about you."

"Ah. Well. You see, I very much like to remain in the background."

"Humility?" I asked, arching an eyebrow.

"Hardly. No, though it pains me to disillusion you, Mr. Brown, I am every bit as egotistical as the next man. I just find that it's ever so much easier to get things done behind the curtains than it is when you're front and center on stage."

The splintered light of the overhead chandelier reflected in his glasses, and when he moved his head to one side to peer at me, he had for a moment the faceted eyes of a mantis watching its prey. I wondered if I looked dangerous to him.

John Hemlock came up from behind me and moved to stand beside Brother Argyle.

"Well, John, I see that you made it."

He had a big smile on his face. The happy host. Dressed in a light-colored suit again, and wearing a faint pink shirt with a white linen tie. Fresh from the Miss America pageant. A pink carnation decorated his lapel.

"You've met Brother Argyle, of course."

I told him that yes, I had met the Beastmaster.

"Pardon?" asked Brother Argyle.

"I was referring to your book, The Coming of the Beast. I saw it on John's desk in his study. It's as thick as my dictionary."

The old man smiled uncertainly. "Thank you, I think. It took me many years to research and write. Have you read it?"

"No."

"Then Brother John must provide you with a copy. I'll sign it, if you like."

"That would make my entire night special," I told him.

John shot me an evil look.

"Honest," I said.

It might have gone a little further had not Allen Hemlock himself shown up then.

"Father," said John deferentially, "I'm so glad that you could come. Christine will be so pleased."

Allen strode up—his legs definitely are long enough that he can actually stride— and shook his son's hand.

Can't get much more personal than that, I thought.

"Wouldn't miss it, son," he said with a wink. "Business will still be there tomorrow. Mr. Argyle, great to see you again. Scott, it's a rare occasion that I get to see you in a suit and tie. Must have been a real project tying the knot, though."

"I got up early to get a head start on it," I said.

Allen was dressed in a lightweight, dove gray suit, pinstriped white, gray, and red shirt with a white collar, and wore a matching tie that is hard to describe. His hair was brushed back, his skin tanned, and he looked like he owned the place, even though it was his son's house. It was a stark contrast to Brother Thomas' Sunday-go-to-meeting black suit and his bald head.

I was beginning to enjoy myself.

"Brother Thomas here was telling me he'd get me an autographed copy of his book, The Coming of the Beast. Isn't that great, Allen?"

Allen was never a guy to be caught short. "Yes," he said, "that's very thoughtful of you, Brother Thomas."

He never broke his smile. You'd think that I just told him that company sales were up thirty percent. Brother Thomas was just as hard to read, although at eighty years old, I imagined facial reactions came a little slower.

"You must be something of an expert on the Beast," I told the old man.

"I have studied the topic for many years," he said, reaching up with a finger and pushing up his glasses. "Although there are many others who have done the same. Hal Lindsay, I believe, is most responsible for bringing the prophecies to the popular attention. Of course, as a popular writer, he was a little naive as concerned interpretation. He erred, essentially, by not being cognizance of our duty to fight the coming of the Biblical Beast. By not recognizing that the Book of Revelations deals only with one outcome for mankind—the outcome we face if we do not do battle against the Beast."

Allen looked at me and I looked at Allen.

Why doesn't the guy just hold up a sign that says "guilty?"

I tried to will the thought over to Allen telepathically, but he must have been tuned to another station.

"This all must sound very strange to you, Mr. Brown. Brother John tells me you're not very religious."

"I'm not much of a Bible reader," I said modestly. "With one hand, it's hard to turn the pages."

It startled him for just a moment. John clenched his hands into tight fists in response to the sarcasm. But Brother Thomas, after an initial double take, laughed pretty hard for an octogenarian. John seemed to relax a little after that. He even cracked a tentative smile.

"Oh, I like you Mr. Brown, even if you are a bit of a heathen," said Brother Thomas when he had quit holding his sides and laughing his hollow laugh.

And I'd like to peel your forehead back and see what kind of marks you've got on your skull, I thought.

Christine, and Dr. Stouffer returned minus the tonnage twins to save us from further discussion. John looked relieved. Allen looked thoughtfully first at Brother Thomas, and then at his son.

As Christine led us toward the dining room, Brother Argyle dropped back and whispered to me in a cadaverous tone, "You and I must talk further, perhaps after dinner," and then picked up his pace to leave Dr. Stouffer and I trailing behind the entourage.

"What was that all about?" asked Dr. Stouffer as she gently took hold of my left arm again.

"Nothing. Just making new friends."

"I'll bet. I don't think I like that old man. He seems... hungry."

"Lighten up," I told her. "Of course he's hungry, we haven't been fed yet."

We stepped into the dining room to meet the rest of the New Apostles.

The Church

Allen Hemlock, the alleged child abuser, sat at one end of the skating rink sized table. Brother Thomas sat at the other, nearest the large window looking out onto the back lawn. Including myself and Dr. Stouffer, there were eighteen other people filling in the chairs.

Dealer always deals to the left, so I'll lay out the seating arrangements in the same way, starting with Brother Thomas as the dealer. I wouldn't put you through the entire list, but before the week was done, one of the people at that table would murder my friend Bob Alby by jamming a gun underneath his chin and pulling the trigger. Try and guess which one.

I would have bet on the one the one who looked like the devil incarnate, but I would have been wrong.

Mr. and Mrs. Houghten, owners of the Houghton Newspaper chain, were the first couple to Brother Thomas' left. They were dead ringers for the husband and wife farmers in the picture "An American Gothic." You remember, the one with the straight faced farmer holding a pitchfork standing next to his obviously frigid wife, with the whole thing set in front of a barn and a haystack. The Houghton's may have been rich, but they didn't look like a fun couple to me.

The next two seats, still going around from Brother Thomas' left, were the Dibell's. Mr. and Mrs. Dibell are a little harder to describe. According to what I learned later, Mrs. Dibell, in her seventies, had inherited the Dibell family oil fortune. She was a smart, but unfortunately homely woman who made Queen Elizabeth look like a knock-out. Roundish face, thinning gray hair on top, a long, pointy nose that belonged on a longer, thinner face, all perched on top of, from where I sat, a flat chested, relatively masculine body.

Her husband, roughly forty to forty-five years old, and has been politely referred to in the tabloids as "the New American Gigolo," was a suave looking devil with a thin black mustache, bright, Latin eyes, and a head of hair that could have been stolen from a game show host. His dimpled chin, wide shoulders- almost as wide as his wife's—and strong jaw line completed the picture. With the right eye-patch, he could have been the poster boy for pirates.

Brother James, wifeless, occupied the next chair, exactly at the center point of my side of the table. I would get a better look at Brother James later, but for the hour or so that we were having dinner, all that I could see was the left side of his face. He was a pretty normal looking guy except for his huge honker. You may think that I'm exaggerating, but I swear I saw a ski slope on "Wide World of Sports" preview that matched my side profile of his proboscis exactly.

Normal brown hair, no glasses, clean shaven, regular looking ears, brown suit, and that enormous nose. What a way to ruin a guy's life. It was only later that I learned of his other disability. His last name, believe it or not, was Dickweed. Brother James Dickweed.

Whenever he turned his head to one side, depending on which way he turned, either Mr. Dibell, who sat to his right, or Mr. Peterson, who sat to his left, would unconsciously pull back to give the pointing device in the middle of his face room to maneuver.

In between us and Brother James were the Peterson's, Al and Louise. Not husband and wife, but brother and sister. Louise we had already met in the hallway. I got stuck sitting next to her; Dr. Stouffer was to my left. At least I wasn't sandwiched between her and Mrs. Boyle.

After Dr. Stouffer was Allen Hemlock, who gets us to the far end of the table, opposite Brother Thomas who was at the other end, as I have already said, next to the window.

That does it for one side of the table.

A thirty or so body builder sat across from Dr. Stouffer. He was a blue eyed, blond haired Aryan with a vacantly shrewd look in his eyes that I twice caught checking out his flawlessly handsome reflection in his china plate. In between primping in the dinnerware, he would smile broadly at Dr. Stouffer whenever he could catch her eye.

I didn't hear his name, but imagined that it was Lance or Rex or something equally appropriate.

The chair next to him was empty, waiting for an unfashionably late arrival. It took someone awfully ballsy or awfully stupid to show up late for a Hemlock dinner. Waiting to see which that it was gave me something to look forward to.

Then the Hemphills, between the empty chair and Brother Peter. The Hemphills looked too old and anemic to donate blood, but, as Dr. Stouffer whispered to me, what they lacked in physical health, they more than made up for financially.

Some people look like their dogs. The Hemphills, with their matching thin white hair, their matching thick glasses, and their pinched, wrinkled faces, looked like they could be stunt doubles for each other. I could really only tell them apart because one was wearing a black dress, and the other a black suit. Their hair was about the same length, so that didn't make it any easier.

Brother Peter was the third Apostle there that night. He was hunkered down in his chair immediately across from the bird-beaked Brother James.

In the Bible, by the time that the cock crowed, the Apostle Peter would have denied Jesus three times. Brother Peter, as he looked to me, would have dimed out the entire Holy Trinity by that time.

He had a shifty look about him. Dark, intense eyes that wouldn't stay still. Always looking back and forth, up and down the table. A face ravaged by acne, with skin that shined an oily gleam. Black, receding hair with a high pointed widow's peak, and a thin, carefully cropped goatee gave him a satanic look.

When he smiled, which he rarely did throughout the dinner, you had to look up quickly to see his uneven, cream-colored teeth before he clamped his thin lips closed again.

The backs of his hands were covered with coarse black hair, and his fingers, though long and elegant for a man only five nine or so, sprouted the same matted dark hair.

You don't see a lot of men like Brother Peter that aren't behind bars.

The Boyles, whom I mentally nicknamed Hemorrhoid and Crotch, were seated between Brother Peter and Christine Hemlock. They were both stout, outgoing people, who waved their hands a lot when they talked. They liked to try to include the entire table in their conversations, which was why I was glad they were down at the other end, near Christine and John Hemlock. I felt sorry for Mr. and Mrs. Dibell, the old lady and her younger boy toy for having to sit across from them.

Christine Hemlock was next, then John Hemlock and that completed the circuit.

I had sized the group as best I could, when Angel ushered in Monica Thomas.

"Everyone," said John Hemlock, after standing to make the announcement, "allow me to introduce Miss Monica Thomas, who has graciously accepted our offer to become the new legal counsel for the Church of the New Apostles."

Dinner was a real treat.

After John introduced Monica, who was squeezed into a shamelessly provocative, shoulderless red dress, to the retinue of guests, she sat down to join her date for the night, whose name, as it turned out, was Lance Warner. If I watched soap operas, I would have recognized him instantly as the actor who had the lead role of Dr. Deersmith in "As the IV Drips," or whatever serial it was that he played in.

Everyone was there for a reason.

Brothers Thomas, James, and Peter were there as three of the twelve New Apostles.

The Houghtons, the Dibels, the Petersons, the Hemphills, and the Boyles were there to be squeezed for big donations.

John and Christine were the evening's sponsors.

Allen was there because he was John's father, although the Brothers would probably try and tap him for cash, too.

Dr. Stouffer and I were there because Christine had invited us thinking that we were John's friends.

Lance Warner and that bitch Monica were there to piss me off.

I think that about sums it up.

"So, you two know each other?" asked Dr. Stouffer.

"Scott and I know each other... very well," answered Monica.

Dr. Stouffer took it well enough. Lance looked a little miffed, and Allen gave me a knowing smile.

"We used to date," I said, emphasizing the past tense.

"I love your dress," commented Dr. Stouffer.

"Why thank you," replied Monica, saying nothing about the doctor's choice of clothing.

"Mr. Hemlock," said Lance, "it's certainly an honor to make your acquaintance, sir."

"Just call me Allen, Lance."

We're all equal here, except those with less than a billion or two.

"Thank you, Allen. Say, when I think of it, after your buying back Global Studios from the Japanese, the two of us are both in the entertainment business."

"Down, boy," said Monica.

I saw her hand go under the table to squeeze something or other of his. She was smiling directly at me when she did it.

"How did you and Monica meet?" asked Dr. Stouffer. "I love to hear how people come together."

"Yes, tell us," prompted one of the wrinkly faced Hemphills sitting next to Monica. The dress led me to think that it was Mrs. Hemphill. But the gravelly voice led me to wonder if the Hemphills weren't the oldest rich cross dressers in the county.

"It was at a party in New York," offered Lance modestly. "I was encouraged by a female admirer to replay one of the recent romantic scenes from my show. Naturally, this would require a female volunteer."

"Naturally," I said.

"And I volunteered, didn't I Lance?" said Monica.

"I was so relieved," said Lance, lifting his hands palm upward toward the ceiling. "Imagine if it had been someone less desirable than you, dear. It could have been that skinny thing with the flat chest that kept staring at me all night."

"I had to save you."

"Yes, and I have been forever grateful."

"And," winked Monica, "he has the best technique. Really, Dr.

Stouffer, speaking clinically, don't you think he has the most delicious looking mouth that you have ever seen?"

"I can see how he got the starring role," answered Dr. Stouffer.

"I would say," said Allen, "that he had a lovely co-star. You should be in films yourself, Miss Thomas."

"We work best as a team," Lance put in quickly.

"And you make such a lovely couple," I added.

Quick, go stand on a wedding cake so I can eat dinner in peace and quiet.

"And how did you and the one-armed man meet?" asked Monica.

"Through a professional acquaintance of mine, a Dr. Richard Kimble," said Dr. Stouffer before I could answer or do anything rude.

The salad arrived and interrupted before I could think of anything to add, but before we could reach for the forks, Brother Thomas kicked in with a request for a prayer of thanks.

"Let us bless this food," he intoned, "before we partake of it. Brother James, would you do us the honor of leading us in prayer?"

"Certainly," said the Nose. "Will you all bow your heads? Our heavenly father..."

About ten seconds into the head bowing and the prayer thanking God for the chicken Wellington that we were about to eat, I glanced up and saw that everyone else at the entire table had their heads bowed except me and Brother James, the Satan look-alike who was staring at me as he led the prayer as though I were on the menu. I carefully raised my left hand and discreetly popped him the finger. He smiled, then bowed his head piously and finished giving thanks.

You and me, buddy, I thought. Anytime.

"Our church has developed into a worldwide force in a remarkably short time," Brother Argyle was saying over dessert. "We have the Good Lord to thank for this, those members of our faith who tirelessly spread the Word, and you, our financial supporters who, moved by the spirit of God provide us the means for outreach."

I hadn't counted on listening to a sermon, but I had to admit it was easier to stomach when you could chow on chocolate torte cake and French roasted coffee.

"In the Book of James, it says 'What good is it, my brothers, if a man claims to have faith but has no deeds? Can such faith save him?

Suppose a brother or sister is without clothes and daily food. If one of you says to him, Go, I wish you well; keep warm and well fed, but does nothing about his physical needs, what good is it? In the same way, faith by itself, if it is not accompanied by action, is dead.'

"And you my friends, are therefore people of action, for you have supported God's Word as well as his people. You have given this church the means to preach God's truths, and you have fed and clothed those in need. You have shown your faith by your deeds."

John Hemlock glanced over at me; we locked eyes for a moment, then he looked back at Brother Thomas, who was getting revved up for the cash pitch. My mind wandered.

Monica Thomas was a way in. John Hemlock had thrown her at me like bait. Untouchable bait.

In addition to the fact that I had no use for Monica, the fact that she now represented the Church of the New Apostles meant she couldn't ethically tell me anything about them. It also meant that we were now adversaries. I would try and take them down, she would try and stop me.

Still, she wanted me and I wanted information. Horizontal interrogation sometimes worked the best, if you left your values at the bedroom door. Trouble was, they weren't always still there when you went back to retrieve them.

I had my suspicions, but I had no proof against any specific individual in the deaths of the gifted children. No hard evidence. I needed a tangible linkage. Listening to table talk wasn't getting me anywhere.

When the proselytizing was through, I needed to get the Brothers alone. Maybe I could stir them up enough to get the linkage that I needed, or feed them a line of crap that would make them think I knew more than I really did. Set them up to do something stupid.

Brother Thomas droned on, his words developing a steady, methodically hypnotic quality.

"But you and I have chosen to be warriors of God as well. We have chosen Paul's words to the Ephesians as our creed. You, as I, repeat every morning and evening Paul's words: Finally, be strong in the Lord and in his might power. Put on the full armor of God so that you can take your stand against the devil's schemes. For our struggle is not against flesh and blood, but against the rulers, against the authorities, against the powers of this dark world and against the spiritual forces of evil in the heavenly realms.

"For it is in the affirmation of this admonition that we differentiate ourselves. It is an affirmation sadly missing in the world. To be soldiers in Christ means more than to suffer, it means that we must prepare ourselves, and then wage war against the dark powers. To be soldiers in Christ, we must fight."

He was on a roll. I ignored him.

The real problem that I was having was that to execute murder on an international scale required a different organization than what I was seeing. People like those gathered around the table, other than me, didn't get their hands dirty, at least on the scale of what I was dealing with. No, I was looking for a well-oiled machine that dealt with torture and murder as just a matter of business. Finding the man that ran that machine and stopping it had to be my primary focus. After that, I could deal with the people that gave the orders and handed out the cash.

In the days of the Inquisition, it wasn't usually the real theologians that did the killing. It wasn't Father so and so that turned the crank on the rank. The Pope and the priests provided the sanction, the rationale, and gave the orders to go ahead with the program. But the executioners, those were different people. There was a parallel as well with Nazi Germany, I thought. Hitler provided the sanction, the rationale, and the orders to go ahead. But there was a psychopath named Heinrich Himmler who organized the killings, and a man named Heydrich who saw that they were carried out.

So, the question was, who really operated the machine?

As the old man droned on, I considered. First, it was most likely a preexisting team of international killers that was being used. People that could move across borders undetected, do their dirty work, and get out clean. Who fit that kind of a bill?

Terrorist groups came to mind. Executing wet orders on a cash and carry basis. Former CIA or KGB type groups. Drug organizations. Crime organizations.

It was getting to be a big list. Sometimes thinking too much just confuses the issue.

Katerina had found out that the man she offed in the Underground Railroad tunnel was untraceable. No history. As if he didn't exist.

Russian. Ex-KGB, she thought.

But did that fit on an international scale? I didn't think so. Terrorist groups were hard to control. Drug organizations had their own agendas. Crime families couldn't be trusted.

Maybe I was missing the point. Perhaps no one organization was used. What if different groups were used depending upon the country? That made more sense.

In the Ukraine and Russia, use ex-KGB. In German, use ex-Stasi agents. In Mexico, use ex-Noriega personnel. And so on. It could be done, if you had a Himmler type at the top. And a Heydrich type executing the plan.

I looked again at Brother Peter. He had the look of someone who would enjoy the work. But for the category of killer that I was hunting, he was a little obvious.

If you look at photos of Himmler and Heydrich, two of the most notorious killers in history, they didn't look the parts, which, I suspect, was in part responsible for their effectiveness.

After the War, in fact, a former classmate of Himmler was lamenting to a friend at how unfortunate it was that their friend Heinrich Himmler had the exact same name as the notorious head of the SS. When the man whom he was making this comment to pointed out that they were, in fact, one and the same man, the former classmate refused to believe him. Maybe that was the type of man that I was looking for. Like Himmler, I mean, not the former classmate.

John Hemlock fit that bill perfectly. An elegant, wealthy man, wanting for nothing, without any rational reason to be involved in the killing of young adults. A pillar of the church—the Church of the New Apostles.

The more I thought about it, the dinner reminded me of Hitler's meeting with industrialists to raise money for his insane programs. None of the wealthy people at our table knew what their donations were really intended for, so they continued to finance the Church of the New Apostles.

I bet I could clear this table pretty quickly if I passed around pictures of what Gregorio and I had found in the Warehouse of the Dead, I thought.

At the far end of the table, old Brother Thomas was in high gear, punctuating his points by stabbing a bony finger viciously in the air before him to emphasize the danger of the coming of the Beast.

After dinner, the group was steered into the living room, but Allen Hemlock, Dr. Stouffer, and I hung back. Allen led us out through the kitchen and onto the back porch, where we sat in lawn chairs in silence before he spoke. The night was a little cool, but quiet, save for the muted voices coming from inside.

The moon hung milky white in the night sky, and I wondered what horrors this night sentinel had seen down through the ages. When full, that lunar light was blamed in the past as the cause of insanity. Hence the word lunacy—as I learned once from a crossword puzzle.

"You've discussed your theory with Dr. Stouffer?" asked Allen.

"He has," the doctor answered for me.

"And what do you think?"

"It's possible, but not proven. Either way, there is no forced linkage to your son."

"It's more than possible," I told him, and relayed what had happened to Benny Franks.

"There is no proven linkage," repeated Dr. Stouffer.

"I'm not a policeman," I said. "I don't plan on taking this to court. That's someone else's job. But I'll tell you something else, Allen. The choice of Monica Thomas as legal counsel wasn't an accident, either."

"I thought it peculiar myself."

"Couldn't she just have been chosen for her abilities?" demanded Dr. Stouffer. "Does it have to be that she was chosen because she was your ex-girlfriend?"

"And when we turn our backs, pigs fly," I said. "Sure it's possible. But it ain't too damn likely. No way. All of this started happening after we saw John."

"But it doesn't mean John's involved," stressed Papa Hemlock.

"No, it doesn't," said Dr. Stouffer.

"Yes, it does," I said. "John's involved one way or the other. It doesn't mean he's killed anyone, or that he has detailed knowledge of what's going on, but he's involved. He was at that conference, so either way he's involved on one side of the balance sheet or the other.

"And I'll tell you this: they're running out of people in other countries to kill. Soon, real soon, it's going to start happening here."

Dr. Stouffer shuddered. Allen didn't notice, being wrapped up in his own thoughts.

"Then what do you recommend?"

"I recommend that we notify Interpol and all of the other relevant police agencies before it's too late."

"We have nothing conclusive," he said stiffly. "Dr. Stouffer, in your professional opinion, could my son be involved in these murders?"

"He's a fully grown man," I said. "Let the police sort this out, Allen."

"I asked Dr. Stouffer."

"My answer," she said, "is that I can't say. I would need more time with him."

"And what alternative can you recommend, Scott, short of going to the police?"

I thought that one over for a minute. I had already worked out the answer, but I didn't want him to know that.

"Give me some serious firepower to play with Allen. Let me yank in some reinforcements and shake the Brothers' cage, see what kind of rats come running out."

"What exactly do you have in mind?"

"You'd better send Dr. Stouffer back inside, first."

"Dr. Stouffer, if you please..."

"I most certainly will not," she said.

But billionaires usually get their way.

When she had slammed the door behind her, I told him what I had in mind. He was rubbing his temples by the time that I was through, but he gave me the go ahead.

Deniability, of course, was understood.

When we went back inside, the party was winding up. I was maneuvering to get Brother Thomas alone, but he stood in the hallway, Brothers Peter and James by his side, thanking the Boyles and the Dibbles for their generous contributions.

Monica was hanging on Lance, Dr. Stouffer stood next to Allen and Christine and John, nodding her head distractedly. Even from where I stood, I could tell that she was still pissed. Allen tried to look supportive in an "it's out of my hands" kind of way.

I made my way over to Brother Thomas.

"Ah, Mr. Brown. Have you enjoyed the evening so far?"

"Sure. It's been interesting," I said. "You're an interesting guy."

Brothers Peter and James inched forward.

"Brother James, that was a nice before dinner prayer."

"Why thank you Mr. Brown."

Brother Peter gave me a discreet smirk.

"We were going to have a little talk, weren't we?" asked Brother Thomas.

"If you're up to it," I said. "I know it's got to be hard staying up late at your age and all."

"Oh, I assure you that I'm quite wide awake. You'll find as you grow to be my age that sleep gets further and further out of your reach. Something to do with the physiology of aging."

"I probably won't live to be your age, Brother Thomas."

"And why is that?"

"I like James Dean's motto."

"James Dean? I don't believe I'm familiar with his creed for living. Are you Brother Peter?"

"No."

"How about you, Brother James?"

"Well, Mr. Brown, then I'll have to ask you to recite it. We're not exactly movie buffs, I'm afraid."

"James Dean said that you should live fast, die young, and leave a good looking corpse."

"Marvelous. But, then, you're not very young, Mr. Brown."

"No, but I live fast, and I've still got the good looking part covered."

"Indeed."

"Indeed," I said. "You want to take a walk?"

"You don't mind if Brothers Peter and James tag along do you?"

"Maybe you ought to leave them behind to cover the remaining guests. Don't worry. You'll be in good hands with me. I've got some experience in bodyguarding. At least half of my clients come back alive. Problem is, I never know which half they are until it's too late."

"That sounds ominous, Mr. Brown," said the old man. "But you seem like a capable young man—young by my standards. I'll take my chances."

*****

We were in the back yard, sitting in the gazebo. I asked the old man if he was cold. He said no.

For a while, we just sat there in the moonlit dark like two dogs circling to see which of them would be first to piss on the hydrant. I lifted my leg first.

"I imagine John talked to you about my visit the other day?"

Old people don't look too good at night. They've got enough lines and shadows on their faces during the day. When he opened his mouth to reply, it was like looking into the mouth of a tunnel.

"Yes, he did. A terrible thing, if it is true."

"You were at that conference, too, weren't you?"

It was a blind shot, but I took it.

"I was. It was a terrible thing, the boiler explosion. And those poor, poor children that were killed."

"Is that where you met John?"

Another shot.

"Yes, it was. It was a sad thing, his blindness. I thank the Lord that it was only temporary."

"You understand that kids that I told John have died since then had their foreheads and hands skinned?"

"So, he said. An awful, awful thing. But why are you telling me all of this, Mr. Brown?"

"Because I thought you might be able to help me."

"Me? Why, however could I help you?"

"You're the authority on the Beast, aren't you?"

"I'm an authority on the Beast, Mr. Brown. But what does that have to do with anything?"

"The thing is," I said, leaning forward toward him, "I believe that the foreheads and the right hands of these children were stripped by someone looking for the mark of the Beast on them."

He waited the right amount of time before saying anything.

"But why would anyone do that?"

"Because that person believes the Beast has already come to earth."

As if he didn't know.

"Still, that would hardly make any sense. It is the followers of the Beast who are to be marked."

"The people I'm looking for, Brother Thomas, they're probably not too… discriminating, if you know what I mean. They've got to be a little fucked in the head, pardon the language."

"Oh."

"And I'm a little worried. I think that you and your fellow Apostles might need some protection."

He opened his mouth again, then snapped it shut. Moonlight danced on his lenses as he shook his head from side to side.

"That's very interesting, Mr. Brown. But why would we need protection? Surely you don't really believe that—"

"No, no, you're missing the point. If this gets out, I'm afraid some misguided people might blame your church and its teachings and attempt to harm you."

"That's very kind of you to be concerned, Mr. Brown, but—"

"There's a lot of crazy people out there," I said, interrupting him again. "These days a group of whackos could do most anything. They don't wait for the kinds of legal proof that you and I would."

"And what," he said carefully, "would that be?"

"The standard. Evidence. Facts proving or disproving a tie-in. Nutcases just act on appearances. That's why they're called nutcases. But they could be armed. They could be former Postal employees. They could be really dangerous. I wouldn't want anyone to get hurt."

"And what do you propose?"

"Maybe I could help. Act as a security consultant. Do what I can to protect you from anybody out there who jumps the gun, who doesn't wait for the evidence to prove your innocence. Somebody with revenge on their mind. You know some of those children were Israeli? They're big on preemptive strikes. And some were Russians. I don't even want to think about that. You get my drift?"

"You could protect us from this? Forgive me, but I know about John's mother, whom you were protecting at the time."

Fuck you.

"That was my first job, and she got away from me. She snuck out, and they whacked her. I imagine you and your group would use a little more common sense than to try and sneak away from your own bodyguard."

"We have a small security staff, already, Mr. Brown."

"Suit yourself, Brother Thomas," I said as I stood up. "Just remember that I made the offer. If things change and you decide you want some help. Just let me know."

"What about your arm?" he called out when I was three steps away.

"I've always shot better with my left hand, anyway," I said without looking back.

Germany

Dr. Stouffer was quiet for the first half of the drive home. She wasn't going to like what I was going to tell her, but it had to be done.

"I'm sorry about what happened back there," I told her. "We've just got different opinions, that's all."

"You cut me out."

"Yeah, I did. But there was a reason."

"Life doesn't have to be some macho fantasy, you know."

I kept my eyes straight ahead on the road.

"This isn't a fantasy. Kids are being murdered. That's real. What would you like me to do? Ask Brother Thomas how he feels about that? Ask him if he is in a happy place? Do you really think that would work? Think he'll crack under the pressures of confronting his inner child?"

"I think you should concentrate on gathering evidence to prove what's really going on."

"I don't understand you. I'm not a cop. I'm not even a private investigator."

"Then what," she flashed, "are you?"

"I'm the fix-it man."

"Like I said, a macho fantasy."

"Your kid's life is at stake here. What are you being so sensitive about?"

"What am I being so sensitive about? I'll tell you what I'm being so sensitive about, you macho asshole. You're trying to remove your guilt for John's mother's death by indicting him without the benefit of a trial or even a jury."

"I haven't touched him yet."

So there.

"But you will. I know you will."

"What's your big deal with John Hemlock? What, are you in love with the guy or something?"

"How dare you?"

"I dare, because I'm running out of excuses for you. What in the hell is the big deal about John Hemlock?"

"He's… he's—"

"He's what?"

"He's innocent until proven guilty."

"Bullshit, that's not what you were going to say."

But she clammed up for the rest of the ride home.

When we pulled up in front of her house, I tried again.

"I'm sorry, Kris."

Her hand was on the door handle, but she hesitated.

"Can I walk you to your door?"

"If you want," she said.

I opened my door. The overhead light came on and nearly blinded me, but I leveraged myself out quickly—it was getting to be a science with me- and closed it behind me.

Before I could get to her side and open her door for her, she was already out and standing there. I missed the view of her getting out. In a car as low hung as a Reatta, it was always a treat to watch a woman in a dress getting out.

The wooden steps creaked in recognition as we walked up onto the porch. A cool, but not cold breeze rustled at the bottom edges of her dress. The outside porch light was on, a yellow beacon welcoming her home, but it was too early in the year for mosquitoes.

"Thank you for taking me tonight," she said, reaching for the screen door.

"There's something else that I need to talk to you about," I said quickly. "Can I come inside?"

"Inside the house?" She looked faintly amused.

"Yes, inside the house, unless you want to stand out here and talk. Look, I'm not trying to get intimate or anything, but I need to talk to you about something else."

She considered it.

"Look, if I get out of hand, I've only got one good arm, so I think you could take me."

"Okay."

I took a step forward, and she put her right palm against my chest.

"But not for very long."

"Sure, if you say so."

"I say so."

The hall light was on when we stepped inside, and it was hardwood with a freshly buffed shine that was interrupted in places by homey throw rugs. She led me to the right, to the living room, and turned on a ceramic-bodied table lamp.

"Nice place," I said, and I meant it.

I couldn't have lived there, but it looked nice. Early American style couch and chairs, a fireplace, an ornate blue and gold Oriental rug, and a cherry wood coffee table. Against one wall was a hutch, which displayed fine china, with intricate patterns. A large front window looked out onto the front porch and into the yard's darkness, past the yellow halo cast by the porch light.

She offered me a seat on the couch, and I sat down.

"Coffee or tea?" she asked.

"No, thanks."

With a graceful movement, she sat down. For a stiff-necked doctor, she moved like a dancer.

"What was it that you wanted to talk about?"

I took a deep breath.

"Your safety. Yours and Bobby's."

I was good at ruining moments.

"You asked to come inside to talk about that? How can you presume to invite yourself inside for that? You really are something else, Mr. Brown."

"I'm worried about you."

For some reason, it came out with the same tone as if I had said, "Shut up, woman."

"Worry about you, Mr. Brown," she said, standing up again. "Bobby and I are in no danger unless you put us there."

"Please, sit down. I'm sorry. Let me try again. Besides, it's not easy getting up and down with one arm."

Her fists bunched, and she propped them against her hips. I was going to get a lecture.

"And that's another thing," she said. "You're always acting the tough guy, but at every opportunity you manage to remind me you're disabled. I don't have to feel guilty that you've only got one good arm. I didn't cause that, you did. So just learn to live with it."

"I'm not disabled."

"Yes, you are. Why can't you just say it?"

"The feeling is coming back. Slowly, but it's coming back."

"Say it. Say 'I'm disabled.' See if you're man enough to say it."

"I'm not disabled," I repeated.

"You are."

"I'm not."

"You are."

"Am not."

That did it. We both had to laugh. It started out a little forced, but in the end, once we got going, it was hard to stop. I hadn't laughed in a long time, and it felt good.

Finally, I said, "All right, I'll compromise with you. I'm temporarily disabled, okay? Is that good enough for you?"

She sat down again, two feet away from me, but she was still sitting.

"It's a start. At least I know now that you can laugh."

"Sure, I can laugh, it's just that in my line of work, I don't get much to laugh at. Or anyone to laugh with."

It just came out.

"Careful, Mr. Brown," she said, but she smiled uncertainly when she said it.

"Sorry, but once the macho mask comes off, it's hard to stop."

"I think that there might be some truth in that."

"Yeah. Anyway. Look, I'm worried about the two of you. Don't interrupt me, please, just let me say my piece. I'm trying to talk nice. The thing is, after Benny Franks died, and Monica was brought in by Brother Thomas and his crew, I started thinking."

"About what?"

Your eyes, I thought. And it was true. I wasn't falling for her, I just liked her eyes, and she really wasn't as bad as I first thought. She was worried about her kid.

"About the fact that these guys know a lot about me, and a lot about you. We're dangerous to them. I think that they're going to make a move against us, sooner or later. And it didn't take me much to find out about Bobby. They'll figure it out, too. They probably already have, a long time ago."

"They why haven't they tried to harm us already, if they already know?"

"I don't know for sure. But here's the fact. Not one kid in the United States or Canada has been touched yet. All the deaths have been overseas. A friend of mine says that they probably thought if they started in the United States, that they were afraid that someone could have caught on sooner. He might be right, but, then again, it might be for a different reason.

"The point is that now things are changing. We know, and they know we know. And that's dangerous. Very dangerous."

Psychologist or no psychologist, sitting there on the couch with me in her yellow dress with her hair down and glasses off, she seemed to me to be a vulnerable woman. A smart woman. A tough woman. But still, a vulnerable woman that I wanted to protect. Maybe I just wanted to help someone that was alive for a change.

She ran her fingers idly down her dress, straightening small wrinkles, thinking about what I had said. The lamp behind framed her hair and face with a soft halo of white light.

"What do you suggest?' she asked finally.

"I'd like to stay the night."

"Here?"

"On the couch, of course."

"Out of the question."

"Come on, think about it. You're out here all alone in the country. Bobby's gone, so no one's going to have to know. Besides, I'm not asking to sleep with you; I just want to spend the night on your couch. All I need is a blanket."

"No."

"Look, I'm not going to beg you to sleep on your couch. It doesn't look that damn comfortable."

"It's very comfortable. I've slept here myself on occasion."

"Great. Share the fun. Let me camp out here tonight."

"I said no. And why do you care what happens to me or my son?"

People always wanted to know that kind of shit.

"I just do. Okay?"

"Not good enough. Tell me why. Say it."

"Why? It isn't enough that I'm willing to scrunch up on this antique thing just to look out for you?"

"Because I like to see you squirm. Turnabouts fair play."

I started chewing on my bottom lip and staring out the window.

She shrugged her shoulders. "If you don't want to tell me..."

"Because I like you. A lot. Sometimes. And I don't want to see anything happen to you or Bobby, even if he is an annoying kid."

"He's not annoying, he's just—"

"Different. Yeah, I know. I want you to let me take him to stay with a friend of mine until this is over."

"Out of the question. What's his name?"

Yes and no. She could put them both in the same sentence.

"His name's Bob Alby. Don't worry. He's not like me. Kids like him. He's a regular Captain Kangaroo. He's not married. Wife died a while ago. He's got two ferrets and a couple of birds. His house is a regular fucking petting zoo. Sorry."

Her mouth crinkled into an interesting smile. She laid her hand on my shoulder, my right shoulder, the one, unfortunately, that didn't have too much in the way of feeling.

"For a generally rude person, someone in your past taught you some good manners."

"Blame my mother and Dear Abby. She always followed Abby's advice religiously."

"Smart woman."

"Uh-huh. So, what about it?"

"You plan on sleeping on my couch every night until this is over?"

"I had a different plan."

"This couch is as close as you're getting," she said, withdrawing her hand.

"I meant you should come stay with me in the lighthouse. It's safer there. Bulletproof glass. Thick, solid walls. Electronic security. All the comforts of home. Maybe I could even play some one-handed piano for you. Maybe we could just turn on the stereo."

"I like my house," she said.

"So do I. It's a lot… homier than my place. But mine's safer. And I'm telling you the truth, Kris, I'm getting a very bad feeling about all of this. These guys, whoever they are, and however they're linked to the Church of the New Apostles, they're scary people. Even for me. And when it started, I was after them. I was hunting them. Now, I think they're going to turn that around. I'm beginning to think we're being watched. Assessed. Targeted by these assholes."

"Why are you so certain that they're linked to the New Apostles?"

"Instinct. Gut instinct. You want to know what made me sure?"

"Yes."

"It was that old man, Brother Thomas, and his buddies. Especially Brother Peter."

I stopped for a moment. James Dickweed. Peter. Dick and Peter. Yeah, it fit.

"What's the matter?"

"Nothing."

I didn't think that she would appreciate the joke.

"They're bad, Kris, I can feel it. I can smell it. Especially the old man. There's no… balance to him."

"Scott, you can't—"

"I know, I can't convict him on my gut instinct. But I'm not wrong. I've got some experience with these kinds of guys. I just don't want to take any chances."

She sighed, and I knew I had won.

"All right, but I'm not cooking for you in the morning. And you're on your own for a toothbrush and a change of clothes."

"I always carry an overnight bag in the car, just in case."

"Liar," she said.

* * *

*****

I dreamed I was back in Berlin.

Karl Schlecter was briefing me on the logistics.

"You understand," he was saying, "that this is not the United States."

"Yeah," I replied, "I picked that up when they asked for my passport before they let me stay."

"The German Polizei are very efficient. Very."

"Sure thing."

"Scott," he said, putting down his pipe, and puckering his thin lips, "you must not think that I am speaking only to hear my own voice. Whatever else may be said about the German people, what we do well, we do very well. And the German police, they are the best in the world. They do not tolerate interference."

"Got you."

He sighed.

"All right, let me continue. The two young people we seek are ages sixteen and seventeen. Hans is the older of the two. His girlfriend Marla is a problem girl. Drug user. I'm surprised she has lived to the age that she has—if she is still alive. Hans' father is director of Hemlock's specialty chemical operations. Hard to believe that a man as fine and distinguished as he has a child like Hans."

"They disappeared three weeks ago. No trace since."

"But you think you've tracked them?" I asked.

He nodded, and his tired eyes were heavy, the whites lined with red, and the eyelids hanging low, as if he were half asleep.

"We have information that they have been involved with a group called the Young Germans. Skinheads. Young Criminals would be a better name. The world will never forget or forgive with young people like them acting out their hate dreams."

Karl was in his early fifties. Named after the great chessmaster who almost toppled Emanuel Lasker from his throne of World Champion, he nonetheless confessed that he was a potzer at the game. He was leaning back in his chair, his desk between us, his black pipe smoldering in the ashtray. The window to his office was open, and the sounds of cars battling for position three stories below were a constant irritant to me.

"We have them located," he continued, "in a building on Reichminster. A very bad neighborhood. The entrance to the building is guarded, but ineffectively so. Only one of this gang has military experience. He should be shot, putting his training to such use. He dreams of organizing the Young Germans into an unofficial action group to carry out the aims of Neo-Nazi groups."

"The police keep an eye on these punks?" I asked.

"Of course, but so far they have, as you would say, nothing on them. So they are now more checking in, as you might say."

"And you think that the two kids are holed up there?"

"Excuse me?"

"Hiding there. You think the two kids are hiding there?"

"Yes."

"How many inside that you know of?"

"Maybe as many as fifteen. Two girls. Don't discount them."

"I never do. Gender doesn't matter when you're holding a gun."

"Just so," he said.

"You got the building plans I asked for?"

"Ya."

"Let's have a look at them."

We went in that night. Karl, myself, and five hired paramilitary guns, lowered to the rooftop by helicopter. Going in through the front door was out of the question. Gunfire in the street, no matter how quiet, would bring the Polizei. Besides, no matter how much Kevlar you wear, some asshole can always get lucky with a headshot.

Our weapons were silenced. I don't like silencers- they can ruin your aim. But at close quarters, that doesn't usually matter much. If we were lucky, we could creep close enough to see their shaved, tattooed heads before we had to fire. There was always the chance that we could catch them totally unawares, but I wasn't counting on that.

For a man in his early fifties, Karl was in excellent shape. He explained that mountain climbing in the Rhine Mountains kept him young. It seemed like a good way to meet Mr. Ravine at high impact speed to me. But he made it down the rope as easy, maybe easier, than the others and I did.

The door leading down from the rooftop to the lower floors was locked, but Otto, who was built like the circus strong man, made short work of that with a set of picks. His hands were big and heavy looking with thick knuckles, but he worked the picks the way that a surgeon works his scalpel. He had it unlocked in less than thirty seconds.

The time was four o'clock a.m.

We were dressed in black from head to toe, wearing ski masks to boot, so that we looked like high priced bank robbers as we made our way downstairs. With our foam-padded boots, we advanced as quietly as night fog.

The infrared goggles were uncomfortable, but necessary. They were the newer models—the type that cut out if a light is turned on so that you're not blinded for life. Always the best for Hemlock's covert ops.

The young Germans were sequestered on the fifth floor. I would have liked to take the elevator, but I didn't want to seem like a wimp. Besides, the bell announcing the arrival of the elevator car might have gotten one or more of us killed.

Fifth floor. Dim white light came from under the bottom of the door. We pulled back the goggles. I took a breath. For a change, I was going in first.

Karl opened the door as smoothly and quietly as he could, but I heard it squeak just as I hit the middle of the floor and rolled up into firing position.

I held up my hand.

The hallway was tiled and narrow. Twenty feet away from me, a man sat slumped against the wall. I would have thought that he was sleeping on the job, were it not for the splash of red three feet above him that trailed down and stopped at his head.

No one behind me, only the body ahead of me. Cautiously, I motioned the rest of the team in.

"Mein Gott," breathed Karl softly.

"Not mine," I said.

We moved silently down the hall to the door beside the body. It was open an inch or two. The team lined up the way the book says, and I gently pushed the door open.

More bodies inside. I felt the weight of death on my shoulders.

A single overhead light hung by a chain in the kitchen, its cold white light illuminating something that I didn't want to see. In the confines of the room, the smell of blood and shit made breathing unpleasant.

With hand motions, I directed Karl to stay with me and others to check the remaining rooms.

Blood was spattered everywhere. On the floor, on the table, on the kitchen chairs, on the furniture, on the walls, and on the bodies themselves. A single splash of blood was on the hanging light bulb, and it cast a shadow on the rusty gray wall.

We inspected the bodies, starting with the ones that still had faces. Carefully, touching nothing we didn't have to.

They had been taken by surprise. Most had been shot where they lay, others were killed more creatively. The girl laid naked over an overstuffed chair, her buttocks an ugly color. Dried blood lined her crack.

"Over here," whispered Karl.

He pointed to the body of what looked to be a young man tied to a chair. His neck was a bloody stump, and his right hand was missing. Blood covered his nightshirt and pooled about him on the floor.

"Ten to one," I said, "that's Hans."

We never found his head or his hand.

I only seem to relive this dream when I sleep on unfamiliar couches.

The Revelation

Things got a little tense the next morning, as Dr. Stouffer regressed into her earlier idea that the whole sleeping over thing was unnecessary. It took me nearly half an hour to get her to agree to my plan again.

Her main concern, as it turned out, was that she didn't understand why it was necessary for Bobby to stay somewhere else other than with us. I had to explain to her that, even though Soldier's Point was well protected, it was probably a known location to the Brothers. If they initiated an action against us, we could hold our own, but I didn't want Bobby around that kind of action. Further, I told her I needed her to be where I was because I needed every bit of help from her analytical brain that I could get.

We took two cars—my Reatta and her Jeep Cherokee. The Reatta was only a two seater, and she needed the packing room of the Jeep. We went directly from her farm to Grandma's.

Grandma didn't seem to like me much. She asked my name, and I told her Ed, my middle name. The doctor and I had agreed that we would not tell her who I was. For her own good.

Bobby promptly called me a liar.

"Your name is Scott," he said.

"It's Ed."

"Scott."

"Ed. You got me confused with someone else."

"Never mind, Bobby," said Dr. Stouffer. "Ed's a friend of mine. Now go get your things."

"But—"

"Now, young man."

"All right," he said.

Cute kid, I thought, but a pain in the ass.

"So where are you from, Ed?" asked her mother. Emphasis on the word "Ed."

Little old women are the best there are at laying fifty-pound guilt weights on your head.

"Ah—"

"Not from around here, mother," said Dr. Stouffer, jumping to my rescue.

"But where from, dear?" asked her mother, fluffing her gray hair with an only slightly wrinkled hand.

"Mother. I don't want Ed to feel like he's being interrogated."

They'd had this kind of talk before, I could tell.

"Well, I just asked where he was from, dear. I didn't ask his underwear size."

"Thirty two," I volunteered.

Dr. Stouffer glared at me.

"Well, I'm proud of it. I work hard to keep a trim waist."

"Yes. Well, mother," said the doctor, "Ed and I are going to a conference, and I want to take Bobby along."

"To a stuffy old conference?"

"Yes, mother."

"They are pretty stuffy, ma'am."

"And you're a psychologist, too?"

"A student of psychology, you might say."

"What kind of psychology?" her mother asked.

I got the feeling that if I answered wrong, she'd whip a flyswatter out of her apron and slap me on my good hand.

"Criminal psychology," I elaborated.

"Bobby, hurry up, son," called Dr. Stouffer desperately.

But I had her mother's attention. The little old lady fairly glowed with interest.

"Oh, but that must be exciting. I love to read true crime stories."

"I do, too, ma'am."

You better not have a letter opener in that apron, I thought as I leaned over a few inches.

"I especially love books about serial killers. They're so... bad."

"I've studied the matter myself a little," I said, "but you sound like you've read a lot. Maybe when we get back, we could compare notes."

"Ooh," she cooed, "I'd like that."

"Mom," said the clearly exasperated Dr. Stouffer.

"Oh, hush, girl. Can't you see we're talking shop? Tell me, Ed, do you think serial killers read books about other serial killers?"

Son of a bitch. I'd never thought about that.

Bobby came to the door with his duffel bag just at that moment, saving me from having to come up with an answer.

"Later," I said with a quick wink at her, "when we get back, you and I have to talk."

"About what, Grandma?" asked Bobby.

"Never you mind, dear. Just a little secret between Ed and myself."

As we walked away, I heard Bobby mutter, "Scott, his name is Scott. Scott Brown."

Like I said, he was a cute kid, but a little bit of a pain in the ass. Dr. Stouffer got her revenge by having Bobby ride with me. She followed at a safe distance in the Cherokee as I led the way to Bob Alby's place.

I was hoping for a mercifully quiet trip, praying that Bobby would be too shy to talk to a nearly total stranger. Some kids don't know the meaning of the phrase "silence is golden."

He yammered all the way there, peppering me with questions.

The temperature was headed to the mid-sixties that day, and Bobby was wearing faded jeans and a lightweight flannel shirt, unbuttoned, and an X-files T-shirt underneath. His hair was neatly combed—Grandma must have gotten to him with a brush- but at the peak of his head, a cowlick sprouted like a weed in an otherwise neatly trimmed lawn.

"So, do you like my mom?" he was asking eagerly.

"Sure," I said.

"No," he said, "I mean, do you really like her?"

"Yeah, I really like her."

"Why?"

"Look, I'm trying to drive."

"Is it against the law to drive with one hand?" he asked, scrunching his face slightly.

"What do you mean against the law? I've only got one hand."

"No you don't."

"Yes, I do."

"You have two hands, I can see them."

"I mean, I've only got one hand that works good. Jesus, do you have to be so picayune?" I asked.

"I know what that means. But is it against the law to drive with one hand?"

"I don't know. I didn't ask."

"Will you have to renew your driver's license like you do if you have to wear glasses, but you didn't when you got your license?"

"No."

It had never seemed so far to Bob Alby's.

"Why?" he asked.

"Do you really care?"

"Yes," he said seriously.

"Okay, then, I don't know for sure. I think it's legal, though."

He considered that for a while.

"But do you really like my mom?"

"Yes, I really like your mom."

"Why?"

I almost ran off of the road.

"What do you mean why? I just do."

"Why?"

"Because she's pretty."

"Is that the only reason?"

"No."

"Then why else?"

"Did I tell you," I asked, "that Mr. Alby has pets?"

"Yes. Two ferrets. One small female, albino, and one male that would make a nice fur collar."

"Don't tell him I said that, okay?"

"Why?"

"And birds, too. He's got a couple of birds."

"What kind?"

"Little ones. I don't know what damn kind they are."

"I had a dog once."

"That's great."

"He ran away and never came back. That was a long time ago."

"That's too bad."

"I loved him very much. My mother said he had to go see the world, but my grandma says that he probably got run over by a car."

I didn't know what the hell to say.

When we got to Bob's, I went through the introductions and the tour of Bob's house, which I really didn't need. Bob lived alone on the edge of town. He'd built his own place, an aluminum sided ranch on one of the lots he'd purchased many years before, certain that the street that ran by the front of his house would be the next up and coming development project. He still owned the only house on the block. While Dr. Stouffer unloaded Bobby's things, Bob, happy, I think, to have the company, introduced Bobby to the ferrets, Niko and Fire Eyes, and the birds, a parakeet named Booboo and a parrot named Yogi. Don't ask me. I didn't name them.

Bob had taken a two-week vacation, leaving the running of his beloved Gibraltar Gazette to Marianne, his assistant of fifteen years. Bobby didn't have to attend school. The kid was so far above the other students that he was in a special program that had ended a month ago. He was free to hang out with big Bob and the wildlife.

Dr. Stouffer grilled Bob for a bit- it must have been a genetic carry-over from her mom- and then hugged Bobby, told him to be a good boy, and to enjoy his little vacation with Mr. Alby. She would be calling him two or three times a day, and especially before he went to bed at night. Also included was the obligatory teeth brushing lecture. Bobby looked to be sixteen or seventeen years old, but it was hard to tell because he was either a little out of sync or too much in sync to be definable.

We were ready to go when I had a thought.

"Say Bobby," I asked, "what was your dog's name?"

"Why?"

I bit my lip.

"In case I ever see him, I'll know who he belongs to."

"Pete," he said. "His name was Pete, but he's dead."

Yeah kid, I know, I thought, and remembered suddenly how I had met Bob Alby.

We parked her jeep in the Reatta in the marina parking lot, and loaded her things, which consisted of one trunk and two suitcases into the boat and set off for Soldier's Point. Neither of us said much on the way over, and it gave me time to think.

Something Brother Thomas had said last night was beginning to bother me. It was the line about the followers of the Beast being marked, not the Beast himself.

The other point that bothered me was that not only young boys and men had died, but young girls and women. The Beast was clearly, from what I had read, a man. Why then, were children of both sexes being killed?

My carefully constructed intuitive leap was falling apart. I was missing something.

I had learned to dock and tie the boat one handed through trial and error, the way I had learned everything else after Mexico. But on that particular day, with my mind on tunnels and death, the Bible and boiler explosions, I hopped off the bough of the boat, holding the rope with my one good hand, and landed on the dock. But not quite enough on the dock, and I spilled back over, my one arm wind milling as I fell backwards, so that I looked like a prop plane with only one engine working, falling from the sky to land nose first into the river.

Although it was clear and sunny, falling into that water on that day was like the time in Finland that I ran outside from a steamy sauna and jumped into a snowbank on a dare. I am a moderately good swimmer, but the pain from my shoulder, and the realization that I had only one arm to swim with, slammed into my thoughts the sudden fear that I would drown. I freaked, and I was mid-scream when the water filled my mouth and I began to choke.

My left hand still grasped the rope, and I yanked and pulled at it wildly, spinning and thrashing about it the way a fish with a hook in his mouth does when he is fighting for his life.

I hit the bottom three or four times with my feet and knees before I remembered that the water was no deeper than my chest.

"Are you all right?" asked Dr. Stouffer from the boat when my head broke water and I coughed, hacked, and swore my way to my feet.

"Don't ask."

But when I made it to the dock, the water was still chest high, and after I had thrown the rope up first, I realized my predicament.

She had stepped out of the boat, and onto the sun-bleached wooden planks and stood there looking down at me, her face full of concern.

"Let me give you a hand," she offered.

"No. I can make it."

"Don't be silly. Give me your hand."

"I can make it. Just tie the boat."

"Fine. You go for it, sailor."

The wooden post that she tied the boat to was too big for me to grasp easily, but when I put my foot against, and then grabbed, I was able to pull myself up a foot. She was watching, but I kept my mind on putting my second foot a little higher on the post.

I was fucked.

The next step up I took, my shoe slipped, I let go, and I was underwater again.

When my head broke water again, she was still standing on the dock, her feet spread apart, her arms folded across her chest, and smiling at me.

She looked good in faded tight jeans and her pale blue blouse opened now maybe one button further than she had intended, but if I could have made it up next to her, I would have shoved her ass right off the dock and into the river.

"I can do this," I said after I had spit out a mouthful of water. "Don't look at me like that."

"Like what?" she asked innocently.

"Never mind. Stand back, I'm coming up."

I tried everything. Holding my body so close to the pole to inch my way up that I got splinters in my face. Floating on the surface and trying to swing a leg up on the dock in a sudden move that only caused me to swallow more water. Dropping down to the bottom in a tight crouch, then shooting straight up and out of the water seemed like a great idea until I propelled my head into the bottom of the dock and nearly lost consciousness.

Scissoring my legs around the pole and trying to scoot up an inch or two at a time was working until a rusty nail head stuck through my scrotum, mercifully going right between my testicles without touching either one.

You wouldn't know it by the way that I screamed, though.

"My God, what's the matter?" screamed Dr. Stouffer.

I hopped and thrashed all over again, swearing like there was no tomorrow.

"What is it? Tell me."

But I couldn't talk. It hurt so badly, and I was so mad that I just couldn't talk. I must have sounded and looked like a Tourette's patient who had just stepped on a thumbtack.

I wanted to hold my crotch with both hands in the worst way.

When she couldn't take it anymore, she jumped in after me. It was a good thing she did, because it's tough to bend over when you've had a nail-head pierce your scrotum without being underwater at the same time.

I still don't know how she got me out of the water and up onto the dock with me wiggling and screaming and yelling at her. But when she shoved me up and onto the dock, I just lay there on my left side in the fetal position repeating over and over, "My nuts, oh shit, my nuts, oh my nuts."

When she'd scrambled up beside me, she got to her knees and leaned over me, dripping water on me—like I gave a damn at that point—and trying to understand what was wrong.

Finally, I said, "I caught my nuts on a nail or something on that damn post." It came out of me like an explosion, so fast I was lucky she understood it.

She reached over, pried my hand away from my crotch, and, seeing the dark stain there, got the picture.

"You stupid, stubborn bastard," she said.

Three hours later, after a trip back across the river to the Gibraltar Medical Clinic and back to Soldier's Point again, we were finally back in the Lighthouse. Her bags were in the spare bedroom on the second floor, and I lay stretched out on the couch with my head propped on a pillow, my legs separated just enough for comfort.

Dr. Stouffer, who hadn't said much more throughout the entire ordeal, brought me a cup of hot tea and set it on the glass coffee table beside the couch.

"Drink it," she said, "doctor's orders."

"I didn't think that you were that kind of doctor," I said.

"Don't even start," she said, pointing her index finger at me as though ready to push my "off" button.

After pulling one chair around to the end of the couch where my head rested, she just sat there and looked at me.

We had both changed clothes. She wore a duplicate pair of jeans, but a plain, pink sleeveless T-shirt instead of her earlier blue blouse. I liked the T-shirt better; it was a little too tight and stretched across her breasts.

"Eyes on my face, please," she warned.

I had on the loosest pair of jeans that I owned to minimize the crotch pain, and a T-shirt of my own that read "Detroit—where the weak are killed and eaten."

"A guy gets jabbed where I got jabbed, and it makes you realize how short life is."

"It's going to get much shorter," she said, "if you don't stop staring at my chest. We need to talk."

"It hurts my head to lean back and look at your face."

"Get used to it. Now, about Allen and John Hemlock..."

"Wait a minute," I said, "you don't want to discuss what happened back at the dock?"

"No. It's over. You spend enough time beating up on yourself. You don't need my help. You're doing a great job. But frankly, if I'd been through what you've been through, and I don't just mean your arm, and if I had all on my mind that you have, I don't know if I would have done any better.

"We should call a truce. The danger in this really hit home to me today when we dropped Bobby off. Before, I was looking at this as a psychologist, keeping my feelings and my fears in the background. And you're not exactly the easiest man I've met to open up to. But, after seeing you roll around on the ground holding your crotch, you seem a little more human. So, I'm willing to take a chance if you are, okay?"

She had her glasses back on, so she looked slightly scientific, but with her blond hair down instead of in a bun, and how she looked in a pair of jeans and a T-shirt, she was one damn good looking scientist from where I sat.

"I can handle that," I said.

"You're welcome. And I mean that, too. So, let's get back to business."

"Deal. What is it you want to tell me, Dr. Stouffer?"

"Kris. Call me Kris."

"But I thought that—"

She cut me off mid-sentence.

"I like to have the choice, you understand? I don't like people to assume that they can ignore my title."

I nodded my head and reached for the teacup.

"You wanted to know what the deal between the Hemlocks and myself is, so I'm going to tell you what I can. But first, let me ask you a question. What do you know about the Hemlock's?"

"The usual," replied. "He owned the company that I was working at when I gassed most of a little town—that's how we met. But I guess you already know all about that.

"Since then, let's see, he calls on me when he's got nasty jobs that don't fit the kind of situation where you can call on the police for help—mostly international, but some here—and he offers me the contract, and if I want the job, then I go in and clean up for him. That's about it, except for that his wife was murdered on my watch, and his son would like to kill me for that."

She took it well enough, probably because she already knew what I was going to say before I said it.

"Now," she said, "I want to take this a step further, but as a friend, not as a therapist. Remember that, as a friend, not as a therapist. Can you handle that?"

"Can you?" I asked.

"Yes, if you're honest with me."

"And in return?" I asked.

"What?"

"You'll be honest and candid with me?"

"Within ethical limits, Scott."

"Forget it."

"Listen," she said earnestly, "you'll have to trust me on this. I think I know what you're looking for, and if you'll help me, I can help you get the answers without having to cross any lines. Will you trust me on that for just a little while?"

I thought it over as much as I felt like it. "Okay, doctor, you've got a deal. But I would have given this a lot more thought if they hadn't jacked me with that pain-killing shot back at the clinic."

She seemed to relax and even put her bare feet on the couch next to my head.

I wrinkled my nose.

"Hey," I complained, "this may be taking it too far."

"Obviously, the tetanus shot worked. You haven't developed lockjaw."

"I surrender. Ask your damn questions."

"I asked you how well you knew the Hemlocks, and you glossed over the question. So let me ask it a different way—do you know as much as you should about Allen Hemlock and his family, considering the impact that they've had on your life?"

"You mean, have I researched them?"

"To be direct, yes."

"No, I haven't. What's to research? He's Allen Hemlock, the famous billionaire, his life's in all of the papers."

"Is it?" she asked patiently.

"Sure," I said. "He's rich, he's famous, and he's widower. The papers love to write about him. He even owns his very own newspaper chain. You want to know his favorite food? It's on YouTube. You want to know who he's dated? Check the Web. The companies he owns? Complicated, but well researched by the press. Get my point?"

"Yes," she said, "I do. But now I want to show you my point. This is where the trust comes in, and you said you'd trust me for a while. Do you know the name of the man that hates Allen Hemlock more than any other person in the entire world?"

"That's a weird question."

"But do you know the answer?"

"I know that he's got his share of enemies in business. I've had to deal with some of them—indirectly, of course."

"But you always went in with a mission, didn't you Scott?"

"A goal, okay, yes. That's the way that I like it."

"You want a job where the customer tells you, here's the situation, I know it's dangerous and people could get hurt, but go ahead anyway and do what you've got to do. I authorize it. Isn't that right?"

"What are you getting at?" I asked. I didn't like the direction that this was going.

"You. In the plant accident, you were traumatized to the point that you don't deal well with unclear responsibilities. You want someone to tell you before you make your moves so that no matter what happens, you're authorized. No questions after the fact. Isn't that right?"

It would have been easy to snap at her. After all, who the hell was she? What gave her the right to go digging into my mind? Could she ever, ever understand what it was like to turn one valve, and kill all of those people, including my own wife and child? Never in a million years. Nobody could.

When the atom bomb was dropped on Hiroshima, the people that dropped it knew what it would do. It was supposed to happen. But when I turned that valve, nothing bad was supposed to happen. No one was supposed to die. I was just doing my job. I had turned valves every day. Nothing bad had happened. But that one day...

"Yeah. That's the way I like it. Exactly the way I like it," I said. "No surprises. And it has to be a one-shot deal. Very specific. I don't like any job that's vague. Someone needs to be spied on, no problem, just lay it out like it is. Someone needs to be found, dead or alive, no problem, just lay it out like it is. There's a bad person that needs to be killed because he's above the law, no problem, just lay it out like it is.

"I need to know my job, and that I'm authorized. If it goes bad, I'm protected. I need to know those two things. You think that's bad?"

Before she could answer, I kept right on going.

"I'll tell you what's bad," I said, "I'll tell you the true nature of bad."

Without thinking, I pulled myself up more to a sitting position, and leaned slightly forward. When I rested my left hand on her shin, she didn't protest, but when I began to talk, she leaned slightly away from me.

"Here it is. Here's the true nature of bad, the reality of horror. A man does a little thing. It's so little that he does it without thinking. He does it every day, day in, day out. It's so little, that he never gives it a second thought. It's his job. He's doing what he supposed to.

"But one day this little thing causes a situation that gets very bad, grows quicker than he can stop it, and expands out of his control.

"It's like being a disease carrier. You're immune, but no one else is. You don't even know that you're carrying the disease.

"But one day you cough. Everybody coughs, don't they? It's natural. But the disease spreads, and other people begin to catch it, and they cough, and more people catch it, and they begin to die. You wish you could take the cough back, but you can't. You've already caused the plague.

"If you'd known that your coughing would cause the plague, you wouldn't do it, of course, but you didn't know. And once done, it can't be undone.

"Little meaningless actions by regular people that get out of their control before they can stop them and that grow into something terrifying and kill other, innocent people. And you started it, but you can't stop it. That's what horror is.

"I was supposed to turn that valve, damn it. It was my job. I was authorized to turn that valve, but nobody ever authorized what might happen. They only authorized what was supposed to happen. Not what did happen. Do you understand?"

"And now?" she asked.

"Now, when I do take on a job, I know what I'm getting into. The client—usually Allen—he pays me enough that I handle what might happen. I check it out first, and then I determine what the worst that could happen is. And I do it my way, so I'm totally responsible."

"You're in control."

"That's right, doctor, I'm in control."

"Every man's dream is to be in control," she said.

"You're not going to go on a gender-bender, are you?"

"No. You're right. It's really every person's dream, especially when they've been traumatized. It doesn't matter by what or by who.

I'm just saying that your reaction is not unique to you, Scott. I've been through it myself. I can't understand exactly what you've been through, but I can relate to the principle."

"You? You've been through trauma?"

The sarcasm was pretty heavy in my voice. She yanked her feet off of the couch, got out of the chair, and began to pace.

"You're such an ass, Scott Brown. I don't know why I ever thought I could trust you."

"Well, excuse me, doctor, but I killed half a town, including my own wife and child, by mistake. You got a trauma that can compare to that?"

When she hauled back her foot and kicked the couch, I cringed. I'd never seen her mad before.

"No, you completely fucked up asshole, I haven't wiped out half a town's inhabitants. Are you happy? Am I supposed to go out and launch a nuclear weapon at an unsuspecting metropolis by mistake before I'm qualified to talk to you?"

The tears came next, and it was better than being screamed at, but not much. I got up—slowly and painfully—but I got up and walked over to where she stood.

"Sorry," I said, and started to put my left arm around her.

She turned and started walking toward the door. "Hey, please, I'm sorry, I am."

She kept going.

"Look, I'd run after you and beg, but my balls hurt too much. I'm really sorry. Please don't make me run. If I do, I'll probably never be able to have children as stupid and insensitive as me."

"That," she said, "would not be so bad."

At least she stopped.

"I was trying to talk to you," she said, turning to face me again.

She'd stopped crying, but tear tracks still glistened down her cheeks.

I really am an asshole sometimes. When I took another step toward her, she put up her hands.

"No," she said. "You get back onto the couch."

"Are you going to get back in the chair?"

"Yes, but you first."

*****

After we were both back seated in our respective seats, I said, "Tell me what happened to you, Kris."

"It isn't like what happened to you," she said defensively.

"I know, I apologize. Please tell me."

"My husband," she said, after giving me the eye, "my former husband, he was... we had... an abusive relationship."

"Go on."

"You're going to have a hard time understanding this. You're strong. You're capable. You can protect yourself. I couldn't.

"He was a brutal man. He would beat me. Humiliate me. It was a terrifying time in my life."

"How?" I asked. "Why did it happen?"

"I told you, he just beat me. Most psychologists make up reasons and justifications for these behaviors. I don't. To me, they're living proof of evil."

The look in her eyes was one of both anger and betrayal. Her shoulders were hunched forward; her fingers twined and released over and again while I watched. It was impossible for me to imagine anyone raising a hand against her.

"I don't want to think about this anymore," she said, "but it's so important that you understand. About Bobby, about John, and about Allen. About everything."

"Then tell me, Kris," I said. "I'll listen."

"He gave me a concussion once. He broke my arm with a wooden chair. He broke my arm with my own kitchen chair...

"I was a psychologist. I am a psychologist. One part of me knew what was going on, but the other part couldn't handle it.

"And then Bobby. He started on Bobby."

I could feel my back tighten. Had that queasy feeling in my stomach that told me bad news was coming.

"I tried to stop him. I tried. I threatened to go to the police. He told me he would kill me and then kill Bobby if I did. And he would have done it."

"I'm sorry, Kris, I truly am. But what has all of this got to do with the Hemlocks?"

"I was counseling John Hemlock at the time. I had an office in the house. But I wasn't using it anymore. Paul wouldn't allow it. Said he wouldn't put up with crazies in his house. Wouldn't tolerate it. He would... hurt me anytime that I brought it up.

"But that night, he was supposed to be out of town on a business trip. My car was acting up. I decided that with him out of town, I'd be safe to have John over to the house that once. They were both going to come, actually. I wanted to speak with them both that night, you see...Allen and John."

"I had a babysitter coming to watch Bobby, but at the last minute, she canceled. Allen and John were already on their way. I tried to get reach them and change the session to another day, but I was too late.

"Paul came home before they could get there. It was six thirty. I remember the clock on the wall. He was drunk. He was furious. He'd been fired. He was shouting. Ranting and raving. Everyone was out to get him, that's what he thought. Everyone wanted to take advantage of him. No one respected him.

"I know this sounds awful. I'm a professional woman. But he hit me again. Slap me around. He knocked me to the floor. Then he reached down and grabbed my hair, and was dragging me across the floor like he was a caveman and I was a cavewoman. Don't ask me if I put up a fight. I tried.

"He picked me up and threw me on the table. He was going to rape me right there on my own living room table...

"Bobby came into the room. And then Paul hit him. With his fist. He knocked Bobby unconscious. He was so small... and there was blood on his forehead.

"I went berserk and attacked Paul. But he knocked me down, then picked me up and threw me on the table again.

"When I tried to fight back, he grabbed my head and started banging it on the table. I blacked out.

"When I came to, my skirt was off and he was...

"Allen and John Hemlock came into the room a few minutes later. They opened the door—I never even heard them knock, but they told me they had been beating on the door when they heard the shouting."

"And they caught Paul in the act?" I asked gently.

"No, Mr. Brown, they caught me in the act. They walked into the room just as I cut his throat with the broken crystal candlestick holder that my grandmother gave us for a wedding present."

"What?"

"They saw me kill my husband, Scott. Now do you understand?"

Lord, love a duck, I thought.

The Polymeric Computer

The phone rang.

"I'll get it," I said, and headed toward my desk.

It was Charlie Kim on the other end, giving me an update. All quiet, he said. Situation under control. I had a lot riding on Charlie, and so did Dr. Stouffer, but she didn't know it.

"Take care of yourself, my friend," I said. "Good instructors are hard to find."

"Ah," he replied, "but great instructors are nearly impossible to replace."

"Who was that?" asked Dr. Stouffer when I had hung up the phone.

"My martial arts instructor, he's doing me a little favor."

"Do you need to leave?"

"No. He can handle things."

"You can leave if you have to. I'll be all right."

"I know that. But I'd rather be here, talking to you. We need each other right now, I think."

"Thank you," she said.

I thought she was going to tear up again.

"You're welcome."

I returned to the couch.

"So, Allen Hemlock and his son John saw you kill your husband?"

"Yes."

"But it was self-defense."

"No, it wasn't. I killed him after he was through. After it was over."

"What does that mean?"

"Just what I said. He fell forward on me. Passed out from the booze. But I was in a rage. It just took me over. I saw the broken candlestick on the table next to me, rolled him over, and cut his throat. He was unconscious when I did it. It was messy, really messy. So much blood. So much blood."

"Wow."

"Yes," she said. "Wow, indeed. Bobby was still unconscious. Allen told me to take him to the hospital. To say nothing to anyone about Paul. To stay away as long as possible."

"And?" I prompted.

"That everything would be all right when I returned. Allen even arranged to have a top neurosurgeon to check Bobby out, and when he had to have some special surgery for the head injury, Allen took care of the bills. But when I came back, everything was cleaned up, and the body was gone."

"But that makes them accessories," I argued.

"If I could prove it, but I can't. Don't you see? I don't know where or how that they disposed of Paul's body. And the broken candlestick, with my fingerprints on it, that was gone, too. They know where the body was disposed of, and they know where the murder weapon is. That means they control me the same way that they control you."

"Whoa. Wait a minute. Allen Hemlock doesn't control me."

"Really?"

"Really," I said. "I'm an independent contractor."

"Being independent doesn't mean that you're in control, Scott."

"It does to me."

"Why then," she asked, "haven't you gone to Interpol or the press with what you know about the killings? Who is in control of the mission, the man who executes the mission, or the man who defines the parameters and selects the target?"

When I didn't answer, she pressed on.

"Answer me this Scott—what if you're intended to be Allen's

scapegoat? What if he's holding out essential information from you? What if you chasing the Church of the New Apostles was planned to keep you away from the truth? Is he capable of that? Has he ever lied to you before?"

"Give me some time to myself, will you?" I said. I was beginning to feel hemmed in by her story and her questions. I needed some time to myself.

"I want to tell you to fuck off, that this is bullshit, but I want to think it through for myself first. I'll be upstairs for a while. Make yourself at home. You've given me a lot to think about. You're okay down here for a bit?"

So, I left her after she reassured me, and went upstairs to the lighthouse cage to think, and to make some arrangements. I shouldn't have left her alone, but I wanted to be by myself. She'd scared me that badly. I did what all real men do today when we're pissed off—I sat down and started surfing the Internet.

It was six thirty, and the sky was darkening. I'd been on the computer for that long. The muted orange sun hung an inch or two above the horizon, getting ready to go down for the night. Purple-gray clouds were scattered across the shaded sky and the river was the glossy black color of a beetle's back.

Lights were on in the windows across the water, and I wondered if the normal people behind the lighted panes were having dinner, talking about the mundane things that happened during the course of their day. Were they laughing and joking, or merely tolerating each other? Were husbands and wives planning family vacations, or was one planning to murder the other? When you live alone for as long as I have, sometimes you think about that crap.

Dr. Stouffer was wrong about me. I always had my doubts about Hemlock, and yes, I was aware that he wasn't always a straight shooter. That sometimes he told me only what he wanted to know. That some of the things that I did for him weren't always kosher. But I had never before considered him as my enemy. I was afraid that if his son turned out to be guilty that Allen might then become my enemy, but I hadn't considered that he was using me all along, setting me up for the big fall. Relationships with people are seldom that simple in real life.

There is a premise in military thinking. The enemy is the enemy.

The enemy may act like your friend, but the enemy is not your friend. Pretty basic stuff, but right on the money. The question was, was Allen Hemlock my enemy? Keep your friends close, and your enemies closer, the Godfather had advised his somebody. But I didn't think that applied to my relationship to Allen Hemlock. I was just a contractor, or so I always thought I was, until Dr. Stouffer had opened her mouth.

In the scheme of Allen Hemlock's life, I didn't amount to much. Some of the things that I did from time to time might have some important damage control implications for him, but he would get along just fine without me. And if he ever thought of me as an enemy, I'd be the part of the photo with a hole where the face used to be.

Still, what Dr. Stouffer said downstairs had me thinking.

There are other categories than enemies and friends. To a man like Allen Hemlock, I was a tool to be used when it was to his advantage. We never developed a close friendship. He had always treated me well enough, but I had kept the distance. I had my friends, and that was enough for me. He used me as a tool when he needed me, and I just did contract work for him.

After the gas accident, I needed clarity in my life, and he gave me the opportunity to achieve that. I was grateful to him for that, but that was as far as it went. To me, he was a customer now. Plain and simple.

Still, what Dr. Stouffer said downstairs had my mental gears turning.

Maybe there was more to Allen Hemlock than I had ever imagined. Like the people across the river in the buildings that I had been wondering about. Like Dr. Stouffer. Like me. Like all of us.

A billionaire who took time out of his busy schedule to help a poor woman who had murdered her husband dispose of the body. Now that's something you didn't hear about every day. But I wondered who had more secrets, Allen Hemlock or Dr. Stouffer.

Dr. Stouffer had said that Hemlock controlled her. He had something on her. The question was, why? To what end? Why bother? In a word, what was in it for Allen Hemlock?

She said that he controlled me, too. Like a pawn on his big chessboard. If that's what he thought, Allen Hemlock was in for a big surprise. I knew how to play chess, too.

Still, what Dr. Stouffer had said downstairs had me thinking.

I reached over and picked up the phone. I got lucky. Gregorio was in.

"Hey amigo," I said, "how'd you like to come visit the one-armed bandit?"

We talked for a few minutes, and then I dialed Katerina. She wasn't in, so I left a message on her machine, asking her the same question.

Next, I got hold of Karl at home in Germany.

I was a busy pawn.

*****

Her mouth was slightly parted, and her chest rose and fell slowly with her breathing. She was asleep on her bed. I stood in the doorway to her bedroom, watching her. She was just like the rest of us, I supposed. When painful memories came calling, she took a nap.

"Hey, doctor, time to wake up," I said softly. "Time for dinner."

No answer.

I walked over and then sat on the edge of the bed.

"Paging Dr. Stouffer," I said. "Paging Dr. Stouffer."

She stirred, but didn't wake, so I took hold of her shoulder and shook her lightly. Her face was framed by a tangle of blond hair.

"Hmmm," she murmured.

"Up and at 'em, doctor. Time for chow."

Her eyes fluttered once, twice, then opened halfway.

"The chef says that it's time to eat."

"What time is it?"

Rolled over on to her back, her arms spread wide.

"Quarter to seven. I don't want you to starve in your sleep."

"I've got to call Bobby."

"Go for it," I said, pointing to the phone on the stand near her bed.

"Thanks for letting me sleep."

"No extra charge," I said.

On an impulse, I took my one good hand and stroked her hair.

"You okay?" I asked.

For an answer, she shook her head yes.

"Good. Then I'll go whip something up for us in the kitchen. That is, if the microwave is still working."

As I started to get to my feet, she grabbed hold of my hand and squeezed it.

"You look nice when you sleep," I said.

"Thanks. Now get out of here so that I can pull myself together," she replied.

*****

I made spaghetti and garlic bread. Thank God I had the strength to open a jar of sauce with one hand and to pop a loaf of store-bought garlic bread in and out of the oven. It made life so much easier.

She had to open the wine, though.

I'd like to say that we had a romantic dinner followed by heavy body contact, but it didn't turn out that way. Bob Alby was going to be murdered while we were putting the plates away.

"So, how's Bobby?" I asked between bites.

"Okay. He loves your friend."

"Bob's a special guy."

"How long have you known each other?" she asked.

"Quite a few years. Bob's a good listener, but he keeps his mouth shut."

"That's the basis for your friendship?"

She sat on her side of the table, I sat on my mine.

"No. But it's a quality I admire in him. Plus, he's good with animals and kids."

"Bobby seems to think so."

"Yeah, I thought he would."

"He runs the newspaper around here?"

"Sure does. It's not much, but it's all his. Bob doesn't want to build a media empire, or control the world. The Web's already done that. He's satisfied with who he is. And yes, before you ask, that's also I quality that I admire in people."

"How about you, Scott?" she asked. "Are you satisfied with who you are?"

"Are we going to talk about me all night?"

"Just answer the question."

"All right. No. I'm not satisfied with who I am anymore. Do you know that Bob Alby is the only one of my friends who hasn't killed someone? I think maybe I could stand to be more like Bob Alby."

"I think," she said after swallowing a mouthful of wine, "that's a healthy sign."

"Yeah, well, anyway, Bob is a special guy. Over the years, he's been the one that I confided in about... me. If you get what I mean. I can talk with anything about Bob. About what happened. About my... my wife and son. About the horror of it all. And he listens. He doesn't try to save me. He just lets me talk.

"He's been through some tough personal times himself. Different from mine, but he doesn't talk about them unless I ask. When he does, I try and show him the same kind of respect."

"A special man."

"The best. Charlie Kim, my martial arts instructor, he's a different kind of friend. In his dojo, I call him Mr. Kim. Outside of those sacred grounds, I call him Charlie. It's a weird relationship, but I genuinely look up to him.

"Leroy or Leo, he's more like me inside. Fucked up. Hard. Carries a chip on his shoulder. I can relate to Leo. I can't always talk to him because he's a cop, and I don't always get along with him, but we understand each other.

"We're all single, we've all got pasts, and we all like to play poker when we can. It's kind of like a club."

"The Lonely Boys Club?" she asked with a smile.

"You've got spaghetti sauce on your chin. No, a little lower. Serves you right, making fun of our club."

"Don't like the name?"

"No. It sounds kind of sad."

She didn't comment.

Another glass of wine for Dr. Stouffer. Her second. I drank coffee. I never drink while I'm working, although I didn't tell her that, because she was holding out on me.

There were a lot of things that still bothered me. I still thought that the New Apostles were tied in with the deaths of the kids. It shows that you're past forty when you can think of teenagers as kids, but that's how I thought of them.

My main problem was that my theory for why the kids were being

killed at all was now kaput. Shot to shit. Whoever was killing these kids wasn't doing it to look for the mark of the Beast. There had to be another reason for the killings, and another reason for the mutilation.

It made so much sense when I first considered it, I hadn't looked at alternatives. Maybe they were looking for something, but if not the mark of the Beast, then what? And why?

Time was running short, and I wasn't much further along in answering either of those questions. I needed to turn the screws on Dr. Stouffer.

"Let me ask you something, Kris," I said. "What would you do if you were me, and you thought that someone you knew was holding out on you?"

She looked at me thoughtfully, and absentmindedly ran a finger around the rim of her wineglass.

"Nothing," she said, "until I knew why."

"Now there's a self-serving answer."

"If you've got something to ask me, Mr. Brown, you just go ahead and ask."

"Okay. Why do you think that whoever is killing these kids is mutilating their bodies afterwards? Your professional opinion."

"I'm not a forensic psychologist."

"General input, then."

"You think I know the answer?" she asked.

"If I thought that, I wouldn't be feeding you dinner."

It mollified her a bit. The wrinkles left her forehead, and she leaned back in her chair. But her eyes were still wary.

"Generally, these types of things are done to make a statement. To send a message. Or, they're part of a ritual with a purpose. Once you understand the purpose, the meaning is clear."

"That's a sick way to send a message," I said.

"They're sick people, Scott."

"I liked Katrina's idea that they were looking for the mark of the Beast, how about you?"

"No. I think that it was naive."

"Why?"

I was a little pissed because she was so matter of fact about it. I hadn't heard her come up with anything better.

"Because there's no real precedent for it."

"What about—"

"The Inquisition? You're talking about a different time, a different era. Those were medieval times, and the Inquisition grew from medieval concepts that just don't apply today."

"Bullshit."

"We're talking," she said, "about something international in scope and execution in the twenty-first century. A sophisticated if sick group of individuals. It just doesn't fit."

I was about to ask her how many times that she had slept with Allen Hemlock, when I decided to take a different tack.

"Okay, how about this—what is the nature of your association with Allen Hemlock, aside from the family counseling bit?"

"It's complicated."

"Try me," I said.

"I mean in the sense that I have consulted for years with him on a very technical if somewhat abstruse topic."

Abstruse always sounded to me like some kind of electrical device ordered out of a sex catalogue.

"I'll try my best to scrape along with my undereducated brain."

"Don't be like that," she said with a sigh. "It concerns the potential integration with cognitive and emotive human capacities with artificial intelligence. Whether or not a computer can think creatively and actually have feelings. Not presented feelings where the software mimes what a person would be expected to feel, but actual feelings. It's an accepted given that someday computers will become self-aware. Some scientists think that evolution has already begun. To Allen, the real question is whether they can experience emotions."

"Why in the hell," I asked, "would Allen Hemlock pay you to consult on such a stupid topic?"

"What did you say?"

"Sorry. I mean where's the utility? Allen's a business man. Show me the money."

"Artificial intelligence is big money, in case you haven't heard, Mr. Brown. Gigantically money. And Hemlock International, in case you've forgotten, is not only a chemical company, but also it is also one of the leading computer software and hardware companies in the world. They're on the leading edge for research in this area."

"There's a big difference between artificial intelligence and what you're talking about."

"Oh really? Are you perhaps limiting the concept by excluding the possibilities of computer self-awareness? Or perhaps by precluding emotions as being low level computationally determined physiological reactions with an as yet undetermined raison d'etre?"

"You talk pretty good for a broad halfway through her second glass of wine," I said reluctantly.

She smiled, which meant that she wasn't going to throw her wine glass at me.

"You're still an ass sometimes," she said, "even if I do like you a little better than I thought I would."

"And why is that?"

"Something Bobby said."

"You going to tell me or am I going to have to beg?"

"Beg."

"Give me a break."

"Bobby said... I don't know if you'll like this."

"Would you go ahead and tell me? Christ on a pony, but you can be a pain."

"Okay. He said that I should be nice to you."

"That's it?" I asked.

"Because even though you acted real tough, you were a nice man. And," she added softly, "he said that you cried inside sometimes. He could see it behind your eyes."

"Oh, Jesus..."

"And he said to be patient with you, but not to cut you any slack."

"What kind of a kid is he?" I asked irritably.

"He's a very special boy, Scott."

"Going to grow up to be a shrink just like his mother."

"I hope not," she said.

"How old is he?" I asked. "It's kind of hard to tell."

She stiffened, then relaxed. It was a sensitive topic, I guess.

"Almost eighteen. I know, I know that he's child-like and his moon face makes it hard to really see him as that old, but he's just shy of eighteen."

"So tell me more about this heavy duty consulting thing that you were doing for Allen Hemlock," I asked, trying hard to change the topic again. "Who did he have you work with?"

"This is all very confidential, you know."

"So? We're mostly past that, aren't we? People are dying over this."

"I'm legally prohibited against discussing it with anyone without Allen's written approval in advance."

"I'm not trying to pry competitive intelligence from you, Kris."

"That's not the point."

"No, it's not. I'll tell you what the point is. The point is that you've implied that Allen Hemlock is a bad man, who might be involved in this."

"I—"

"So don't backtrack on me. Give me what I want."

"It's not that simple," she protested.

"The fuck it's not. Tell me it's not relevant."

"I don't know what's relevant."

"Then just tell me."

"Don't shout at me," she snapped. "I won't tolerate being shouted at."

"Except by the man you're protecting—Allen Hemlock. How many times have you slept with him?"

The table was up and over and slammed in my lap before I had a chance to get out of the way. Dishes crashed and cluttered onto the tile floor while I was knocked backwards, chair and all, onto the floor. My head hit the floor and I said good night to the world.

"Wake up, you stupid bastard. Open your eyes, damn you."

Those were the first words I heard as I struggled back to consciousness.

"My head..."

Her hands grabbed my shirt, ripping out a few chest hairs in the process. With a solid yank, my chest was up and at a forty-five degree angle to the floor. My head lagged a little behind. She straddled me and zoomed her face in to within an inch of mine. I could smell her breath.

Lambrusco, I thought.

"How did you know? Tell me, how did you know? Did he tell you? Did he brag about it? You smug son of a bitch, you knew all of the time. I poured my heart out to you, and you knew all the time."

She let go, and I cracked back onto the tiles for a second time.

"I hope you die," she said, and got off of me.

Things had been going so well.

"I feel like I'm going to die," I said.

"Good. I hope you do. You're as bad as he is."

She was shoving chairs around, sending them teetering, tottering, then crashing to the floor. After exhausting all of the chairs, she stomped over and kicked me in the leg.

She was pissed.

"Damn it," I yelled. "Quit kicking me. I didn't know."

Her foot flew at my leg again, but I rolled out of the way.

"Liar," she screamed. "You're a bastard and a liar."

I sat up and started scooting my ass backwards, out of the way of her feet.

"You were holding out on me," I explained quickly.

"It's my business," she yelled, thumping her fists on her chest. "My business. Nobody else's. He blackmailed me into it. Blackmailed me. It's my business. My shame. My humiliation. How dare you?"

"You talk to me because of some bullshit legal technicality. Allen Hemlock blackmailed you into having sex with him, and you won't even take a stand against him? So you murdered your husband. I don't give a shit. He deserved it. Now do something to get back at Allen. Be a man, for God's sake."

"Be a what?" she screamed and reached for an unbroken wine bottle on the floor.

"Let me rephrase that," I said quickly.

"Rephrase this," she said, and threw the bottle.

It's hard to duck a high-speed incoming bottle when it's launched from only four feet away. The kick in the leg hurt less than the

Lambrusco in the chest. I was on my back again before I knew it, swearing up a storm. It hurt like hell.

"Damn you—" I began, but was cut off when the next one hit me in the thigh. I howled and then scrambled to my feet.

"Whatever happened to partners?" I yelled.

"I don't want to be your partner."

"You want a stupid partner? One that only hears what you tell him? One that you can lead around by the nose?"

"Yes," she screamed.

She was definitely winning the volume contest.

We were on the couch, surveying the disaster.

"You sure make a mess when you get mad," I said.

"Screw you," she said.

"We don't know each other that well."

"What do you want?"

She was running out of steam. Her shoulders were slumped forward, and her blond hair hung down, covering her face.

"I want the truth. Tell me about this secret project. What is or was it all about, and who in Allen's company were you working with?"

"Dr. Estes," she said without raising her head.

"His full name."

"Dr. Nathaniel Estes, out of Toronto."

"And what is or was it about?"

"Was," she said. "It was about an artificial intelligence, a new type of computer memory, and a new theory of programming and information transfer."

"Here. Swing your feet up onto my lap, lean back against the arm of the couch, and relax. Then tell me everything."

"It's classified."

"Put your fucking feet up here."

"No."

"I'm too sore to dick around with you. My crotch hurts, my head hurts, my chest and hips hurt, and, well, I hurt about everywhere."

"It's your own fault."

But she put her feet in my lap and leaned back against the arm of the couch like I asked.

I'm a clean person; normally I wouldn't leave red wine to dry on the floor and broken plates and wine glasses scattered everywhere, but I hurt too much to bend over and pick them up.

"I'd take your shoes off and massage your feet, but there's glass on the floor, so I'll just leave your shoes where they are. Now start talking."

"It's classified. Top secret."

"By whom?" I asked.

"By the military. By the federal government."

I gave a low whistle.

"Sounds interesting. Tell me everything."

"If someone finds out," she said, "I could not only be sued, I could be sent to a federal prison. Don't you see? I can't risk that. If something happened to me, who would take care of Bobby?"

"Nothing is going to happen to you. I'm sure as hell not going to tell anyone. Secrecy is a way of life with me, so spill."

"Dr. Estes is a genius," she began.

"Not another one?"

"Yes, another one. He had a new theory of information transfer that was given to defense department funding. Dr. Estes works for Allen. Did I tell you that?"

"Yes, now get on with it."

"He had this idea and the Defense Department funded it. You have to understand that I mean major funding. If what Dr. Estes theorized was true, it would change the world. His theory was that radical."

"But if he was wrong?" I asked.

"Then the whole thing was a just another huge waste of the taxpayer's money."

A question occurred to me, and I put it to her.

"Who would own this new technology?"

"The government, of course. They were paying for it."

"And if it didn't work?"

"For a small amount, the ownership of the work in progress would transfer back to Hemlock International."

"And what specifically was he doing?"

"Dr. Estes was working on several things. One was the transfer of information via ELF, another area of investigation was a new processor material, and the capstone of his efforts was to be the initiation of self-awareness, including creative and emotive capability."

"A computer," I asked, "that would be alive?"

"In a word, yes."

"What about the new processor material? What was so special about that?"

"Dr. Estes was experimenting with the use of polymeric materials."

"Plastic?"

"In laymen's terms," she agreed. "Plastic. Today's computers are silicon based. Dr. Estes was attempting to create a plastic that, using the molecular structure and the component chemical attributes, would function to process information. Only with an organic platform."

"I don't mean to burst your educated bubble, Kris, but plastics don't even conduct electricity."

"But you're wrong," she said. "There are plastics in use today that can conduct electricity. And if plastics can conduct, they can be gated. That means that the electricity can be routed throughout the molecular structure in a controlled fashion. Considering the complex structure of polymers, a sheet of this material could have more processing power when inserted into a system than a Cray supercomputer."

"Did it work?"

"Not officially, no."

"Let me guess. He was wildly successful, but under Allen's direction, Dr. Estes fudged his research, declared it a failure, and Hemlock International bought back the project."

She nodded.

"So the taxpayers bought and paid for it, but Hemlock International owns it. Bought it for pennies on the dollar, if that. Wonderful. Allen will make all of the money on it. But if he owns it now and can exploit it, then why has no one ever heard of it?"

"Because Allen has kept it under wraps. Only a handful of people know. If word got out to a competitor, Allen could lose his development edge and the government might go after him. He wants to keep it from them, to be the only one with this technology. To develop it to its fullest potential and then introduce it. If he introduces the technology in a completely developed format, he thinks he will keep it under his control. The barrier to market entry for competitors—especially development time—will be insurmountable. And Allen will claim that it was his company that made it work after the government failure, so he'll be safe from the government. The longer he holds back on introducing it, the more credible it will sound."

"Okay," I said, "so he's got a new type of computer. What's that got to do with you?"

"Everything," she replied. "He wanted it to think like a human being. That's where I came in. I'm the expert in differentiating computer cognitive simulation from human thinking. The measurement standard in the field is called the Stouffer. As in Dr. Kristen Stouffer. Allen knew that he could blackmail me into silence. I was the perfect person for what he wanted. One of those happy for him, unhappy for me coincidences."

"What was all of this stuff about information transfer?" I asked.

"Dr. Estes theorized that human mental content, our programming in a sense, could be transferred to this new organic platform."

"Pardon me?"

"Our brains are electrical in nature. He theorized that the electrical process of thinking could be monitored and fed directly into the new organic media. Essentially, he wanted to use the electromagnetic radiation that the brain emits to transfer our thinking process to the new polymeric processing platform."

"And?"

"And I don't know anymore. Dr. Estes ran into some problems. I don't know if he ever completed the work. But I do know that he ran into the problem that there is essentially too much information in the brain for a quick transfer to be accomplished. Our cognitive skills and patterns develop over the course of a lifetime, although as adults they don't alter much. Am I boring you?"

"No," I said, "I'm just trying to understand what the hell, if anything, that this could have to do with the murders. Or if it has any relevance at all."

"And?"

"I think that I'm not doing too well in the analysis department. Intuition and action are my specialties. Maybe I should stick with them. What do you say we clean this place up a bit? I'll pick up the furniture, sweep up the broken dishes and the glass, and then we can put the plates away."

The Assassins

I'm reconstructing this after the fact, but this is, as best as I can tell, what happened:

At or around 8:55 p.m. that night, a van with the words "Gibraltar Gazette" blazoned across the side pulled into Bob Alby's driveway. Two men, wearing light jackets with the same words printed on the back of their jackets, got out of the front seats of the car and went to Bob's front door and rang the bell.

Had Charlie been positioned on the other side of the house, things might have turned out differently. We disagree on that. I say that Bob would still have been killed, and that it was my fault for sending the kid to him. Charlie thinks that it was his fault. It really doesn't matter who's right.

Bob is still dead.

The front light snapped on as three other men, who got out of the van's side door, slipped around the back of the house to cover the back door. Charlie saw one of the first group of men pull a gun on Bob when the front door opened, and the two men forced their way in, closing the door behind them.

Charlie headed to the back of the house to gain entrance, and that's where he ran into the three well-armed stooges. He said that they were quick, and well trained. It was hard for me to tell after the fact by looking at their bodies.

Dead men just lie there, especially after the fire.

No big deal about how he killed them, he said. Charlie covers ground so quickly in the daylight that it's hard to follow his moves. At night, the first man who raised a gun to point it at him didn't, I imagine, bring it up enough to aim before he was cut in two.

The remaining two men didn't see him coming, and when the butt handle of Charlie's sword smashed the next man in line's windpipe and snapped his neck, he probably didn't know what hit him.

Charlie took out the third man by bringing his sword round and up in a wide arced swing that cut open his abdomen. When I first saw the man's corpse, his sliced, fried crisp intestines were mainly on the outside of the body.

That left two bad guys still standing, inside Bob's house.

Bobby was already in bed when this all started, but still awake. He heard the voices, and heard the cough of the silenced gun that fired a round into the soft underside of Bob Alby's chin and blew out the back of his head.

The door to the guest bedroom where Bobby was resting opened, and he saw the dark figure of a tall man framed in the doorway by the light from the hallway.

It must have been a terrifying sight. A grown man might have demanded something stupid, like "who's there," but Bobby dove under the covers and pulled them up and over him and lay there shivering like a puppy who's been caught in the wastebasket.

The tall man grabbed where he thought Bobby's leg was and pulled hard, lifting Bobby and the covers off of the bed and slamming him into the dresser. I saw the cut on the kid's forehead and the bruises after the fact.

Charlie came onto the man who had offed Bob Alby next, after using the key I had given him to get in silently through the back door. He'd sheathed his sword and drawn his pistol. He shot the killer once in the throat, in case he was wearing a vest. The blood splattered and blended with the bloody mess that decorated the same wall where the back of Bob's head had impacted. Charlie told me that the clock on the wall, which Bob's wife had bought for him as a birthday present on his thirtieth birthday, was smeared with red. Odd what sticks out as important at times like that. When the remaining man stepped out of

Bobby's room, Charlie shot him, too.

It was nine forty-seven when Charlie called me, gave me a short, coded message, and told me he was looking forward to seeing me soon. That was it.

Dr. Stouffer and I had cleaned up our mess, and she was playing some stupid song on the piano that I had liked before Charlie called.

She continued to play, halting occasionally, pecking for the proper note. I leaned up against the desk, my field of vision narrowing as though I were experiencing the wicked migraines that I had as a child. The air I breathed seemed sweet and strangely thick.

Bob Alby was dead.

There are some people that, when you receive news of their death, you feel as though your own life has dimmed. It is as though their lives were so strongly intertwined with your own that their passing weakens the fabric of your own life. Dimmed and weakened, that's how I felt. But Dr. Stouffer continued to play. I watched her, amazed that she could continue to exist unaffected.

Another dead body to add to the running total. This one, however, was someone that I knew. Someone that was my friend. Someone whose only crime had been to try and protect an innocent.

"Kris," I said, loudly enough for her to stop playing.

"What?" she asked.

"Do you know how to handle a weapon?"

She saw the look on my face.

"What's happened?" she demanded.

"War has been declared," I said, "and I'm drafting you."

While I waited for Charlie, I told her what I had learned from Charlie's coded message. Bob was dead. Bobby was safe in Charlie's care, and Charlie was on his way over.

Charlie arrived within the hour; I picked his boat up on the night vision cameras mounted around the island. He came in clean, with no one following him.

"Is Bobby with him?" asked Dr. Stouffer.

"Yes, it looks like it."

"What do you mean, it looks like it? Is he there?"

I swiveled the chair to face her.

"Look for yourself. That monitor. There. You see? There are two shapes that you can see every now and then on the floor of the boat. One of them is Bobby. He's covered to keep him safe in case anyone would try and pick them off on the way in."

We were up in the Lighthouse cage. I had my holster on, with the Beretta tucked in it, fully loaded, and my Benelli pump shotgun, the one with the strap on it, leaning against one of the workstations.

"Then why is he coming here?" she asked.

"It's safer than trying to arrange a meet. Didn't you ever wonder how the bastards knew to make the hit on Bob's place?"

"I was... too worried about Bobby."

"He's alive. Bob's dead."

"That's not fair—"

"Don't freak on me, I need you in peak form, doctor. I'm not blaming you. It was me that put him with Bob in the first place. I never expected anything to start this soon. Never."

"Then no one would be hurt if we hadn't—"

"You'd be dead already and probably Bobby right along with you."

"I'm so sorry."

"Me, too. But one thing we've got to do, is to quit telling each other that we're sorry. We're on a war footing now, and we don't have time for it. You and I are on the same side. The only people that we want to be sorry are the people who dealt the hit on Bob. Deal?"

"Deal," she said.

We tracked Charlie's boat all the way in. I spent the time showing her the way the system worked. It was like trying to train a new air traffic controller in fifteen minutes, but I did the best I could.

"They're docked," I said.

She rose from her chair to go downstairs.

"Sit down," I said.

"I've got to go get Bobby."

I stood up, blocking her path.

"You want to help your son? You stay right here with me and watch the monitors. This is the most dangerous part for them, and they need you to be their eyes and ears for them. I'll go downstairs and let them in."

"Why you? I'm his mother."

"Because I'm a better shot than you."

"But he—"

"Watch the monitors, Kris. I've got no time to argue with you and Bobby needs your help."

But it went off without a hitch. Charlie carried Bobby in. He had crossed the ground running low and fast, and when I opened the door, he was through, and I slammed the door behind him so hard that it must have sounded like gunfire because Dr. Stouffer came running down the stairs.

"I heard—"

"It's okay," I said. "It was just the door."

Charlie lowered Bobby to his feet and took the blanket off.

"He's a brave boy, Dr. Stouffer," he said.

"Mom? Mom, I had to—"

Nobody was finishing sentences that night.

While she fussed over Bobby, and he over her, Charlie and I left to retrieve the other bundle. Neither of us spoke a word to the other as we walked, each brooding over his private loss.

My senses were surprisingly acute. The sound of each step seemed magnified to the point that I could hear each plant being crushed beneath my feet. Each stone felt larger than it was beneath my shoes, and the sound of the river was like a beast lapping hungrily at the shores.

The moon overhead shone so brightly that the island was highlighted by an eldritch silver glow, and I felt as though we were walking through a secret place seldom trafficked by the living.

Charlie's face was like a primitive mask formed of a dull brass, and his eyes reflected a dark light. He moved like a robed judge on his way to deliver the ultimate penalty to a defendant. I could feel the unyielding sense of purpose within him. A dull rage was fermenting inside me, too, and my own steps were those of a predator going to claim his prey.

Somehow the bound and gagged man beneath the blanket had struggled to a sitting position to face us by the time we got to the dock, and for a moment I imagined that the boatman Charon had delivered another hooded soul to the Isle of Hades.

Charlie got him out of the boat and slammed a fist into the man's stomach. When he doubled over, Charlie threw him over his shoulder, and, without even flexing his knees to absorb the weight, followed me back.

*****

"Well, Lance, long time no see."

Lance didn't look so good. Charlie had kneecapped him.

"You were talking good the last time I saw you at the dinner party," I continued. "Charlie, you didn't cut out his tongue already, did you?"

"Not yet. I been nice to him so far."

"You hear that, Lance? Charlie's treated you nicely so far. Don't worry. You can talk, go ahead. You can scream your fucking head off if it will make you feel better. No one can hear you down here."

His hair was a mess.

"Don't you want to know where you are? No? I'll tell you anyway." I leaned my face over until it was a few inches from his. "You're down in my tunnel. I've got a lot of experience in tunnels, Lance. But you probably already know that, don't you?"

Sweat was pouring down his forehead.

"All dressed in black and everything, aren't you, Lance? Look at this shit, Charlie. Lance here's a real pro. Dressed like a ninja and everything. And tough, too. Me, I'd be passed out if I took a bullet in the knee, but Charlie here is a good medic. He's had practice. Bound and dressed it real good so you can stay awake to talk to us.

"You see, Lance, we want you to live. You're going to tell us what we want to know, and then I'm going to let you go.

"That's because Charlie says you didn't kill Bob, the other guy did. And, you didn't kill Bobby either. That was thoughtful of you. So, I vote that you live. Since you didn't kill anybody tonight.

"Instead, you can just look over your shoulder for your bosses to come after you for the rest of your life. Bob would like that. It has kind of a poetic justice to it. Don't you think, Charlie?"

By way of answering me, Charlie looked around my underground workshop for some appropriate tools. He selected the pliers. They were a good set, with red rubber sleeves on the handles. Craftsman.

Bought them myself on sale.

Lance was tied to a chair, each of his legs bound again separately to one of the chair legs so that his knees were spread a good foot or so apart. His arms were tied to the chair back, again individually secured.

Charlie and I left Lance where he was for a few minutes, stood just out of earshot, and he filled me in about what had gone down. Lance kept his mouth shut and practiced tough-guy silence.

When we returned, Charlie walked over to Lance and kneeled in front of him.

"You're thinking of that old joke, aren't you, Lance?" I asked. "But, no. Charlie just wants to adjust your nuts a little. They need a tune up."

Charlie spread the pliers' jaws, placed them appropriately, and gave a little squeeze. I bet Lance didn't scream so loud when Charlie shot him.

"Damn, that must hurt, but at least we know you can still make noise. But you better try it again, Charlie, just to make sure that it wasn't a one in a million fluke."

While Charlie torqued down on Lance's other nut, I was considering the facts. Blood loss. No arteries cut that I could tell. Lance was a little in shock, but not enough that I gave a shit. Keeping him alive to feel the pain so that he would talk was all that I really cared about. My biggest worry was the amount of time that it would take to make him talk. We were running on borrowed time, and Charlie and I both knew it.

After loading Bobby and Lance into the van, Charlie had moved the three bodies in the backyard into the house, set the place on fire, and then moved out. It would confuse the trail, but not for long.

Sheriff Leroy Croton had already contacted me when I was inside the lighthouse telling Dr. Stouffer that Charlie and I had things to take care of. I had told Leo that Charlie was with me and that we would be on our way. That bought us maybe another hour before we had to head out to the station. Not exactly long enough for the normal torture sequence, and too short a time for me to balance the books in the right way.

"I want to show you that we're serious here, Lance," I told our guest. "And look around, we've got lots of things here that we can use to be serious with."

There were four rooms underground that I had had built over the years, halfway between the lighthouse and by a passage that opened behind the work shed. They were built with the idea that sometime, sooner or later, someone would come looking for me. I had sleeping quarters, a computer and communications room, a kitchen and bathroom, weapons room, and the workroom, which was where we were then. A separate generator provided power in case everything else went down.

The work room was set up like a mechanic's repair shop, including basic electronics repair equipment, a tool bench, drill press, band saw and some metal working equipment primarily used in weapons maintenance and repair. For a few years, I admit I had a bomb shelter mentality.

When Lance's head had stopped thrashing from side to side and his screams had settled to a low moan, I said, "Well, Lance, you feel like talking? Or should I just let Charlie continue?"

He didn't look so pretty now. I wondered who he really was. An actor by day, killer by night?

"Whose payroll are you on, Lance?"

"Fuck you," he finally said.

At least he was communicating. It was a start.

"Not an option, buddy. Let me tell you what your actual options are. One, you tell me everything that I want to know, and you do it quick. If you don't, I'll figure that you're a lost cause, and I'm going to rub your face down with sulfuric acid so that burn victims will look good compared to you. Charlie's going to completely crush your nuts, and then I'm going to use an acrylonitrile glue to seal off forever the end of your limp dick—you know, like they use in hospitals to close skin together, and then set you free like I promised. The whole thing will take a half an hour to forty-five minutes tops, and then you'll be on your way. We'll drop you someplace by the side of the road.

"Or, you can tell me what I want to know and leave here with your good looks and your nuts and the rest in good working order.

"You may think that you know a lot about me, Lance, but buddy, you don't even have a clue as to how bad I can really be. You know the movie called The Good, the Bad, and the Ugly? Well, I'm the Ugly."

"I know you better than you think," he sneered.

Lance tried to look tough. Maybe he was. Maybe he was acting. It didn't really make a lot of difference at that point. It was a question of how far that Lance thought I would go.

"Time to find out. Who are you working for?"

"K-Mart," he said.

"Have it your way. I gave you the chance."

I walked over to the workbench and found the super glue. The acid was in a metal cabinet marked "chemicals". I wasn't looking at Lance when I opened the doors and took the glass bottle out and set it on the bench, but when I took it back and set it on the floor a few feet away from him, his eyes were wide open and bloodshot. I got the Superglue and came back again.

Charlie had stood there the whole time looking at Lance. Lance avoided his eyes, looking instead at the floor, the ceiling, at me. Anywhere but at Charlie.

"There's nothing I can tell you," said Lance nervously.

"Have it your way," I said as I unzipped his trousers.

"He'd kill me."

"I won't," I said, as I uncapped the glue. "Oops. Wait a minute. These days it's better to be safe."

I went to the chemical cabinet and took out a box of disposable latex gloves.

"Who knows where your dick has been," I explained.

"You're crazy. You're fucking crazy."

"You want to know a secret, Lance?" I asked. "You know that time I gassed the town?"

He nodded his head mutely.

"I did it on purpose."

"What?"

"Yeah. I knew what would happen. Kind of funny that I was the only one in the safety suit with an air hose. You ever think about that? Just me. Everyone else died."

"No."

"Yeah. They burned from the lungs out. Hydrogen fluoride is a bad gas, but I like it. It does the job. Sulfuric acid is a bad acid. I'm going to wipe your face with it. I won't use much. Too much would kill you, and all I want it to do is eat away enough of your face that you'll never look in a mirror again."

"He'll kill me if I talk."

"Like I said, I won't."

It wasn't the most fun I've ever had to pull his dick out, but the look on his face made it worthwhile.

"Don't," he pleaded.

"Since you won't tell me what I want to know, Lance, you're going to have to piss out your ears for the rest of your life, because your dick's going to be sealed off tighter than the Pharaoh's tomb."

Charlie folded his arms across his chest and kept up The Stare at Lance, while I squeezed a drop of the glue out on the floor. I took my time about it. I Let Lance eyeball the liquid as it came out the tapered end of the cap.

"This is going to hurt."

As I bent down, he said, "You'll let me live?"

I straightened.

"If you give me answers. That's the deal."

I bent down again, slowly. Charlie's dark eyes met mine. No emotion there. He knew the truth, and so did I.

"What do you want to know?" he asked. His voice cracked when he said it.

"I don't like bending up and down, Lance. If you don't tell me everything, or I think you're lying to me, I won't stop. That's the deal."

"Okay," he said. "I'll talk."

Charlie kept up the Inscrutable Stare.

"What do you want to know?" he asked again.

"Who are you working for?"

"Hemlock," he said, "Allen Hemlock."

Confirmation. Confirmation that I didn't want to hear.

"What's he after?"

"You don't know?"

"I want to hear you say it."

"You don't know, do you?"

I didn't say anything, but looked down at his flaccid dick.

"All right. Don't touch me. He wants to protect the device from them. The implant. They're crazy."

"From who?" I asked.

"Brother Thomas and the rest."

"Tell me about the implant."

He was fucking Monica, I thought. I imagined the two of them rolling around, pounding it out. Her tongue in his mouth, his hands on her breasts. I was going to kill him.

No man alive has ever really gotten any woman out of his system. We all hate at some level a man who touches a woman that we want or have had. It's our nature. We can't escape it. We can deny it, but it's still the way we are.

"One of the kids has it in their head—the implant, I mean."

"Which one?"

"I don't know," he said. "Only Hemlock knows."

"And Brother Thomas?"

"He wants it, to find it and destroy it."

Two powerful men. A bunch of teenagers and young adults in the middle. All for an implant. Whatever that was.

"The implant," I said, "it's..."

"The new computer. It's almost time to remove it, and those religious freaks want to find it first and destroy it. They're crazy."

"And John, Hemlock's son, which side is he on?"

"I don't know anything about him."

"Lance..."

"He's got nothing to do with this. Nothing that I know. He hates his old man."

"Then who's doing the hunting?"

"I don't know what you mean."

"Who's killing the kids?"

"They are. They're fanatics. Have you checked them out? They're all over the fucking world. They'll do anything to find the implant before it's done learning."

"Who are you really?" asked Charlie. It was the first thing that he had said to Lance.

"What do you mean?" His voice had a different tone when he said it, a wariness about it.

"Background. Tell me now."

"Do I have to talk to him?" asked Lance.

I shrugged.

"I would, if I were you."

Try to imagine what it must have been like for Lance. Tied down, his dick hanging out. Not sure if he was going to die, but willing to say anything to save himself. He knows that I'm crazy, but thinks maybe he can deal with me better than he could Charlie.

Then, the guy who shot him, trussed him up like an animal, and brought him to me, the guy who cranked his nuts with a pair of pliers and has eyes with no mercy, wants to know who he really is.

He's willing to squeal on his buddies, tell us anything about them. But now, this Korean who cut up his team wants to get a handle on him, maybe for future reference. Scary thought.

"I'm a contractor."

Charlie picked up the pliers again.

"Government. I used to be with the government. Now I act. That's a cover. Hemlock set it up."

"Real name?" asked Charlie.

"Wil. Wilhelm Dieter."

"What government you work for before?"

"German. East German."

Stassi. The East German secret police. Since the dissolution of East Germany and the reunification of their country, there were a lot of Stassi agents out of work, looking for money, and hiding from the new government. Not all of them spoke with German accents. The good ones spoke English better than most Americans.

"Tell me about Hemlock's shadow organization, the real covert crew," I put in.

And Lance, alias Wilhelm Dieter, began to talk. He held back a little as he picked up some confidence that he might live and that he could hang on to a few bargaining chips. Professionals always do, if they feel like they've got a real chance.

He was willing to change sides, he said, for a price.

But I killed him anyway, and Charlie and I dropped his weighted body in the middle of the Detroit River on our way over to see Sheriff Leroy.

The Polymeric Brain

Things were falling into place, but they didn't look good. For example, Hemlock had sent a team out to grab Bobby. Brother Thomas and crew hadn't made a move on the American kids yet. The bad news was that there were two groups of bad guys to deal with, not one.

Also, the good news was that I now knew what this was all about. Money on the one hand, religious mania on the other. That was also the bad news. Give guns to businessmen or religious zealots and everybody else was in trouble.

A biologically compatible polymer that was "learning" from a human brain, according to Lance. One group that wanted to control it, the other that wanted to find it and destroy it. I had enough to go the police for their help, but I'd changed my mind. Let them do their own dirty work. It was time to play both sides against their common middle—me.

It was just past midnight when Charlie and I arrived at the police station. The lady at the desk called back to Leroy, and a flunky came to get us and take us back to Leo's office.

The Gibraltar police station was about the size of the town's Post Office, which is to say that it wasn't very big at all by most standards. From the front, it had two post globe lamps that flanked an arched doorway inset against the brick facing. Over the doors, a frosted half circle of glass had the words Gibraltar Police Department stenciled on in it. The building was two stories in height, half a block long, and if you didn't read the sign over the door carefully, the mailbox out front might have confused you into thinking that it was the Post Office.

Inside, the walls were cheap wood paneling from the floor up to my waist, and chalky white drywall from there to the ceiling. The night clerk was a middle-aged hard ass woman with short dirty blond hair and a chunky body. She looked as though she had been born and would someday die at her desk.

The kid that took us back to Leo's office was tall and lanky, and wore a tight uniform to highlight his lack of body fat. He swaggered the short distance to Leo's office. The effect didn't come off as planned. With his brush cut, and pole thin body, we could have hung him in a field without scaring away the crows. Crows can tell the difference between a hard ass and a tight ass. So could we.

"What took you so long?" growled Leo when we got to his office.

The kid turned around without saluting, which I thought was bad form, and returned back to wherever he had come from, to finish reading his copy of S.W.A.T. magazine.

"Damned boat engine wouldn't start."

He didn't offer us chairs, but we sat down anyway.

"Hell of a mess," he said.

"What started the fire?" I asked.

"A somebody started the fire."

"You get Bob's body yet?"

"We've got to figure out which body is his," he said.

"How do you mean?" asked Charlie.

He could get away with the inscrutable bit. Straight faced and straight back worked for him when he used it.

"I mean," said Leo angrily, "that there were five bodies in the place. It's a damn nightmare."

"No shit," I whistled. "Five bodies. You know who they were, yet?"

"Not a clue. I was hoping you might tell me something."

"Me? I don't know anything. He never told me he was having half of Gibraltar over to his place."

Leo grunted.

"It's a goddamned shame. Bob Alby is—was—a fine man. One of

the finest men I've ever known. I'm going to get to the bottom of this if it's the last thing that I ever do."

Charlie shook his head in agreement. "He did not deserve to die. We lost a good friend tonight."

"Damn right he didn't deserve to die."

"I hear you. You say someone set the fire."

"Near as we can tell. Too early to say exactly, but we'll figure it out. This got anything to do with what you told us the other night?"

"I don't know, Leo," I lied.

"I'm asking you as a police officer. You know anything about this mess?"

"I'm in the dark. There was no reason for Bob to die. He didn't have anything to do with anything. I don't think that the two were related. If it was my body you found, I'd say yes, but if it had anything to do with what I'm working on, they got the wrong man. Bob didn't know enough to be dangerous."

"Maybe he was digging around," suggested Leo, "and got under the wrong person's skin. You should have left him out of it."

"He wasn't in any danger. Cut me some slack here. What did he know? That I had suspicions about a possible conspiracy? Bob was too smart to go digging around for the dope on things. Too old. The Gibraltar Gazette is a community paper. Not exactly the Washington Post. I don't see any connection."

Leo looked down at his desk and then shuffled around a few papers with those big hands of his. His eyes were shot red, and his cheeks sagged. I noticed for the first time that Sheriff Leroy Croton was getting gray hair.

"I loved that guy like he was my own brother," he said at last.

"We all did," offered Charlie.

"Got me through after Heather." He cleared his throat, but still didn't look up. "Bob always wanted to be cremated," he said, "but not like this."

"No," I said.

The three of us were silent for a minute or two, an unspoken memorial of quiet dedicated to our friend. I remembered the splash that I heard when Lance's body hit the water. I don't know what the other two were thinking.

"You know," said Leo, "we were just playing cards with him the other night. Who would have thought that it would be the last time we'd ever see him alive?"

"Monica know yet?" I asked.

"Left a message on her machine. Nobody home. What a thing to come home to. Maybe you better go by there in the morning."

"Maybe you better go by. She'd take it better if it came from you."

"You think so?"

"I know so. She's always leaned on you more than me. She and I haven't been close for a long time."

"She tell you that?" he asked.

"What?"

"That she leans on me..."

"You're the only one that doesn't get it, Leo. Stop trying to camp out at arm's length from the woman. She's going to need you."

The idea that I might burn in hell for what I was doing crossed my mind. Deflecting Leo with concerns about Monica. Playing on his feelings. But I was just doing what I had to do. I needed some time, and I needed some space to work things out. Besides, what I had told him was true, even if Monica didn't know it yet. He'd be good for her. And I wouldn't hate him for it. At least I didn't think that I would.

"Monica was his lawyer," I continued. "She'll know what he wanted."

"Yeah, you're right."

"You going to see her?" I asked.

"Sure," he replied, "somebody's got to. Might as well be me."

"Let us know what's going on," I said. "Call if I can help. Other than that, I think I'm going home and drink myself to sleep."

"Yeah, I might do that myself. You okay, Charlie?"

"No. He was my friend."

"I'll find whoever did this and put him behind bars for the rest of his life," said Leo.

"There is refuge, sometimes from the law. But there is no refuge from justice, whether in this life or the next."

There was nothing to add to what Charlie had said, but I hoped he was right.

By the time I got back to the lighthouse, it was nearly two o'clock in the morning. Charlie and I had some loose ends to take care of, like getting rid of the van. He had gone to Bob Alby's house on his motorbike. After the killings, he had loaded Bobby, Lance, and the bike in the van and driven them to my dock, where he had taken my boat to Soldier's Point. I liked the way he handled things, including torching Bob's house afterwards. Bob didn't have much in the way of relatives, and it was the best thing to do under the circumstances to obscure our involvement.

I asked him to come back with me, but he said no, that he had arrangements to make, and would come tomorrow. When I pointed out that somebody might be waiting for him at home, he said that he hoped so.

Point made.

Dr. Stouffer was pointing her Beretta at me when I opened the door.

"Hi honey," I said, "I'm home."

"You look terrible."

"You look dangerous. Put that thing down, will you? How's Bobby?"

"All things considered?" she asked.

"Yeah."

"He'll make it. Physically, he's okay. Mentally, he understands what occurred. Emotionally, it will be a long time before he can sort this out. The same applies to me. I can't understand anyone wanting to hurt your friend. He didn't do anything wrong, he was just watching Bobby.

"As a psychologist, I understand it doesn't have to make sense, but as a person, I'm still vulnerable to the same feelings that everyone else is, including Bobby. But how are you?"

"Me?"

"Yes, Mr. Brown," she said getting off of the couch. "How are you?"

"I don't know."

"Maybe that's not true," she said gently.

"Maybe it is."

"How do you feel?"

I thought it over.

"Well?"

"I think that I'd like you to shut the hell up and go to bed with me."

If looks could kill, hers would have dropped me in my tracks.

"You asked me how I felt, and I told you. I didn't say that I wanted to have sex with you. I would just like, for the first time in years, to wake up in the morning and have someone that I'm protecting lying next to me. Safe. Bobby too. Like a..."

"Like a what?" she asked. "Like a family?"

"I didn't say that."

"I know you didn't."

"But yeah, sort of like a family. A family that I knew I could protect. That trusted me, and I took care of them when they needed it. And in the morning, they would still be... safe."

She put her arm around my shoulder, and squeezed me gently.

"Come on," she said, "let's go lie down."

"All of those kids," I said, "and now Bob. And I—I just want to do something that makes it over now."

"Come on, time to rest."

"I don't want to rest."

"Then you can watch over me while I sleep."

"Bobby," I insisted, "I want him in the same room. You two can have the bed; I'll sleep on the floor in front of the door. All I need is a pillow."

"I don't want to scare him when he wakes up in the morning."

"I don't want anything to happen to him," I told her. "Please, just for tonight. We can all sleep in the room. In the morning, we can all laugh about it. Or something. Tomorrow I'll be okay. Promise."

"Come on," she said again. "We'd better get to bed before morning gets here first."

*****

When I opened the next morning, Bobby's face was two inches from mine.

"Hi," he said. "Why are you here?"

I almost went for my gun, but stopped myself.

"I live here," I said, after I remembered that I did.

"Oh," he said. "Do you have any cereal?"

"Yeah, tons of it. Now could you give me a little room so that I can get up?"

"What kind?"

"Uh...I got bran flakes."

"I don't like that kind. Do you have anything with sugar?"

"Sugar's bad for you, kid."

"You shouldn't frown, my mom says it will give you wrinkles."

"Bobby," came Dr. Stouffer's voice, "let the grumpy old man get off the floor."

"Do you have to go to the bathroom?"

"No. Yes. Maybe."

That's my business.

"Bobby..."

"Okay, mom."

I stood up slowly, painfully, the way I always seemed to be doing those days. Daylight. They were both still alive.

"It's all right," I told Bobby, "I'm just waking up, my brain's a little slow."

"Good morning," said Dr. Stouffer.

She sat cross-legged on the bed, wearing the same clothes that she had had on the night before.

"You know," I said, "you're a mess, but you look great."

"Told you he likes you," said Bobby to his mother.

"Let's get him some breakfast," she said to me, "before I have to stuff his mouth full of tissue paper."

"Can I see the rest of your house?" asked Bobby.

"Sure, kid."

"My name's Bobby," he said.

"Yeah, Bobby, I know."

"Your name is not Ed."

He smiled, like I'd learned a new trick.

Blue jeans, a new T-shirt that said "Rock the Planet", and a big smile. Same cowlick.

Downstairs, I straightened from beneath the cupboards and announced, "Good news, I've got Frosted Flakes."

"Yay," said Bobby.

"How old are those things?" asked Dr. Stouffer.

"How old? How am I supposed to know? I think they were here when I bought the place."

"The box isn't rusted," said Bobby.

"Cardboard doesn't rust," she said.

"It's a joke, mom."

"It doesn't say," I told her.

"Give me that box."

She marched over, her sandals flapping on the floor, making a noise like my third grade teacher rapping her fingernails impatiently on her desk.

"The expiration date," she scolded us, "was three years ago."

"That's the date it has to be sold by, mom."

"Yeah, mom, what he said."

"There're probably worms in this box," she said, holding her ear to its side while she shook it.

"Cool," said Bobby.

"I don't think that you can hear worms," I warned her. "They don't make any noise."

Ignoring us both, she put the box on the counter, opened it, and tipped it over slightly, checking for any little creatures that might be hiding inside.

"I don't see anything..."

"I'm hungry, mom."

"Worms are a good source of protein," I offered.

"Don't you have any other newer boxes?"

"I don't eat Frosted Flakes very often. I save them for special occasions."

She wagged her finger at us. "If you two get sick..."

"We'll puke," said Bobby.

We started laughing, and Bobby smiled.

The Frosted Flakes tasted like shit until Bobby explained to me that when they go stale, you've just got to pour more sugar on them.

After we'd eaten and I'd showered, I told her I had to go.

"Where to?" she asked.

"Charlie will be here any minute to keep an eye on the place while

I'm gone, and then I've got to go see Brother Thomas. After that, I'm going to visit the Hemlock family. But before I do anything, you and I have got to talk. Privately."

Bobby was still sitting in front of the computer, happily playing whatever the newest version was of Gears of War was. She glanced at him, then told me, "let's go stand in the kitchen next to the sink. He won't be able to hear us since he's busy destroying half of the universe."

Outside of the kitchen window, the morning was cooking along just fine. It was a boating day for the masses. The river would soon be littered with yuppies in sailboats, and the occasional idiot on a Sea-Doo, or whatever they called motorized skis. People would wander in from Detroit to fish down where they thought the river was cleaner.

Don't reel in Lance, I thought, he won't look so good.

Sometimes I wondered if anybody had jobs anymore. Monday morning and the sky was as clear and uncluttered as a 1950s prom queen's conscience. Yeah, they'd be out in droves. Workday or not.

"So, what is it you want to talk about?" she asked.

"I've got to ask you something first. Could this organic thing, this new plastic that can function as a processing device, could it learn by being implanted in a person's head? Don't look at me like that, I'm serious."

"Learn how?" she asked.

"By constant exposure to the brain's electromagnetic field."

"That's pretty far fetched. The brain doesn't generate much of an electromagnetic field."

"But what," I persisted, "if it was left in a child's head for years, while the child was developing. Couldn't that be a long enough time for changes to be absorbed?"

"You think that Allen Hemlock had Dr. Estes implant the polymer into a child's skull?"

"Maybe just under the scalp. That would explain a lot."

"That's fantastic."

"Well…"

"No, I mean, that's just plain ridiculous," she said.

"Think about it. If you were going try to transfer the patterns of the brain to this polymer by exposure, and it needed to be a child so that the developing patterns would be integrated into the polymer, what kind of a child would you choose? If you were that insane."

She chewed on her lower lip for a minute, and then her mouth dropped open.

"I'd choose a child with an extremely high intelligence quotient—a gifted child."

"Walk with me a little further, Kris. Let's suppose that someone found out what you had done, but didn't know which child it was. And that this someone only knew that it was one of the children that attended that conference. And that person thought that what you were doing was evil, and just happened to tell the head man of the Church of the New Apostles. Are you keeping up with me?"

I had her attention like I'd never had it before.

"Now, let's also suppose that Brother Thomas, the head guy, thought that this device was the Beast referred to in the Bible. If you grant me all of that, what do you think might happen?"

"The murders. Brother Thomas and his followers killing the gifted children that attended the conference, and Allen Hemlock trying to put a stop to it. How in the world did you figure this all out?"

A pair of pliers, a tube of Superglue, a bottle of acid, and somebody who knew what was going on tied to a chair, I thought. The rest was easy.

"Luck, mostly. But, even though the chances are that the organic strip or piece that was inserted into the kid's brain isn't too damn likely to work, the results would be the same. A witch hunt. Or a Beast hunt. What do you think?"

"It works for me," she said. "It frightens me, but it's a solid piece of inductive reasoning. Mycroft would be proud of you."

"Who?"

"Mycroft Holmes, Sherlock's older brother."

"Uh-huh."

"Sherlock did deductive reasoning, and Mycroft did—"

"Inductive reasoning," I finished for her. "I never knew that."

"See, having me here rounds out your education."

"I can see that."

"You've got a lot of rough edges that need to be rounded off, you know?"

"So I've been told. But now I'd like to go knock a few rough edges off of some other people, namely Brother Thomas and Allen Hemlock."

She placed the palm of her hand on my chest.

"They're dangerous people. If you're right, they might target you next."

"I just want to rattle them, Kris. That's all. Rattle the cages and watch what the animals do."

"Is this what you were talking with Allen about the other night?"

"Yes," I said, "in a way."

"But now you know why he is willing to back you. Do you still have to go? He doesn't want the Church of the New Apostles to find the child with the insert. And now we know why he doesn't want you to go to the police. So, why not turn the tables on him? Why not just turn the whole thing over to the police now? You could stop both groups without exposing yourself."

"Because," I said, "I thought about what you told me. You were right. The chances are that if I took what I know to the police, that I would probably be the one that goes to jail. Allen has probably been using his time and money to plant enough incriminating evidence on me I wouldn't have a chance to defend myself.

"You know about what I did before. Who's going to believe me, the man who gassed an entire town? Me against Allen Hemlock, who has probably got me set up as the murderer already. They'd hang me, Kris, as soon as they could get their hands on a rope. And if the courts didn't do it, the media would. I wouldn't stand a chance. I'm the perfect patsy, you were right. Hemlock's probably already had made up computer-altered photographs showing me trying to leave Los Angeles in a white Bronco.

"And Allen Hemlock and the Brothers Bad would be free to go on their merry way. No, going to the police would not only fry me, it wouldn't stop the killings or expose Allen. I've got to take everybody down."

"By yourself? You'll excuse me, but I think that you're outnumbered."

"No. With the help of my friends. I've got Charlie, you, Leroy unless I can help it, and an international team of people like me on their way here already. People that I know I can count on."

"Then why don't you wait? Wait until they get here before you go off on your own?"

I looked out the kitchen window again. I had been right earlier. The boaters were coming out in force. There ought to have been a law. Maybe there was, but no one paid attention to it.

"I'd like to wait," I said when I turned to face her again. "But time is short here, so I've got to use it. They went after Bobby, killed my friend, and don't forget what they did to Benny Franks. We've got to rattle the cages now, before the animals escape."

"Let me go with you."

I shook my head.

"No, not a chance. You're safer here."

"This isn't about me being safe. If you go and get yourself killed, who am I going to throw plates at? Besides, I know enough to help you. I'm not just a beautiful psychologist," she said, "I'm also the consultant that Allen Hemlock paid to contribute to this project. You need my input. I can help."

We argued a little while longer, but in the end I gave in, because it occurred to me she was right, although not only for the reasons that she was giving me.

I really did need her to be with me, when I thought about it, so that I could make sure that she was out of Hemlock's reach. If he put the big-time blackmail move on her, would she tell him what she knew about what I had learned?

In a perfect world, she would keep her mouth shut out of loyalty, and trust me to stand by her. But, as I had learned in Mexico, this isn't a perfect world.

The Beast

When Charlie arrived, I told him about the others. Gregorio would arrive tonight, Karl tomorrow morning, and Katerina, who had to come in via Chicago, would be in tomorrow afternoon. I asked Charlie about Korea. He told me that all was well. But even if it wasn't, I realized later, he wouldn't have said anything in front of Dr. Stouffer.

Bobby took to Charlie a little more slowly than his mother and I would have liked. The episode the night before had shaken him. Charlie was his savior the night before, but the bodies, the fire, and cruising across the river with a blanket over his head and a wounded, tied up bad guy as a traveling companion had left Bobby a little in awe of my Korean friend.

He stood fidgeting next to his mother for the longest time. When Charlie offered his hand, Bobby shook it, then yanked it back quickly with a nervous smile.

"You know, Bobby," I said, "last night must have been a little scary."

"I've never seen a real ninja before," Bobby admitted.

"Ninja?" asked Charlie, pretending to be offended. "Ninja are Japanese. I am Korean."

"Korean?"

"Yes, you know how to tell the difference?"

Bobby looked from his mother to me to his mother, then back

again.

"No."

"Koreans," said Charlie, smiling his big smile, "are much better looking."

"They are?"

"Yes. Much better looking."

"But if you aren't a ninja, what are you?" asked Bobby.

"Just a friend."

"Are you here to protect me?"

"Mostly," deadpanned Charlie, "I came here to play with someone my own size. Do you like video games?"

"Some of them."

"Me, too," confided Charlie with a wink. "I know where Mr. Brown here keeps the good ones."

"You do?"

"Come on, let's get rid of these tall people so that we can do some serious playing."

Dr. Stouffer and I took the cue, told them not to tear the place apart while we were gone, and left. Okay, so it didn't take that long for Bobby to take to him.

I called Brother Thomas' office from the car. Surprise, surprise, he was willing to see me, even though I didn't have an appointment. We took I-75 straight in to Downtown Detroit, past the refineries and chemical stacks belching their multicolored pollutants into an otherwise nice day. From a distance, the yellow brown clouds coming out of the one set of stacks might have looked particular striking had I not known that the gas that gave it the color of autumn leaves was a mixture of nitrogen dioxide and nitrogen tetroxide, lovely gases that are also class A oxidizing poisons.

Hydrogen sulfide, sulfur dioxide and a variety of other noxious gases hung over the Detroit skyline in a dirty pastel haze. Carbon monoxide was there as well, but it's the least offensive of the crap that's pumped out over city skies. At least it's invisible. You know enough about bad gases and you begin to understand Michael Jackson and his oxygen tent. Almost.

We exited on Gratiot, and followed it in to the burned out city proper. These days, under the new mayor, Detroit is making something of a comeback. I don't envy him the responsibility. You have to look hard sometimes to see the changes. But it's easy to notice the evidence of what a decade or two of carpet bagging and drug dealing has done to a city that was once the premier industrial center of the free world.

Even if I hadn't looked at the buildings, the litter alone was enough to make me sick. What I remember best about Toronto is that it's a clean city. In Detroit, you look at the streets and you think that the garbage truck had a hole in the back when it went by.

The Church of the New Apostles was on the corner of Cass and Gratiot. Formerly the First Presbyterian Church, it covered the entire block front. Half for the church, half for the parking lot. A shiny new cyclone type fence enclosed the entire parking lot with spiraled rows of gleaming sharp barbed wire along its top. A well-muscled security guard in a crisp blue uniform greeted us as we pulled into the entrance.

I rolled down the car window, and told him we were there to see Brother Thomas.

"Brother Thomas? That'd be on the seventh floor," he said.

"I've never been to a church before with seven stories."

"Not the church itself, sir, although it's tall enough, if you count the spires. I mean in the new Sunday School and Mission Training Building next to the church. You'll see the signs in the lobby, then you just take the elevator up and somebody will meet you and steer you the right way after you clear the metal detectors."

"Thanks," I told him.

As we pulled into our space, I said to Dr. Stouffer, "Did that guy look like Mike Tyson to you, or was it just me?"

"Just you," she replied, unbuckling her seat belt, "that guy didn't have a gold tooth."

"I wonder if you can clear the metal detectors with a gold tooth."

"Let's go," she said.

Both the old church and the new addition were faced with the same quarried stone blocks, which gave the effect of strength, age, and stability. I remember from the Bible the part where Jesus spoke about building on a solid foundation. For enough money, anyone can buy a solid foundation. If you're into literal translations, that is.

The inside of the new addition, however, was shiny and new. Shiny, crème colored linoleum, bright white walls, and doors with windows that were free of smudges and fingerprints. No smoking signs notified newcomers that smoking was not allowed in the temple of the Lord—or His offices.

On the way to the elevators, we passed an eight-foot long mural depicting the battle against the Beast. A victorious Jesus stood looking down at his fallen foe, and the armies of Light and Goodness were making short work of the wimpy powers of Darkness.

"What do you think of that?" I asked Dr. Stouffer, as we paused to glance it over.

"It certainly is impressive," she said. "It must have cost a fortune."

"Psychologically speaking, I mean."

She pursed her lips, folded her arms in front of her, and said, "Psychologically speaking…"

"Yes?"

"It must have cost a fortune."

"Send me a bill," I said, and grabbed her arm to usher her towards the elevators.

We got off on the seventh floor and said good-bye to linoleum, and hello to richly plush carpeting so white that I knew why there were shoe racks near the short red brick foyer when you stepped out. Fifteen or twenty pairs of shoes were hung on rubber tipped silver pegs.

"Full house today," I commented.

"Holy ground?" she asked the woman at the desk beside the airport style walk-through metal detector.

"No, honey, we just like to keep the carpet clean. Looks beautiful, doesn't it? I don't want to tell you how much it takes to keep it clean, though. Brother Thomas ordered it special from the factory in Georgia. All that logo on the floor up ahead. Now that, nobody walks on, just because the dye doesn't hold up well under foot traffic, shoes or no shoes."

I looked down the hallway and saw four posts set three feet apart to form the corners of a perfect square. Red velvet ropes connected them to protect the royal blue and gold insignia of a cross. After we cleared the metal detector and got closer to it, I saw that the quote from Ephesians that Brother Thomas had related over the dinner table the other night ran along the bottom of the insignia.

Over the cross were the words Warriors for Christ.

We followed the hallway to it's end, where an elderly woman who looked a lot like Dr. Stouffer's mother and sat behind a bigger desk than I have in the lighthouse greeted us.

"You're here to see Brother Thomas?"

The guard had called ahead.

"Yes, ma'am," I said.

"And your names?" she inquired.

"Scott Brown and Dr. Kris Stouffer."

"Please be seated. Brother Thomas will see you in just a minute. Would you care for something to drink?"

"Ma'am?"

"Coffee or tea perhaps?"

"No thanks," said Dr. Stouffer.

"I'm just fine, too. But thank you for asking."

We sat down in two fine and comfortable brown leather chairs while we waited. There were magazines on the table in front of us, but I preferred to look at Dr. Stouffer. She was wearing a blue business suit with a skirt that, unfortunately, was mid-calf length. The slit in the back that went a little higher up was on the wrong side for me to stare at. She had on a light pink blouse that was high collared and had a little dark blue bow where the collar came together. Her hair was up again, and she had on her glasses. She looked like a professional, sat like a professional, and ignored me like a professional by sitting there reading a religious publication.

Twenty minutes passed before the sweet old lady at the desk announced that she would show us into Brother Thomas' office.

"I do apologize for the wait. Brother Thomas is so busy these days. Especially for a man of his age. I don't know where he gets his energy."

"Clean living," I suggested.

Dr. Stouffer discreetly elbowed me, then walked on ahead to follow her. My foot had just crossed the door when I heard Brother Thomas' voice.

"Deborah, thank you for showing my young friends in. Can you please take these notes and type them for me?"

I saw him hand Deborah a flash drive, and then straighten the brown suit and tie that he was wearing. Old people are always straightening their clothes. Nothing seems to hang well on an eighty-year-old body.

"Well, well, Dr. Stouffer, it's so nice to see you again. Nice to see you too, Mr. Brown, but it's always my practice to greet the pretty ladies before the men. At my age, I can do that without fear of misinterpretation. You remember Brother James and Brother Peter, don't you? It's like a small reunion."

We said hellos all the way around. Brother James turned his big nose toward me and I wanted to reach out and honk it. Brother Peter smiled and came right over to shake my hand and hung on to it for a fraction too long, as though he were prepping for a trip to San Francisco. His skin had a waxy, feminine feel to it, and I finally had to pull back to break his grip. He smiled at my annoyance.

"You have a marvelous office, Brother Thomas," said Dr. Stouffer.

"Please, call me Thomas. And, yes, it's quite nice, isn't it? What do you think Mr. Brown?"

"I've seen smaller bowling alleys."

"What? Oh yes. Bowling, eh? Well, we have to have our staff meetings here. And the couches and chairs give an at-home feel to visitors. The bookshelves," he said, waving his hand at the rows and rows of books on dark wood shelves, "were the only thing that I insisted on."

"What's that?" I asked.

I pointed at a corner of the room near his desk that looked like a shrine. Black and white photos covered the walls where they came together. And on a stand in front of them, on a velvet cushion, lay something bright and shiny. Surprisingly, the old man's voice dropped a bit, losing some of its vitality, and became more serious when he answered.

"That," he said solemnly, "is my place of remembrance, dedicated to all of those around the world who have died in the terrors of the great wars."

"World War I and II?"

"Come," he said, "let me show you."

Brothers James and Peter hung back but stayed standing. Dr. Stouffer and I followed the old man's halting steps.

"My God," breathed Dr. Stouffer, "it's horrible."

"Quite," he said. "I keep this so that I will never forget, never feel too proud, never too vain. This lithograph here is about the Inquisition. You see the poor devil on the rack? Here the head of a Muslim on the pole of a Christian's spear. And the head of a Christian on a Muslim's spear. And this, this is a reproduction of a very famous photograph from near the end of World War II—you see the outline of the person on the melted concrete? The atomic blast at Hiroshima left us many such remembrances of the influence of the Beast in the world."

"How can you keep these photos here, in your office of all places?" asked Dr. Stouffer. "How can you stand to look at them every day?"

"Oh, Dr. Stouffer, I begin my every morning looking at them, and end the day by contemplating them again. This photo here has recently dominated my nightmares. You see, a young man who recently converted to our faith captured the image, and he brought it to me to purge his soul of its horrors. Who could imagine that an All-American football hero from Purdue would one day cut open the stomach of a pregnant Vietnamese woman and remove and butcher her unborn child? My, my. Do these photos bother you as well, Mr. Brown?"

"I can think of better things to look at."

"So can I," said Dr. Stouffer, turning away.

"The better things in life are everywhere to be seen, Mr. Brown. Our country is a very happy country. Ignorance is bliss, they say. Such an equation. Ignorance equals bliss. No wonder the world is in such trouble. Pretend that there is no evil, and it shall be so. Bring unto me the little children, said Jesus. Have you wondered why? It is because they see what they see. Both the good and the bad. They have not learned to rationalize like we adults."

On the velvet pillow that lay on the stand in the midst of his shrine was a dented aluminum cup. I hadn't wanted to ask, but I couldn't figure out what the hell it was there for, in the middle of all the displayed carnage. Finally, I couldn't take it anymore.

"What's with the cup?" I asked.

"Now there's a story to that," he said, "a very special story. It is the counterpoint to all of the terrors displayed on these walls. Would you mind terribly if I told you both about it, Dr. Stouffer?"

"Could we sit down first?"

"Of course. I'm afraid that I wouldn't last a minute in high heels. Here, sit down on the couch next to Mr. Brown. Brother James and Brother Peter, you've heard this story many times. Why don't you leave us, and I won't bore you again with it?"

Bowing dutifully, the devil and his consort left, closing the door behind us. I imagined that after we left, Brother James would be back to sniff the chairs. Meantime, somebody had to operate the hidden microphones.

"You don't much like Brother James, do you?" the old man said to me when we were all seated.

"Not especially," I replied.

"Well, there's quite a story behind the man. Never the same after Iraq. Never the same at all. Perhaps sometime I'll share the indelicate details with you. But I was going to tell you the story of the cup.

"Did the two of you know I was in World War II? Indeed I was. Every war has its casualties. I was almost one. I never went to college. There was no need after the war. What could any man teach me after what I had seen?

"I understand you are a big fan, Mr. Brown, of the music from The Good, the Bad, and the Ugly—the Clint Eastwood picture."

"Who told you that?"

"Miss Thomas. She seems to know quite a lot about you. Quite flattering, really. Anyway, it's true that you like the music?"

"Yeah," I said, "more than I like Miss Thomas."

"Oh, it's like that, is it? Well, she seems quite taken by you. Anyway, that music was the backdrop to a movie about the Civil War. The title, I think, has captured my imagination, as well as yours. I even gave a sermon once about the Good, the Bad, and the Ugly. Compelling—if I do say so myself. Really compelling. The content was easy to construct; I just drew on my experiences from the Second World War.

"Every element of education and learning could be found in that war. Honor, dignity, treachery, malice, to name just a few. Good, evil, and beyond. I saw the fruits of science and technology there, such as they were at the time, and the uses to which they were put by an enlightened humanity.

"I was even both privileged and disgraced to see mustard gas in action. Most associate it only with the first war, but the bad things sometimes come back at us like an encore." He shook his head. "Imagine. A lethal gas named after a hamburger condiment. My, My."

"About the cup…" I prodded.

"Forgive me, please, I tend to ramble. The privilege of age, I suppose, but an annoying trait to the younger people sometimes.

"At any rate, the cup that you see here was my own. I was a soldier. It was my water cup, but there was a day when I had no water, when I was alone, separated from my fellows, wounded—that's why I limp, you see—and dying of thirst. In the middle of a raging war, it was the last thing that I would ever have expected to die from. A hail of bullets, perhaps, a grenade, an unfortunate step onto a landmine, or even impaled on the end of a bayonet blade… that's what I would have predicted. But to die of thirst… no way at all for a soldier to die.

"But I was dying. A man can go without food for some time, as you are no doubt aware, if he has water, but without water, we go quickly. And it must be good water. Good drinking water in times of war can be something of a problem. With so much death and dying, there is always disease."

Up to this point, Brother Thomas had done most of the talking, and we just let him lead on. The implicit idea was that the more we knew about the way his mind worked, the better off we were.

He had a corner office with two big windows, both of which had their drapes closed. It could have been because daylight hurt his eyes like it did other vampires and ghouls, but I doubted it.

On the other hand, I thought, there was no sense looking at Detroit if you didn't have to.

"You get the idea, I think," continued the old man. "I was dying. I was an American dying in France, and not of dying of a broken heart like in a poem. There is no romance in death—none at all.

"I was not a Christian then. War, it is said, makes believers of us all. But it had not yet happened to me. Fear and hatred did not bring me to God. I was a Methodist on paper, but in my heart I was an unbeliever. I had never seen God, don't you know? Such a trivial, meaningless thing to keep a man separated from his Creator.

"That is why in the Bible, when God opened Adam and Eve's eyes that the Fall ensued. Because we could see everything except God. Until that time, we could, I believe, actually see the Almighty much as we now see the rest of the world. We could see the angels, and the devils, too. After the Fall, we could see only the material world. We could see, and therefore we were blind. Now there is poetic justice for you.

"But I digress. I could not see God, therefore I did not believe. I was dying, and still I would not believe. It took a German soldier to open my true eyes, to show me the reality of good and evil, God and the devils. It was this German soldier who saved my life, who gave me water, when by all rights he should have killed me.

"His name was Franz Mueller. I will remember him until the day I die. He looked a little like you, Mr. Brown. Tall, rugged looking, square features like yours. You have light blonde hair, however. If you were in Germany during the war, I suppose that you would have qualified for the SS.

"Franz made the mistake of having black hair, and one eye, unfortunately, that was lower than the other by perhaps a quarter of an inch. It was a genetic anomaly that he paid for by being put in the front lines. The German Blood, you understand, could not be contaminated by those such as he. God forbid he should marry and reproduce to the disgrace of all The Fatherland.

"He, too, was separated from his troops. Wandering. Alone. Afraid. A man alone with his thoughts can be a dangerous thing. Franz had had much time to think. He was a remarkable man, a man of depth and insight, and a sensitive soul at heart. The war was a black thing to him, and he struggled with what had led his country to such depravity.

"Was it Adolph Hitler? Was it the ideals of the Nazi Party? What had turned his people in to animals?

"Franz's father had been a minister, like my own father was, and he began to wrestle with his angst from a different perspective. For the first time in his life, wandering in the desert of war, he began to truly remember and think on the Bible, and the Book of Revelations in particular. And he came, in time, to the conclusion that his country had been brought under the influence of dark powers, of the spirit of the Biblical Beast.

"His revelation was that there was only one enemy of all men, and it was not their fellow man—it was the spirit of the Beast. The spirit of the Beast that was responsible for the enslavement of his people to an evil cause. Adolph Hitler was a powerful and persuasive man, but do either of you think it was his words alone that changed the soul of a nation sufficiently to bring the vileness of Nazism into their hearts?

"Can a man like Heinrich Himmler, the man responsible, more than anyone else, for the SS and the death camps, can he be explained by any rational means? Did he suffer an impoverished upbringing? Did he not suckle long enough at his mother's breast? Was he abused sexually? Was his self-esteem too low? Are there are any true answers to such questions within the normal ken of human experience?"

"So he gave you a cup of water and saved your life?" I put in. "That's pretty much the story?"

Brother Thomas shook his head, and Dr. Stouffer, bless her pretty face, frowned at me. I couldn't help it, though; the guy was putting me to sleep.

"Yes, I suppose you're right. He gave me water, saved my life at the risk of his own, demanding only that I swear my life to the battle against the powers of darkness so that good could ultimately triumph. I forget that the television generation likes so very much stories that are quick, simple, and to the point. You require sound effects, music, high drama, and above all, action, action, action."

Dr. Stouffer jumped in to save the day.

"Please tell us more, Brother Thomas. My attention span is a little longer than Mr. Brown's, and I do find what you're telling us to be compelling."

"I'm a little harder to compel, I guess," I said.

"You're sure that you don't mind?" asked the old man.

"Knock yourself out."

"The equivalent of 'break a leg,' I hope."

"You've got it."

"Where was I?"

"Franz gave you water, and you joined the cause."

"Thank you. You have a gift for simplicity. Anyway, to continue, A German soldier, of all things, saved my life. The very enemy that I had sworn to destroy saved me.

"Most people believe, Dr. Stouffer, that I founded the Church of the New Apostles, but it was in fact Franz Mueller who was its founder. Franz's gift was the power of his insight; mine the power of organization. He was my mentor, I his student. He saved my life by pouring water from his canteen into my cup. He saved my soul by commissioning me as a warrior for Christ.

"So, you see, that cup symbolizes to me that we can all be saved, that we can all be commissioned as warriors for Christ. I believe we must not be deceived into thinking that when a war is over that the war is over.

"The Bible teaches us that we are at war always until Jesus Christ returns and claims his victory over the Beast. It is our calling, our duty if you will, to recognize the true enemy of mankind and fight against him each and every day. There will be casualties, as in any war, and there will be sacrifices. Innocent people will die alongside the not so innocent, but such is the nature of war, as I have seen for myself.

"But even in the most depraved of battles, there can be one soldier, one warrior, who offers the gift of life and salvation to another. That is what that cup is there to remind me of. In the midst of horror, there can be redemption."

"What a fascinating and revealing story, Brother Thomas," said Dr. Stouffer. "Tell me, whatever happened to Franz Mueller?"

"He died seven or eight years ago, doctor. A terrible, terrible loss to the world. His heart. He was not in the best of health anyway, and he came across a news story in the paper one day that caused him great distress."

"A story killed him?" I couldn't believe it.

"Yes, Mr. Brown, a story. Not just any story, you understand."

"What was it about?" asked Dr. Stouffer.

Brother Thomas seemed a little uncomfortable, and squirmed around in the chair, as though his underwear had slipped up the crack in his ass, and he was trying to dislodge it. Finally, when he had quit fidgeting, he continued.

"You are familiar with the phrase the Abomination of Desolation?"

"No," she said.

"The sacrilege in the reconstructed temple in Jerusalem," I said.

"Very good," said Brother Thomas with a curt nod in my direction. "Franz had read a story about plans by the Israelis to rebuild the temple, and to include in that temple the most powerful computer in the entire world. A computer that would link the temple to the ends of the earth to link all of God's people together. The electronic antidote to the Diaspora—the forced exile of God's people from their homeland, Dr. Stouffer."

"Why," Dr. Stouffer pressed, "would that cause him to have such a violent reaction?"

"Because he had a vision. A vision that this supercomputer, with all of its power, was to become a tool of the Beast. Perhaps the tool of the Beast, whereby this monster could attempt to control the world.

"You look unconvinced, Mr. Brown," the old man said with a frown.

"Well, if he died after reading this story," I asked, "how in the hell do you know what his vision was all about?"

"Because I was standing by his side when it happened. He made me swear, before he died, that I would do everything in my power, make any sacrifices necessary to prevent that great evil from occurring."

"And you bought his story, that this was actually a vision from God?" I asked.

"Oh, yes, I did," he leaned forward with such a look of dark intensity that I was reminded of Roger Chillingworth, the villain from the Scarlet Letter, "and I would do anything, anything in my power to prevent that from happening.

"But enough of my past," he said with a sigh, "what is it I can help you with here in the present?"

"The day after tomorrow," I said, winging it as I went, "I'm going to hold a press conference to announce what I've learned about the unfortunate murders that I told you about and their linkages, in the hope that a public outcry will galvanize the world's police organizations to action. I was wondering if you would like an opportunity to condemn these murders to the media at the time. To lend the moral force of your office to the cause, if you will."

A minute passed, maybe two before he said, "I should very much like to think about that Mr. Brown, and discuss it with my Council. Can I call you tomorrow with an answer?"

"I knew I could count on you," I said, standing up after looking at my watch. "Got to go now, though, we've got a meeting with the local FBI office now."

"Yes," said Brother Thomas, "I'm sure you do."

Christine Hemlock

"What in the world was that all about?" asked Dr. Stouffer as we peeled shoe leather out of the parking lot. "What appointment with the FBI?"

"I was making it up as we went along," I said. "I was beginning to think that we wouldn't make it out at all if we didn't have somewhere else to go where we'd be missed and the alarm bells would go off if we didn't show up."

"That was your escape plan? To make it up as you went along?"

I took my hand off of the wheel and, seeing a like blink on my dashboard, pulled over to the side of the road. Leaning over, I punched in a code into the in-dash computer. On the screen the words:

Security system violated:

Emitting device detected

Foreign power device detected

flashed in bright green letters.

"Get out," I screamed.

We were half a block away when the Reatta exploded into a bright orange-red fireball, spewing hot metal projectiles into the air and clouds of dark, billowing smoke. The noise was so loud that cars two blocks away screeched to a halt, and the few pedestrians reacted by stopping in their tracks and covering their face with their hands instinctively.

Dr. Stouffer was immobilized by the spectacle of it, by the realization that if we had been in the car, we would be dead now.

"Keep walking," I yelled.

"Where?"

"Follow me."

"Where are we going?"

"Anywhere but here—just follow me."

We left behind a gathering of gawkers, the sounds of sirens in the distance, and the beginnings of a major traffic jam. I led her in one side of a parking garage and out the other, entering the sidewalk again at a casual walk. Nothing stands out more than a white man and woman running away down a sidewalk in downtown Detroit. It's a reverse stereotype, but I wasn't about to be picked up by the cops for it. We could sort out the racial harmony considerations later.

In front of the huge McNamara Building, I gave some thought to disappearing into the Government Bookstore inside, but remembered that the FBI and Bureau of Alcohol, Firearms and Tobacco were located inside. They had metal detectors there. I had retrieved my gun when I got back to the now vaporized car, and though it was tucked safely underneath my jacket, I didn't want to be explaining its presence to Federal Officers after the electronics picked up the metal.

Two blocks, later of Detroit city walking, we were in front of the Hotel Plaza Ponchatrain Building without having been mugged. Not wanting to press our luck, we went inside.

"What now?" asked the doctor.

"Don't sweat it," I said, "we're going to go into the cafeteria to have some coffee."

"We're what?"

"Act natural. Just keep on walking. That's the trick."

"But—"

I pulled her arm gently.

"We're alive and well, that's all that counts. Don't sweat the small stuff. They fired a round, but they missed. Come on, let's stand in line with the rest of the good citizens."

She played the part well enough for someone who had never been near a car bomb explosion before. One of her legs was shaking, and she wasn't even aware of it. If she didn't pass out, I figured that we'd be okay.

We got two cups of coffee, and a slice of banana cream pie for me, paid the cashier, and then found a table away from the rest of the people. We were lucky; it wasn't the lunch hour crowd yet.

"How can you act so...so... so unaffected?" she asked.

On a scale of one to ten on the bewilderment scale, with one being normal and ten being a nervous wreck, she was about a six. Not bad for a first timer. I swallowed a piece of pie and washed it down with coffee before I answered her.

"Because I'm alive. We're lucky, Kris. We walked away from something that we shouldn't, so I can handle it. You're not doing so badly yourself. The only thing that I'm really upset about is that I loved that damn car. Buick only made them for three years. You know how hard it will be to find another one in good condition?"

"Who cares about your automobile? We could have been killed."

"Yeah," I said, "now we know what comes sneaking out when we rattle Brother Thomas' cage—a bomb. Maybe C-4 or something else."

"See for what?"

"C-4. It's a plastic explosive. But keep your voice down. There's no one close by, but sound does carry."

"You're crazy, Scott Brown," she said. "I'm a psychologist, and I know what I'm talking about."

"Brother Thomas is crazier. What did you think of that bullshit that he laid on us?"

"I think that he should be put in a cell right alongside of you."

Sarcasm. That was good.

"You can't put two predators of different species in the same cell."

"Different species?"

"Yeah. I'm human. I don't know what the hell that he is. Lousy coffee, isn't it?"

She looked at me and her eyes widened.

"You're trying to deflect me. To take my mind off of it."

"It's my job," I said.

"I can handle this, you know."

"Never doubted it."

"I've just never been almost blown to pieces before."

"Yeah. So, what is your professional opinion of Brother Thomas?"

"Shouldn't we be getting out of here? Doing something?"

"No. I haven't finished my pie yet. What did you think of him? You did come along to help, didn't you? To give me the benefit of your professional input..."

While I forked another piece of pie and stuffed it into my mouth, she glared at me. When I didn't pay attention, her lips tightened, and then relaxed as she thought of what to say.

"He has," she said at last, "an obsessive personality."

"I'd say so, but is he acting the part, or is he genuinely off the deep end?"

"He's long past acting, hon." She said the word "hon" as if she had just bit into a lemon. "Most of what he was saying was from his stock and trade—he didn't have to think of what to say, he was just regurgitating. But his eyes, the way he fixed his eyes on you, that was scary.

"And I'll tell you something else," she said. "Did you notice the fact that he wasn't the least bit nervous about sending his associates away? That he didn't feel the least bit threatened by us?"

"It registered. He figured we wouldn't be coming back. He didn't buy the bit about the FBI, of course. I think he got a kick out of it. But the message got across."

"So what do we do now? I'm calmer."

"Nothing like a little run followed by a couple of block stroll to calm the nerves, is there? What we do now is, I finish this pie, and then we go catch a cab to Dearborn. We go to the bus station at Telegraph Rd. and Michigan Avenue, and we take the bus to Trenton. From there, we catch another cab back to Gibraltar and pick up your Jeep. Then we go visit one of the Hemlocks."

"Which one?" she asked.

"Haven't made up my mind yet," I said.

It's the little things that can trip you up, but I pay attention to those details. You can't just leave a burning car on a main street of

Detroit and expect that you won't have to be interrogated by the police as to what the hell is going on unless you've planned in advance. It never occurred to Dr. Stouffer, though.

The police would have taken us into separate rooms and gotten our stories. Why were we in Detroit? Where had we been? Whom had we seen? Did anyone have a reason to try and kill us? Did we like our burgers with or without cheese? Little details like that.

And the press would have gotten involved. After hours in the police station, there would be the inevitable reporters. We would have made the news, been stalked by microphones. None of which we had time for, and I couldn't afford the notoriety, anyway.

Lucky for me, I didn't own the Reatta.

It was owned by an offshore company, which was owned by another offshore company, which in turn was owned by another, and so on and so forth. Same as the lighthouse.

In the end, of course, I owned the entire shell game, but my accountability was way down. If either the police or the press tracked me down as the owner of the Reatta before the second millennium, I'd be real, real surprised.

"Where to?" asked Dr. Stouffer.

"John Hemlock's."

"Shouldn't we call ahead so he'll know to expect us?"

"We did that once today, and look what happened."

"Good point," she said.

*****

After retrieving her Jeep, she drove, which was a relief for me. Her Jeep was a stick shift. Personally, I see no reason for anyone to drive a damn stick shift. I've listened to all the crap about fuel efficiency but there's nothing to it. Then again, it may just be that I didn't like them because it took two arms to drive the damn things.

Angel opened the door and asked us if Mr. Hemlock was expecting us. Someday I will drag a dead body to the door and see if she shows any emotion.

"No," I said, "we were just in the neighborhood."

"Mr. Hemlock is out just now," she told us.

"Will he be gone long?" asked Dr. Stouffer.

"He did not say."

Christine Hemlock called out from somewhere inside, "Who's there, Angel?"

"Mr. Brown and Dr. Stouffer, ma'am, to see Mr. Hemlock."

"Well, show them in. They can wait, if they like. He won't be away long."

"Would you like to come in?"

"Yes, thank you, Angel," I said. "We don't mind waiting at all, do we Dr. Stouffer?"

Dr. Stouffer shook her head no, and then followed me inside.

It took me a few takes to peg the woman who met us in the foyer as Christine Hemlock. The electric pink lipstick and the frizzed hair confused me, but what really set me back were the tighter than snug shorts, the half open, barely decent halter top, and her come-hither stance. She was definitely "open for business."

"Well, hello, Mr. Brown," she said. "You can go back to your chores, Angel, I think I can handle Mr. Brown all by myself. John isn't here right now, Mr. Brown, but I can keep you entertained until he comes back. That is, if you don't mind."

Angel said, "Yes, Mrs. Hemlock," and disappeared where to wherever it is that servants go to do whatever it is that servants do when their mistress turns embarrassing.

I wanted to look at Dr. Stouffer to check her reaction to Christine Hemlock's Marilyn Monroe imitation, but I couldn't take my eyes off of the temptress in the tight shorts. Despite the fact that the last two times that I had seen her, she had looked like Suzy Sweetness, there was no denying that she looked damned good in her new role as Suzy Sex Goddess.

For a brief moment, I wanted to ask Dr. Stouffer to go outside and play in traffic while Christine and I stayed inside and played hide the salami. This was an entirely new Christine, and I found her equally as believable as I had the earlier version. It was as though she were an actress playing each part with believable conviction.

Dr. Stouffer cleared her throat. "Well, Christine, thank you for inviting us in. Where shall we wait? Would you like to show us to John's office?"

"You can wait in that stuffy old office if you'd like, honey. I'd like to give Mr. Brown the grand tour of my home. I'm planning on redecorating a few choice rooms, and I'd like to ask a man's opinion. Won't you help me, Mr. Brown?"

"Uh, sure, if that's okay with you, Dr. Stouffer?" I said.

To my surprise, she nodded in the affirmative. She looked almost sorry for me.

"Then let's go, sugar," Christine said, grabbing my arm and leading me toward the stairs leading upstairs. "You know your way to the study, don't you, Dr. Stouffer? There's things that might interest you in there, especially some of those big, fat, stuffy, moldy old books."

"Why thank you Christine," said Dr. Stouffer, giving a curt nod of her head. "That's very thoughtful of you. You two take your time, I'll look after myself."

Tension.

Angel was, at that point, at the top of the stairs, walking down. Christine led me up, hugging close by my side, and if Angel thought that there was something peculiar about her employer looking like a strumpet and the fact that we were heading up the stairs and toward the bedrooms, she never said a word about it as she passed us.

Dr. Stouffer was showing herself to John's study, and by the time that Christine and I reached the top of the stairs, I was certain that she had seen this side of Christine before. She must have been counseling the entire damn family.

"I like the stairs," Christine was saying, "because they keep my thigh muscles firm. A girl should have firm thigh muscles, don't you think, Mr. Brown?"

"You can call me, Scott."

"I think I should call you Mr. Brown, because you're old enough to be my daddy."

"Wow," I said.

"How do you like my house so far?" she asked.

"It's a nice place," I said.

She put her arm around my waist and squeezed.

"You haven't seen the best parts yet. There are so many rooms. Just me and all of these rooms. It gets very lonely."

It was like being in a hotel. Long, carpeted hallway at the top of the stairs. Door after door down the hall, closed and unidentified. Lights concealed beneath elaborate molding that ran along the walls a foot or so down from the ceiling to light the hallway, which, with the doors closed, would have been dark without their soft, white glow.

"Lot of rooms," I agreed.

"Lots," she repeated. "We've got secret rooms. Play rooms. Very fun. Lots of rooms. Lots of secrets."

"I like secrets, Christine."

She stopped, and brought herself in front of me, her one arm still around my waist. The top of her head came up only to my chest, but she pressed in close and leaned her face up. As she did so, I felt the palm of her other hand flatten against my crotch, rubbing softly.

"You're a naughty man, aren't you, daddy?"

"Yes, I am Christine."

"I can be a good girl, but sometimes you have to punish me."

Okay, so this was across the line, and if I didn't have an erection, I would have said that I was just doing my job, trying to find more dirt on the Hemlocks. But this young woman wasn't teasing, or playing at being the temptress. She was the temptress. Up close as we were, I could smell her perfume, a faint lingering scent that blended with the heat of her body to make a heady, female odor. Her skin was smooth perfection and there was a bright flush in her cheeks. She looked up expectantly directly into my eyes, wanting my approval, needing to be reinforced.

"But you try to be good, don't you?" I asked.

"Oh, I do, daddy, I do."

"Then you'd better show me a secret place, because you need a spanking."

"But I try to be good," she pleaded.

"Then show me quick."

"I can be real quick, daddy," she promised, "like a bunny."

She moved ahead, pulling me by the arm.

"Hurry, daddy."

Daddy was hurrying.

Daddy was about to see the other side of John Hemlock.

It was a room connected to the main bedroom through the closet. There was no door to the outside; that would have been bad. Someone might have wondered someday what was behind the door. It might have been accidentally left unlocked. And that would have been very bad.

Twenty feet by twenty feet of mirrored walls, leather straps, clamps, and audio/video equipment. Two beds a foot apart in the center of the room for the couple that craved double the fun, double the action. A trapeze over one of the beds.

Really.

A mirrored disco ball over the other with colored lights aimed at it from various points in the room. Speakers and an overpowering stereo. A cabinet full of lotions, oils, and powders.

A big screen television and VCR was mounted at an angle from the ceiling between the feet of the beds, so that whoever was looking up from the mattresses could watch whatever show was playing.

A desk, a chair, and two file cabinets. Pictures were fanned out across the desk.

I walked over to the desk, ignoring Christine, and looked at the pictures. There were six in all. Christine in braids and a little girl's frilly white dress, kneeling before a man, her hands tied behind her back, giving him head. Christine naked, stretched over a man's lap on the bed, him shoving something where it shouldn't go. He had a hairy stomach and arms. His head was bent over so that I could see only the top of his head, but the tip of his nose was sticking out.

I knew that nose.

Brother James.

He really was a dickweed.

I scooped all of the photos up, and put them in my inside coat pocket. There would be time to look at them later, right then I wanted to explore inside the file cabinet.

"Daddy, I'm ready."

I shouldn't have turned my back on her.

Sometimes you feel the movement before you see it. I slid to my right and turned as I did. That pivot saved my life.

I saw metal, hard, pointed, and shiny, flash past where my back would have been. The tip of the knife made a solid, final sound as it sunk a good quarter of an inch into the desktop. I snapped my forearm into the side of her neck, stepping into her with enough weight that it shut off the blood flow from her carotid artery to her brain, and she fell over onto the desk before she rolled unconscious to the floor.

Like husband, like wife. Let them get their hands on something sharp and they immediately want to stick it into somebody.

I was getting tired of the whole family.

The files were locked.

A key was taped to the bottom of one of the desk drawers. It fit both file cabinets easily enough, but only opened one. I rifled all four drawers, selected three files that I shoved under my shirt, and then tucked my shirt back into my pants, and left the way that we had come in.

The best that I could tell, the psycho in the halter-top was still breathing when I left.

I passed Angel in the vestibule. She ignored me as usual when I went to retrieve Dr. Stouffer, but when we were going out the door I heard her say softly "Vaya con Diaz."

"Where to now?" asked Dr. Stouffer when we came to the first intersection.

"Home."

"So, how was your tour of the house?"

"Fuck you, doctor."

"Excuse me?"

She slammed on the brakes. I didn't have my seatbelt on, and slammed forward into the dashboard. If we would have been going any faster, my head would have broken the windshield.

"What the hell is wrong with you?" I yelled.

"Me? You're the one who waltzed off with Mrs. Hemlock to visit the bedrooms."

"You could have broken my neck with that stunt."

"Next time, wear your seatbelt."

I reached over and grabbed the back of her hair before she realized it had happened, and yanked her head back against the headrest. She tried to backhand me, but I slid behind her arm and leaned into it.

"You lied to me, doctor," I shouted, my mouth an inch from her ear.

"Let go of me," she screamed.

"Why?"

"Because—"

"Why did you lie?"

"Let go of me, you son of a bitch."

"I ought to let them have you. You deserve it. When did you call? You were gone a few minutes to get your car while I was in the bathroom back at the marina. Is that when you did it?"

"Did what?"

"Called," I yelled into her ear.

I hoped it ruptured her eardrum.

"I don't know what you're talking about."

I released her hair and moved back into my seat.

"Drive," I ordered.

"I didn't tell him anything."

"Drive."

"I only said that we were going to come over."

"Put the car into gear and drive the goddam car."

"You're not my husband."

"I know that, lady. I'm still alive."

If looks could kill, the rage on her face could have sent me straight to the morgue. She tried to backhand me again, but I blocked with the edge of my forearm, and then whipped my hand over, twisting the palm at her face as I slapped her hard enough on the cheek that her eyelids fluttered and she almost blacked out.

"Had enough?"

She started to cry.

It didn't bother me at first; I was still too mad.

Then she brought her arm back, and collapsed forward onto the steering wheel, bawling her eyes out, sobbing.

"Could you please stop that?"

"You're a bastard," she said, and began to shake.

I couldn't take it anymore and leaned over to her.

"Hey, come on," I said.

She swung her elbow into my face before I even saw it coming, but I heard the crunch as my nose broke, felt the warm spurt of blood through my nostrils and blacked out before I could say "ouch".

*****

* * *

"Mr. Brown," said Dr. Shakapura, "you must be more careful. I have so many patients, and so little time. Next week I will be on vacation. Perhaps you should stay indoors where it is safe until I return."

The rotten little bastard was smiling when he said it.

"I am serious, sir. Your health is my responsibility. I am concerned about your balance. You seem always to be falling and hurting yourself. Did you hear a ringing in your ears before you fall?"

I was sitting up on his examining table, gritting my teeth.

"No."

"Did you perhaps feel dizzy?"

"No."

"Come, come. I cannot help you unless you tell me the complete truth. I feel that there is something that you are not telling me. What happens before you fall? Is there anything that is common to both incidents?"

"Yes."

His face lit up.

"And what would that be, sir?"

I motioned him forward with a crooked finger. When his face was even with mine I said, "Same damn woman, both times."

The Endtimes

Two strips of adhesive tape held the gauze bandage over my nose in place. I had to breathe through my mouth. I didn't feel like talking.

"I said I was sorry," she repeated as she pulled into the marina parking lot.

"I heard you the first time."

"I know you heard me, but you haven't admitted it was your fault."

"My fault?" I said. She was driving me crazy. "My fault? You bust my nose and it's my fault? The doctor thinks I'm a complete klutz. Says that he is going to need an additional nurse just to look after me. He told me I should stay indoors while it's safe next week while he's on vacation. I should have broken his nose. And what are you laughing at?"

"Nothing."

"Good."

"You just sound so funny with that thing on your nose."

"Well, you put it there."

"I'm sorry. I told you I'm sorry."

"You know, since I met you, I've got stitches in my balls, and stitches in my nose. What's it going to be tomorrow? Is my tongue going to have to be sewn back into my mouth?"

"Not," she said with a smile, "if you watch what you say."

I shook my head. She was unbelievable.

"Come here," she said, "let me fix your bandage."

"Uh-uh."

"Don't be a sissy. Come here."

"You're not going to smack me again, are you? Okay, okay, I was just asking."

When I leaned over, she put her hand on the side of my head, pulled me forward a little further, and kissed me quickly on the lips before she let go.

"I thought you were going to fix my bandages."

"I lied. Are you complaining?"

"All these stitches, and that's all I get?"

"You are a sissy," she said, but she kissed me again anyway.

We were halfway across the river when I noticed the motorized water sled coming straight for us. Sometimes you get the feeling that something's not right. There was nothing I could identify as a problem. It took two hands for the rider to maneuver the thing; which wasn't an ideal way to move in for the kill. What could he do, run us over?

Three sailboats, and a few motorized water sleds ring dinging along, scaring the fish away from the two boats half a mile away or so. And the kamikaze coming straight at us.

The afternoon was clear, and Dr. Stouffer was steering. My first instinct was to pull out my gun and shoot him before he got too close.

"Jam the throttle," I said, "we've got company coming."

She turned around to look at me, saw the water sled, and shoved the throttle to the full tilt position. The twin Mercs kicked into overdrive with an angry roar and we started making tracks across the water.

The water sled veered to intercept us. I keep a few handy things aboard the boat in a small chest. Flare gun, medical supplies, night vision goggles, Beretta with a silencer, a grappling hook with fifty feet of cable. The usual. Nothing that felt right for what I needed then.

The first burst blew out the windshield. The second stitched a pattern of holes in the side of the bow. I could see the flashes from the front of the water sled, but couldn't hear the silenced shot over the sound of the engines.

Dr. Stouffer crouched down in her seat so low that her head was barely high enough to see over the top of our boat. I did the same, dropping to my knees and scrambling to undo the latches on the chest. It was either the Beretta or the flare gun. I opted for the flare gun.

We were closing in on the shore, aiming right for the docks.

"Swing to the left," I yelled. "Aim for that patch of ground by the big tree, and don't slow down."

I loaded the flare pistol and snapped the barrel back into place.

"Don't slow down?" she asked.

"You heard me. Don't slow down until we're on dry land."

"You're crazy."

He was still coming straight at us.

I fired the flare gun at the same time as he pulled the trigger and another burst ripped into one side of the boat and out the other directly between Dr. Stouffer and me. If I'd been sitting another foot forward, the bullets would have taken out my legs.

The flare hit him square in the head, knocking him back and off of the sled. His leg was caught somehow, and he dragged behind it, his head burning like a torch. The water sled tipped to one side as he fell off, continued skimming the water for a few seconds, and then sank out of sight, taking him with it.

Dr. Stouffer had been looking back at that moment and, when she saw what happened, she yelled excitedly, "You got him."

"Now who's a sissy?" I asked.

"What?" she asked. "I can't hear you over this—"

"Jump," I screamed.

She turned in time to see the shore rushing at us and leaped out almost as fast as I did. We both hit the water as the boat hit the shore and skipped like a skimming stone up from the surface of the water and into the air. I was underwater when the boat splintered into pieces against the tree.

*****

"Nice driving," said Charlie with a smile when I came downstairs after a shower and putting on dry clothes.

"She was behind the wheel," I told him again.

"We saw it all upstairs from the lighthouse cage. Nice escape. Fancy shooting, too. "

"Okay, Charlie, I got the message."

"What message?" he asked innocently.

"That life isn't like the dojo. I've got to watch more carefully."

"In the dojo, we have but one purpose—to study combat. In life, it is easy to get caught in the crossfire of many different purposes. In the dojo, it is usually one on one. In life, it is not that way. Some are good distractions, some are not, but they are all distractions."

The phone rang and saved me from having more oriental wisdom pounded into my head.

*****

It was Gregorio. The Latin connection had arrived. I told him we would be right over to pick him up, and then added, "And Gregorio. Keep your eyes open. The bad guys are out in force."

When I had hung up the phone, I asked Charlie if he would take the remaining boat and pick Gregorio up.

He had been gone about ten minutes when Dr. Stouffer came down the stairs wearing leather sandals, khaki colored shorts, and a sleeveless white blouse. Her legs, I noticed, were nice looking, especially when I got to see them coming down the stairs first.

"Where's Bobby?" I asked.

"In bed," she replied.

"In bed?"

"He was pretty wound up. The last two days have not exactly been normal for him. We led a peaceful life until I met you."

"Believe it or not, my life in the past when I'm back in Michigan has been peaceful, too. This is the first time that I've been through something this action-packed on my home turf."

We had walked over to the couch and sat down, closer to each other than we normally did.

"So, what do you do most of the time when you're here?"

"Pardon?"

"When you're home and not in some other country playing Mr. Fixit."

"Oh. Usually I just, I don't know, work out, keep the place in order, play with the computers, clean the lighthouse windows, or pine away for the perfect woman psychologist to drop into my life."

"I doubt that..."

"Ask anybody on this island."

"You're the only person who lives on this island."

"See?"

"That's the other thing—you spend so much time alone. Does it ever bother you?"

She was back in mode. I knew what she was getting at. I wouldn't have answered her except that she was asking, as best I could tell, as a woman, not a shrink.

"You want a serious answer?"

"That's why I'm asking."

"I've been atoning."

It was the kind of answer that I couldn't have given to a stranger.

"Oh."

"Everybody has to work things out their own way. That's one thing that I've learned over the years. I know that I've isolated myself here, and I know why. Isolation equals insulation, that's one. Isolation equals deprivation, that's another. Mainly, though, isolation equals time to think things through that you normally don't get when you're surrounded by other people."

"And are you through atoning?" she asked.

"Almost," I said.

"Almost?"

"Yeah. I might even deserve a future. Maybe. After I take care of the killers."

I said it with a smile, but it made her mad, anyway.

"Everybody deserves a future."

"I don't believe that," I said. "Once you're grown up, you earn things. The right to a happy future isn't in the constitution. It says the right to the pursuit of happiness. There's no guarantee there of a happy outcome. If you're not naturally lucky, you've got to earn it. Since most of us aren't naturally lucky, we have to earn things.

"Like trust," I continued. "I have to earn your trust and you have to earn mine. I don't want people like the Hemlocks or the Brothers

Grimm coming between us. John Hemlock had a file on you, among other people, did you know that?"

"No, but I should have guessed. How did you know?"

"I found it in one of his special rooms."

"And you left it there?"

"No. I took it."

"Then where is it now?"

Her voice had a tense edge to it.

"It's at the bottom of the Detroit River, along with the other two files. I had them tucked under my shirt. Didn't even realize that they were gone until we got on land. Maybe it's better that way."

"But you never mentioned the file on me before," she said.

"That's what I mean. Trust me, I wasn't holding out on you. It's just that with us arguing, you busting me in the nose, and us being shot at, it slipped my mind. That's all that it was, honest."

She chewed her lower lip for a minute, and then asked, "Did you see what was in the file?"

"No," I lied.

"Nothing?"

"No. I was in a hurry to get out. I just saw your name, took the file, and bugged out."

"You didn't even take a quick look?"

"I told you—no. I wanted to get out before John got home."

"Scott Brown, are you lying to protect me?"

"No."

I wasn't. I was lying to protect me.

She bought it.

"What were you two doing upstairs?" she asked. "How did you find these... these files? And what was in the other two?"

"Let me ask you something before I answer you. How long have you known about Christine Hemlock?"

"Too long," she replied. "Way too long."

I tried again.

"What specifically is wrong with her, and don't give me that confidentiality bit again, okay? Our lives could depend on details like this. Yours, mine, Bobby's, and my friends."

She could have gotten pissed off like before, or stalled, or approached her answer obliquely. But she didn't. She got right to the point.

"Christine suffers what is commonly known as multiple personality disorder. Pretty rare compared to what most people and some psychologists think, but it's real enough."

"What caused it?" I asked.

"A massive psychological trauma. Her father. Christine's maiden name was Manuel. Does that tell you anything?"

"What was his first name?"

"William Manuel, as in 'Bill the Butcher."

"What?"

She nodded her head.

"The one and only. The man who announced himself as the Great Beast of the Apocalypse in his posthumously published diary."

"Oh my God."

Bill the Butcher, Cincinnati's black mark. The man who practiced, it was reported, black magic. Sacrificed virgins to his dark master, then had sex with them afterwards so that they died virgins. His daughter, whom he forced to watch and made her kiss them on the mouth after he beheaded them. Bill the Butcher, who killed his mother in front of his little girl, and then, it was said, ate the woman, making his daughter share in the "feast."

"Christine was the little girl."

"That's who Christine Hemlock is?"

"Yes."

"So," I said, "when she called me Daddy…"

"She called you Daddy?"

"Yeah."

"Oh. That's bad, that's very bad."

"Tried to put a knife in my back, too."

"What was going on up there?"

"I real freak show," I said. "She took me into the family Inner Sanctum, where she and John act out their sick fantasies. And not alone, I might add. Some of the Brothers of the New Apostles were in on the circus as well."

"What happened when she tried to stab you, and what do you mean by sick fantasies?"

"I laid her out, as in knocked her out cold, and I mean very sick fantasies. Wait a minute, the pictures. I forgot all about the pictures that I stashed in my coat pocket. Maybe they're still there, if the water didn't ruin them."

We got off of the couch and headed toward the stairs when the phone rang.

"My coat's in the bathroom," I told her. "I'll get the phone, you get the pictures."

It was Leroy.

"Hey Leo," I said, "how's Monica?"

"About as well as you might think," he said.

Pause. Pause. Bigger pause.

"And?" I asked.

"Uh—I, uh, spent the night at her place."

"That's great."

"It was more or less in an official capacity," he added quickly.

"She was taking it that hard, huh?"

"Well, she, uh, she was pretty upset. Nothing much happened."

"Jesus, Leo, will you spit it out? I've told you a hundred times that I'm not involved with Monica."

"You don't have any… feelings left for her?"

"We were over a long time ago, buddy."

"Thanks, Scott."

"For what?"

And I thought that I was bad.

"For… hey, I remember what I was calling to tell you."

Avoidance, that's a good sign in a man.

"What?"

"You know that guy that got flattened?"

"There was more than one?"

"Smartass. Benny Franks. The one that used to be with the Army Security Agency. What do you think about that?"

"Doing what?"

"Cryptography. His specialty was remote computer penetration."

"I'm guessing you're not talking about cyber-sex."

"Hacking. He hacked enemy computer systems for the Army."

"Son of a bitch."

"It gets better," said Leroy. "Just don't ask me how I found any of this stuff out..."

Leo was in the army, Leo has friends still in the army, blah, blah, blah...

"How in the hell does it get any better than that?"

"According to Mrs. Franks, who was a tough nut to crack by the way, he was contracting part time with your friend Allen Hemlock."

Uh-oh.

"Doing what?"

"Computer stuff. That's all that she knew. He had some kind of a confidentiality agreement. Poor Benny couldn't even talk to his wife about what he was doing."

"No lie."

"No lie, Scott. You got any idea of what this means?"

"Not a clue yet, Leo. But I'm going to find out."

"Not without me, you're not. Besides, I need to talk to you about what we've found out about Bob and the other bodies in Bob's house."

I didn't want to talk to him.

"You want to meet?" I asked him anyway.

"Damn straight. When can you make it?"

"How about tonight? Eight o'clock at the River Hut. I'll buy you dinner."

"You want me to wait that damn long before I eat?"

"I've got a problem with my nuts, caught my bag on a rusty nail, believe it or not."

Stop it," he said, "it makes me hurt just listening to you. Any permanent damage?"

"No, I can still have ugly kids, but it hurts like hell every time I practice ballet."

Or jump out of an exploding car, or hop out of the way of a knife.

"All right. But you sure are getting to be a sissy."

"Yeah," I said, "so I've been told."

We had just locked the photos away in the safe that looked like a computer upstairs in the lighthouse, when I saw that Charlie and Gregorio were docking the boat. Dr. Stouffer was still fuming from what she had seen in the pictures I had pilfered from the Hemlock's Inner Sanctum.

"That's the first recruit," I said, pointing down at Gregorio to take her mind off of what she had seen just seen.

Alongside of Charlie, Gregorio looked even bigger than he was. He carried a trunk over one shoulder and a suitcase the size of a stove in the other.

"That's a big soldier," she said.

"Yeah. I should have remembered to stock up on groceries. Every time he eats, you'd think it was his last meal. Burns all the calories off by talking all the time."

"He's the one that went into the tunnel with you?"

"Actually, he went in first. I followed."

"Why did he go in first?" she asked.

"It's a tradition," I said. "We flipped a coin. Ever since then, he goes in first."

"All right, Mr. Macho. Let's go downstairs and greet your friend like proper hosts."

"I like the sound of that," I said.

"I knew you would."

"Ola, Scott," said Gregorio, "so you finally have a missus Scott. I'm so happy to meet you, senjorita. How did he convince such a lovely person as you to be his woman?"

I shook my head quickly from side to side. Dr. Stouffer's mouth was still open.

"Oh, so you are not his woman. Then you are not only beautiful, you are muoy intelligent."

"Dr. Stouffer," I said, stepping in before I got into too much trouble, "may I introduce the not-doctor Gregorio Tarancon."

"It is my pleasure," said Gregorio with a deep bow.

"Scott didn't say that you were so charming," she said.

"He's not," I told her. "It's all a front."

"You wound me, amigo."

"I like him already," said Charlie.

"Give me one good reason," I demanded.

"He carries his own bags."

"Why don't you show our guest to his room?" asked Dr. Stouffer.

"Yes, I am very weary from traveling. I hope you have a big bed. I do not sleep well when my feet hang over the edge."

"Come on, Miss Muffet," I said, "let me show you where the spiders hang out."

"Buenos nochas," said Gregorio to Bobby.

"He says 'good evening,'" Bobby told me. To Gregorio, he said: "Buenos nochas, senjor. Soi Roberto Stouffer. Como esta usted?"

"Muoy bien, gracias," replied Gregorio. "He is as beautiful and intelligent as his mother."

"I'm a boy. Boys are handsome, not beautiful."

"Oh, I am sorry. Sometimes my English is not so good."

"I can help you," said Bobby proudly. "I speak eight languages and read several more, including ancient Egyptian and Aramaic."

"Where in the hell did you learn to speak all of those languages?" I asked.

"I—"

"Never mind," I said, waving my hand in front of his face. "I don't want to know."

"Then why did you ask?"

"Yes," chimed in Dr. Stouffer, "why did you ask?"

"It was a rhetorical question—and don't define rhetorical for me, okay? I know what it means."

"So do I," said Bobby.

"Me, too," chimed in Charlie. "Hey Bobby, do you know Korean?"

"Not yet, but I want to learn if you will teach me. I like to learn."

"I can't stand this," I said, "I'm not used to so many people talking at once in my house."

"Calm down, dear," said Dr. Stouffer with a smile, "I'll make you some tea and go get you your shawl."

"Do you wear a shawl?" asked Bobby. "I thought only old women wore shawls."

"Oh, no, my little friend," said Gregorio, "whiny old men wear them, too."

"That does it, I'm going outside for a walk. At least the frogs still respect me."

"They do?" asked Bobby.

They were still yakking when I closed the door behind me.

A lot of people believe in power spots. I don't; I think it's a load of crap. Still, sometimes when I need to think and it's warm enough, there's this place on the Canadian side of the island where there's a tree stump that I sit on and look out of the water. I like that about Soldier's Point. It's smack in between the United States and Canada.

Although technically the island is American, I liked to think that it was a separate country by itself. My own country. I was the ruler. I had no human subjects yet; the frogs, birds, and insects filled in until some loyal bipeds could join me.

The tree stump is my throne. I can sit and contemplate my country's policies in peace and quiet. Someday, I had promised myself that I'd get a first rate velvet cushion to sit on to keep from getting tree stump splinters in my ass.

On that night, however, I was thinking about something else entirely different from affairs of state. I was remembering the children, now teenagers and young adults, that were being murdered by edict of an old fanatic named Brother Thomas. I imagined them alone and afraid in the hands of their captors, chained and unable to protect themselves from what was about to happen. I couldn't see them, but I knew about down below whatever passed as my conscious mind.

The cries of innocents filled my ears, the screams of terror, the sound of the blade as they were butchered.

Bill the Butcher. Christine Hemlock, his daughter. Children, savagely mutilated. Brother Thomas, Brother James, Brother Peter, and their brutal minions. Who actually did the killing? Could I stop it before another child died?

Allen Hemlock and Lance, his hired gun, now lying at the bottom of the river, being eaten by the fish. Allen Hemlock, I now thought, a man with the black secret that lay behind the killings.

Strange days.

If I believed Brother Thomas, the End Times were coming. The advent of darkness. The uncovering of the Beast.

Not if I could help it.

The Men in the Van

Leo wiped the sauce from his mouth with the back of his hand.

"You've still got class," I told him.

"You're just mad because you'd have to put down your fork to wipe your mouth. What, what'd I say?"

"Nothing," I told him. "I was just remembering this friend of mine in the Ukraine that took a bullet a little while back."

"I look like him or something?"

"Not even close," I laughed. "He was handsome."

Sometimes you remember friends that have died at the weirdest times. Kris might say that it was defrayed or delayed mourning. The mind can't handle the grief all at once; so it dishes it out later, a little bit at a time, chunk by chunk when you least expect it.

"So, this friend of yours, how'd he buy it?"

He put it on his MasterCard, I thought.

"We were down in this underground rail tunnel, me, him, and his wife. Looking for these missing teenagers. We found them, all lined up in a row. They were... cut up. Hadn't been there that long, I don't think. You know the way that stiffs are when they've been there a while. Anyway, they were sitting up against the wall, and... one of them wasn't a stiff. We didn't figure it out in time. Boris took a bullet. It could have been any one of us, you know? Just happened to be him. I don't even know why I'm thinking about it. I think that I've seen too much death, Leo. Too much."

"Kind of fucks you up sometimes, doesn't it?"

"Sure does."

He raised his beer glass.

"Here's to the dead. To Bob, and all of the others that died before they should have."

We clinked the glasses and downed the beer, like so many men before us had done over the years for fallen comrades. And like so many before us, we didn't have a clue about what the events that had killed them meant.

"Another round?" asked Leo.

"Damn straight," I said.

The River Hut was made for men like Leo and me. The waitresses were too young and pretty to waste time on beat up survivors like us. They left us alone to talk. And there never seemed to be so many customers that we couldn't get a table away from everybody else so that we could talk privately.

After Judy, or Julie, or whatever our waitress's real name was had cleared away our plates and brought us another round, Leo told me what was on his mind.

"The coroner and the crime team from the Wayne County Sheriff's Department found some pretty interesting things at Bob's place. You care to guess what?"

I didn't say anything. There wasn't any need. He knew that I knew.

"Bob was shot in the head before he died. A machete or some kind of sword had hacked the rest of the bodies up, except for one that was shot. One of the bodies was cut clean in half. None of the bodies other than Bob's have been ID'd as of yet. I'm willing to bet that they never will. What do you think?"

Leo would tell me which way he was going with this when he was ready. It was dangerous to give a man like him feedback until he'd made his move.

"No guesses, huh?" he continued. "Didn't think so. It's a real mess, Scott. You don't like to read the online news or watch TV, but this whole thing is pretty famous now. Even got some national coverage. My ugly face was even on the tube. Wayne County Sheriff's

Department is getting most of the exposure, though. Makes it easier on me.

"Damn thing is all over talk radio, too. Buddy Nelson, the AM radio mouth is hammering away at us, making Gibraltar sound like Dodge City. Everybody's calling in to him with an opinion. Saying Bob Alby was probably into drugs or some kind of racket. Lot of ' I heard this' or 'I think that.' Makes me sick. We're going to clear his name, you and me. You with me on that?"

"I'm with you, Leo."

I'd been trashed way back when by the media—I knew the pain and the rage of having your life analyzed in public by people who didn't know you, who wanted a hot story more than the truth. I could understand it in my case. I didn't like it, but I could understand it.

But Bob Alby was a straight guy. He had been a victim; he hadn't been responsible for anyone else's death like I had. There was no reason for them to be destroying his reputation after he'd been murdered.

Bob Alby a drug dealer?

My ass.

"Then you've got to start dealing me some straight cards here, partner. I'm not going to go official on you. I resigned today. I won't starve. I've got some money saved up, and to tell you the truth, I'm pretty damned tired of playing by the rules. I want somebody's ass on this one, and I don't think that whoever did this is ever going down in court."

"I've got no argument there, but I don't see any reason you had to resign your job."

And I didn't. Leo Croton had been the police chief long before I had moved to Soldier's Point to leave the bad memories behind. He was good at his job; he was good for the town.

"Scott, I'm going to tell you something that I've never told a living soul. I think you'll understand when I'm done why it is that I have to do this."

I knew what was coming, but I wasn't going to tell him that. Leo and I were too much alike for me not to have already figured out what had really happened to Heather's ex-husband, the guy who had shot her and left her for dead.

"As a policeman, I'm not proud of what I'm going to tell you. But as a human being, after all of these years, God help me, I'd still do the same damn thing.

"You know I went kind of crazy after Heather died; I had a real bad time of it. He killed her, but he did it because of me. Told her after she left him he'd never let another man have her. I told her it was just him talking to hear himself talk. I told her I'd protect her. Didn't do such a good job of that, did I?

"No, don't bother answering me. I truly believed what I told her. I just plain didn't see it coming."

He paused for a moment, his eyes seeing the past instead of the present. His eyes were clear and sharp the way that a person's sometimes are when they are watching the history of their own soul playing itself out again in the private theater of the mind.

"Everyone thought that the man had made a clean getaway. No one ever tracked him down. That's what they thought. That's what I told them. Must of thought that I was losing my touch.

"You know how far he really made it?"

I shook my head no.

"Well, his car was found broken down and abandoned on King Road between West Road and Fort Street. They figured he must have walked from there, hitched a ride somewhere and just kept going. They were right.

"It must have been one, two o'clock in the morning when I saw him walking. I was just cruising around in my car, trying to understand what the fuck had happened. Trying to ride out my guilt. I turned down King Road, going toward Fort Street, and who do you think I saw?"

"Him," I said.

I needed to say something, just to show him I was paying attention. Leo took another swig of beer and wiped his mouth with the back of his hand.

"Him," he said. "The son of a bitch who had shot Heather, a woman that never harmed anybody in her entire life. There he was, walking like he had a right to breathe and move like anybody else. He's got his thumb stuck out for me. So, I stopped the car, nice and slow like I didn't have a clue what kind of scum he was.

"When he gets to the car and opens the door and says, ' Thanks, mister,' he sees me pointing the gun at him.

'Get in,' I tell him.

"He's thinking about making a run for it. You know how sometimes you can just see it in their faces? Well, I could see it in his. He's thinking, 'Can I make it? If I just turn and peel off into the night, would he shoot me in the back?'

"I don't let him take it too far. I'll tell him that if makes a wrong move I'll kill him and say that it's self-defense.

"Then he starts thinking that maybe he'll just play along, and then go for his gun. I let him know real quick what will happen. He got in the car.

"As he's sitting down and turning his back on me to close the door, I nailed him in the back of the head with the butt end of my gun. He went to sleep real peaceful like then."

Leo paused again, absorbed in the replay. I waited patiently.

"So, I cuffed him, then drove him out to the right place, and then I shot him in cold blood. I didn't talk to him, explain why he was dying. Nothing like that. He was just an animal going to slaughter, and I was the butcher.

"He cried and screamed, but out where we went, there was no one to hear him. He sounded just like a pig being prodded up the ramp, crying and squealing, knowing that the slaughterhouse was waiting for him at the end of the line."

"What'd you do with the body?" I asked.

"You know, cops think a lot about that kind of stuff. How to commit the perfect crime. How to get rid of the body. I'd worked that out years ago. There's nothing—and I mean nothing—left of him for anybody to find. Now you know."

"Yeah."

"Now you know both halves of why I can't stay in the job. Because when we find the son of a bitch responsible for Bob being killed, I'm going to do the same damn thing all over again. And I can't do that again if I'm a cop. I did it once. But I just can't do it again wearing a badge."

"You want another beer?" I asked.

"What the fuck do you think?"

I raised my hand and waived the waitress over.

When she had come and gone, Leo said, "But I figured you'd already worked out what happened a long time ago. Am I right?"

"You're right."

"We're too much alike, aren't we Scott?"

"Yeah, we are. I figured that out a long time ago, too."

"Well, I hope," he said, "that you sleep a lot easier than I do."

"Not usually," I replied. "You ready to get going on this tonight?"

"What do you have in mind?"

We had let the River Hut and drove in Leo's car to a small office building on the corner of Eureka Road and I-75 to meet with Joey Clives, the private investigator that I had contacted to shadow and investigate Brother James, the former Viet Nam vet. Joey used to be with the Military Police, and he still had his contacts.

Equally important to me, Joey was divorced, with no children. His parents had died when he was younger, so that there was no one for Joey to worry about but Joey. I liked that—a guy who could be focused, a guy who didn't have a family to endanger. It was a gruesome consideration, but one that I thought had to be taken into account considering the situation.

The light was on in Joey's office, and I buzzed the intercom. It was one of those jobs with a built-in video camera.

"Who's your friend?" asked Joey's voice through the wire grating.

I depressed the "talk" button.

"Friend of mine."

"What's his name?"

"Leo Croton."

"Chief Leo Croton?"

"Former Chief Croton," said Leo testily.

"Since when?" asked Joey's voice.

"Joey," I said, "I'm getting tired of pushing this damn talk button. Can you just let us in? We can talk about this shit inside."

I heard a different buzz, then a click, and I opened the door. Leo followed me inside.

The vestibule was lit by an overhead light that lit the otherwise dimmed hallway.

"Down here. You know the way," called Joey.

Joey Clives's office looked like it belonged to an accountant. Anymore, any really good investigator was an accountant. Following money trails was just as important as following people. Most crime, after all, was about money in one way or another.

He had only a banker's green shaded lamp on, and the office was cast in shadows from file cabinets. We stepped inside. Joey Clives himself looked like a regular guy. Average height, average weight, light brown hair, blue eyes, average looks, average build, wearing an average gray suit, sitting behind an average looking desk stacked with papers, and aiming an average looking silenced Beretta nine-millimeter at my midsection.

"Don't bother sitting down, fellas," Joey said, "you won't be here that long."

"Friend of yours?" asked Leo.

"Used to be," I said.

"Oh well," said Joey.

He stood up easily, the gun never wavering. Moved like a professional.

"Who's paying you, Joey?"

"No time to talk, Scott. Your ride is here. When you called from the restaurant and said that you were on your way, I called and they said they'd be happy to come and get you."

Car lights had suddenly brightened the shades behind his desk, and then vanished.

"I hope they're paying you a lot," I told him.

"They are," he said with a grin.

"Money's not always good for your health," said Leo

"It's always been good for mine. But I'll tell you something, asshole. I'm not doing this for the money."

Joey's smile transformed into a sardonic sneer. Obviously, there was something more to this prick than I had figured.

In life, Charlie had said, it is easy to get caught in the crossfire of many different purposes.

"I got a call today from a friend of yours."

"Who was that?" I said.

I felt movement behind from Leo. Time was short, though. Whoever was in the parking lot was either on their way in, or they wouldn't wait long if we didn't come marching out with Joey behind us.

Leo was left-handed, and his left side was behind me. He was carrying, I knew that much already. He wasn't a cop anymore, but Joey Clives wasn't the only one carrying a silenced pistol that night.

"Johnny Hemlock. He gave me a little information about you I didn't know."

"And you believed him?"

Hurry it up, Leo.

"I never made the connection. Scott Brown. You know how many Scott Brown's there must be in the world? But you had to be the one, didn't you?"

Oh, shit.

"You had to be the one and only one. Scott Brown," he chanted, "'turned a valve and killed a town.' You know who lived in that town, you asshole?"

Innocent people.

"That was a long time ago, Joey," I said.

"A long time ago," he nodded.

"It was an accident."

"You're about to have an accident, too. Now there's justice for you, huh? You probably can't remember all of the names of all of the people that died, can you? Just numbers to you. Remember this one, though—Shelly Weeks. Now move. Your ride is waiting."

I felt the barrel of Leo's gun in my back, and with a quick prayer, I stepped to one side, turning toward the door as naturally as I could. Heard the silenced shot that sounded louder than you can imagine in that little room, and saw the blood on Joey's suit before he dropped straight down to the floor with a surprised look on his face.

"One down," said Leo.

The grim look on his face was something that I had seen in my own mirror too many times.

"Out the front," he said.

"No. Wait."

"There's somebody waiting outside that ain't going to wait much longer before they come in after us."

I had a crazy idea.

"Nobody knows you're here, Leo. No one knew you were coming along."

"So?"

"Chances are whoever's waiting for us doesn't know Joey Clives from you."

"For fuck's sake, what are you trying to say?"

"I'm going out first. You follow with the gun in my back, just like Joey would."

"What the hell for? We've got to get out of here. I just killed a man."

"Because I want whoever is in that van. We need to know whatever they know."

I didn't wait for him to argue it out with me, I just started walking toward the back door exit.

It was your classic black van waiting out in your traditional dark parking lot with the engine running just like in the movies. Couldn't really ask for much more unless it was that whoever it was that was in the van was wearing a ski mask.

Leo didn't look at all like Joey, which was the only flaw in the whole plan.

Aside from being scared shitless, I felt like a total asshole walking out with one hand held up. It was fifty/fifty whether or not they knew that the other one wouldn't go up.

I walked around to the sliding door side of the van, which someone inside slid open for me. The dome light was out, so I couldn't get a good look at whoever was inside.

Hard to peg. One driver, one man I could see in the van. How many more? My bet was none. How many men did it take to make a simple pickup?

We were five feet from the open door when Leo shoved me aside and shot the man inside, then shot the driver through the passenger side window. He fired twice for good measure.

They're alive.

They're dead.

That's the way it happened.

Broken glass and an engine idling as though there was someone still alive left to drive it. Otherwise, the only sound was street traffic.

I had my own gun out by then.

Leo had seen two men; he had killed two men. That should have been it—if there were only two to begin with. The seconds ticked by awfully slowly as we waited it out. Couldn't stay, didn't want to turn, walk away, and be shot in the back.

"Fuck it," Leo said, and started pumping rounds into the side of the van.

The last guy dove straight out head first from the van, landing face down, flat on his stomach on the asphalt.

"Freeze," I yelled.

I had always wanted to do that.

No need to have said anything, though.

He was already dead.

*****

Charlie was still up when we got back to the lighthouse. Dr. Stouffer had just turned in a half an hour or so ago, he told me. Gregorio had crashed, too, being tired from the plane ride. Bobby was long since gone.

I got Leo a blanket to sleep on the couch. Charlie was staying up. I told him good luck, I was going to bed. I was beat to rat shit.

Along the way to the bedroom, I stopped off at the bathroom, popped two pain pills to kill the pain in my nose, the pain in my nuts, and to just generally turn my mind off. I wasn't used to this kind of crap going down on my own turf.

I brushed my teeth, don't ask me why, and gave myself the once over in the mirror. Busted nose, oily, messed up hair, oily messed up face. I washed clothed the areas of my face that weren't bandaged, dried off, and looked again. Cleaner, drier, but still haunted by the past. No matter how hard I tried, I couldn't remember the name Shelley Weeks.

Had she been his sister? Was she an adult, or was she a child? His child? No matter, she was dead. I closed my eyes and leaned my forehead against the mirror.

I remembered the moment that I had woken up in the acid suit, still breathing, still alive. The first body that I found. The skin burns from the hydrogen fluoride gas converting to hydrofluoric acid in the presence of moisture. It wasn't healthy to sweat in a plant that used big quantities of hydrogen fluoride.

Dead bodies on the floor, outside in the parking lot.

The image in my mind shifted and I saw headless bodies in crates. Bodies in the Warehouse of the Dead. The smell filled my nostrils as though I were really there. Too much death, too much death. So much death that I had run from the living, and isolated myself in my lighthouse tower, locked away except for forays out to experience more death.

My son would have been older than Bobby was now. Many times I tried to imagine what he would be like if he were alive now. A son, someone who would love me. A son that I could love and protect.

What would he enjoy? Sports? Music? Camping?

What would it be like to be called dad? How would it feel to see my son every day, to talk to him, do things with him, and grow with him?

If the Darvocet didn't kick in soon, I might, just might, start to cry like I had back in the Ukraine.

I didn't bother turning on the light when I went in my bedroom, but closed the door behind me and undressed in the dark. I left the clothes where they fell; plenty of time to throw them in the clothes hamper in the morning.

I was going to stop whoever had killed those kids in the Warehouse of the Dead and around the world. I couldn't bring back my wife and kids or any of the people that had died in the gas leak, but I could revenge the kids that had been murdered in cold blood, and save those that were left alive, if I had to kill everyone involved. After I got a few hours sleep.

As I pulled back the covers, I realized how deadly alone I felt.

Except that when I crawled under the covers, I wasn't.

"Hard night at the office?" asked Dr. Stouffer softly.

"I'm dreaming, right?"

"Yes," she said, "but it's going to be a nice dream."

She snuggled close and put her arm across my chest. Her touch was tender and reassuring. She smelled clean and fresh the way apples look when you shine them. And warm. She was so warm.

"I got a nail between my legs," I reminded her.

She kissed my ear lightly.

"That's normal under the circumstances."

"No, I mean I got a nail, a real nail in the balls today. Remember? I'm not exactly in the best working order."

"Shut up," she said.

The Plan

"Good morning, Mr. Brown," said the cheery little face standing next to the bed.

I could feel Dr. Stouffer's naked hip next to my own. Her hand, resting on my thigh, gave a gentle squeeze.

If I kept my eyes closed, maybe he would think that I was still asleep.

"Good morning, Mr. Brown," he said again.

I was lying in bed with his mother, for God's sake. Hadn't he ever heard of privacy?

"Mr. Brown, are you awake? I can see your eyes moving under your eyelids."

"He's very tired, Bobby," said Dr. Stouffer in my defense.

You should know, I thought, you kept me up half the night.

"But I have something to tell him."

"I'm awake, kid—Bobby. I've just got my eyes closed."

"Why?"

"Because, uh, your mother and I—"

I could hear Dr. Stouffer suppress a laugh.

"Because what?"

Take a deep breath, get control. He's just a kid. He won't bite you.

His face was only three inches from mine. Eyes wide open. Eager. Innocent. I closed my eyes again.

"My mother doesn't sleep around, Mr. Brown."

"Bobby," chastened the doctor.

"Well, you don't."

"Thank you, son, but sometimes—"

"I like Mr. Brown," he rattled on. "And his friends."

"You do?"

"Yes, Mr. Brown. Sometimes you're funny, and sometimes you're scary. That's cool. And you're not boring. It's okay to open your eyes. I have something to tell you."

"How's this?" I said suddenly, popping my eyes open wide.

"You're not always funny," he said gravely, "but you try."

"Oh."

More suppressed laughter from Dr. Stouffer.

"I heard you talking. And I heard your friends talking. Everybody whispers, but I heard parts of what you were saying."

I was all attention now, and I could feel his mother's hand tighten on my hip.

"What have you heard, Bobby?"

"Most everything, I think. I have a very good memory. I can reassemble conversational bits and pieces in my head until they fit together like a puzzle."

"Bobby—" began Dr. Stouffer.

"I have to tell you about the Beast."

"What?" I asked.

"Have you read the Revelations?"

"Yes."

I felt my stomach muscles tighten, trying to squeeze off the unease that was growing inside me.

"Did you know that there were two Beasts?"

"I don't think that we should be talking about this with you," said Dr. Stouffer, sitting up, clutching the sheets to her.

"Two Beasts?" I asked.

"Yes, there were two. The first dies, then comes back to life, and the second Beast tells everyone to follow the first, because coming back from the dead shows how powerful the first is because he was stronger than death. In Revelations it says, 'One of the heads of the Beast seemed to have had a fatal wound, but the wound had been healed,' and later it says, He—that's the second Beast—'ordered them to set up an image in honor of the Beast who was wounded by the sword and yet lived.' Now do you understand?"

"I believe you, Bobby, but why is that important?"

"First," he said, holding up one hand, and began to tick off his points on his fingers like a midget university professor, "it says one of his heads was hurt. Do you understand?"

I nodded, impervious to the increasingly painful pressure on my hip from his mother's fingernails.

"Second, both beasts are clearly masculine. Third, the definition of death at that time was different than—"

"Bobby, that's enough," interrupted Dr. Stouffer. "I forbid you to carry this conversation further. Leave the room, and close the door behind you. I want to speak with Scott—Mr. Brown alone. Please."

"But, mom—"

"Now, young man. You and I will talk later."

"Okay."

"Thank you, Bobby."

"I love you, mom."

"I love you, too. Now go on."

I felt the classic lump in my throat as I watched him leave the room, his head tilted forward, as though he had been caught doing something bad. Slowly, I was beginning to realize that caring for people was a mixed bag. Especially people as complicated as Bobby.

"Did you have to stop him? He was trying to help."

There were tears in her eyes. Her hair was beautifully mussed, one side of her face a soft red color from lying on that side while she slept. The sheets hung on the tips of her breasts as she fidgeted with the wrinkles in the fabric.

"Do you know," she said, "how difficult it is to raise a child who is so much smarter than you are?"

"No."

"He has adult thoughts. Analyzes and remembers better than you would think possible. But he's still a child, less than a teenager emotionally sometimes, but more emotionally strong and vulnerable than anyone I have ever met. He is a very special person. But he's also my son. I'm supposed to raise him, but how can I raise a boy who is so special?

"I don't want him thinking about these murders, or biblical Beasts. Do you know what that can do his mind? I don't. Being exposed to Bob Alby's death will scar him for years. What do you think being involved in the analysis of the horrible mutilation of other children will do to him? I can't begin to imagine the impact that will have on him, in spite of my training. He's my son, not my patient, and I don't want him traumatized. I don't want him hurt.

"He's just a boy, Scott. I don't want him thinking about these things. You and your friends are heroes to him. Fighting bad people. But he doesn't really understand what bad is.

"Mutilation and murder. That's what we're talking about here. Prophecies about the coming of the ultimate evil. A boy his age isn't equipped to handle these things. Please don't involve him more by talking about it to him."

When she put it that way, I could understand the tears. I could feel the unease in my stomach twist, as though it were trying to break free and overwhelm me.

"I'm sorry, Kris. I just didn't think. I got so caught up in the idea that he knew something important that I screwed up. I'm sorry. It won't happen again."

She put her hand on my cheek, and stroked it softly.

"He may think he's Sherlock Holmes," she said, "but don't encourage him by playing Dr. Watson."

"Wasn't Watson the dumb one?" I asked.

She nodded, and then kissed me lightly on the lips.

"You said it," she said with a quick smile, and then leaned her head forward to rest on my chest.

*****

"We got a small fucking army here," said Gregorio, "but I think we need more men."

"How about another woman?" Katerina asked.

Leo, Gregorio, Charlie, Dr. Stouffer, myself, Katerina, and Karl Schlecter, fresh from Germany. And Bobby, upstairs in the lighthouse cage, playing with one of my computers. His mother and I had agreed that he should stay out of the meeting, and we both thought that hanging out with the electronic horsepower in the top of the lighthouse would keep him occupied.

"How about a plan, instead?" growled Leo.

The day had passed quickly enough. Charlie and I had worked out in the morning while Bobby sat on the ground and watched. To my surprise, Charlie would stop frequently and explain to Bobby not only what we were doing, but why, and the history of the art. He peppered their talks with frequent Korean words and phrases.

I got a bigger surprise when Bobby responded in Korean. I began to appreciate what Dr. Stouffer had been saying about him.

"There is only one difference between a hapkidoist and a criminal," Charlie told him.

"One's a good guy and the other's a bad guy," Bobby had said.

Big smile from Charlie.

"In essence, you are correct. It is the principles of a man of honor and his understanding of them that separates the two men, even though both may act aggressively. Destructive force is destructive force, Bobby, but it is the code of the man initiating such force that differentiates the two."

"I saw the Karate Kid," said Bobby proudly.

Charlie grimaced.

"Oh, the old guy was Okinawan, not Korean."

"That's not the point, Bobby."

"I'm sorry."

While I took a breather, Charlie sat on the ground next to Bobby and put his arm around the boy's shoulder.

"Korean, Okinawan, Chinese, Japanese, American—distinctions like that aren't important. What I was shaking my head about is that you must learn to concentrate without thinking. Words are only signposts, pointing the way toward the ultimate meaning. Movies are like rest stops. You like that example, Scott?"

"No," I said. "It's not oriental enough."

Charlie winked at Bobby. "He's a purist."

"I know," said Bobby.

"It's nice to take a break at rest stops," continued Charlie, "but you don't go anywhere if you stay there. Get the point?"

"I think so," said Bobby hesitantly.

"Good." Charlie got to his feet again, tussling the Bobby's hair as he did so. "Back to work, Scott. Time to meet Mr. Ground again."

No rest for the purists.

After we had finished working out, Charlie and Bobby took off to scout the island and talk. I had gone inside to shower, check information bases on the computer, and think. Everyone, including Dr. Stouffer, had left me alone.

I called John Hemlock during a break.

"Hey, John," I said, after he had come to the phone. "I came over to talk to you, but you weren't home. Your lovely wife entertained me instead. We had a nice time."

Silence on the other end.

"Are you there, buddy?"

"Yes, I'm here," he said at length.

"Good, I like talking to you. Your wife is also fun to talk to—she has so many different sides to get to know. Is she narcoleptic, John?"

"Why do you ask?"

"She fell asleep while I was talking with her."

Click.

Dial tone.

I called for Allen Hemlock, as well. He wasn't available, but his man said that he would return the call at his convenience. Was there a message?

"Sure," I said, "tell him that I'm working closely with the therapist that he assigned me, but that we're not making much progress."

Bite on that, big guy.

"Brother Peter?"

He was next on my list, and, surprisingly, he answered his own damn phone.

"Yes?"

"This is Scott Brown."

"I know who you are."

"Well, I've been going over your military service record, and you appear to have been one bad-ass mother fucker, if you'll pardon the language."

"Is there a point to this call, Mr. Brown?"

"Yes, there is."

"And what might that be?"

"I've been living a little harsh, lately, and I was wondering if you could maybe meet me and talk me through some of my problems."

"Living harsh?"

"Walking the knife edge without shoes. You know."

"I see."

"Well," I said, "how about it?"

"I'm afraid that my schedule is just too crowded these days."

"Too bad. I had these pictures that kind of symbolize what it is that I need to talk through, and, well, since you're in some of them..."

"Pictures?"

"What's that noise?" I said nervously.

"I don't hear any noise."

"Be quiet for a minute."

"I still don't hear any noise."

"I did. It sounded like someone grinding their molars."

"You know, Mr. Brown, after checking my schedule more closely, I do see some openings. I must have been confusing my weeks."

"Happens to me all of the time, Brother Peter. Can't hardly go to the bathroom without my monthly planner anymore."

"When," he asked, "did you have in mind for us to meet?"

"If you're busy," I said, "I've got this newspaper friend of mine that I can go to for advice."

"A live one?"

"Yeah," I said, fighting back the bitterness at the reference to Bob Alby, "I get around. I know quite a few newspaper people."

I'm going to peel back your forehead with a butter knife, I thought.

"Ah," he said smoothly, "I hear it now, too. And you're right. It does sound like someone grinding their teeth. Indeed, it does."

And then I'll cut your eyes out and feed them to the crows.

"I'll tell you what," I said, "I'm going to firm up my own schedule, and then call you back."

"At your leisure, Mr. Brown."

The line went dead before I could hang up.

"Like I said," repeated Gregorio, who had come in with Leo while I was talking to Satan, "I think we need more people."

"Gregorio," I said, "you always think we need more people. I could have an army regiment backing us and you'd think that we need more people."

"I like lots of company," he admitted.

"And I like to have a good plan," said Leo again.

*****

We were camped out around the table like the Magnificent Seven on coffee break. It was my show, and as I looked around the table at them, I thought I had never seen such a disparate group of similar people in my life.

"Leo told me earlier that he thought we needed a good plan," I said, "but before I tell you what I've got in mind, I want to bring everyone up to speed on what's happened, from my end, then have each of you fill in anything that I've missed, especially anything that you've found out independently to make sure that we all have all of the same information.

"How about some more coffee first?" asked Leo. "I didn't exactly sleep well last night. Anybody else?"

"We should have had this meeting at MacDonald's," said Gregorio.

"Bring the whole damn pot over and set it there," I said to Gregorio, pointing at the end table that we had pulled over next to where we were sitting. "And Gregorio, before you ask, I don't have any breakfast muffins."

Ten minutes later, when everyone's cup was filled, we got into it.

"By now, everybody knows everybody," I said. "And you all know about the conference for gifted children in Riverview that happened a long while back. You've all had time to look at the summaries that Dr. Stouffer prepared this afternoon, and the information packages that I yanked out of the Internet."

"Si," said Gregorio.

"Da," said Katerina.

"Ya," said Karl.

"Don't even say it," said Leo to Charlie. "Christ, could everybody please speak English?"

"Si," said Gregorio.

"Da," said Katerina.

"Ya," said Karl.

"Okay, okay, I wasn't going to say it," grinned Charlie.

Leo grumbled a response, but it was too low to hear.

"How can you all be so cavalier about this?" demanded Dr. Stouffer.

It was the way she said it that brought everybody to attention. She was seriously upset. I was so wrapped up in what we were about to do that I hadn't even noticed that her fuse was lit until she was ready to explode.

"Because," said Leo, "not all of us might be around when this is over, Doc. I don't know these people very well, but I think I like them enough to want to see everybody's smiling face when it's over. Problem is, it's not too likely to turn out that way."

"Dr. Stouffer," said Katerina, "I assure you we all take this very seriously. The men that we are seeking are responsible for the death of my husband. They killed him in front of my eyes."

"And I have seen first-hand what they can do, Fraulein," said Karl. "They are dangerous people who have no souls. They kill children."

"They killed my friend," added Leo simply.

Gregorio shrugged his shoulders and smiled. "Me, senorita, I'm merely along for the tacos. But if I should chance to meet the people who did what the one armed bandito and I found in the Warehouse of the Dead and in the tunnels in Guadalajara, then I will gladly send them to Hell."

I left her on her own to answer them. She didn't need me to talk for her.

She looked around the table at the group assembled before her, allowed her glance to linger on me for a moment, then cleared her throat. "I'm sorry," she said. "Please forgive me. I'm not accustomed to..."

"Please, Dr. Stouffer," interrupted Charlie, "you don't have to apologize to us. This is not an easy thing for any of us we are about to do. We are all here of our own free wishes, including you. To work together, it is necessary that we all understand each other. You must not ask forgiveness for questioning what it is that is necessary for you to know."

"Thank you," she said, "all of you."

"Motives and methods," I continued, "are what we all need to be sure that we understand. Dr. Stouffer, I believe that motives are your department..."

Last night with Dr. Stouffer had been different. While she talked to the group about motives and the psychology of the Hemlocks and the Brothers, I was remembering her making love to me last night. Gentle, but insistent. Strong, but needful.

Monica had needed a man to get off. Who he was, was just sort of the icing on the cake, so to speak. I had been used to that sort of sex for too long myself.

Once, after I had broken it off with her, she tried to get me back by reminding me, "We used to screw like bunnies."

"You've fucked too many other rabbits in the meantime," I'd replied.

She'd thrown a glass at me. Like an idiot, instead of moving out of the way, I had whipped up my right hand to block it. The glass had shattered on impact, and when I opened my eyes, I saw, for a few suspended seconds, a long piece of glass embedded in the edge of my hand, red blood trickling down it as though from the edge of a knife and dripping to the white ceramic floor where it splattered to form a gory Rorschach.

Tough love isn't what it's cracked up to be.

The group droned on, discussing Brother Thomas' psychological profile. My mind still wasn't hooked on the topic. Psychology was only psychology. Me, I pretended to pay attention to it, but mainly, when faced with psychological complexities, I vote for the cattle prod.

My mind drifted, and again I remembered sex with Dr. Stouffer. I remembered having trouble breathing through the bandages over my nose while she straddled me and slid back and forth along my length, her breasts moving along the sweat that wet my chest and stomach. Each time that she pushed back, the pain in my nuts caused red and white sparkles to explode like fireworks on the inside of my eyelids. But the final burst when the grand finale came round lit up the darkness in my head with such an intense light show that her gasping, urgent cries sounded like crowds disappointed that the show was over.

Afterwards, when we lay next to each other, the night sky behind my closed eyes was dark and clear, quiet and warm like when the crowds have gone home and the night is wide open in purple summer darkness.

"At some level, in my opinion," she was saying when I tuned back into the group discussion of the New Apostles and their head honcho, "Brother Thomas believes that he himself is evil and wants to die. In his own subconscious mind, the repeated murder and mutilations of children around the world, is confirmation of his inherently sinful nature and his desperate desire to be judged and executed. Conversely, his prolonged existence is only allowed by God because he is hunting an evil worse than himself."

"Dr. Stouffer," said Karl, "aren't the two views somewhat contradictory? He's evil and should die, but he is obsessed with killing children—a reprehensible agenda—to serve a greater good."

"It is within the bounds of human nature to do evil in the name of good, Mr. Schlecter," answered Katerina solemnly before Dr. Stouffer could respond. "You and I must only look to our own countries for confirmation. Germans murdering Jews in the name of racial purity. Stalin murdering thirty million people in the name of ideological purity."

"That is well put, Katerina," said Dr. Stouffer. "The human mind can both fortunately and unfortunately rationalize contradictory thoughts and behavior by compartmentalization of disconsonant implications."

"Whew," whistled Gregorio, "I don't understand what you just said, but the way you said it..."

"Simply put," continued the doctor, "we can say one thing and do another. But Brother Thomas is inherently unstable because although the mind can do this, it cannot sustain the stress transformation. Madness or catharsis are the only options to restore mental balance."

"So, he's either going to go out of his mind, or confess and get it off of his chest," said Leo.

"He's too far gone to repent," I told him. "You can knock on his head, but I don't think that there's anybody home to answer the mental front door."

"But he will not stop until either he locates the child that he seeks and destroys him or her, or until we kill him and those who serve him," said Karl. "Is this substantially correct?"

"Or put him behind bars," corrected Dr. Stouffer.

"Kill him," said Gregorio.

"He's too old to be put in prison," said Leo.

"But if Brother James is arrested—"

"The old guy will just hire more guns. We've got to kill him. End of story."

"Or kill the child," said Charlie.

"Whoa, Charlie," I said.

"I mean," he explained, "that we make it appear that we have killed the child. To buy time."

"I like it," said Karl.

"Too complicated," said Leo. "I mean, we don't even know who the kid is."

"That's true," confirmed Dr. Stouffer. "We don't know the identity of the child."

"We could have each child x-rayed. Or have them undergo MRI." said Katerina.

"Mr. Brown knows, don't you Mr. Brown?"

It was Bobby's voice from the stairs. Everyone turned to stare at him.

"Bobby," said Dr. Stouffer, "you go upstairs, right now."

"But he does, don't you Mr. Brown?"

I kept my mouth shut.

Dr. Stouffer and the others turned their stares on me.

"Is this true?" she asked.

"What's the game, Scott?" asked Leo.

I looked at Bobby.

"Tell us," pressed Dr. Stouffer.

Still, I kept my mouth shut.

"It's me, mom," said Bobby. "I'm the one they want."

The Objection

"He's not the one," I said.

We had pulled up the last folding chair in the house for Bobby, who now sat at the table between his mother and I, the center of attention.

"You're the decoy, son," I explained.

Dr. Stouffer's mouth was tightly set.

"You have never mentioned any of this to me."

"It was only a hunch, anyway," I said.

"How could you keep this to yourself?" she demanded.

I didn't want to tell her it had been in her file, the one that was now at the bottom of the river, or that I hadn't told her to keep her from freaking out on me.

"Because it never really crystallized for me until Bobby just told me he thought the same thing."

"I'm a decoy?" asked Bobby.

"Spit it out, Scott," said Leo, "tell us what's going on here."

"Maybe I better have Bobby tell it," I said carefully. "It's about time, I think, that we start getting his ideas on this."

"But we talked just this morning and—"

"I know we did," I told her, "but he's put his nose in it now. Plus, we need his help on this, Kris. He may be just a teenager, but he's got the brain of an adult when it comes to analysis, according to what you said. If you disagree with me, just tell me, but I've been thinking about what we discussed this morning, and I believe that, in spite of everything that we said, we could sure as hell use his help. A lot of other kid's lives are riding on us. There's just too many of them for us to make mistakes because we're afraid to ask a child's help. No offense, Bobby."

"That's okay, Mr. Brown. But why do you think that I'm only a decoy?"

"I'll tell you when you've given me your analysis. That is, if it's okay with your mother."

Dr. Stouffer bit her lower lip.

"Tough decision, I know, Kris," I said, "but I'm telling you honestly—we need his help."

"Mom?"

"What, Bobby?"

"I know you want to protect me, but can I tell you something?"

She sighed. "All right, but I haven't made up my mind yet."

"Okay. Well, you know, I know that it's hard raising a kid like me, but sometimes you make it too hard. You don't want to make a mistake, and I know that you'd like me to grow up real slow so that you don't feel like everything is out of control. It would be sweet if I was like other kids, but I'm not.

"And Mr. Brown's right, mom. I'm not helpless. I don't always need to be protected. Sometimes I need a chance to fight. Every boy has to grow up. Even if they have special problems.

"You know how it is to be a mom for a boy like me, but you don't know what it's like to be a boy like me. It's the same for the other kids like me, too, their parents don't understand. We're the ones that these people are trying to hurt and... kill.

"The people who are after us are very smart, mom, and very organized. They haven't been caught yet. But they're not as smart as us kids. We're real smart, mom, and we don't need to be protected by being left out."

"How do you know what the other children feel like, Bobby?" asked Charlie.

"Because we... talk."

Dr. Stouffer's mouth dropped about the same time that mine did.

"But, but how?" she stammered.

"Through the Internet, mom. It's not long distance."

"You talk?"

"Yes, mom. Mom, are you okay?"

She looked dazed and confused, as though she had just stepped through Alice's looking glass.

"Son of bitch," I said. "You've been using my computers to do it."

"Yes, Mr. Brown. I'm sorry that I didn't tell you before, but I know how mom feels, and how the other kids' parents feel."

"How many kids have you talked to, Bobby?" I asked.

"Three," he said proudly. "I didn't talk to everybody. Just the smartest ones that I thought could help."

"Bobby," said Dr. Stouffer, "you may have put them in danger."

"I think I might have helped them to stay alive, mom. And they have good ideas. We need each other."

"Good ideas?" asked Katerina. "Such as what?"

"Such as, we went into all of the kids medical records. All hospital records are on data bases these days."

"You did what?" I said. "Bobby, that's not possible. They've got new privacy laws everywhere these days. And computer security is a lot tighter."

"Maybe for you, Mr. Brown, but we speak all of the languages required, and getting past the computer security screens—including their firewalling at the hospitals— was easy enough. There are certain languages which we didn't know, but they weren't relevant search parameters. In other words, we didn't need to know them. Such as Nigerian."

"Why not?"

He shrugged.

"Can I have something to drink, mom? I'm thirsty."

"I'll get it," offered Gregorio. "What you want kid?"

"My name's Bobby, Bobby Stouffer. And I'd like a Coke. I'm not a kid."

"Sure thing, little buddy. Coke coming up."

"Bobby?" I prompted.

"Well, psychologically speaking, Mr. Hemlock is most likely to be prejudiced. He wouldn't want a black person's brain for the work with his polymeric processor. There's no scientific reason for it, but he would act out the matrix of his stereotypes. He would want whoever he chose to be as much like him as possible. They would have to be white, and they would have to be male. It's intuitively obvious to the discerning observer. Mr. Hemlock, at one level, acts like a god. And God created man in his own image. Mr. Hemlock would do the same, since this would a secondary reinforcement of his own self-perception. Wouldn't you agree, mom?"

You really had to be there to get the flavor of this. Here was this kid sipping a Coke and discussing his psychological evaluation of one of the richest men in the world as though they were two old colleagues just kicking the psycho-shit around. The kid was awe-inspiring.

"Well," said Dr. Stouffer as though she were operating on automatic pilot until she could sort all of this out, "it sounds... reasonable. But—"

"But what mom? The guys a freaky geek on a power trip. Admit it, he'd want the implant to go into someone who reminded him of himself."

"And," I said, "as a nasty son of a bitch, he'd want a decoy to sick the wolves on if they got too close," I said.

"Me," nodded Bobby. "I see what you mean, now. But what are my qualifications as a decoy?"

"Your head wound, Bobby. When you had reconstructive plastic surgery on your forehead, Allen Hemlock was careful to pay for all of the bills and even suggested the doctor. Your mom went in and saw someone who said he was the doctor. But I'd bet that the real guy who operated on you was named Dr. Estes.

"Head wound plus surgery. He probably put a regular sheet of medically accepted plastic into your head. If someone were to check your medical records, they'd think that they'd found the secret. If they checked your head, they would find what they would think would be the real implant. Only it wouldn't be.

"But it would be deniable in case the police got involved. This way, not only the Brothers would be discredited, but the very idea of a computing polymer installed into some gifted kid would be ridiculed as well. Now do you understand what I meant?"

"That's very perceptive, Mr. Brown."

"Bobby, wouldn't the man who installed this shit be the guy to collar and grill?" asked Leo.

"What did you say?" asked Katerina.

"Very good, Mr. Croton," replied Bobby. "Except for the fact that, according to the databases, Dr. Nathaniel Estes is dead."

"Oh," said Leo. "How did he die?"

"A pulmonary edema." answered Bobby.

"Bullshit," grinned Gregorio. "A bullshit set job to pull him out of circulation and keep him under wraps."

"Okay," said Leo reluctantly, "I'll buy the idea. But if they iced him to keep him out of trouble, where did they hide him?"

"Bobby?" I urged.

He frowned, and then closed his eyes for a moment.

"How do you think," said Dr. Stouffer angrily, "that he's supposed to know the answer to a question like that? He may be a genius, but—"

"Mom," said Bobby patiently, "I'm thinking."

"Oh. Sorry."

"Okay. I've got it. I know how to find him."

I was really rooting for him, because I had no damned idea even where to start looking.

"I was confused," Bobby explained, "because I thought it was me they wanted."

"The New Apostles do want you, Bobby," I said, "you and every other kid that attended that conference until they get a lock on who has the real thing in their head. We've got to stop them before Hemlock feels the pressure and throws you to them to make them think that they've got what they wanted."

"Can I use your computers again, Mr. Brown?"

"Do it. Just don't leave any electronic footprints wherever you're going in cyberspace."

"Trust me," he grinned, and then scooted out of his chair and up the spiral stairs.

"That's some kid you've got there, Dr. Stouffer," said Leo.

"Um-hum," she said, watching his tennis shoes disappear up the stairway.

"You are very quiet, Mr. Brown," observed Katerina. "What

occupies your mind?"

"I was thinking," I told her, "about what it would be like to be twelve or thirteen years old and have some psycho after your head with a scalpel."

"Here's what else I was thinking," I said to the entire group. "Our first concern is the Church of the New Apostles. Get rid of their leaders, and the killing will stop. I think that they have been contracting out the killings, for the most part, although there is one of them named Brother James that I think from time to time does some of the work himself just because he enjoys it. Anyway, if we take out the players within the church, there will be no one left to pay the bills, and that will be that. You don't pay your killers on time, they cut off their services."

"Sounds reasonable," said Leo. "But we would only get one shot. You sure that you know who to take down? We've got to get them all the first time."

Karl had been silent for a while. As the oldest hand in the bunch, he had known where this was going for a long time. When you reach his age and you're still doing people, you've made your piece with it a long time ago.

"Have you selected a killing field?" he asked calmly.

"Scott, is there no other way?" asked Dr. Stouffer. "The police—"

"I'm not taking any chances with these kid's lives, Kris. A quick execution is the only way to get this done. Period. It's the death penalty, plain and simple. No police, no courts, no prison sentence. I can understand if you want to leave the room.

"I'll do the killing myself. The rest of these people are only here to cover my ass so that I can get the job done."

I turned back to Karl.

"Yes, to answer your question. A right unusual one."

"What you got in mind, buddy?" asked Leo.

"The salt mines," I said, "under Detroit. I'm going to put my experience to good use. I'm going to gas them in an enclosed area. There's a place I built in a section that's down deep where I planned on hiding out if I ever felt the need. The mines themselves are closed down, so no one else will be in danger. After I gas the Brothers, there's plenty of space to dissipate the fumes into the rest of the mines.

Whatever doesn't dissipate will react out with the salt."

"Gas them?" asked Gregorio. "What do you mean, gas them?"

"Poison gas. Going to make them a nitrogen dioxide gift pack. A little metal, a little nitric acid, some dark brown clouds, and then they can breathe deep the gathering gloom. A couple of serious pulmonary edemas later and they won't be bothering anybody again."

Nobody likes poison gas. It's one thing to point a gun at someone and blow their brains out. That's understandable. That's tough. They've got a gun; you've got a gun. It sounds fair. But poison gas is something else entirely. Poison gas is not fair.

And nitrogen dioxide isn't like carbon monoxide. It's not colorless, it's not odorless, and it's definitely not painless. Your eyes start to burn; your nasal passages get scorched about the same time. It's because the humidity in the air acidizes the gas. Your lungs burn like they are on fire; they begin to fill with fluid. And your heart ends up with a problem. Your heart dies. That's a big problem.

The rest of you dies, too.

"I'm going to seal them off and gas them."

"How you going to get them in?" asked Gregorio.

"I'll be the bait," I said.

"And how," asked Katerina, "do you plan to get out?"

"Same way that I did last time. Gas mask and an acid suit."

"You're loco," said Gregorio. "They'll have hardware. They'll shoot your ass. An acid suit won't stop bullets."

"This is crazy," said Dr. Stouffer. "There's got to be another way."

I shook my head.

"I have to kill them where there are no other people around to get a stray bullet in the process. There's no way that I'd win a gunfight against as many people as they could bring in to finish the job. But if I trap them and gas them, nobody else is going to get hurt. I've just got to seal them off before they start shooting."

"Let me get this straight," said Leo. "You're going to get them to walk into a room that they can't get out of, but that you can get out of. This sounds like bullshit, Scott."

"They won't have a chance," said Dr. Stouffer.

"That's the idea," I told her.

"The little ones," said Gregorio, "they had no chance."

"But this is murder. You'll be no better than they are."

There. It was out. Finally.

"If you can get them into this room," she continued, "couldn't you just leave them locked in there, and then notify the authorities to come get them?"

"Kris," I said as patiently as I could, "we have no evidence that would hold up in court. If we did, I'd use the police—if I thought that Allen Hemlock wouldn't shut down the investigation using a lot of cash and some national security bullshit.

"Remember, he brought me on board because he wanted to keep the Brothers away from his son. That's the only reason. He wants us to shut the Brothers down. He just doesn't know that we know about him. Otherwise, you and I wouldn't be sitting here talking. We would be dead."

"Do you mean to tell me that if Allen Hemlock thought that we would expose him, that he'd have us killed?" she asked.

I looked around the table.

"Anybody here," I said, "who thinks that Allen Hemlock wouldn't have us killed raise your hand now or forever be silent."

Dr. Stouffer's eyes went from Leo to Katerina, from Katerina to Karl, from Karl to Gregorio, from Gregorio to Charlie. No one's hand popped up.

"I now pronounce us in as much danger from Allen Hemlock as we are from the Church of the New Apostles."

"But Allen Hemlock is a respected businessman," she protested. "He may have grease for ethics, buy I can't believe that he would have us killed."

"Who inserted a new polymeric supercomputer into some unsuspecting kid's head and probably put a dummy into Bobby's to use him as a decoy if he needed him? Not to mention the shit that he's done to you. Have you forgotten about that?"

You know what would be a great invention? An electronic billboard that you could put on someone's forehead where you could read what they were thinking in bright red letters instead of having to try and guess what the hell was going through their mind. I'd buy stock in that.

What was going through Dr. Stouffer's mind was impossible to decipher. She was having a hard time of it, though, that much I could tell.

"I just don't know if I can agree with killing these people in cold blood. Is that what you plan to do to Allen Hemlock, too?"

"No," I said, "him I planned to shoot. Just for old time's sake. After the Brothers are taken care of."

"You can't be serious. You can't just shoot Allen Hemlock."

"Sure I can. And his jerkwad son right along with him. Who else is going to do it?"

"Are you so convinced that someone has to do this?"

"Aren't you?" I countered.

"I don't care about them," she said, "I care about you."

"And I don't know if I'm worth caring about. I've got too much blood on my hands—innocent and guilty."

"But that could all be past."

"Maybe. You are what you've done, Kris."

"Scott," said Charlie quietly, "a man is what he does. And a man does what is in his heart. We make new choices every day."

"Are you saying that I should just let this go?"

"No," he said, "I am saying that you should think before you act. Think carefully. It is a warrior's obligation."

"Charlie, do you think I want to kill these people? Okay, you're right, I do. They need killing. Not because I want to kill them, but because they've crossed the line."

"Who elected you their judge?" asked Kris. "And who says that you have to be judge, jury, and executioner?"

Think, Charlie had said. What the hell was I supposed to do, find an "elegant" solution to an inelegant problem?

"Mr. Brown?"

It was Bobby, coming down the stairs.

"Yeah?"

"I heard what you were talking about again. Sorry."

"It's not your fault. We get kind of loud."

"But I want to help. I think that your analysis is wrong. They could hurt each other."

"Look, Bobby—"

He was at the foot of the stairs, walking toward me.

"Do you love my mother, Mr. Brown?"

"Ah—"

"Do you love yourself?"

I couldn't think of what to say. He was standing next to me by that time. His eyes wide and direct, staring straight at me without blinking.

"I don't know about that kind of... stuff, Bobby."

"Mom, do you love Mr. Brown?"

"Bobby, this isn't the time or place—"

"If you don't tell him, I think that he's going to get hurt real bad."

He waited for one of us to answer, but neither of us did. We were, after all, adults.

"You're his friends," he said to the group at large. "If I figured out a different way, one that wouldn't make my mom cry, would you make him listen? I know who has the polymeric processor implanted in their head. I know where Dr. Estes is. I know a way to end this without any of you killing anyone."

"You do?" asked Katerina.

"Where no one else would get killed?""Almost no one," he said hesitantly.

"You know who has the processor implanted in their brain?" I asked.

"Scott wouldn't have to kill anyone?" asked Dr. Stouffer.

"Almost no one," he repeated.

"What you got in mind, Bobby?" asked Leo.

From the corner of my eye, I saw Charlie looking at me, watchful as a cat near a birdcage.

Somewhere along the way, I realized, it had become Bobby's meeting.

The Abduction

My plan was out; Bobby's was officially in. The one where almost nobody had to die. As plans went, I had to admit that it was pretty slick. I wasn't happy that Dr. Stouffer had made me promise not to gas everyone, but I had another plan in mine. The one where almost everybody died.

Leo, Karl, and Katerina had already left to snatch Dr. Estes. Charlie and Dr. Stouffer were staying behind on the island to watch over Bobby and maintain a base of operations. Gregorio and I were on our way to nab John Hemlock.

Bobby had compared it to chess. While I had been concentrating on the big picture, it had never occurred to me that the other side's—both of them—most important piece was vulnerable. If, that is, you knew who the most vulnerable piece was.

"It's his son," Bobby had explained to us. "His son fits the parameters. He put the polymer into his own son's head. Dr. Estes, who is operating under an assumed name, is probably his doctor."

"Let's say I buy this," I had said. "How can we know for sure?"

"John Hemlock's doctor, according to his medical records in the computer databases that I penetrated, is Dr. Fred Frylander, who lives at 1543 Garvey Rd. in Sterling Heights."

"So how do you know that he's really Dr. Estes?" asked Leo.

"Because seven years ago, Dr. Fred Frylander died at the age of forty-three in Buffalo, NY."

"Maybe there were two doctors with the same name." I suggested.

"Oh, no, Mr. Brown. In the computerized history of the American Medical Association, there has only been one doctor by that name. Tactically, because of the rarity of the name, they made a mistake. A doctor named Smith or Jones would have been a superior choice. There must have been a reason behind their choice, perhaps ease of assumability, but it was still a tactical error. Dr. Estes has become Dr. Frylander; he is even using the same credit cards, which is kind of hard, since the real Dr. Frylander is dead. Dr. Frylander's area of expertise, by the way, was neurosurgery."

"This would also explain why I was called in as John's therapist," said Dr. Stouffer distractedly.

"Sure thing," I said, "the expert in discriminating between human and artificial intelligence is told to become the guinea pig's personal therapist. Slick move on Allen's part. If there's a problem, you're there to sort it out."

"He turned his own kid," said Gregorio, "into an experiment. You should shoot him anyway."

I could feel Dr. Stouffer staring at me. Gregorio could be a real shithead sometimes.

*****

"Hey amigo," said Gregorio, "you shouldn't have lied to the kid."

"Shut up," I told him, "I took you to a Mexican restaurant, what more do you want?"

He was finishing his third taco and washing it down with a swig of pop.

"Yeah, but it was bad to lie to the kid."

"Don't leave those wrappers wadded up on the floor," I said, "this is my good car—my haul-a-hostage station wagon; I don't want it looking like a pig pen when we pick up Johnny. He's used to classy things, you know."

Gregorio grinned.

The station wagon was outfitted specially with a sliding window of bulletproof glass like they have in taxicabs in New York. The back of the front seat was metal plate. Doors in the back that you couldn't lock or unlock except from the outside, dark, tinted windows in the back seat and storage area, and restraining chains in the back seat.

It was a pretty grim vehicle.

"I mean it, I like this car clean."

He scrunched the taco wrappers and the pop cup into the bag, wadded the entire thing up, then threw it over his shoulder through the half open dividing window into the back seat.

"Clean enough?" he asked.

"Asshole."

"This is a clean park. What you want me to do, throw it out on the grass? You want to make it look like Mexico City?"

Elizabeth Park is where I go when I want to think. It's a lot easier to do when I'm alone.

"Look at this place, eh?" he continued. "Green grass, little yellow flowers—"

"Dandelions," I corrected him.

"Yeah, whatever. Trees. It even smells clean. Swings, and teeter-totters and shit. You can see the river over there. And quiet—nice and peaceful."

"Used to be," I said.

"You missed me," he said with a wink, "I know."

"I'm trying to think, Gregorio."

"About what?"

"About how to get you to shut up."

"Oh. I get it."

I didn't want to lie to Bobby. I hadn't meant to lie to him. I was leaving extra maneuvering. It was just that even though I had seen the files at John Hemlock's house, I didn't know if they were real or red herrings. These days it didn't take jack to computer alter a photograph. And I didn't trust either Hemlock anymore, but I especially didn't trust John. He was whacked out enough without a plastic life form tied to his brain.

The natural beauty of Elizabeth Park seemed more real to me than it had in all of the years that I had been coming there to relax. Okay, so it really wasn't "natural" natural beauty, what with the county maintenance people mowing the grass and what not, but the trees and the grass and the bushes and even the goddamned dandelions were real. There was so much plastic shit in the world that it was actually nice to be around things that grew right out of the ground instead of being injection molded into existence.

Down the road a way, I could see the ice cream concession stand where the little kids would drag their parents so that the parents could buy them chocolate and vanilla ice cream. They didn't carry eight million flavors there, just chocolate and vanilla. For some reason, on that day I found the lack of options comforting.

In the late afternoon, if you walked by the ice cream place, you could see brown and white blots of ice cream that had melted down over chubby little fingers and dripped onto the blades of grass.

Beyond the ice cream stand was the pony place. A little plank shed of rough, gray-white wood and a rickety corral where for fifty cents your kid could ride the ponies around the circular fence. In their little imaginations, it was probably as good as or better than the rodeo. I liked the smell where Gregorio and I were parked.

Even pony shit stinks.

But they had these little stagecoach-like wagons you could rent, and a pony would take you down this trail that wound through the woods. The trees and vines and bushes lining the trail walled off the world and it was like you really were in the wilderness for a moment, released from the binding ropes of time.

Every now and then when I walked through the park, I would go and stand in the bushes and watch the parents and their kids and the ponies clopping along the packed earth trail.

If my family were still alive, they could have been us.

"Hey, Gregorio," I said, "what do you think of this plastic brain stuff?"

"Pretty weird, amigo. Like science fiction. I think it's bullshit. Scientists are bullshit."

"Yeah," I said.

"I don't believe anybody's ever been to outer space, either. I think that's bullshit, too."

"What?"

"You know, I think they do all that crap in Hollywood. Make it look real, you know. That's crazy, people walking around in space. I heard that's what the Russians did."

He slapped me lightly on the shoulder.

*****

Gregorio and I took a walk.

"I got a friend," he continued, "who saw one of these Russian docu-things—about walking in space that was so bad, you could see the strings if you look real close. What about that shit, hey?"

"Gregorio, what the hell are you talking about?"

He leaned closer to me, his browned skin glinting with a glow from the sun.

"Listen, man," he said, "they put in artificial hearts and lungs now. How long did you think it would be before they started replacing our brains? Scientists got no soul, man. They're like crackheads looking for a pipe. They measure this, they build this. You know why they do that? It's power, amigo. Scientists are the most dangerous people in this fucking world. Power is crack to them.

"I seen this researcher once in this medical lab. You know, I was doing some checking around for some shit contract for this one company. Well, I go into this lab and there's only this one person there, this lady, and I mean lady. Ooh, a beautiful, magnificent woman. Ahhh."

"Gregorio—"

"Oh, but she was tall, and gorgeous, and she had this long black glowing hair and these eyes. Magnetic eyes. You know, like she could hypnotize you or something. And when I tell her I'm there to see the lab director, she tells me she's the lab director, and asks how she can help me. How can she help me? I'm thinking that if she takes off that white lab coat and drops to the floor—"

"You ever tell Maria this story?" I asked.

"Huh? No way, man, no way.

"Anyway, I tell her I need to talk to her, and she says she has to check her experiment first, and then we can go into her office. So I think okay. When she's turning around, though, I notice these little red dots that look like blood on her sleeve, but I think, 'no way.'

"But I follow her back to this little lab room, and what do you think it is that she was checking on?"

"I don't have a clue," I sighed.

"You're fucking right you don't have a clue," he said. "You could guess for a thousand years, and you'd never even get close. She's got these little white mice tied to this plywood. You know, little trash tie wires go through holes in the wood and each of their little feet and hands are tied back to the wood like they was in fucking mice prison. It was weird shit.

"And these mice are tied, so they're like standing straight up. They look like little people in white furry suits. And they're alive."

"So?" I asked impatiently.

"So? I'll tell you so. She's got their stomachs or something cut open and peeled back and thumbtacked back to the wood. And she's got these little teeny stainless steel clamps fastened on these tubes inside the mice that you can't hardly see except she's got these rectangular magnifying glasses mounted on stands. One in front of each poor little mouse.

"I ask her, I say, 'Senorita, what are you doing here?'

"And she's real happy to tell me. She lights up like a freaking Christmas tree when I ask. She thinks maybe I'm a scientist, too, or something.

"She says that she's clamped off their pisser tubes."

"Their what?" I asked.

"You know, the tube that goes to their little dicks so that they can piss. I forget what name she called them. Anyway, she's clamped them off. They were all guy mice, see?

"I ask her why, and she tells me it's to see how long they can live with their dicks shut off. This is a sick bitch, man. Very sick. But she's a scientist, so it's okay. There's something wrong with scientists. Better living through chemistry, my ass. They just want to keep us alive longer so they've got more time to fuck with us."

"What the hell are you trying to say?"

"I think that brain plastic is the real thing, amigo. People who play with mouse dicks will play with anything."

We'd been walking aimlessly for about fifteen minutes.

"So you going to tell me, or what?" asked Gregorio. "I mean it's a nice park, but..."

A brown squirrel ran across our path, then stopped and looked up at us, as if daring us to take another step into his territory. I stopped and looked at him, eye to eye. He wasn't going to back down. I stomped my foot. He didn't budge.

"I outweigh you by a hundred and eighty pounds," I said.

Gregorio grinned.

"Hey," he said, "we could catch him and cook him for dinner."

The little furball sniffed the air, checking me out.

"I've got a gun stuffed in my waistband under this jacket," I said.

"He knows you won't shoot him."

I turned and looked at Gregorio.

"That's it," I said.

"What?"

"I've gone soft."

"Bullshit."

"Really, I got a thirteen-year-old telling me what to do. Running my operation."

"He's a smart kid."

"Yeah, but that's not it. I've got this bandage on my face that makes me look like the mummy, stitches in my balls, scars and shit on my arm from that prick in Mexico. I've done my time, Gregorio. I'm a hard guy."

"So?" he asked.

"So why am I folding like a cheap card table?"

"Ah, so that's it. You're in love, muchacho."

"Fuck you."

"No, fuck you. You're in love, really in love. Before, you were always a circle jerk of one."

"A what?"

"Now you find something... something wonderful, and it doesn't fit in with the way you see life. You been feeling safe that the world is cold and bad. So, her and the kid scare you, and you want to push them away. You want to walk away, go down in flames like Romeo did on Juliet."

Gregorio smacked me hard with his open palm on my good shoulder. "What's the matter, you got low self-esteem? You need a support group or something? You ain't soft, you're scared, you dumb shit.

"Maria always been after me to hook you up with a Spanish woman. I tell her, 'leave him alone. Someday, a good woman will find him.' Hey, today's your lucky day."

I looked around to the squirrel, to see what he had to say about it, but he was gone. The squirrel had taken a tough stance, but underneath he was a chickenshit, too.

*****

The bridge between Grosse Isle and Trenton was one of those turning bridges that rotated on a central axis to turn sideways and let the big boats through. It had an operator's office halfway across and up in the metal beams with windows on all sides where this guy would sit all day and jack off unless he had to throw the switch and turn the bridge, which happened about once or twice a day.

The whole bridge was maybe half a mile long, but only the middle fifty percent turned. There were railroad flasher bars that fell down to hold back traffic on each end when that happened.

John Hemlock would be coming across that bridge. It was the only way to get off of the island since the toll bridge at the other end was being repaired.

Karl, Leo, and Katerina had insured that he would be coming by nabbing Dr. Estes and holding a gun to his head while he called John and said that he needed to see him in his office.

For our part, Gregorio and I, after parking the car next to the operator's special parking place, had gone up to the bridge command office, and camped out with the operator himself. He had other ideas when he saw our ski masks and gloves, but when Gregorio put a gun to his head, the guy quieted down a bit.

The timing was going to be a little tricky, but we could handle that.

When I saw John's car through the binoculars coming down the Grosse Ile Parkway, I walked back down the metal steps, and hid behind two broad silver I-beams.

We were lucky. Traffic was pretty much nonexistent, except for John's convertible Mercedes. Convertibles always made it easier to grab the guy driving it. Even when the top is up, they don't do much. Cloth tops aren't bullet proof, and they're easy enough to cut open with a blade if you need to get at who's inside.

It had been a long time since I had been really lucky, but that day I was.

When the convertible was thirty feet from the midpoint of the bridge, Gregorio flipped the switch that turned on the flashers, dropped the guard bar, and pushed the button to turn the bridge.

Hemlock slammed on the brakes, uncertain what to do. With the bridge starting to slowly move in response to the high-pitched grating of the big motors, there was no way off. I waited where I was, pretty damned sure that he would be walking my way soon enough.

I didn't hear him coming. The bridge-turning motor was too damn loud. But when I saw him on the walkway, I stepped out of the shadows, aiming my gun straight at his heart.

"Don't even think about running, Johnny, if you want to live to see tomorrow."

He was dressed nicely for someone who was responding to a call to go see his doctor on short notice. You can always pick out rich people in times of natural disasters, like earthquakes or war. They're the ones still wearing clean clothes while everyone else is in rags.

"You did this?" he asked.

He had on a white-gold shirt, light gray slacks, and matching gray shoes and socks. On his left wrist, he wore the regulation rich person-Rolex.

"No, John," I said, "I just happened to be standing here with a gun in my hand. Don't be stupid. No bullshit, it doesn't really matter to me whether you're dead or alive. So don't screw with me. You see my car over there? Just walk to it, get in the back seat, and sit down. You do that, and I won't have to shoot you."

"What's this all about?" he demanded.

"First mistake, John. You open your mouth again, and I'll wax you. Now move."

He sized me up the way they always do—but in the end, he turned and did what I told him to do.

When he was in the backseat, I manacled both of his wrists to the chain that went to the iron ring set onto the floor. Before closing the car door behind him, I waited to hear the satisfying click of the metal wristlocks engaging. Then I put the neck ring around his neck and locked that into place. He wasn't going anywhere.

The rear windows were blackened on the station wagon, and with the animal control magnetic sticker I fixed to the rear door, we looked street legal enough to get us where we were going.

I had taken John's car keys, so I got into the Mercedes, and pulled it up right behind my car and put the top up so that Gregorio wouldn't muss his hair when he drove it. Next, I went back up and told Gregorio we were on track. He punched the buttons to set the bridge right again, waved good-bye to the operator laying on the floor whom he had cracked on the head and shot up with a little sleep inducer, and we went back down the stairs and got into the cars. We were headed to the salt mines to meet up with the rest of the crew.

The weather was good enough, but what was really making my day was cruising down the road with John Hemlock shackled in the back seat like he was on his way to death row. I turned the radio on.

"You like gangster rap, John?" I asked.

"Not particularly," he said.

"Good."

At the next stop sign, I slid the bulletproof glass that ran along the back of the front seat so that it was nearly closed, turned up the volume, and slid the speaker switch to rear speakers only. I could feel the back of the seat vibrate from the sound.

Yeah, I was having a good time.

"Where are we?"

"We're in Oz, John," I shouted, "I'm going to ask the wizard about getting you a real brain."

*****

And Oz was where we were.

Miles and miles of underground darkness, abandoned over a decade ago for a variety of reasons, but the main being was that it was unsafe to operate. Caverns the size of football fields. Abandoned excavation and hauling vehicles three stories tall. Conveyor systems that stretched for miles. Walls, ceilings, and floors of crystalline white. The interior of a human anthill. We were in the salt mines of Detroit.

In the nineteen fifties, when air-raid shelters were the rage in the United States, people in the Detroit area didn't feel the need to join in and build shelters to protect them from nuclear attack. The entire city, it was thought, could go down into the salt mines and be safe. That should give you an idea of how big the place is.

The tunnels extended outward underground for over ten miles, like the spokes from a gigantic, underground wheel. Superheated steam was shot out along these tunnels to flush back the brine, which was then evaporated to yield the salt.

When the steam injections were removed, so much salt that roads over ten miles away started to cave in, the suburbs started to bitch. Parts of Grosse Isle even caved in. So, the salt company yielded to public pressure, and closed down the business. Now the salt mines are completely abandoned and off limits. Which is why I like them. No chance of being disturbed if you're doing something you shouldn't.

"Fucking spooky," said Gregorio.

I had a blindfold on John Hemlock, tied so tightly that he was lucky if he got blood to any part of his head higher than his eyeballs.

"Watch your step, John," I warned him.

"You'll pay for this," he said through clenched teeth.

"Not likely," I replied.

We had gone over a half a mile to get to the abandoned underground warehouse that I had claimed five years ago as my headquarters-of-last-resort. It was a metal structure, two stories high. The only place in the awesome darkness where lights shone, reflecting out on to the milky white crystalline walls. The salt ceiling overhead was lost in darkness.

"You need a name for this place," said Gregorio.

"Got one," I said.

"Yeah?"

"The Cemetery. What do you think of that?"

"Too happy," he said. "Can't you think of something more depressing?"

"I think it fits. I always figured someday a lot of people would be coming after me and were going to die down here."

"Like I said," said Gregorio, "you shouldn't have lied to the kid."

I shoved John Hemlock ahead of us toward the warehouse. He stumbled, so I pushed him again just for the fun of it.

"This is going to work," I told Gregorio.

"So, you going to run this whole show down here alone?"

"I can do it," I said.

"You know—" he began.

"Don't say it," I warned him.

"I think you need a lot more men."

Insanity

I had ditched Hemlock's car in a parking lot in Taylor long before we got to the salt mines, leaving the key in the ignition. It wouldn't last long. Even though Taylor is in the Downriver area, there's this joke that should give you the flavor of the town. It goes like this: What do you say when you meet a woman from Taylor?

Answer: Nice tooth.

Hemlock's car ought to be in two hundred pieces before bedtime.

Gregorio, Leo, Karl, and Katerina were preparing the welcome arrangements for our expected visitors; I was headed back to meet with Allen, whom I had finally got a call back from on my portable phone. He would meet me at his private office at Detroit Metropolitan airport.

While Gregorio and I had been picking up John Hemlock, Katerina had acquired his physician and brought him to the salt mines. Dr. Estes hadn't been at all what I had expected. He didn't look evil enough. Movies have taken typecasting to such an art form, that sometimes real villains are disappointing. I found myself thinking this can't be Dr. Estes; it must be some kind of a mistake.

At first glance, he was a kindly looking old man. Thin. Stoop shouldered. Bald on top, but with a fine, white halo of hair that horseshoed his head. His facial skin was loose. His cheeks were splotched red, and blossomed like spidery flower tendrils.

Katerina had strapped him into one of the office chairs. His light brown suite, white shirt, and burgundy silk tie were rumpled, and he had a haggard, vulnerable look.

"Are you in charge here?" he demanded. "What is the meaning of this?"

John Hemlock was in another room, out of hearing range. It was just me and the doctor. Everyone else had disappeared to carry out the details of our plan.

"Did I tell you you could ask questions?" I asked. "Did I?"

"I demand to know why I'm here."

His voice had a screeching, crow-like quality to it. When he spoke, I noticed he had the sunken-faced look of old people with dentures. I wondered how he would sound without the false teeth.

"I don't give a rat's ass about what you demand."

"Who are you people? Why are you doing this?"

The effect that his voice was having on my nerves reminded me of crushed glass rubbed against abraded skin.

"Dr. Estes. That is your real name, isn't it?"

For an evil little prick, he had weak blue eyes, the color of water in a toilet bowl with one of those tablet dyes added to the tank that had been flushed way too many times. But when I said the name Estes, he squinted at me as though he had found a new specimen that he wanted to dissect.

"Who told you that?"

"You know," I said, "for a guy strapped in a chair, you sure are pushy. I don't like pushy people. I don't untie pushy people. I only untie cooperative people. You know what I do to uncooperative people? I tie off their dicks and sit back to wait and watch until they explode."

Okay, I got the idea from Gregorio, but I liked the way it sounded.

"Why are you doing this to me?"

"Because I really don't like you, Dr. Estes," I said. "But Brother Thomas says that although I can torture you as much as I want, I can't kill you just yet."

His face was already too pale to turn any whiter, but by the way his facial muscles tightened, I'd say that he already knew all about Brother Thomas.

"You're with Brother Thomas?"

I nodded gravely.

"You people are sick," he said, but he pulled his head back in fear when he said it.

I pulled up a metal chair, turned it so the back faced him, and straddled the seat.

"At least we don't go around cutting open kid's heads and putting abominations inside."

"Abominations? You call my work an abomination?"

"I do."

"What do you know of it? What do you know of what I have accomplished?"

"I know that I've got a low threshold for mad scientists."

"Mad scientist? Is that what you think I am?"

"You tell me," I said.

"Why should I talk to you? You're all religious fanatics. What do you know of reason and science?"

I leaned over the back of the chair a little.

"Try me, Doc, and you just might live through the night. I'm a hired gun, not a true believer. You got a story that will explain all of the shit that's been going on, I'll let you go. But if you're as crazy as the Brothers say, I'm going to waste you right now—orders or no orders."

While we sat there, Katerina, and Karl were setting the explosives into place. I'd given them maps of the salt tunnels, and told them to be careful—like they needed to hear it. Leo was standing guard over John Hemlock. I would have rather handled the explosives myself.

Dr. Estes, who didn't know he'd been fingered by a teenager, was considering my offer.

"You'll listen with an open mind?" he finally asked.

I assured him I would.

"You're lying."

"Suit yourself," I told him. "You can wait and talk to Brother Thomas and his crew when they get here."

He yanked as hard as his old arms would let him, but the straps binding his wrists didn't budge.

"You keep bouncing around in that chair, and it'll tip over. You'll probably break your neck, or maybe just sever your spinal cord.

Hard to run when you're quadriplegic."

"Let me out of here," he screamed.

"Okay," I said.

"Really?" he asked.

"Got you," I said.

"What do you want from me?"

"I want you to tell me the truth about what you've done, Dr. Estes, like I said. I'm an impartial audience for now. Like I told you, I'm not a believer. But I'm nobody to fuck with. And if you lie to me, I'll deliver you to Brother Thomas."

I could almost see his resignation in the way that his frame seemed to suddenly sag, as though there was no point anymore in trying to put up a fight. He looked so pathetic, that I might even have felt sorry for him, but the memory of all of those dead kids kept getting in the way.

The Warehouse of the Dead.

Crate upon crate of Latin American kids stacked on pallets. Drums of hazardous wastes. Labels with skulls and crossbones. The smell of death.

"I've done nothing wrong," he said at last. "My technology will benefit the entire human race."

Dramatic pause, seeing if I would buy in.

"I've invented an entirely new technology. It's taken my whole life to do so. What we now call supercomputers will become obsolete."

He was leaning forward, more animated now. There was a spark of life in his rheumy eyes.

"Listen to me," he said, "I know you cannot understand the technology that I have created, but you can understand the general concepts, and it is vital to all mankind that this work not be lost. If my work is successful, I will have created a living computer. Do you understand? A living computer."

"A living computer? Bullshit."

"No. The final leap forward in evolution. It will be a new life form. A thinking polymer."

"So, I'll finally be able to talk to my sandwich wrap? Cool."

"Please take what I'm saying seriously. I don't know who you are, I don't know your background, but—"

I reached underneath my jacket and pulled out the Beretta. His eyes widened as I stood, walked over to him, and put the barrel to his head. I could smell the urine as he wet himself.

"I'm going to count to ten, Doc. If you don't tell me my name by the time I do that, I'm going to blow your brains out. One."

"Please..."

"Two."

"Listen to me."

"Three."

"I can make you a rich man."

"Four."

"You don't know what you're doing..."

"Five."

"We're talking about the fate of the world."

"Six."

"No one else can complete this experiment. No one."

"Seven."

"Oh, God, my heart..."

"Eight."

"Brown."

"Nine."

"Scott Brown."

I put the Beretta back under my coat, went back and straddled the chair again.

"You were saying?" I prompted.

He was still shaking. He couldn't talk.

"You want me to start counting again, Doc?"

"No, no," he said quickly, "I just—"

"You're just a little nervous. Is that it?"

"Yes, that's it."

"Ready to start talking again?"

"Yes, I'm ready."

"Go for it."

"I'm sorry. I shouldn't have lied to you. I knew who you were."

"No, you shouldn't have."

"I was—"

"You were just a little nervous," I said again. "We already plowed that ground once."

He took a deep breath, trying to get control of the shakes. I waited him out.

"You see," he said, "this technology is so revolutionary that it's worth—uncounted billions of dollars. A new life form. The first in the history of mankind. A created life form. The first in the history of the planet."

"Unless," I pointed out casually, "you happen to believe in God."

Dr. Estes, a.k.a. Dr. Frylander, looked at me as though I had lost my mind.

"God?" he asked. "God doesn't exist, Mr. Brown. God is a myth."

"A persistent one, you have to admit."

"Fah," he said contemptuously, "next you'll be telling me you believe in the objective existence of good and evil."

Now there's a thought.

"I thought that this polymer was a computer. How do you figure that it's alive?"

"Oh, it is alive. You understand that polymers have a crystalline content, don't you?"

"Sure thing," I said.

"Do you know what piezoelectric crystals are?"

"Apply stress to a piezoelectric crystal, and it produces energy. Is that about right?"

"Very good, Mr. Brown. Very good."

Blow me, I thought.

"Not only does my polymer have both micro and macromolecular gating, it also has a piezoelectric crystalline content. An advancement in the understanding and usage of piezoelectric physics as far ahead of its time as Nicola Tesla was above Thomas Edison. It reacts to the presence of energy; the movement of energy is to my polymer what food is to our own biochemical bodies. Electromagnetic movement is its lifeblood. You are familiar perhaps, with the oriental concept of chi?"

I nodded.

"Chi," he continued as though I wasn't there, "is the movement of energy throughout our bodies. The vital fluids, as it were, of life. Our bodies, however, are inefficient vehicles at best. My polymer needs no biochemical interface with the subtle energy of chi. It is specifically designed for direct interaction with it. The intake and out-take of energy with my polymer, energies that the human body so inefficiently if at all handles, is the basis of its living qualities. What blood is to the human body, energy is to my polymer. The flow of blood through our bodies is analogous to the flow of energy through my polymer. Hence, it is alive.

"And it can think.

"Thinking is programming, in the ultimate sense. Our DNA programs us. The ELF of the host is absorbed over time into the polymer, and in that way it is programmed to think conceptually, freed from the confines of the body. The life force of the thinking host becomes the programming for the polymer. The polymer, once removed from the host, continues, in the beginning, to operate under the programming of the host human being. The personality itself, the history, and the essence of the host is transmuted from the dross of the body, to the gold of the new being."

"You're getting pretty fucking weird, Doc."

He just kept on talking as though I hadn't said anything.

"It will be free of disease, free of aging, free of the contamination of human emotions. It will be a—"

"Soulless piece of plastic," I offered.

"Pardon," he said, blinking his eyes.

"It will have no soul," I said. "A living, sentient being free of the messy burden of having a soul. And none of that bullshit about a conscience, either."

"Yes," he said happily. "Exactly."

I should have shot him right then and there. Later, I would regret that I hadn't.

"But how could I have known," he said, his voice suddenly dropping to a plaintive whisper.

"Known what?"

He didn't answer right away, but instead stared at the back of my chair as though it was an understanding colleague.

"Known what?" I repeated.

"About the poison," he said softly. "The oligomeric species

migration into the blood stream. It never occurred to me. The phenomenon was unknown until recently. How could I have known the dangers?"

He raised his head to look at me defiantly.

"What the hell are you talking about, doctor?"

"Oligomers. Short chain hydrocarbon contaminants that are soluble in organic fluids and can be leeched into the human body."

"You mean," I asked, "that the plastic was contaminated?"

"Residual by-products of the reaction that formed the plastic remained in the plastic. Small amounts that we never considered a problem back in the days when I first created the plastic. We had so little experience with plastics remaining in the body for prolonged periods of time. Such small amounts. We didn't know how to purify plastics back then. We never gave it much thought. It didn't seem to be necessary."

Gregorio had been right. Scientists were dangerous people.

"And what are the effects of these oligomers on the body?" I demanded.

He shrugged.

"We don't exactly know in this case. In other documented cases, they can cause, or seem to cause cancers or they can act as a poison. But this is a new type of polymer, you understand."

"But what do you think it causes?"

Jesus, it was tough getting a straight answer out of technical people.

"I think it might cause... insanity. Bizarre behavior. Distorted thinking patterns—"

"I know what fucking insanity is, you stupid prick, I'm looking straight at it right now."

John Hemlock suddenly became a lot more understandable. His plastic brain-buddy was leaking.

*****

Christine Hemlock was sitting in Allen Hemlock's airport office in one of the chairs across from his desk. Allen rose when I was admitted. I hardly paid attention to the way the place looked; I was still remembering the last thing that Dr. Estes had told me—that John Hemlock had known all about the transplant into his head before the operation was ever performed. And he had agreed—eagerly. John Hemlock had been one screwed-up kid.

"Scott, I'm so glad to see you."

Allen's greeting brought me back to attention.

"Yeah. Hello Christine."

Christine was wearing a peach chiffon colored dress with a high white collar. She looked like the Priestess of Purity. I wondered if I had left a bruise on the side of her neck.

"Hello, Mr. Brown," she said back with a tentative smile. "It's so nice to see you again. I just wish that it were under different circumstances."

"I don't understand," I said.

"Please, sit down," said Allen, motioning me toward the empty chair as though I needed his help to see that it was the only empty chair in the place. "I have terrible news."

The polymer computing platform has disappeared, and, oh yes, your son is gone, too.

"And what's that?" I asked as I dropped into the chair.

Christine sat a good three feet away from me in the other brown leather chair. I supposed I was safe enough unless she was hiding a machete under her skirt.

Allen Hemlock settled back into his own chair, his big hands spread wide apart in front of him as he told me about John's disappearance. Men like Allen performed well under stress. As he told me about his grief and worry, I felt like I had front row seats at Hemlock-on-Avon.

Christine did a lot of hand wringing and did the occasional teardrop thing. She didn't seem to remember trying to knife me the other day, but with the Hemlock family, how the hell could I ever know for sure?

Multiple personalities in one body. Like that meant something. She didn't need a shrink, she needed an exorcist.

She kept smoothing her dress, which didn't have a wrinkle in it in the first place. I wondered if it was a form of compulsive behavior, or if one part of her just liked the way that the fabric felt.

As the two of them continued to prattle on with their respective lines of bullshit, I began to wonder whether her father—the infamous Bill the Butcher—lived in Christine's head with her. If he did, he could sure get off on peeling back a few foreheads.

The thing was, people like the Hemlocks could move back and forth across international borders like the rest of us walk from one room in our house to another. With the kind of money that they were dealing with, anything was possible. Was this pretty young woman involved with some serious skin peeling and beheading?

Her hands were fine china white, with long elegant fingers that I already knew had some practice wielding a knife. As a child, she had seen and participated in horrors that even I didn't like to think about. Yet here she was, looking like a grown-up version of Little Miss Muffet. Sometimes, I realized, looks were not only deceiving, they had damn little to do with reality.

I nodded at the appropriate moments, expressed anger and concern myself, but all the while I was wondering if, in fact, it was Christine Hemlock's hands that had held the knives that had cut back the skin on the kids who had been butchered. Her dad would have been proud.

"It's Brother Thomas and his people, Allen," I said. "I'm sure of it. I've done some deep background checks with my computers on some of his key personnel, and they're former military special ops. Black bag shit. A snatch like this would be simple for them."

"Then why," he asked pointedly, "weren't you watching my son?"

"Because he wasn't an official attendee," I replied evenly. "John was there because you sponsored the conference. He wasn't logged in as one of those invited because he was too old. The age range was between five and seven years old. We looked at it, and when we realized he wasn't actually on the invited list because he didn't fit the age requirements, we discounted him immediately as a possible target."

"Well, you were obviously wrong. This is the second time that you've let one of my family members go missing."

His normally regular-guy face was reddened to the point that I thought he would burst a blood vessel. Even his ears were colored. Losing control of a potential revenue stream in the billions of dollars range and world domination to boot would have been hard on Attila the Hun himself. Allen wasn't holding up too badly, all things considered.

"Look, Allen, I know you're worried, but my assignment did not involve bodyguarding John. If you wanted that, you should have spelled it out, and I would have told you to fuck off right from the beginning. I don't do bodyguarding. I tried to tell you that last time around, remember?

"Now, we can either call in the FBI and the police like I advised you in the first place, or you can have me go get John myself. That kind of work I do handle. Besides, I'm tired of tiptoeing around these fuckers. I can't prove that these assholes are behind all of this shit, but I know they are. Unless you've changed your mind, I say you turn me loose like we talked at that dinner party and let me take the Church of the New Apostles apart from the top down.

"All you've got to do is make the call. Which way do you want this crap to go down? Street legal, or my way?"

"No one will be hurt, will they?" asked Christina nervously.

Not like you'd give a shit, honey. But maybe you'd like pictures of the dead bodies for your collection?

So, both father and son had known about the implant. But son John was a card-carrying member of the Church of the New Apostles, the group that was carrying out the killings. Was it him who had put the whole thing in motion in the first place as an insider? If that was the case, why? Was his cable box broken, or what?

From what Dr. Estes had told me about the impurities leaking into John's blood stream, maybe he had gone legitimately nuts instead of just being a genuinely evil little kid. If he was now a certifiable nutcase, maybe he had maneuvered Brother Thomas into his plastic Beast hunt to either kill off the potential competition, or just for the fun of it.

And I thought Beavis and Butthead were bad.

My involvement had to be just an added bonus for John, if that was the case, since there was no way to predict it. John hated me for his mother's death; Dr. Estes and Kris had confirmed that much. But he couldn't have seen my involvement coming. Nobody was that fucking smart. Unless he was, and had been manipulating me long distance through his father.

On the other hand, maybe dear old dad was involved in the machinations. But that didn't make any sense. Why bring so much risk to the entire operation?

Son against father. Only the father didn't know it.

I decided that if I didn't figure out the whole mess soon, I would have to take two aspirin and call myself in the morning.

Allen slapped his open palm down on the desktop. It sounded like an M-80 had gone off on the desk.

"You do it," he said. "You take whatever you need to get the job done, and you do what you've got to do. I don't care if there's anybody left standing by the time this is over except my son. Is that perfectly clear?"

He stood up quickly, towering over the desk and looking down at me with a rage in his eyes that I had never seen before. The mind behind those eyes was capable of anything.

"Sure thing, boss," I said.

The Death of John Masters

Bobby and I had had a little talk about the Biblical Beast before we had all left on our kidnapping spree. As he had explained it to me, John Hemlock could, from the standpoint of a bonafide religious nutcase like Brother Thomas, fit the expected bill.

I hadn't had much to do with church since my town gassing days. Christians were usually pretty good about forgiveness when it came to things like screwing somebody else's wife, simple theft and all the way up to grand larceny if you said you were sorry, and the occasional ax murder if you claimed the devil made you do it. But when it came to accidental toxic gas releases, it sounded a little too much like Auschwitz for their tastes.

But I'd read the Bible. I wasn't illiterate.

Neither was Bobby.

John Hemlock held, by virtue of his family name and his profile as one of the leaders of a large religious denomination, a place on the world stage. He could literally communicate with the entire world via television because he was a VIP.

He was influential. If you've got money like the Hemlock family, you're automatically influential. You can buy and sell influence. You could even fund the third rebuilding of the Jewish temple and a new generation supercomputer to gain a few points for a margin call to be held down the road.

He was internationally connected. There was a Hemlock International corporate office in every country that could be called a country. The company dealt even handedly with Jews and Arabs. With free nations and totalitarian slave states.

Throw in a dash of evil at the right moments, and you have a portrait of what most us would look for in a Biblical Beast. In my personal opinion, John Hemlock had the bases pretty well covered. He had the name, money, and yank to get the Armageddon ball rolling downhill. If you believe in that kind of stuff.

"Brother Thomas," I was saying into my cellphone. "I think I've found what you're looking for."

I could imagine Brothers James and Peter with their ears pressed to the extension phones.

"And what is that, Mr. Brown?" he asked.

"He was right under your noses all the time," I continued.

"I don't understand," Brother Thomas said carefully.

"If you're not interested…" I said, and let it hang.

One one thousand, two one thousand, three one thousand… I had made it to twelve one thousand by the time he bit.

"Right under my nose?" he asked.

"For two hundred points, Brother Thomas, what unpopular drink did Socrates suck down?"

One one thousand, two one thousand, three one thousand…

"You expect me to believe that?"

"Did you know that his lovely wife is actually the daughter of Bill the Butcher, the Beast of Cincinnati?"

"Christine Hemlock?"

I could hear an intake of breath as loudly as if a major vacuum seal had been broken.

"Check it out, Brother. Think on it for a while. I can call you back, if you'd like."

Pause.

"That might be good, Mr. Brown."

"Oh, did I tell you that the young man in question has apparently been kidnapped? I just left his father, and the poor man is going nuts. He thinks that you're responsible. But I know you're not. And I know what this is all about now. You should have told me in the first place.

I would have been on your side from day one."

Real big pause. I forgot to do the one one thousand thing.

"Don't toy with me, Mr. Brown."

"I don't know about all of this religious prophecy stuff, Brother, but what I've found out scares the living shit out of me. I know a little bit about computers, and if it's true, we'll all be in bad shape if someone doesn't put a stop to it. Computers control lots of things these days. Like satellite weapons. You know that bit in Revelations about the Beast calling down fire from the sky?"

"Yes," he said cautiously.

"You send the right computer generated signal to one of those birds upstairs, and you'll have some major fire on its way down here. Am I making myself clear?"

"I underestimated you, Mr. Brown. Is there a chance of finding our… target?"

Got you.

"That's a done deal, Reverend. I'm going to throw a party for a certain young man tonight, but I don't know enough about the occasion to make sure I do it up right. What say we join forces on this one and attend together? We could snuff out the candles together. I've got the place all picked out."

"Hmm…"

"But, Brother Thomas, if I'm on your side, I'm on your side. I don't want to wind up missing after the party, if you understand what I mean. I've got friends that would get real pissed off if that happened, and that would be bad for you."

If I didn't threaten him, he would think that it was a setup. Brother Peter would think so anyway. Wet work guys are warped. I know; I've done a little of it myself from time to time.

"It would be bad for you, Mr. Brown, if you were lying to me."

"Would you like to know where he is right now?"

"Yes, I think that I would," answered Brother Thomas.

"Should I speak a little more loudly so that Brothers James and Peter can hear?"

"As you wish."

"Then I'll be calling you back with the information."

I hung up the smartphone without telling him.

Benny Franks had gone into work feeling pretty good and had left in a body bag with a two dimensional head. What was beginning to bother me was whether the Brothers or a group working for Allen Hemlock had in fact killed him.

Detective work, from my perspective, was a waste of time. Little things like the law and evidence make things complicated. Complicated is inefficient. When I was a kid, I used to read detective stories. Gather the evidence, make some deductions, and voila, they had the killer.

Bullshit.

It always came down to some fancy piece of reasoning in the end. Like real people do that sort of thing. I had a better idea of how to find things out. You start by beating on suspicious people until they tell you what you want to know. Lance was a good example of the proper approach, although a little extreme, I admit.

Then you take the next suspicious character and do the same, and so on. It's messy, but it works. You take your chances; they take theirs.

The last thing that I needed were clues and fancy deductions. What I wanted were answers. Clues are for sissies.

The plant manager where Benny worked knew a lot more than he had told us. I was sure of that. I'd let him ride before because there were so many more important things to do.

Now, I was thinking that before the final showdown, I needed to clear up that loose end or I might trip over it and turn up dead. That would be bad.

Details, details.

So, I followed John Masters, the plant manager, as he left his facility. It wasn't hard. He wasn't exactly expecting me. Besides, he drove a bright red car.

We were in the middle of a country road when I accelerated, made like I was going to pass him, and slammed my car side-wise into his, knocking him off of the road and crashing him into a ditch between us and a major cornfield.

I saw the look on his face at the moment of impact. The raucous scraping and sound of crunching metal was more satisfying to me at that moment than the best blow job that Monica Thomas had ever given me. I jammed the brakes down hard just as I saw his airbag inflate and pin him safely against his seat.

His fancy sports car was pretty well ruined. His whole day was ruined when I opened the passenger side door and pointed the Beretta in his face.

"Hello, Mr. Masters," I said.

He squinted his eyes, as though he didn't recognize me. Dazed. Confused. I wished that his employees could see him now.

After disentangling him from the airbag, I hurried him along to my car by jamming the barrel of the Beretta into his back as though it were a cattle prod. Twice he slipped in the rushes and fell forward into the ankle high water. When I kicked him hard in the upper thigh, though, he got up and kept going. His starched white shirt was a mess, although his name tag—John Masters Plant Manager, still looked pretty good.

At the back door to the station wagon, he hesitated when he saw the manacles inside. A quick crack to the nose with the gun barrel, and he saw things differently. If I had to walk around with my nose bandaged, everybody ought to take a turn at it.

Three simple snatch jobs in one day. I was beginning to like my work again.

When he was all comfy and leg-ironed into place, I got back into my car and drove off, never looking back at his sports car, which now lay sideways in the ditch like a discarded red toy.

I kept the bulletproof glass window closed between us during the ride—if I heard him start to whine, I thought I might just turn around and shoot him before I had a chance to rough him up. I was way past being tolerant with these people.

Benny Frank's wife had been nice to me on the day that I had met with her. A little old lady now alone in the world. All because people like John Masters had a hard-on for Biblical prophecy.

There were plenty of places to take John Masters for what I had in mind, but the important thing was that it be somewhere where no one would see me come or go. If it turned out that John had known what would happen to Benny, he wasn't going to be leaving with me. If he hadn't known, I would have to let him go.

The chances of him going to the police afterwards were, in my estimation, slim and none. He was involved in something that he shouldn't have been. Should his role in the death of Benny Franks ever come out, he would be ruined. I thought that he would keep his mouth shut.

Benny had been in the ASA when he was in the army. He was someone who knew a great deal about penetrating secure databases. What I wanted to know was whose computer databases he had been killed for penetrating—the Church of the New Apostles, or those of Hemlock International? Or both? By the time that I got done with John Masters, I was hoping that I would know the answer.

"Out of the car," I said.

I opened the passenger and pointed the Berretta at him. The car engine was still running.

Masters was a little slow getting out. I couldn't say that I blamed him. Whatever was coming his way, he was reasonably sure that it wasn't going to be good.

We were outside a small corrugated metal shed on the grounds of the abandoned Gibraltar Quarry. The property was fenced in by wicked looking barbed wire rolls atop a cyclone fence to keep the kids out. Over the years, the quarry had filled with water, and the kids had liked to use it as a swimming hole. Hence the barbed wire enclosure.

"I remember you," he said when he was out of the car.

"You didn't think that you'd seen the last of me, did you?"

"Why are you doing this?"

"I'm getting tired out of that question," I said irritably.

I had unlocked him from the iron rings in the back seat, but left him shackled with the chains—prisoner style. With the exception of his tie, he looked like he would be right at home in a Georgia state chain gang.

"But I've done nothing," he protested.

"Walk."

He walked where I pointed him, to the rear of the car. I whistled aimlessly while I secured his chain to the back of the car.

Whatever else he expected me to do, he didn't expect me to climb back into the car and put it into gear. Before I started driving across the rocky ground toward the edge of the cliff overhanging the water, I had slid back the bulletproof glass divider so that I could see out of the rearview mirror a little better. His face showed real concern when I popped the gear and depressed the accelerator down lightly. He followed behind like a man on his way to the work camps. Nervous. Afraid. Praying for a miracle.

By the time that we got a short distance from the edge of the sheer cliff, I could see that he had caught on to the idea.

I stopped the car, put in park, but left the engine running. The fuel gauge still read a half a tank of gas.

"Let me tell you how this will go," I told him when I got out and walked to the back of the car to face him. "If you don't want to tell me what I want to know and do it quickly, I'm going to force the accelerator down, throw the gear into drive, and send you and this car out into space. The car will drag you right along behind it. If you don't break your neck when you hit the water or get crushed by the car, you'll go straight down and drown. If you don't tell me what I want to know.

"If you cooperate, I'll just unchain you and leave you here."

"How do I know you won't kill me anyway?" he asked.

"You don't, but if you ask me another stupid question like that, I'm going to go ahead and do it just to feel good about myself. I'm tired of people lying to me and asking me stupid questions."

It was getting to be late in the afternoon. We were in a beautiful place. Wild grass and white stone. A wide expanse of glassy water below. The wind was as soft as cotton against my face. No one but the two of us in sight. If it weren't for the fact that I was probably going to kill him, it would have been a nice enough day.

For a moment, I forgot why I was there, and looked up towards the sky, looking for shapes in the puffy white clouds. I could make out the figure of a hooded figure in one, the outline of a casket in another.

"Who told you to call Benny Franks back to the plant?" I asked.

He looked down at the ground and didn't answer me. With his head bowed, I noticed for the first time that he had a bald spot at the back of this head. It was an attractive target, but the Beretta would make short work of his head, and then how would I learn anything? I considered it anyway.

"I'm not going to ask again. If you don't tell me, I'm just going to do it," I told him, pointing at the car. "The beauty of it is that no one ever comes here. There's nobody to save you, Masters. We're surrounded by barbed wire, and even if somebody was as good at picking locks as I am, they aren't likely to be looking for someone chained to a car bumper like you. So, I'm not personally too worried. If they ever do come looking for you, I'll be long gone by then, and you'll be too dead to care.

"Last chance. Tell me or die. It's up to you."

He was looking at me; really seeing me. Maybe the bandages over my nose made me look more sinister than I was. More than likely, it was the fact that I had him chained to a car with its engine still running that was parked five feet from the edge of a sheer rock cliff that descended straight down to a very deep quarry lake. It seemed to be sinking into his tiny management brain that I would actually do it; I would actually send him over the edge to his death.

"John Hemlock," he blurted.

"The two of you are pretty close?"

His lips compressed until his mouth looked like little more than a straight line cut into his face two inches above his chin. Dirty stains on his white shirt, rumpled creases, a tear in his left shirtsleeve, and wing tipped shoes still soaked with water that squished when he shifted his weight from side to the other.

John Masters had a slight frame made worse by the narrowness of his shoulders. His body had the look of a gawky boy waiting to get past the puberty mark. A gawky boy who had conspired with John Hemlock to murder Benny Franks and leave his old wife a widow.

"How much did he pay you?" I asked, when he didn't answer how close that he and John Hemlock were.

Sometimes you can see it in their faces.

Guilty.

"What do you mean?"

"You want to take a ride behind the car?" I asked. "Look, your new sports car. I know that you didn't buy that out of petty cash money. So, how much did he pay you?"

"Thirty thousand," he mumbled.

"Thirty thousand? That was it? You help make Mrs. Frank a widow for only thirty thousand dollars?"

Judas did much worse, however, for only thirty pieces of silver.

His face went slack; his eyes seemed to lose focus.

"He was trying to hurt the church," he said finally.

"You did it because John Hemlock told you that Benny Franks was trying to hurt the church?"

He nodded, his eyes on the ground.

"Liar," I said.

He was screaming something when I went round to the driver's side, leaned over and slid the shifter into "Drive" and got back out again. Being a conscientious person, I closed the door as the station wagon began rolling inexorably forward.

The car was idling slowly, but that wasn't the real reason that it seemed to take so long to get to the edge. It was the fact my mind went into slow motion, and made it seem as though reality was advancing forward just a few frames at a time.

I heard him begging and pleading, but I tuned him out the moment that he lied to me. I could hear the noise, but noise was all that it was to me.

As the car began to slide forward at an incline, it made a grating noise that reminded me of something, but I'll be fucked if I can remember what it is. John Masters was kicking, swaying, and screaming too much for me to bother him with such a small detail.

I took a step or two forward so that I could observe the car as it disappeared over the edge. John Masters, for a brief moment in his otherwise uninteresting life, took on heroic proportions as he did an imitation of Custer's last stand and Sisyphus combined. Only, there were no Indians and he was being dragged, not pushed. Honestly, it's hard for me to think of an analogy that fits how this guy looked trying to plant his feet on the ground and stop the forward momentum of a station wagon that weighed over two thousand pounds by nothing more than willpower.

When it made it past the halfway point, though, it was all over. The chain snapped tight and flipped him up into the air. The car and John Masters disappeared in a quick fast forward, and time returned to normal for me. I hurried to the edge and looked down to see the grand finale.

The car was hurtling down toward the water with John Masters stretched out behind it. He looked like Superman flying after the car to save it before it hit the water. I stood transfixed at the edge of the precipice, watching to see if he could grab the car in the nick of time, pull up before he hit the water, and fly back triumphantly.

Instead, when the car impacted the water, John kept going and hit the rear window, which, unfortunately for him, was bullet proof.

Question: What's the last thing on a bug's mind when he splats onto a windshield?

Answer: His ass.

And so it was with John Masters.

My Mom Doesn't Sleep Around

Another day, another car destroyed. At this rate, I'd soon be able to get bulk buying discounts from the car dealers.

The walk back to the Lighthouse Marina took me a little under an hour, but it was time well spent. It wasn't that great on my nuts, but it helped me think some things through that had been bothering me. Like, for example, the look that would have been on Dr. Stouffer's face if she had been standing next to me while I chained Masters to the back of the station wagon and sent him to his death over the cliff.

Disgust?

Horror?

Disdain?

Clinically speaking, what a woman like her would ever want with a guy like me was impossible to say. She really could have her pick of any man that she wanted. Dr. Stouffer had brains, looks, style, and about anything else that a man could want.

My mom doesn't sleep around, Mr. Brown.

Yeah, well, I had that going for me.

A man with a past.

A woman with a past.

A couple with a future?

Not too damned likely.

Still, aside from slashing her husband's throat, she had been a victim more often than not. I couldn't say the same for me.

So it was hard for me to believe that any woman would be interested in me for long. The more they really knew about me, the worse they would think that I was. If Kris had seen me send John Masters to his death, I doubted she would be interested in me for much longer.

Afraid, yes; interested, no.

Applying logic fairly to both sides is a bitch. If she should be afraid of me, did that mean that I should be afraid of her anytime I caught her with jagged glass in her hands? What came to mind was that she was basically a good person who did what she did in future self-defense. I wondered if that would hold up in court.

She would never hurt me.

Right.

God, I was getting a headache.

At least the kids from the Gifted Children's Conference were no longer in danger. Thanks to Bobby the Brilliant, the killings would stop. Take out the target, let everyone know who the target was and that he was out of commission, and the hunt by the New Apostles was over. Almost no one had been killed so far.

Without Bobby, I don't think that we would have ever found out who the target was until it was way, way too late. Who the hell would have ever thought that Allen Hemlock would have had the polymeric nightmare implanted in his own son's head? Worse yet, who would have thought that the son would have agreed to the idea?

Trying to please his father? I suppose that would fit Dr. Stouffer's analysis of John Hemlock. Always trying to please his father, but never being able to actually do it.

What's that dad, you want me to let the doctor's cut open my skull and implant this chunk of plastic?

Sure, but could I finish lunch first?

What a family.

I suppose from a shrink's standpoint, it made sense, though. Crystal clear psychology. It was just that I was having trouble buying it. There must be another reason that John had for going through with the operation. He might have wanted to please his father as a child, but he hated Allen, too.

Crystal clear with a drop of poison. That's what John Hemlock's psychology was really like. The crystal clear part was him going along with the operation to please his father. But where was the poison?

And if John and his father were so fucking brilliant, how come we had been able to figure out the whole mess? That was the part that I really didn't like. I still felt like I was being manipulated, although I couldn't tell at that point by who or for what purpose.

I just knew that in some way I was being had.

There were too many loose ends.

I don't like leaving loose ends, and there was one person who came to mind as I walked back toward the lighthouse that might be able to provide me with some of the answers that I didn't have. Answers to questions such as why John Hemlock, knowing that the implant was in his head, was a prominent member of the cult that was trying to find and kill whoever had the implant in his head. Fortunately, there was one person who knew both John Hemlock and me and some of the inner workings of the Church of the New Apostles.

Monica Thomas.

Now that she and Leo had spent the night together, maybe she would talk to me. Leo was a better man than I was. He was more understanding; committed to working with Monica to put bad parts of her life behind her. I was probably a thing of the past to her. Everything forgiven and forgotten. Maybe not. She was, after all, a woman.

Men hold grudges a long time, too, but our memories aren't worth a shit. So we're theoretically easier to get along with when we're not making asses of ourselves.

By the time that I got back to the marina to get another car, I was hot to drive over and talk to Monica. I called her office on my cellular phone and found that she was in, and, yes, she would see me if I could get my butt over there before she left.

I had only one car left to drive—a nineteen sixty-eight convertible black mustang. It wasn't exactly inconspicuous, but I didn't think that that would be a problem anymore. All of the players knew who I was, and with John Hemlock in custody, I doubted that Brother Thomas' flock would screw with me.

Allen Hemlock was a different matter. He didn't know yet that I had his dearest little son captive, and, in fact, thought that I was on my way to rescue him. There was no percentage in Allen putting a team on me, though, unless it would be a surveillance team, and I hadn't seen any sign of that yet. But with the right equipment on his side, I wouldn't know I was being surveilled, anyway. I hate drones. Especially the itty-bitty ones.

As I pulled the Mustang out of its storage shed, I tried to think of what might yet go wrong.

Dr. Stouffer and Bobby were in good hands with Charlie. Although I couldn't completely rule out an attack on the island, it didn't seem too damn likely. The basic idea, if someone decided to put the moves on my island fortress, would be to snatch Dr. Stouffer and Bobby as hostages so that I would play ball with whichever side got them.

Certainly, no one would be stupid enough to think that I had John Hemlock stashed there. Or would they? Nah. The place was too secure. Besides, the timing was wrong. The time to make a move on Soldier's Point would have been earlier in the game. That's the way that I would have done it.

I took the cellphone out of my coat pocket and called the lighthouse. Charlie answered the phone on the second ring.

"All quiet there?" I asked.

"Sure thing, Scott," came the answer. "Any reason for it not to be all quiet?"

"No. But I was just thinking that somebody might be stupid enough to hit the island. That's all. Looking for hostages to keep me in line."

"You got a premonition or something?" he asked.

"No. Just watching the details like you taught me."

"Don't worry. Big trouble comes, we go underground. You want to speak to Dr. Stouffer?"

"No. Yeah. Sure. Put her on."

A minute or two elapsed while he went to get her.

"Hello?"

"Hi, Kris. It's me. Just checking in. How's Bobby holding up?"

"Fine."

"How are you holding up?"

"Worried about you," she said.

"Worry can give you an ulcer."

"Bacteria give you ulcers. Worry gives you heartburn."

"My mistake."

"Scott," she said softly, "be careful. Come back in one piece."

I didn't know what to say.

"Are you still there?" she asked.

"Yeah. I'm here."

"What's wrong?"

"I think that I'd rather be there with you than talking to you over the phone, that's all."

"It will be okay, Scott."

"Does my past bother you?" I asked, not wanting to hear the answer.

"If you can handle mine, I can handle yours," she said.

"I was just wondering. What if it's pretty bad?"

"Go to work, Mr. Brown. Get this over with and then come home."

*****

Monica Thomas' office was as bold and brassy as the woman herself. Her desk was so large that you could have shot pool on it. It was so expensive that you wouldn't dare.

Her luxurious red hair spilled back over the chrome and leather chair behind the desk and the fire in her green eyes made me feel uncomfortable. It was something in the way that she sat, or looked, or smelled. She just radiated dynamic tension.

On the walls were paintings by a famous somebody or other that were like explosions of brilliant colors captured on canvas. I've never been much for art so I didn't try to understand what the artist was trying to communicate. I just thought that the colors were pretty.

Back when we were a hot item, Monica used to make the attempt to explain what it was that the artist was trying to say. I figured that whatever he was trying to say was his business and I wasn't that damned interested anyway. Like I said, I just thought that the colors were pretty.

Monica's office was a power office. It was on the twelfth floor of an important building and she had not one, but two windows. The chair that she sat on was much bigger than the ones that her guests sat on. She'd confessed to me once after a night of sweaty sex in her office that her chair was six inches higher than the guest chairs as well. Taller and bigger. Now that's power.

The office carpet was pure white. I supposed that was so clients would constantly worry about leaving dirty footprints, like children who were visiting the neighbors with their parents.

Afternoon sunlight shone in through the windows from behind her desk. That was a textbook power tactic as well. Make sure the light is in their eyes, not yours.

"So, what's on your mind?" she asked casually, her lips forming the words with sensuous precision.

Beautiful women can be such a pain in the ass.

"I need some help."

She was toying absently with a gold pen, rolling it between her fingers. It seemed faintly sexual, like everything else she did, including breathing.

"Oh?"

"You're not still pissed at me, are you?"

You would be, if you knew what I did to Lance.

"No. Leo and I talked about it. He told me I should just accept you for what you are. I told him you're an asshole. He modified his position and said that I should accept you for the asshole that you are."

"I'm here about the Church of the New Apostles, Monica."

It was an even bet that, as usual, that she wasn't wearing underwear.

"You understand I am their legal counsel."

Stockings, not panty hose. She never played fair.

"So, what are you telling me?" I asked.

"That there are limits to what we can talk about."

"Maybe you'll rethink that after you hear what I have to say."

"I doubt it."

"Don't be so quick to judge."

"You know," she said, leaning forward and propping both elbows on her desk, "someday you're going to learn to quit telling me what to do."

"I'll leave that joy to Leo."

"Leo? What's he got to do with anything?"

"I thought that the two of you..."

"Because we slept together? So, one quick sperm deposit at the bank of Monica and I belong to Leo? Using that logic, you own more shares in me than he does."

The twinkle in her eye almost made me lose it.

"What are you telling me here? That there's nothing between the two of you?"

"His cock was between the two of us the other night. You were looking for something more permanent?"

"He loves you, Monica."

She actually laughed.

Actually.

A sinking feeling.

A bad feeling.

My shoulder muscles bunched so tightly that they hurt. Maybe it was an act. A tough girl act to keep from being vulnerable.

"He loves me? So what? Does that mean I'm supposed to be faithful to him or something? That I'm supposed to deny myself what I want when I want it?"

"Is that the most important thing in life to you? Your immediate gratification? Don't you ever feel like you need more lasting feelings?"

"Don't you?" she countered.

"Sometimes," I replied. "Yes."

"You mean to say that you don't want to do me?"

Now I knew why even lawyers looked down on lawyers.

"No, Monica, I don't want to do you. I'm big on faithfulness, or don't you remember that?"

She stood up and stretched. She looked so good that it hurt to look at her.

"I was married once," she said, walking over and sliding up to sit on the desk in front of me.

"You blew that, remember?"

With a casually insensitive motion, she crossed her legs. Her black, high-heeled shoes shone with a patent leather shine.

"Nobody owns me."

"Being faithful doesn't mean somebody owns you, you stupid bitch. It means that you care enough to be honest."

"Oh, I was honest," she said with a wicked grin. "Al knew about everything. Everything."

I shook my head.

"Honesty isn't just about telling the truth, anybody can do that. It's about keeping your commitments. If you don't want to make a commitment, then don't make it. The problem with you is that you've got no honor. But Leo's an honorable man, Monica. You shouldn't fuck with people who are honorable."

She licked her lower lip and said, "but I like to play with my food."

I had to get out; my knees were starting to tremble. There was no reason for me to have come in the first place. She was a user who wanted to be used. Trying to control my breathing to calm myself, I stood up.

"Once more for old times," she said, tilting her head up to look at me.

"How about once for Leo?" I asked.

She uncrossed her legs eagerly.

I turned slightly, then whipped my left hand around in a short arc and knocked her flat on her back.

She was screaming at me as I left, but what else was new?

*****

River Rouge.

South and a little west of Detroit. A suburb of dirty streets, abandoned factory buildings, corrugated warehouses, and weeds sprouting through heaved concrete cracks in empty sidewalks. Steel mills poured their hot sparks and black particles in the air. Rusty railroad tracks with solitary cars waiting for engines that never came. Half a mile away, the Detroit River, filled with the maximum allowable level of pollutants, wound its way in shameful silence past the carnage on its banks.

I chained the gate to the salt mine property shut, got back into the car, and drove to the gutted building that concealed its entrance.

The salt mine was owned by a company out of Pittsburgh nowadays, who had closed it after its operations had caused a cave-in to occur ten miles away from where I parked the car. There had been another accident that happened only two hundred feet west and a long ways down to bury two men and a woman in tons of salt rock. After that, the place had been permanently closed.

There was supposed to be a security guard on the premises at all times. That was the corporate policy, but in a cost saving move, they had sacked that idea and gone with electronic alarms. Fortunately, I have some experience in that area. In fact, skirting the average industrial security system is much easier than getting past a guard. People have this odd habit of being occasionally unpredictable.

Electronics are electronics.

You can always count on silicon.

It seemed like for the last few years, most bad things for me were coming to a conclusion underground. And, to tell you the truth, I had become somewhat resigned to the idea. Bad things belonged underground. You had to finish them off where they lived.

And the Hemlocks were bad.

But even a card carrying member of the Cynic's Union like myself was hard pressed to believe how one family could cause so much unnecessary death for such bullshit reasons. John Hemlock had known all along that he was the one. Yet he had started Brother Thomas on his Beast hunt. I still questioned whether or not he was on inside track with the Church of the New Apostles because he chose to be, or whether his father had put him up to the whole scam. Either idea was chilling in its own right.

Christine Hemlock was either just crazy or crazy and involved somehow. Before the night was over, I planned to find out. The feeling that she might possibly be the one who had wielded the knife on occasion was in the same league as the emotions that the other Hemlocks raked up inside me. I think "the putrid slime that clings to the walls of Hell" is a pretty apt description of those feelings. H. P. Lovecraft would have loved the Hemlocks.

On the way to the salt mines, I had called ahead from the car to my team to make sure that everything was ready. It was Karl that answered the phone.

"Any problems, Karl?" I asked.

"Nein," he had replied. "All is set here. Charges are in place, and everyone is in position."

"How about our two visitors?"

"In good health, if the doctor does not die of a heart seizure before you get here."

"The old prick is a bit nervous, eh?"

"Yah."

"And the other?"

"A very different type of man, the young one is. He has no fear. He acts as if he knows something that we do not. I do not like it at all."

"He knows a lot that we don't know. They all do. Both sides. I've got a feeling we're never going to understand this whole thing. But I think that Bobby's idea of taking him and notifying Brother Thomas that John Hemlock is who he's been after was a smart move that will stop the killing. Now we've just got to dish out the judgment. Starting with the Hemlocks.

"Anyway, is Gregorio still asking for more men?"

"Always. He speaks incessantly."

"It's a birth defect," I explained. "He's missing the gene that would allow him to close his mouth."

"As you say."

"Put him on for a minute, will you, Karl?"

There was an apologetic pause, and for a second, I thought I'd gone through a bad mobile cell zone.

"He is not here."

"Well, where the hell is he?"

"In the mines. Checking."

"Checking what?" I asked.

"He didn't say."

With the explosives in place, Gregorio Tarancon decided to indulge his long time fantasy of taste testing various locations in the underground salt mines of Detroit.

"Well, get his ass back there, Karl. The Brothers of Death are on their way. I called them with the location not five minutes ago."

"At once."

"Katerina and Leo are set?"

"To the death," he said.

"Jesus, Karl, don't be so fucking deadly serious. It's bad enough as it is."

"It is a serious business."

"It's not like I'm asking you if you know any good jokes. Just chill out a little. Don't go stiff on me. And, Karl?"

"Ya?"

"I appreciate what you're doing here. I know it's bad going up against Allen Hemlock, but we're doing the right thing. Are you there, Karl?"

"You will see soon enough what I think of Mr. Hemlock and his family."

"One more thing. You're all to be out of there before the timer is set. You guys have done enough. Nobody hangs around to cover my ass. That goes double for Gregorio. I don't know what that asshole is up to out there in the dark, but he gets out with the rest of you. You make sure of that personally, will you old man?"

"I will take care of everything," he said, and then hung up.

A Prussian to the end.

I thought about saluting the phone after he closed off the connection. Karl was an old style German, for sure. He was the type of man who only looked natural in a formal tuxedo or a uniform. If things took an unexpected turn, like something unexpected happening to me, I knew the others would turn to him instinctively. He had the brains, the experience, and the discipline. Man did he have the discipline.

Betrayal

The first time that I had driven down the road that descends into the salt mines, it had truly seemed as though I was entering the land of Oz. Glittering walls of whiteness surrounded me, reflecting a diffuse milky white glow back at me in the harsh edged sodium lights. I had gone on a tour, back when they still gave them. Cruising the eighth wonder of Detroit. More impressive than the Edsel.

The city of Detroit was and always had been unimpressive to me. But the city beneath the city of Detroit, that was a different story. It was like being in Mammoth Caves sans the spikes of congealed rocks that form the forbidding stalactites and stalagmites that give those caverns the look of gigantic torture chambers.

As the road descended deeper and deeper into the blackness, spiraling down further into the cavernous blackness, the walls receded beyond the reach of the headlights, and it began to feel as though I was descending far beneath the sea, where light from the surface world never dared venture.

When the road eventually eased in pitch and straightened out, I was in the first of the main caverns. Normally, I would park the car soon and walk the rest of the way. There was no real reason for parking the car instead of driving it the rest of the way, but I the unreasoning fear that the ground would crack from the weight of my vehicle dictated the choice. The ground was actually quite safe. It was the ceiling and the walls that were most dangerous during the mining operations of days gone by. Still, fear is fear, reasonable or not.

My idea for what was coming was that I needed to drive the car in all of the way. I was a little nervous about the timing, and I might need the additional exit speed the car would give me. So, I tried not to think about the fact that I didn't like driving so deep into the mines and just kept on trucking.

It was too dark for me to see the tunnels that radiated out and away from the central cavern, but I knew they were there. The headlights showed me only what they could penetrate ahead through the unforgiving blackness before me.

Through the silence of the mines I drove, the only sounds were the hum of the engine and the crunch of salt beneath the tires. They were the inexorably lonely sounds of a man going where he should not go.

I had been having bad feelings about the whole business and how it would conclude for some time by then. They didn't stop me from doing what I thought had to be done, though. But I won't deny thinking that everything was going to turn to shit.

It was the whole business of the Beast.

I don't like prophecy anyway. The whole idea that the universe is planned out in advance gives me the creeps. It's like a big con job that we're playing on ourselves or that someone upstairs is playing on us. I'm not sure what the difference is. We go through our lives with the idea that we can do something about the future. In a way, that concept is the core of our existence.

Striving to do better is only meaningful if in fact we have the freedom to make a difference, for better or worse, to succeed or fail. If that's all worked out in advance, striving is kind of pointless. I mean, why get all worked up if everything we're going to do is a done deal already?

It gets especially creepy if the Biblical Beast is in the cards. I didn't really believe that John Hemlock, screwed up as he was, was the Biblical Beast, but the whole business had me thinking. In a place like the Detroit salt mines, thoughts about a coming Beast were especially unsettling. It would have been a whole lot easier to digest on a beach in the Caribbean.

The light from the building where we held Dr. Estes and John Hemlock was like a beacon in the darkness. There were drums and pieces of metal equipment parts scattered at random around the front of the building, giving it the look of an underground junkyard. The power for the lights came from a generator unit that I had installed. I'm big into independent power sources.

I parked the car around the side of the building and entered through the front. There wasn't a security procedure for identification other than that anyone who had walked through that door who wasn't one of us would have had their head blown off.

Karl was waiting for me a short ways into the building, gun aimed at my head until he determined for a fact that I had come alone. In the dim light that spilled into the hallway, he appeared gaunt and deadly. His face was half in darkness, but I could just make out the grim set of his jaw.

"I come in peace," I said.

He lowered the weapon. It was the one coded sentence that we had between us.

"How much lead?" he asked.

"Forty-five minutes. Fifteen minutes either way. Depends on the size of their team and how they mobilize. How are the twin pillars of evil?"

"As before. Come, I will show you."

I had other things on my mind as I walked down the hallway. When Karl came to the door to the room and stood to one side to let me go in first, some part of my brain should have remembered that I never go in first. But that time I did.

Madness waited inside that room.

The door opened inward and to the left. Since we entered via the far right hand side of the room, the opened door obscured what lay behind it. It was the smell of blood-burned powder that assaulted my nostrils before I saw the bodies. Arms sprawled wide in death for Leo Croton. Blood pooled and congealed next to his half open mouth. He lay on his stomach, his back was drenched with more blood. Ragged holes ripped through the fabric of what used to be his army green shirt.

Katerina lying on her back, her arms folded across her chest as though by a mortician. Face half blown away. Splintered skull and brain exposed. Crusted dark gel, black-scabbed blood rusted in what hair remained.

For once in my life, the agony of personal loss commingled so completely with the rage that when I saw Allen, John, and Christine Hemlock and a triumphant Dr. Estes standing near the bodies, their faces searching me for a reaction, I had none to give. John and Christine were pointing guns at me. Karl no doubt was doing the same from behind, too smart to touch the end of his barrel to my back, knowing the consequences of being too close.

Failure.

I had failed my friends.

Scott Brown called his friends to meet their ends.

But Gregorio was nowhere in sight.

"Yes," said Karl from behind me in a bitter voice. "Your Spanish friend has vanished. But we will find his body. He cannot have crawled far."

"Forget his body," said Allen Hemlock. "I saw your shot. You hit him with a solid round. He's down. He won't be back."

"Get his weapons, Christine," instructed Allen.

"Why?" I asked when I finally found my voice.

Although I stared directly at Allen, there was no way not to see the dead bodies of my friends. When Christine placed one delicate high-heeled shoe directly onto Katerina's stomach and walked over her body, reality seemed to waiver before my eyes. An elegant, tan colored shoe, the point of the heel pressing onto Katerina's dead body as though she were stepping on road kill, and then she was over her and moving toward me.

"Why what? I think that you know as much as you need to know."

Christine removed the Berretta. Her hands roamed carefully over my body, removing the extra rounds, searching for anything else that I could use to cause trouble. She smelled like peaches. A pretty woman, the smell of peaches. The sight of death. The top of her head as she bent before me, probed me, felt me.

"Remember that I am here," said Karl as though I could forget.

Christine stood up before me, a beatific smile on her face, looking for acknowledgment, encouragement.

"Blow me," I told her.

She stood on tiptoe and kissed me lightly on the cheek, then, with a soft rustle of skirts, backed away to join her husband and hand him my gun.

"Bring him in," said Allen.

"Move," said Karl. "Slowly."

"You didn't have to kill them, Karl."

"Shut up and walk," he said.

"You know that I'll have to even the score."

He kicked me square in the ass, sending me sprawling forward and onto the floor. As I hit the hard tile, I took most of the weight on my left shoulder, but I spread the fingers of my right hand and took some of the shock with it as well. The significance of what had just occurred hit me harder than the floor.

"Get up," ordered Karl.

My right hand had some feeling in it. The impact was a painful jolt to my right arm that traveled all the way up to the shoulder, but in that moment, I was oblivious to the pain.

I raised my head and found myself looking directly at Leo's face, the small pool of his blood that had leaked from his mouth.

"The religious cavalry is coming," I said.

"We know," smirked John. "We're waiting for them."

I should have figured that. Everyone seemed to know what was going on except me.

"Tie him to the table, Karl," said John.

"We don't have time for that," said his father.

Father and son.

Together again.

"But I promised Christine," said John.

"We don't have time."

Uh-oh, thought David, Goliath brought his whole fucking family.

I was on my knees, looking up at them.

"Don't piss him off," I told Allen.

Allen Hemlock. Chairman of the Board, an easy enough job to get when you owned the entire company.

Allen Hemlock. What would his employees think if they could see him now? Standing tall, looking handsome, but with blood on his thousand dollar shoes.

And where did his secretary think he was?

Allen Hemlock, his Mr. Rogers face a little harder now.

"All I need from you is a little information," he told me.

"But you promised," said Christine to John.

"He lied, whatever he said," I told her.

"All right," sighed Allen impatiently, "tie him to the desk. Let's get this over with."

Dr. Estes, the modern day Frankenstein, smiled wickedly. Some bad shit was going to happen to me. Gregorio was right. I should have used more men.

"You're such a pussy, John," I said. "Daddy still runs you."

"Karl," snapped Allen.

I glanced furtively around the room. A few worktables, scattered chairs, and Gregorio's machete lying on one. Scattered pieces of rumpled paper. A rusty screwdriver, almost in reach. An ancient stapler. A broken clipboard on a desk. Wire in and out baskets. Fluorescent lights overhead. Everyone with a gun but me.

I was screwed.

Except for Gregorio's machete lying on the desk.

He must have been in a hurry to get out.

I thought about Dr. Stouffer, Bobby, and Charlie. The three of them would have to be eliminated, either by the Brothers or the Hemlock's. No loose ends.

Three can keep a secret, wrote Ben Franklin, if two are dead.

Handsome John Hemlock, the man with two brains, was looking at me. He smiled, a gentle, knowing smile. He was casually dressed, but, as usual, looked like a million dollars- although worth considerably more.

John Hemlock looked at Christine, the modern day Whore of Babylon who was equally at home in bobby socks or spike high heels. They exchanged knowing glances.

John Hemlock, gun in hand, turned to his father, the man who controlled more companies than I had stitches. There was something like sadness in John's eyes as he shifted the position of his gun slightly and pulled the trigger. The bullet caught his father in the throat, blasting a ragged bloody hole and sending a spray of blood and shattered spine out the back of his neck.

Christine smiled a delighted, rapturous smile and appeared to say something, but over the sound of my Beretta, I couldn't hear her words of ecstasy.

Dr. Estes frowned.

This, he seemed to be thinking, is bad science.

The body of Allen Hemlock dropped to the floor.

Another one bit the dust.

Christine Hemlock started clapping her hands, but I still could not hear.

Obviously, Bobby's plan had turned to shit. He had forgotten that most fundamental tactical possibility—betrayal. It was hard to fault him. I had forgotten it, too.

"Oh, my God," John was saying to me when my hearing returned, "you've killed my father. Scott Brown, how could you do such a thing? What will the media think when they find out? Although, I suppose I should thank you. Karl, Mr. Brown has made me an even richer man. What will I do with all of that money?"

"Whatever you wish, young sir," replied Karl gravely from behind me.

"Christine, dear," continued John Hemlock, "would you mind terribly if I chat for just awhile with Scott before I turn him over to you? I've been waiting to do this for so many years."

She frowned and tugged at the belt that cinched her dress together at her waist. Her lower lip stuck out a little, as though she were pouting.

"I'll give him to you right afterwards," said John, "I promise."

"But—"

"Christine," he said, with mock severity, "be nice. I promised."

"Oh, all right," she said, "but don't touch him, please."

"Thank you, sweetheart," he said.

John stepped backward and politely got a metal desk chair and rolled it over toward me.

"Sit," he said, and then got one for himself.

"Are you happy, now?" I asked Dr. Estes when I was seated.

"What?" asked the old man.

Dr. Estes looked at me with unfocused eyes. I could almost hear the circuits firing in his brain. He looked down at the untidy messes on the floor, and shook his head, then leaned back and sat his ass on the edge of a metal desk, lost in his thoughts.

"Perhaps you think it is a tactical mistake to take time to reminisce together..."

I looked back at John, now sitting three feet away from me. The machete and the screwdriver called to me, asking what the plan was.

"It's your show," I shrugged.

Somewhere behind me, I heard Karl move.

Where the hell was Gregorio?

"Not quite, although I do play a major role, I must admit. Do you believe in prophecy, Scott?"

"Is this a James Bond thing with you?" I asked. "Bad guy captures good guy, bad guy explains his entire life fucking history to good guy, bad guy leaves good guy with henchmen, good guy escapes and kills bad guy. Because if it is, you're doing this all wrong."

"You hardly qualify as a good guy," he laughed. "How many good guys kill half a town's population, let a woman that they're bodyguarding be murdered under their noses, and then go to work as a hired gun for a man like my father? Oh, and lest we forget, let all of those innocent children die without ever stopping the man responsible for it all? Well?"

He had a point.

"Just don't talk me to death," I said. "That's all I ask."

"You have my word. Christine is in charge of that area. Trust her to do good work. She's quite the woman, don't you think?"

"Quite the women, you mean. How many people live in that pretty little head of hers?"

"Ah, yes. Perhaps five or six. And, her father, of course. Quite a happy family when you think about it. You had a happy family once, didn't you?"

"You've been playing with me all along, haven't you?"

"Oh no," he said, wagging his finger in front of his face, "you don't have to stall. I know the timetable. Everything will be just fine. Painful, but fine. Your Spanish friend," he said, leaning forward conspiratorially and dropping his voice, "is alive and well."

He straightened abruptly in his chair.

"Thanks for the tip," I told him.

"A gift," he said, waving a hand as though to brush it off. "But of course, Karl will find and kill him soon. So don't count on his help."

"Yeah."

"Do you like poetry, Scott?"

"No."

"Listen carefully to this: 'One will die, one will born. Come to earth, star of morn.' Do you like it? I wrote it myself."

"No."

"One will die, one will born," he chanted, "Come to earth, star of morn."

"I said no."

" It sounds much better in French, I assure you. Much. And, it's prophetic, you see. Everything, all of this is about prophecy. Realized prophecy. That's what's important. I will realize prophecy. A heavy burden, but…"

"What the hell," I asked, "are you talking about?"

"That's why I like you, Scott. You're so utterly clueless. Did you understand any of my poem?"

"No."

"Do you read the Bible?"

"Sometimes."

"Which of the many glorious editions?"

"What the fuck is the difference?"

"Yes," he said seriously, "what the fuck is the difference? There's a sage question if there ever was one, as Dr. Stouffer used to say. Although I would say that she's only mediocre in bed, don't you think?"

I thought of the file lying at the bottom of the river.

"Monica, whom you don't appreciate as much as you should, is so much better. I think that that's special, don't you? That we share so many of the same women, I mean. The same women, and different parts in the same destiny play. I, a major role, you a bit part, but an important bit part. Actually, if it weren't for you, the next acts couldn't happen at all."

"And what are the next acts?" I asked.

"Did you sleep with my mother?"

"No. I didn't."

"Neither did I," he said, glancing at his father's body. "But that's beside the point. Really. I would have, you know, if you hadn't let her be killed. I'm irresistible to women. If it weren't for the fact that," he looked quickly at his watch, "about right now your lighthouse is being blown to oblivion by a minor rocket attack, I imagine that your Dr. Stouffer would be willing to sleep with me again without the slightest bit of coercion on my part."

The look on my face caused him to break into a grin.

"They might survive, you know. Charlie Kim is a resourceful man. I find that most Koreans are very tough. It's a stereotype. Be that as it may, please don't make any stupid moves, because then Karl would kill you instantly, and you would lose the chance to know if they survive. Really, I don't care. But it's irrelevant, you see, to the bigger plan."

"If you—"

"Trust me. There's a chance that they survived. You have that wonderful underground bomb shelter that they could have escaped to, remember? I just wanted to be polite and let you in on the action that's going on while you're sitting here talking to me, you know."

God, I wanted to get my hand on that machete.

"But we haven't much time. You don't really care that I maneuvered Brother Thomas into the killing to find the Beast and that it was all a little joke to me since we both know who the Beast really is. You don't really care about the particulars of how I managed it. I'm sure, however, that you've guessed that my lovely wife supervised personally many of the... cranial explorations, shall we say."

"I'd figured that much out."

He clapped his hands together delightedly.

"Excellent," he said.

"Elementary," I said.

If they made it into the rooms beneath the Lighthouse, they could still be alive. He was right. And if they were still alive, that was, at that moment, the best that I could hope for.

"And you want to know why, of course. I was bored. There was no other reason. And lonely. Brother Thomas and his flock were just what I needed. Such a perfect vehicle for transformation. They are comrades. Brother Thomas will march forward into the future with me. His sect is so useable you see. Yes, the church of the New Rome.

"Remember, One will die, one will born. Come to earth, Star of Morn. And why come to earth without a following?"

"John," I said, "you are seriously whacked out, man."

"Oh," he said seriously, "you have no idea. But you will. Yes, you will. One will die, one will born. Come to earth, Star of Morn. Remember my poem, it will explain a lot for you later."

"You're going to let me live?"

"Oh no, you're going to let me live—again."

His eyes glanced quickly at the machete, then back at me again. The natives, Christine and Dr. Estes, were getting restless, but John kept right in my face.

"Ever hear of the ten nation confederacy?" he asked.

"No," I lied.

"Well, here's the thing. I'm going to create it. The EuroGovernment is the key, of course, but I'll reshape it to make the exact number of members to be ten. I have to. Prophecy rules, you know."

"You got a point to this, John?"

"No," he winked, "but somebody up there does."

"You've got Beast on the Brain, buddy."

"More than you believe, for now."

Okay, I admit it, I was getting seriously spooked, but you have to remember the circumstances. Three bodies on the floor. One that I didn't care about, but two that I did. Outgunned and helpless to do anything about it. That about sums it up, I think.

And Gregorio, somewhere out there, alive and on his way.

Or not.

"Why are you important to me?" he asked.

"Just shoot me and get it over with, please," I said, and I was beginning to mean it.

"I'll tell you why you're important to me. There is a reason besides the part you have still to play."

He leaned over and tapped me on the forehead with his finger.

"It's what's inside here," he said. "Your soul."

"Oh, yeah, that."

"You see, you are a man who realizes guilt, futility, and unworthiness before God. You have both killed unintentionally and intentionally. You have killed by accident and with malice, yet you have not gone entirely cold. Do you believe in salvation?"

"Fuck the theology. Please shoot me."

"You do, I know, but you know that you are unworthy. Others feel that they are worthy or unworthy. But you have true knowledge. Fascinating. The Fear of the Lord is the beginning of Wisdom. Of course you know that proverb."

"Blow me."

"And you do fear God, don't you, Scott?"

"So, this is what happens when plastic leaks into your brain? You turn into a raving maniac? You know about that shit in your head? Leaking into your fucking gray cells?"

"Why yes," he said quite seriously, "I do. Wonderful isn't it? Do you know where I come from?"

"Hell," I said.

"Quite."

"You've grown up to be a real spooky tune, man," I told him. "You're right out of your mind. Look at your whacked out wife pacing around over there. And have a little sympathy for Karl standing behind me, holding that heavy gun. Just have him go ahead and shoot me, for Christ's sake."

"Be the machete, Billy," he whispered, and winked at me again. "It's time, Scott Brown. Time to turn another valve."

He jumped to his feet suddenly, and pointed over my shoulder, yelling, "Karl, behind you, look out."

Darkness Into Light

Gregorio.

I dove for the machete, clamped my hand around it, and in the most beautiful move of my life, prepared for by twenty years of martial arts training, I pivoted, swung its blade around in a wide circle, and cut off John Hemlock's head in a vicious chop. The instant before the blade struck, I swear to you he smiled. He didn't even try to duck.

The chop spun me around to face a bewildered Karl.

Uh-oh.

No Gregorio.

My hand went numb when Christine fired, and the machete jumped out of my hand. For the second time in an hour, my hearing went bye-bye. I bent over reflexively, and saw John Hemlock's bloody head staring up at me.

Christine was on me before I could recover, knocking me straight back over and onto the desk, forcing the air out of my lungs. The butt of her gun cracked against my head, and I tumbled into a well of pain and darkness.

*****

They were all over me in the dark. My speech was still slurred, my awakening vision was dark and blurry and shadowy shapes moved over me. I was bound and tied with rope. Immobile. I felt the cutting edge of the clippers at the base of my left thumb. Heard her loving voice as the blades began to cut into my skin, and then withdraw. Warm fluid trickled across my wrist.

Soft confusion flowed through my head. She kissed me lightly on the lips. Lingered. Kissed me again.

Gentle fingers pulled back my lower lip, and then the metal shears cut it clean down to the base of my chin. Quick and bloody and then released. My hand could not move to press the two sides together, and I felt a nauseating wetness fill my mouth and drench my neck.

Metal clattering against metal and scratching like fingernails across a blackboard as she selected another implement. She was singing in a childlike voice a song that prickled the hair on the base of my neck. It floated by me, a soft lullaby of death and mutilation, and she had cut off my half my ear before someone shot her.

I'm coming to meet you, Mr. Van Gogh.

I sighed, then shuddered when the point of her butcher knife punctured clean through my right lung and out the other side as the weight of her body fell against me, then slipped down onto the floor as her dead arms slid across my chest.

A second shot, and blood sprayed my face. The other person fell peacefully across my waist, his split-open abdomen smearing my stomach with an ugly slipperiness.

Impaled, I thought. Smeared with death. Impaled.

Floating.... floating in sharp-edged pain.

"Jesus," I heard Gregorio say, "all this for some fucking tacos."

*****

We cut it pretty thin, according to what Gregorio told me later. Once again, he bound me up as well as he could and loaded me into the car. We passed Brother Thomas and his men trekking their way in full combat gear across the salt mines main cavern. They fired as we roared by.

I would have fired back, but I was unconscious.

Gregorio raised his hand in salute as we tore by them, holding the remote activator in his hand, and pushed the button.

If I had been awake and not bleeding to death, I would have heard the explosions, felt the awesome rumble as the charges broke through the rock barrier separating the salt mines from the Detroit River and thousands of gallons of water began pouring into the mines traveling at terrifying speed.

Gregorio must have driven like a stock car racer up the spiral road. Some rides are easier on the nerves when you're unconscious.

The only part that I regret is not getting to watch Brother Thomas and the rest being turned into saltwater fish.

*****

"Mr. Brown, are you awake?"

They had survived. I could die in peace.

"Shush, Bobby, shush. Let him sleep."

Her voice cradled me in concern as I lay there.

"He has so many bandages, mom."

"I know, son. That's why he needs his rest. He's going to be all right."

"How many stitches does he have?"

"Ooh-ay-ee," I said.

"Shut up," she said.

"Eh-ah."

"I mean it," she told me.

I'd have told her to quit ragging on me, but I conked out again.

*****

"Hey, gringo, you're a fucking mess. They got you bandaged up like the mummy from hell."

When I got out of the hospital, I was going to tell Maria that he had been a prick to me while I was recovering.

"But you look better than the two that I wasted. I never shot a woman before. I stabbed one once, but only in the leg. She was trying to cut my nuts off."

"He needs his sleep," said a nurse.

"Yeah, but he can't talk back."

I couldn't open my eyes, but I knew he was grinning.

His chair creaked as he leaned forward, and put his face next to mine.

"I told you," he whispered, "that we needed more men."

*****

In a troubled dream, I saw Katerina linking her arms through Boris's. They were walking toward me, and a diffuse white light shone through their bodies.

I was crying, could feel the tears trickling down my face as they had when we were together in the Ukraine, and I wanted to speak, but I was so ashamed that they had died.

When they had come close enough for me to see their faces, I saw her smile forgiveness my way the moment before they turned to vapor before my dreaming eyes.

*****

"You're going to live with us, Mr. Brown."

The three of us were in the hospital parking lot. It was many weeks later, and my injuries were healing, as the prick of a doctor had told me, "nicely." Bright sunshine hurt my eyes as she wheeled me down the ramp into the daylight.

"Bobby Stouffer," I heard her say from behind me.

"She's going to marry you," he whispered as he walked beside me. "Don't tell her I told you, though."

I winked at him, and he winked back.

"What are you two up to?"

"No good," I said.

"I figured that."

Getting into her Jeep was like climbing Mt. Everest with ankle weights on. But with the two of them helping me, I only almost passed out from the pain once.

Sitting upright, willing the pain to subside, I closed my eyes, heard Bobby scramble into the backseat, heard the back door slam, and imagined how good it would feel to be home.

When she climbed into the driver's seat and started the engine, I told her, "As soon as they take the stitches out of my lip, I'm going to kiss you until you run out of air."

Bobby started laughing in the back seat.

"Say something, mom," he said.

She turned to look at him, looked at me, then looked back at him and told him, "Sometimes actions speak louder than words, young man."

*****

It was some weeks later.

Dr. Stouffer was at her office with a patient. Bobby was on the computer in the farmhouse. I sat on the swing, gently rocking back and forth as the chain overhead creaked against the I-hook, absent-mindedly rubbing my recovering arm.

Charlie Kim had been by earlier to see how I was doing. Gregorio had called earlier to tell me he knew where I could get a new lighthouse cheap. No trade-in value, he had said, for the old one.

Monica Thomas, I had heard, had broken down and cried uncontrollably when she heard that Leo Croton was dead. After a prolonged two days of mourning, she had spent the night with someone she met at a fundraiser.

Leo Croton was too dead to give a shit.

I was in the news again, over the destruction of the buildings on my island. This time, the story was that someone had found out who I really was—perhaps a relative of someone that I had gassed—and was seeking revenge. Just your average relative with a surface to air missile.

It would blow over.

If it had happened in Lebanon, the coverage would have gone on forever. But the entire Downriver area could be annihilated by a comet, and people would get tired of hearing about it after a week.

Still, I was worried.

John Hemlock's head was what was worrying me. I had killed him, plain and simple. A machete through the neck is fatal, plain and simple. But the thing inside his head. Had that died too? Had it ever been alive? If Dr. Estes had been correct... if, if, if. It was driving me crazy.

Did it in fact contain the essence of John Hemlock, and if so, had I really killed John Hemlock? Or would he be resurrected if Dr. Estes had lived and, after removing the polymeric processor, inserted it into the computer matrix that had been waiting for it for so many years?

Gregorio had sworn to me that when he came in and shot Karl and Christine, both Dr. Estes and John Hemlock's head were gone. Estes might have made it out. I don't know how, but he could have. It bothered me that, as I sat there swinging on the porch, Dr. Estes could be hooking up the polymeric processor after cutting open John's head and removing it.

Was it in fact alive? Would it have John's personality and memory and would it therefore remember death?

I had killed John Hemlock. Would Dr. Estes resurrect him as part of a new polymeric computer system in the rebuilt Temple in Israel? Or remove it and insert it in someone else's head?

I remembered the smile on John Hemlock's face just before I had beheaded him. Had I started in motion some biblical prophecy? What, really, had I done?

Scott Brown turned a valve and killed a town.

The little things we do, not meaning to do wrong. Turn a valve, kill innocent people. But had I initiated something worse this time?

I needed to relax.

I needed to think.

I needed to find that head.

www.ingramcontent.com/pod-product-compliance
Lightning Source LLC
Chambersburg PA
CBHW060938120726
47910CB00002B/390
9780989866941